Gloria Cook was bo rarely ventures beyond its border. Her village upbringing fostered a love for the surrounding countryside and coastline which permeates her writing. She is married with two children.

PENGARRON PRIDE is her second novel, and like the first, PENGARRON LAND (also available from Headline), is set in and around the dramatic scenery of Mount's Bay, Penzance, during the 18th century.

Pengarron Pride

Gloria Cook

HEADLINE

First published in 1993
by HEADLINE BOOK PUBLISHING PLC

First published in paperback in 1993
by HEADLINE BOOK PUBLISHING PLC

10 9 8 7 6 5 4 3 2 1

ISBN 0 7472 4189 9

Typeset by Keyboard Services, Luton

Printed and bound in Great Britain by
HarperCollins Manufacturing, Glasgow

HEADLINE BOOK PUBLISHING PLC
Headline House
79 Great Titchfield Street
London W1P 7FN

To the memory of my father, Ted,
and my father-in-law, Percy.

Chapter 1

After five long days at sea, drifting for mackerel around the Wolf Rock, the Perranbarvah fishing fleet sailed back through a heavy swell and made its way into Mount's Bay, heading for Newlyn's fish market. As the black-stained luggers made their way past the inhospitable granite headland of Pengarron Point, the fishermen were in good humour. At regular intervals they soaked down the most recent catch with sea water to keep it fresh; an excellent catch was already salted down in the fishrooms of their boats. This meant food on the table and a few extra shillings to invest in the maintenance of the boats, or, if the vessels were rented, something to put by towards the dues.

The fleet came from a close-knit community of men and boys of three generations from fifteen families, of whom many had intermarried down the centuries. They put to sea together and returned home together. They kept a close watch on each other's interests and shared the same griefs and fortunes. When one family ate, they all ate; more often they went hungry.

The fleet would soon tie up at Newlyn, the catch would be unloaded, weighed, and sold for either local or overseas consumption. Then the luggers could finally sail for home. They would be washed down, their equipment assessed for loss or damage and the fishermen could at last take a short, hard-earned rest.

The sky this morning was taking longer than usual to lighten and usher in the dawn. The wild coastline of the little horseshoe-shaped Trelynne Cove was barely visible.

A short time later, as the fleet neared its home village, the strong south-easterly wind that had been whipping up the waves suddenly dropped away, as though two giants quarrelling at the south and east ends of the earth had ceased their puffing and blowing. A dense fog swept over the boats with uncompromising speed.

All talk in the boats came to an abrupt halt, as though a mighty voice had cried 'Hush!' and the fishermen had obeyed it without exception. Within seconds the fog spread a shroud of chilled damp air in all directions, obliterating sky, landmarks, horizons and fellow vessels. The fishermen lit more lanterns against the gloom. Some of the men fidgeted with nets and tackle or tried to count the slithering mass of oily blue- and green-backed fish of the most recent catch. The older fishermen remained still, their weathered hands clamped into fists as they peered through the thick dank air and tried to locate a familiar landmark, looking for reassurance that they were not heading too close inshore towards the congregation of silent deadly rocks.

With the drop in the wind, which had been on their backs and driving them into Mount's Bay, the boats were becoming increasingly difficult to navigate as they were tossed about on the heavy swell. The fishermen held on to masts and gunwales as the open vessels were swept up to the crests of high waves and bounced down seconds later only to repeat the stomach-churning motion. The sea smelled strong and salty. The malevolent fog swirled about the men as if it sought to cut off their air supply.

Uncertainty at setting foot safely on land again filtered into the minds of some of the younger, less experienced fishermen. Thoughts of the girl waiting on shore to welcome them home, a satisfying meal served on a table, or the night's drinking ahead were all pushed aside. Their breathing grew heavier, sounding strangely inside their own heads. They relaxed slightly when they recognised the unique sound of the iron mooring rings on the short pier of the village being clanged by their womenfolk to guide them away from the dangerous cliffs. The wives, mothers, daughters and sisters of the Kings, the Drannocks, the Laitys and the others, all clanging the rings in turn.

Two of the fog-bound luggers riding out the heavy sea were the *Lowenek* and the *Young Maid*. The *Young Maid* was skippered by Samuel Drannock and crewed by his seventeen-year-old son Bartholomew, his close neighbour Jonathan King, and Jonathan's three sons, Jeremy, Christopher and Josh. They could just make out the fuzzy outline of the boat in front of them, but they were unable to identify it as the *Lowenek*, manned entirely by more Kings.

Samuel Drannock watched the other lugger with anxious eyes. He hoped it would draw further away but did not attempt to alter the course of his own boat for fear of colliding with an unseen vessel to his port or starboard.

'Damn this fog, why now?' he muttered to himself, irritably pushing a lock of greying hair away from his colourless eyes.

The *Young Maid* was a brand-new lugger, expertly crafted in Mount's Bay, working her first week at sea. Even though the lugger was owned by a wealthy man at Marazion who took the greater share of the boat's profits, it was the

3

consummation of the dreams Samuel had held all his working life. The last thing he wanted now was to have the craft damaged by ramming the boat ahead. When a few seconds later the hazy outline in front of him disappeared, his hard face relaxed a little.

'Thank the Lord,' he breathed, and Bartholomew, who had been watching his father intently, nodded his dark head in agreement.

But it was too early to thank the Divine. As the *Young Maid* was swept up to the top of the next wave, the *Lowenek* was in the deep gully below it. *Lowenek*'s skipper, Nathaniel King, known locally as Grandfather King, was the first to sense impending danger and the only fisherman on his family's lugger to see the *Young Maid* tossed off the wave to plunge down on top of them.

His shout of 'Look out!' had barely left his thin, cracked lips when forty feet of heavy timber, masts, yards and sails and several stone of fish crashed down, snuffing out life, tearing off limbs and almost cleaving *Lowenek* in two. The noise was deafening over the turbulent waters. The fish-wives paused in their clanging at that same moment, as though premonition of tragedy had stilled their hands.

At his shout Grandfather King had risen to his feet. He was swept overboard with the speed and grace of a swooping sea bird, hitting the cold, inky-black water with no more than a dull splash. He had no regrets at facing death now. Better to die at sea as a working fisherman than to end up as a slinger, left by old age and infirmity to watch on shore with the women and children for the return of the fleet.

His two sons, Jonathan, and Solomon with his left arm ripped off, were thrown out of their boats immediately after him. The waves swept them quickly away into the fog, their cries growing fainter and fainter until they were no longer heard. Both men fought for their lives, both lost them, not content as their father was to leave their fate to the elements and their Maker.

Terror and confusion possessed the survivors on the *Young Maid* as it rocked crazily on the rushing sea. Clinging to the mast after a desperate attempt to clutch at Jonathan King's body, Samuel Drannock was brought forcefully to his knees. When he regained his feet the lugger was steadying itself, the sea was a little less angry, the waves had lost some of their awesome strength. Although grateful to have a stable albeit damaged boat under his feet, Samuel's horror did not lessen. His inbred Cornish superstition rose to the fore at the uncanny changes in the weather and the sea.

'We'll pay for this, boy,' he hissed to his son who was looking at him anxiously from his position at the bow.

'What's that?' Bartholomew shouted above the moans and exclamations of the other survivors on the *Young Maid*. He saw with despair that nearly all their catch had been lost overboard in the collision. Five days' tedious labour and sweat all for nothing. Bartholomew wiped blood off his chin where it had struck the bottom of the boat. Furious at what had happened, he swore profusely and for once did not care if his dour father heard every oath.

Samuel did not repeat his gloomy prophecy but looked about the lugger to count the heads of his crew. Bartholomew had survived, thank God, and thank God his younger brothers Charles and Jack were lying abed at home recovering from the measles. Jeremy, Christopher and Josh King were on board. Only Jonathan King had been lost. But how many had survived from the smashed vessel?

5

Samuel shouted for silence, straining hard to listen for cries of survivors in the water. He was rewarded almost at once. A muffled cry was heard through the gloom.

'Sounds like Paul!' shouted Jeremy King. 'Sounds like my cousin.'

The *Young Maid* was swept into the next gully and the upper half of Paul King, clinging desperately to a length of spar and canvas lugsail, bobbed into sight. Tears of relief joined the salty wetness on the young fisherman's face and with renewed strength he kicked his long legs, characteristic of the tall King family, to bring himself up to the hull of the boat.

Samuel and Bartholomew leaned over the lugger side by side. They snatched at Paul's hair, neck and shoulders and struggled to haul him in between them. Paul stretched out one free hand towards his rescuers but fear kept the other hand clamped to the wreckage.

'Let go of the bloody spar!' Bartholomew shouted.

The lugger, its crew and Paul King, still holding on precariously to the spar, were swept up the crest of another wave and the volume of water that smashed into Paul's face and filled his gaping mouth tore the spar from his grasp. He panicked. Without realising it he fought against Bartholomew's grip on his shoulder and Bartholomew would have toppled into the water with him if Christopher and Jeremy King had not grabbed his legs and thrown themselves on to the deck, battening themselves down hard. Bartholomew screamed in agony at the over-stretching of his body until the King brothers could scramble to their knees and hold on to him more gently.

Samuel had managed to get a painful grip on Paul's hair and with his legs braced against the side of the boat he used his other hand to cuff Paul heavily on the face. It brought

Paul to his senses; he stopped fighting them and made himself go limp, and Samuel and Bartholomew were able to get a better grip on his coat and shoulders. As they desperately dragged him towards them, Paul's body was slammed against the hull of the boat. With loud grunts and straining muscles they hauled Paul up until his torso was slung over the gunwale. Christopher and Jeremy let go of Bartholomew's legs and grabbed their cousin's body, pulling him fully into the safety of the *Young Maid*.

Collapsed in a water-sodden heap, Paul gave a hacking cough and gasped for oxygen. As the lugger hit the crest of the next wave he was thrown on to his back and stared up stupidly at the grim faces of his rescuers.

'So it was the *Lowenek* we hit,' muttered Samuel, wiping a wet, calloused hand over his stony face. He knelt at Paul's side. 'Are you hurt, Paul?'

Paul shook his head, but his hands travelled to massage at the red marks and bruises on his throat and scalp. Then his relief at being rescued vanished as quickly as the fog had first appeared. He was too breathless to speak but using Samuel's body as a lever he prised himself up beside Bartholomew and scanned the short limits of the sea under the thick cloying air, looking for other members of his family.

A full five agonising minutes passed when a startled outburst came from Christopher King at the stern. 'Somebody's climbing in!'

Eager hands reached out to help another sodden fisherman to safety. It took the combined strength of all those on board, clinging to each other's wet coats and avoiding slipping legs, before the exhausted body of Matthew King, Solomon's eldest son, was safely on board. A giant in stature, Matthew King had used his massive strength to

7

swim through the waves in the direction of the shore and had hardly believed his good fortune to find the stern of a lugger in front of him.

'How . . . many . . . of us . . . have 'ee . . . pulled in?' he rasped out moments later, granite-faced but hopeful, while gulping in lungfuls of chilled air.

'Just you and your brother Paul,' Samuel answered him gravely.

Shaking off his helpers, Matthew's eyes eagerly sought his brother. 'You all right, boy?'

'Aye, Matt, I'm all right,' Paul replied solemnly. 'No need to worry about me. I'm ruddy glad to see you though, afraid I was goin' to be the only one to . . .' He didn't finish the sentence and Matthew turned to Samuel.

'Were it your boat who hit us, Samuel?'

'Aye, it was,' Samuel replied in a small voice.

'Have 'ee lost any on board here?'

Samuel nodded. 'Aye, Jonathan. He went over the side on impact.'

'Ruddy hell!' the big man exclaimed unbelievingly. He moved about the rocking boat as best he could and stared into the grim faces of each of the fishermen on board to reassure himself of their presence and safety.

'Only five of you!' he cried in anguish a moment later. 'For heaven's sake, Samuel! There's only five of you here! Where's Josh?' Glaring wildly at Samuel, Matthew gripped his shoulder. 'Where's young Josh? Where's the boy!'

'But, but . . .' Samuel wrenched himself free and whirled round to the bow, pointing agitatedly. 'He was there, beside Bartholomew, I counted him. I did, he was there!' Samuel appealed to his son. 'Did you see him, after the accident?'

Bartholomew gulped. 'I . . . I didn't notice . . .'

Samuel's thin mouth gaped open and his eyes glazed over.

8

He had witnessed Jonathan King's tall frame being hurled overboard and probably to his death. Had Jonathan's youngest son gone over too and without anyone noticing? Samuel looked at each taut face in turn with the question etched on his features. In return he received either a shake of the head or a blank stare.

Matthew King grabbed Samuel again and shook him roughly. 'Where is Josh!' he screamed in sheer frustration.

'For goodness sake, Matt!' Paul shouted fearfully. 'Leave him be or you'll have this boat over too!'

Matthew heeded Paul's plea shamefacedly. He let go of Samuel with a slight push then patted his arm in a gesture that said he was sorry for the outburst.

Bartholomew, who had been on the verge of coming to his father's aid, spoke up firmly over the roar of the waves. 'We may yet find the others, Matt. We mustn't give up hope but we're not going to hear their cries for help if we panic.'

The fog was gradually lifting, the waves becoming smaller and more manageable. The fishermen silently acknowledged the youth's words and all turned about to lean over the gunwales to resume the search for signs of life.

Matthew brushed tears from his eyes and muttered prayers through his bristly brown beard. He had no idea where the *Young Maid* had been tossed to, no familiar clanging of rings could be heard, either from his own or a neighbouring village. Paul stood close beside him, his knuckles white as he gripped the gunwale. Though numb with grief, a small part of his brain marvelled that he was still alive and he found comfort that the sea had spared his amiable giant brother, who, if their grandfather, father and uncle were really lost, was now the head of their family.

Bartholomew nudged Paul's arm. 'Some of them may be picked up by the other boats.'

It was a comforting thought. 'Could be.' Paul gave the other youth a grateful smile. 'Never thought of that.'

'Shush, you two,' Matthew hissed through the corner of his mouth.

The sky was slowly clearing, soon the coastline would be in sight and the fishermen would be able to ascertain their exact whereabouts. Silence reigned on the *Young Maid*. Then Samuel Drannock's voice came in a rasp, 'Hark, I thought I heard something.'

The fishermen straightened their bodies and became alert, turning their heads this way and that to pick up any human sounds.

'There it is again,' said Samuel urgently. 'Did any other of 'ee hear it?'

'I b'lieve I heard something,' Christopher King replied, hoping it would be his father Jonathan or his brother Josh.

'There it is again!' cried Matthew, jubilantly repeating Samuel. 'To starboard. At least one more out there's still alive. Someone get me a rope to tie round my waist. I'm going in after him before this lugger is swept too far away from him.'

'Let me do it, Matthew,' Samuel said, catching the giant's arm.

'Tes someone in my family out there, Samuel,' Matthew returned solidly, taking the rope held out to him by Christopher. 'Tes my place to go, and besides, I'm the strongest swimmer here. When you feel me jerking on the rope, pull us back in.'

'Please, Matthew,' there was an urgency in Samuel's voice. 'I feel partly to blame for what's happened and as skipper of this lugger I'm the one with the right to say who goes and who stays.'

10

'I don't know about that—'

'Let Samuel go, Matt,' Paul broke in, frightened at the prospect of his brother leaving the safety of the boat and becoming lost with the other members of their family.

Matthew King hesitated for a moment but it was long enough for Samuel to snatch the rope from his huge hands and begin tying it in deft knots round his own waist.

Despite the rocking motion of the boat, Bartholomew was quickly at his father's side. 'Father, don't,' he pleaded, grabbing Samuel's arm.

'I'll be all right, Bartholomew,' Samuel said, momentarily resting a hand on his son's broad shoulder. 'I'm leaving Matthew in charge. Listen out for more survivors.' Giving Matthew the other end of the rope, Samuel lifted his legs over the gunwale and lowered himself into the cold, hostile sea.

Salty spray washed over Bartholomew's angry young face as he leaned over the side and watched his father's tossed-about form becoming rapidly swallowed up in the fog.

'Don't 'ee worry now, Bartholomew,' said Jeremy King, as Bartholomew lifted his dark head and angrily wiped dripping water off his cut chin. 'Your tas is a good swimmer, he'll be all right.'

'Against these waves?' Bartholomew said harshly. 'He'd better be all right.' He was furious with his father. Why did he have to act the hero? The skipper of the *Young Maid* wasn't responsible for what had happened, it could just have easily been his boat struck by another vessel. Anything could, and did, happen in seas like this. Perhaps another lugger in the fleet had come to grief as well as theirs and the *Lowenek* this morning. Bartholomew looked at the almost empty fishroom. The cruel sea had won again; there

11

seemed to be no way a young man could earn a living from it and better himself.

Jeremy watched Bartholomew nervously for a moment, guessing what was going on inside his head. Jeremy feared an outburst of the temper Bartholomew was liable to display when his father was not about. But he remained still, glaring down into the fishroom. Jeremy sighed deeply and moved away to stand beside Christopher. They linked arms across their shoulders and looked out to sea. If all went well, who would Samuel bring in? Their grandfather, father or uncle? Their brother Josh who had mysteriously disappeared from the boat? Or one of their cousins, Mark or John?

At regular intervals Samuel stopped his laboured swimming strokes to listen for the cries of the survivor, which were weakening. He was bumped and jarred by waves and wreckage and once a dead fish slapped against his face. His mind was half on reaching the survivor and half on the plight of the *Young Maid*. Would its owner blame him for the accident? Would he lose his precious rented boat after all these years of longing to skipper a brand-new one? Then there was the question of the damage caused to the boat. Samuel's family was poor; if he was forced to pay for the repairs, where would the money come from? His wife Jenifer had been so happy for him when he'd secured tenure of the boat, it would be as much of a blow to her as to him if the worst happened.

Samuel's limbs were aching unmercifully and his lungs were near to bursting at the end of the thirteen arduous minutes it took him to reach the survivor. He saw a pitiful small figure clinging desperately to one floating battered half of the *Lowenek*.

As he closed in on the figure, salt water stinging his half-closed eyes, Samuel called out loudly, 'Who are 'ee?' although there was no need to raise his voice now he was this close; it was something the fog made him do.

'J . . . John King . . .' came the feeble reply. 'C . . . can't . . . hold on . . .'

Samuel trod water for a moment and wiped water from his eyes. 'Now don't 'ee take on so, John,' he called to encourage the boy. 'I'll soon have 'ee away to safety.'

He reached John and slid an arm under his armpits and over his narrow chest. Samuel held on to the wreckage for a short time to regain his breath.

'I . . . I can't . . . s-swim . . . very well,' John stuttered in fear and cold.

Samuel said into his ear, 'Tes all right, boy. You can leave go now. When I tug on the rope round my waist they back on the *Young Maid* will pull us in. Your brothers are waiting for 'ee on board. You're safe now, the fog's thinning out and we'll soon see to put ashore.'

'I'm scared, S . . . Sam . . .'

'You'll be all right, John, I've got you now,' Samuel tried to reassure him, but he was exhausted and fearful himself.

When he felt the pull returned on the rope, Samuel had to prise John's frozen fingers from the wreckage. He made sure the boy's face was raised above the waters as he swam off. He knew that no one on the lugger could hear him but he shouted, 'Matthew! I've got John!' And thought grimly to himself, 'At least this one's saved.'

A bare second later Samuel's head was smashed by the side of another lugger seeking shelter out in the fog. He had not one moment for memories or regrets before he died. His arm was flung out from John King's body and the boy's screams went unheeded as the youngest King at sea that day sank to join the skipper of the *Young Maid*.

Chapter 2

Hours later, a few short miles across Mount's Bay,
Kerensa, Lady Pengarron, arrived on the arm of her
husband Sir Oliver at Tolwithrick, the stately home of the
wealthy mine-owning Beswetherick family. With at least
one hundred other guests invited from all over the county
of Cornwall, they were gathering for the celebration of Sir
Martin Beswetherick's seventieth birthday.

'I shall enjoy the party tonight,' Kerensa said brightly,
peering through the crush of people. 'I hope Martin does,
he's been so looking forward to it.'

'Your presence alone will ensure that, my love,' Sir
Oliver said as he acknowledged and returned a greeting
from Sir John St Aubyn of St Michael's Mount.

Kerensa was greeted too by Sir John, but not all the
gentry, the bankers, magistrates, landowners and the inevitable interlopers who appeared at such a high social
occasion would afford her the same courtesy. She was
not born of the same blood or money, nor had she any
connection with them before her marriage. But while
Oliver would have been angered on her account, Kerensa
was not offended by any of the cold stares, quickly averted
eyes or tosses of haughty heads she received as she looked
around the banqueting hall. She cared only about the
proud aristocratic man standing protectively at her side and

those among the people here who, like the Beswethericks, were their friends.

'After this though,' Kerensa went on, 'I shall be glad to get home. I can't wait to see the children again and find out what they've been up to.'

'You did enjoy the last two days and nights though?' Oliver asked, his dark eyes gleaming brighter than the hundreds of candles lighting up the hall.

Kerensa knew that gleam intimately. 'The last two days were wonderful, my dearest, the last two nights even more so . . .'

Oliver lifted her hand and kissed the warm fingers. 'Buying that little cottage at Mullion so I can take you away and have you all to myself for a day or two was a master brainwave of mine. I'm rather proud of it.'

'So I can see,' Kerensa replied, smiling up at her husband who constantly and openly lavished love and adoration on her. She had been bonded to him in marriage for eight years and except for the first few months they had been blissfully happy in each other's company. She loved Oliver Pengarron with the same intensity with which he loved her. Everybody who knew them knew that too, although no one would have thought their marriage would turn out this way. Kerensa had been forced to marry Oliver, who had wanted to buy the little cove, formerly Pengarron property, which she and her grandfather had lived in. Her grandfather only cooperated when Oliver agreed to take Kerensa to wife. Oliver had been furious and Kerensa heartbroken that she could not marry the youth she was betrothed to. But the first year of their marriage had taken many unexpected turns and ultimately they had fallen in love.

None of Sir Martin's guests who witnessed Kerensa bringing Oliver's hand to her own lips were surprised at

16

the gesture. Sir Martin often remarked on their marriage as a fairy tale come true and Kerensa likened those who shunned her to witches and dragons who would like to spoil it for her. She would not allow their disapproval to taint her happy life.

The display of affection between her and Oliver was interrupted by a maidservant, and, laughing, Kerensa allowed herself to be whisked away to the bedchamber of Sir Martin's daughter-in-law, Lady Rachael Beswetherick.

Kerensa entered the bedchamber and nearly turned tail again to escape a confusion of harassed maidservants and the overpowering odours of perfumes and powders. But Lady Rachael caught sight of her from her seat in the powder room where she was being attended by three maids.

'Yoo-hoo! Here I am, Kerensa, my dear. Come in, come in.'

Kerensa stepped over several discarded gowns and pairs of dancing shoes and made her way through a haze of powder to Rachael's side.

Rachael sent the maids away in a sudden scurry and stood up. She fluttered her heavily jewelled hands up and down. 'Well, what do you think?' she asked.

Kerensa stared at the other woman, gloriously arrayed in jewels of every colour, and an over-decorated gown of vivid orange with spiralling purple motifs, her wig elaborately dressed twenty-two inches high and graced with huge colourful feathers, more jewels, and stuffed birds of paradise. Lady Rachael looked, to even the kindest observer, little short of ridiculous. Kerensa blinked, swallowed, smiled widely, and blatantly lied. 'You look beautiful, Rachael, perfect for tonight's occasion.'

'Of course I do,' Rachael purred. 'And you look your

usual picture of glowing beauty too, Kerensa, my dear. One can easily see that you've had the most divine time alone with your husband, but then who wouldn't with the most gorgeous man in the county.' Rachael pursed her painted lips and risked the position of her wig by putting her head a little on the side. 'I suppose you had the most terrible time wrenching yourself out of his arms.'

'Of course I did, Rachael,' Kerensa smiled.

Rachael laughed with a loud snort then swung round to survey herself in a full-length mirror. 'Do you think I have enough jewels on, my dear? I simply must look my best for tonight. Old Marty won't be seventy years old on every day of the week, and who knows, he might not be around much longer. Did you know the dear old thing wanted to hold the party in his tiny little house in Marazion? The very idea. There's not enough room to comfortably hold twenty guests in there. I've got six children old enough to attend the celebration, so with them and William and myself, and you and Oliver that makes ten people for a start so I got William to insist . . .'

Kerensa couldn't get a word in edgeways, or near the mirror to check on her own appearance, so she sat on the only chair not draped with discarded clothing and listened patiently.

'I hope I've ordered enough food and wine to cope with the evening,' Rachael continued, pressing another black patch on her chin in an attempt to conceal a wavy-lined wrinkle. 'I don't want to let old Marty down and I want the county to talk about the event for years. Talking of children, I was just now, wasn't I? I'm waiting for Ameline to come to me, she has no dress sense at all, you know. My other older girls know exactly how to dress but I have to check on Ameline on every occasion, it's so tiresome of

18

her. I keep telling her, you only have to emulate your dear mama and all will be well.'

Kerensa smiled behind her fan and managed to get in a few words on a pause of Rachael's breath. 'That was strange weather we had earlier today.'

'Was it, my dear? I was too preoccupied with the preparations for tonight to notice.'

Kerensa didn't have any more time to remark on the weather. There was a timid knock on the door and Ameline Beswetherick appeared. Ameline took one look at her mother and came into the bedchamber quite fearfully.

Downstairs Oliver was joined by Sir Martin who handed him a glass of the finest white wine. He'd had a look of disappointment on his chubby face as he'd watched Kerensa disappear up the stairs.

'I thought we would have trouble getting here through the fog,' Oliver said, after appreciating the wine, 'but it lifted almost as quickly as it fell. Kerensa kept saying there was something strange in the air, but you have a fine clear spring evening to celebrate your birthday, Martin.'

'The fog spread across the bay and drifted out to sea in a very short time according to some of the talk I've heard tonight. Don't know why people want to keep on about the weather when there's more important things like my birthday to celebrate,' Sir Martin ended grumpily.

'My humble apologies. Happy birthday, Martin.' Oliver raised his glass.

'Damned old I've become, damned old, Oliver, my boy,' Sir Martin sighed, then with a wicked glint in his yellowing eyes, 'But not too old to appreciate a slender neck and a graceful step, and,' he emphasised, 'the flash of wonderful red hair. So tell me why that little wife of yours was taken off like that before my very eyes! Haven't had my arm round her tiny waist for far too long and that's a fact!'

Oliver smiled indulgently from his great height. 'Kerensa was taken up the stairs to join Rachael and Ameline. I fancy that Rachael requires her as part of her grand entrance.'

'Oh yes,' Sir Martin bellowed. 'Rachael and her grand entrances! She insists on carrying them out even if the occasion is not in her honour, as it isn't tonight. And she'll make the most of it, you can be sure of that. This is about the only year within the last ten or so she hasn't been with child. Damn me, boy, it would be a sight indeed to see her fall down those stairs one of these days, all preened up like a hysterical pheasant.'

'A sight indeed,' agreed Oliver, turning his dark head and looking up the wide stone stairway.

'Whose birthday is it anyway?' Sir Martin said peevishly. 'I wanted the celebration at my house in Marazion but Rachael badgered William into insisting I hold it here. Henpecked and beaten down, that's what William is, not like you, Oliver. You're master of your own house, as I was when my dear Amy was alive. Amy, Kerensa – they're what real women are all about, they know how to treat a man, keep him content and satisfied in all his needs. Don't seem to be many men with backbone about these days.'

'What about young Martin?' Oliver asked. 'I hear he's doing very well for himself in the regiment.'

'Well, I'll concede the point in his case, but that's because he tries to emulate you rather than William. A fine grandson that boy is, a man couldn't wish for one better, he's a credit to the family.'

Sir Martin broke off his ramblings to greet two of his guests, elderly brothers, John and Alfred Sarrison, who wore matching clothes and pumps and identical idiotic grins.

'What a pair of silly old fops,' he snorted, when the brothers moved away to talk to other acquaintances in the noisy crowd. 'They're no fun,' he complained. 'Most of the people here tonight have no humour at all. Most of them have no class, all of them are boring. Except for you and Hezekiah, there's no one here worthy of a bit of sport or a good session at the card tables. I may be getting on in years, my boy, but I can keep up with the best of 'em.'

'I look on you as a most enduring ancient of days, Martin,' Oliver said, with humour and sincerity.

'Yes, yes, quite,' the small, elderly gentleman nodded, with a dismissive wave of a podgy hand, 'but if Rachael has not appeared within the next ten minutes, I shall order the musicians to begin the dancing. I'm paying a pretty shilling for them and this is still my house!'

Oliver sipped his wine with a wry grin. 'However long it takes Rachael to get herself ready and make her appearance with your granddaughter and my wife, I'll wager you that Hezekiah will take a good deal longer.'

'Well, I won't take you up on that,' smirked Sir Martin, with a lift of bristly eyebrows. 'Never have been one to put my money on a losing bet. Pity Judith passed on,' he mused sadly, suddenly changing tack. 'The best and most loyal servant the Beswethericks have ever had. She would have liked to have seen my seventieth . . . dear old Judith . . . but she didn't suffer at the end, carried away by the angels in her sleep. Hope I go the same way when my time comes.'

'Your time is a long way off yet, Martin,' Oliver said firmly. Oliver Pengarron was a man renowned for his lack of patience but he had an unlimited supply with regard to the other baronet, who had taken to rambling more and

21

more as the years progressed. 'You may have had your three score and ten but you're far from on the wane.'

'Mmm, you could be right, Oliver. Where is that wretched woman?' Sir Martin stamped his foot then cried out, 'Ouch, damn me!' because of his rheumatism. 'I sent William up half an hour ago to hurry her up and he has disappeared. The trouble with Rachael is that ever since she learned what some of the ladies will be wearing at the coronation later this year she's been trying to outshine the lot of them.'

At that moment William Beswetherick, Sir Martin's eldest son, appeared at the top of the stairs with a serious-faced gentleman dressed in subdued autumnal colours who looked distinctly ill at ease.

'Here comes William at least,' Oliver said. 'Who is the man with him? One of your guests, Martin?'

'Ah, that is James Mortreath, he's an acquaintance of William's.'

'Mortreath, you say?' Oliver's strong dark features became alive with interest. 'There are Mortreaths back in my family history. I wonder if there is any connection. As far as I know they all died out years ago.'

'You can ask him presently, it may prove interesting to you. He is a lawyer by profession, a very efficient one by all accounts and also has banking interests. He's come down to Cornwall from the capital city to arrange the sale of a considerable amount of property he has inherited at Truro. William met him there at the races and since then he has called often at Tolwithrick – Ameline is the attraction.'

'That is hardly surprising, Ameline is a most attractive young lady.' Oliver gazed at James Mortreath. 'Will he make a suitable husband for her? He doesn't look comfortable in society and he appears to be much older than

Ameline. The difference in their ages seems more apparent than my own to Kerensa.'

Sir Martin was smiling as he watched James Mortreath descend the stairs at the side of his son. 'I've made enquiries about him. I wouldn't allow my dearest granddaughter to marry just any young fop. William and I are in agreement. Mortreath's a fine man, upstanding, successful and highly regarded and wealthy in his own right. I fancy he'll ask for Ameline's hand in marriage tonight.'

'I grant you he sounds the ideal suitor for any young lady of quality,' Oliver said, looking around for another glass of wine.

'He is. I hope Ameline will have him willingly. He's a good churchman too, doesn't have any sympathy with this Methodist nonsense. Can't think why you of all people tolerate it, Oliver.'

'Each man to his own way of believing, Martin. I haven't heard anything yet in Wesley's or his laymen's preachings that I can take exception to.'

Sir Martin gave Oliver a sideways glance. 'You don't take all their prattlings to heart either though, do you, my boy? Haven't given up smuggling, for instance. You don't think of it as "an abomination". You're too much your own man.' He looked back up the stairway and tut-tutted in extreme irritation. William and James Mortreath's progress was being impeded by the enormously overweight Countess of Nansavellion. 'Huh!' he grunted. 'Now Rachael's wretched mother is delaying William!'

Scanning the animated crowd for a footman with a tray of wine, Oliver was delighted when a young man in an officer's uniform of the 32nd Regiment of Foot handed him a full glass.

'Martin! How good it is to see you and how good you look in the red and white. It makes me wish I was back in the regiment again.'

'I'm sure I don't look half as good as you did, Oliver,' the younger Martin Beswetherick said. 'I'm not as tall and straight as you are, but I do admit I'm proud to be wearing the uniform and to be following in yours and late Uncle Arthur's footsteps.' Pushing back the lock of light brown hair that had persisted in straying over his eyes all his life, Martin turned to his grandfather. 'A very happy birthday to you, Grandpaps. This looks like it will be a grand celebration.'

'We'll give you one for your coming of age at the end of the year, Martin,' the elderly baronet beamed indulgently. 'Bigger and better than this if I have anything to do with it. A worthy grandson I have here, Oliver, and a worthy heir to the Beswetherick fortune after his father. Do you know, not one of the others of my large brood could be bothered to put in an appearance tonight. Well, damn me, who cares? If they can't be bothered to come, I won't have to send the stable boys to shovel up after their horses, eh? Mind you, we could really get things warmed up if that tiresome mother of yours would hurry up and show herself, Martin.'

Martin laughed. 'I'll dash up and escort her down myself, Grandpaps. Is Kerensa with her?'

'She is,' Oliver replied.

'Wonderful! I can't wait to see her again. She is sure to outshine all the other women here tonight as usual. I won't allow you to claim all of the dances with her, Oliver,' Martin rejoined.

'You'll have to keep an eye on that young man, he adores Kerensa,' Sir Martin teased as his thin, wiry grandson bounded off to take the stairs in leaps, waving at his father and James Mortreath as he passed by them.

'Well, Father,' William Beswetherick said, rubbing his hands together when he finally made his impatient parent's side. 'I'm afraid it took us rather a long time to disengage ourselves from the Countess. Where has Martin gone in such a hurry?'

'To fetch Rachael,' his father told him peevishly. 'Why didn't she come down with you and Mortreath?'

'I'm afraid she insisted I leave the bedchamber. She said she would be no longer than ten minutes and to leave her to get ready in peace. It was like taking my life into my hands up there, I can tell you.' William smiled graciously at Oliver. 'Ah, Oliver, allow me to introduce you to James Mortreath. James, Sir Oliver Pengarron.'

The two men briefly shook hands and both were about to speak when, on a signal from a footman, the musicians changed tune to the notes of a fanfare and the guests in the suddenly hushed banqueting hall watched Lady Rachael Beswetherick descend the stairs on the arm of her eldest son. Ladies tittered at her appearance behind their fans while all male eyes were upon the lady on Martin's other arm, Kerensa, Lady Pengarron.

James Mortreath sucked in his breath. 'Lady Rachael looks radiant tonight,' he whispered to Oliver, 'but who is the beautiful child with her and her son?'

Oliver looked from the ridiculous to the beautiful then fixed James Mortreath with a hard stare. 'That child, Mortreath, is my wife.'

'Your wife!'

'And,' Oliver added, to underline the fact that his wife was no longer a child, 'the mother of my children.'

'Children? . . . I . . . um . . .' James Mortreath's face

turned crimson. He jumped back two paces. He was not unaware of this tall man's reputation for outbreaks of bad temper, of his arrogance and strong will, and that he was said to be particularly sensitive on matters pertaining to his wife. How could he have possibly known that this auburn-haired vision of beauty, youth and innocence now gliding gracefully towards them was Sir Oliver's wife? He'd assumed she was one of Ameline's friends. 'If . . . if you'll excuse me, Sir Oliver, Sir Martin, I . . . I will go and find out where Miss Ameline has got to.' James Mortreath retreated like a fox before hounds.

'Now, now, Oliver,' Sir Martin bellowed. 'That was most wicked of you. You've frightened the poor man half out of his wits.'

'Oh dear,' Oliver said, amused. 'You know, Martin, this is going to be one of your best parties yet.' With his handsome head raised and dark eyes twinkling, he held out his hand to claim Kerensa's.

Ameline Beswetherick thanked her maid and after a final check in the mirror of her own bedchamber she left and hurried towards the stairs. She had two small flights of five steps each to patter down before pacing the long corridor to reach the main staircase down into the banqueting hall.

At the last moment Ameline had suffered a mishap which turned out to be a blessing in disguise. She had meekly endured her mother's frequent changes of mind about her appearance and her inane chatter and exhortations on how she should behave, how she should dance and with whom, and how she must be careful not to drink too much wine because it went so quickly to her head. She had suffered the indignity of her mother pinning fripperies to her gown, spoiling the maidenly effect of its dainty neckline of deep pink bows. Nothing more was needed to complement the pale pink satin, white silk petticoat and single layer of white lace sleeve ruffles. Resentment was heaped upon her frustration when lavish silken flowers, made in France and costing more than her gown, were thrust into her hair.

When Ameline viewed herself in her mother's mirror she could have cried. She was a plain young woman of twenty-one, awkward in stature with ordinary brown hair. Compared to Kerensa, who retained a perpetual beauty and simplicity in dress and ornamentation, she usually felt like an unripe fruit. But now, thanks to her mother's garish ministrations, she looked like a bowl of stewed strawberries.

Then had come the mishap for which she had been most grateful. The clasp of her single dropped ruby necklace came apart to send it bouncing off her skirts and skimming under her mother's elaborate bed. Martin had knocked and entered at that point and he had got down on his hands and knees with Kerensa to search about under the bed for it.

'Leave that now, the servants can retrieve it,' Rachael said, laughing so shrilly Ameline wanted to put her hands over her ears. 'My little lambkin can wear something of mine.'

'It's all right, Mama,' Ameline hastily asserted, determined never to wear any of Rachael's fussy jewellery. 'I'll return to my own room and put on my pearls.'

'Don't be too long, sis,' Martin said as he got to his feet and helped Kerensa to hers. 'Grandpaps is steadily growing redder in the face with impatience to get the party under way.'

'We have been rather a long time, Rachael,' Kerensa said diplomatically.

27

'You go down without me, I don't want Grandfather to have a seizure on my account,' said Ameline and fled before her mother had time to argue. She was pleased to have this excuse to escape from taking part in one of Rachael's 'grand entrances'. Ameline hated them as much as the silly pet name her mother called her and she wished she wasn't her parents' firstborn; the younger her brothers and sisters were, the less attention they received. She told her maid not to hurry looking for the pearls, wanting to delay her appearance until the party was under way and she could slip down the stairs unnoticed. She removed all the non-essential ornaments from her hair and gown.

The last note of her mother's fanfare had died away long before she neared the end of the corridor. Ameline wrinkled up her face, then smiled. She must remember to smile all night, her mother often stressed it was her best feature. This was true. It lit up her face to transform it from ordinary to, in the secret thoughts of James Mortreath, perfect loveliness.

'A very good evening to you, Miss Ameline.'

'Oh! Captain Solomon!' A hand flew to her cheek. 'I had not expected to find someone else still up here. I fear I am late going down.'

'You are indeed, Miss Ameline, and so am I. If you'll permit me, I would consider it an honour to escort you safely down the stairs.' At all times the voice of Captain Hezekiah Solomon was clear, precise and strangely musical.

Ameline had known this dapper gentleman sea captain from childhood. He was a close friend of Sir Oliver's and less so of her grandfather's and gambled with them until the small hours of the night. As with most people who knew Hezekiah Solomon, she was fascinated by his eccentricities, his fastidious manners, decorative colourful clothes and long, shiny white hair.

Ameline was about to say something in reply but the words died away. An unpleasant tingle touched her spine. With her eyes unwillingly locked to his, she placed her hand on the bright gold-brocaded satin of his arm, bent ready to receive her hand. Hezekiah Solomon made her feel that he could see right into her, even read her thoughts. Until now she had felt nothing to fear from this effeminate looking creature and although he was smiling at her as one might imagine an angel would, there was something odd about his eyes tonight. They were so queerly blue, steely blue and somehow icy cold. A chilled bleakness crept up from her toes to the top of her head and remained with Ameline throughout the night.

Hezekiah Solomon escorted Ameline to her grandfather's side and left her with a gracious bow. He danced as often as was possible with Kerensa Pengarron. Throughout her marriage, from their first meeting on her wedding day, he had looked for opportunities to be close to her without arousing Oliver's protective or territorial instincts and probable wrath. When Hezekiah relinquished Kerensa, after the last dance he could ask for without infringing the proprieties, he drew Oliver aside for a private talk. They slipped into William's study and helped themselves to his brandy. Hezekiah was careful not to mention Kerensa.

'What do you want to discuss with me?' Oliver asked, stretching out his long legs from William's chair.

'Oh, it's nothing important or secretive, Oliver, just curious.' Hezekiah stood before a scroll-framed mirror smoothing his hair with the palm of a perfectly manicured hand. 'I was passing through Marazion a few days ago and I came face to face with a youth who bore, I have to say, more than a passing resemblance to you.'

'Really?' Oliver grinned. 'That comes as no surprise to me, Hezekiah. I am believed to be responsible for siring every brat of sixteen years or under who possesses black hair or dark eyes and dwells hereabouts.'

With a smile Hezekiah continued, 'This was more than just a physical resemblance, Oliver. When I first saw him he was fully involved in a drunken brawl outside the Commercial Inn. It was most enjoyable to watch him. He laid out three other men, all older and bigger than himself, in not many more minutes. He would have given that King fellow, the one known as the Barvah Giant, a run for his money. Then he threw back his head and stood with his hands on his hips. I thought of you at once, it was a stance I have seen you adopt often. I watched him walk away after that and he wouldn't give room for either gentry or uniform. I'll warrant the youth shares your stubbornness and pride too.'

'I see,' Oliver said thoughtfully. 'Do you have any idea who he is? This likeness of me?'

Hezekiah inspected the false pads in his hose to ensure they were giving his legs the shape he desired. 'I made enquiries at the inn. Apparently he is a young fisherman by the name of Bartholomew Drannock. He lives with his family at the little village of Perranbarvah. I don't doubt you know or at least know of him, Oliver. Nothing escapes your notice in the parish. Ah, I see by your face that you do.'

'Yes, I know Bartholomew Drannock. I agree with you, he does bear a likeness to me. I've pondered on it since I first noticed it a few years ago when he helped to save my life. He was no more than a boy at the time and helped to drag me out of the sea in Trelynne Cove. I'd gone in to save a girl from drowning and was caught in undercurrents by the rocks. I got her to safety but was too exhausted to pull myself out. In fact, Hezekiah,' Oliver grew serious, 'the boy may have been wholly responsible for saving my life. I shall never know if Clem Trenchard, who was the only other one there on the rocks at the time, would have pulled me out if he'd been alone.'

Hezekiah stayed his brandy glass midway to his mouth. 'Clem Trenchard? That is quite a thought, Oliver. Will he ever forgive you, I wonder, for marrying Kerensa?'

'Probably not,' Oliver replied bluntly, 'and that's too bad for him. As you said, it is curious about Bartholomew Drannock. I've never been with his mother, Jenifer, although I would like to have been, once upon a time. She was quite a beauty when young, the daughter of a ship's chandler, then she got herself pregnant by a poor fisherman and the youth in question was born. I was not on Cornish soil when he was conceived and born, or I would surely have been held to blame for it. I like the youth, Hezekiah, he must be seventeen or eighteen years old now. He fishes with his po-faced father and some of the ever-increasing King family. They're very poor of course. That wretch Peter Blake owns most of the boats in the village, luggers, and seines for the pilchards, and takes more than what is fair of the profits.' Oliver drained his glass and rose. 'Yes, I'll have to take a closer look at Bartholomew Drannock. It's something I've kept meaning to do.'

'What will you do?' asked his white-haired friend, examining the lace ruffles clustered at his wrists.

'Who knows. Now, let us get back to the party.' Oliver smiled wickedly and winked. 'I promised Kerensa I'd dance more than I'd drink tonight and I want to learn more about this fellow Mortreath.'

James Mortreath never enjoyed social gatherings of more than half a dozen people and only endured the crush of the revelries in the hall for the opportunity it gave him of being near Ameline. For the past few minutes he had watched her dance a quadrille partnered by the persistently grinning Mr Alfred Sarrison. The clammy, heavily scented atmosphere crowded in on him. He felt he would suffocate. He was sweating profusely and although painfully thirsty he had no head for alcohol and refused all offers to replenish his empty wine glass.

He longed for the night to be over, while wishing over and over again that he could detain William Beswetherick for more than a few seconds at a time. But William, being a sociable man with a love of partying, was gaily dashing from one to another of his father's guests. James hoped he would catch him before the speeches and toasts began; they were likely to go on for ages. If he could only talk to William now, the speeches could include an announcement concerning himself and Ameline.

He had his own speech meticulously prepared: Sir, would you allow me the honour of asking your daughter Ameline for her hand . . . It was an excellent petition and he knew he would deliver it well. He had never faltered over a single word in the courtroom.

James was confident he was looked on favourably by William, Lady Rachael and old Sir Martin, and he considered himself a suitor of whom he himself would approve if he had a daughter of his own. Ameline seemed to like him, she was always polite and showed an interest in his topics of conversation and appeared to enjoy dancing with him.

On the other hand there were one or two things that might go against him. He was quiet and serious and might be considered rather stuffy by the high-society Beswethericks and their circle of friends and acquaintances, who tended to socialize often and noisily. It had been his only concern until the introduction to Sir Oliver Pengarron. The infamous Sir Oliver was one of the Beswethericks' closest friends and James would have done better to have made a good impression on him rather than spark off his ill humour with that unfortunate remark about his wife.

James wiped away the sweat on his upper lip. If only he could speak to William and obtain permission to ask Ameline to marry him. Then it wouldn't be improper to suggest to her that they step out on to the balcony together to breathe in some welcome fresh air and get away from all these dreadful people. He was fairly confident she would accompany him; Ameline had looked uncomfortable all the evening herself.

James momentarily toyed with then dismissed the notion of approaching Lady Rachael who was in close proximity to him. Apart from the breach in etiquette, Ameline having a father and grandfather present, he felt he could not guarantee a sensible hearing from a woman with an aviary piled on top of her head.

He moved through the nauseating combination of sweating, over-perfumed bodies in the hope of finding an opened window. The bright light from the hundreds of candles and dazzling jewels hurt his eyes. The spread of swishing gowns made from silks, satins, muslins, batistes and, in the latest fashion, cotton, caught at his legs and impeded his progress. Rouged faces seemed to loom up on him. The hum of voices, the background of music, the squeals of laughter, all made his head ache.

He eventually located an open window but it did little to

refresh him as the air outside was warm and clammy. He looked round for Ameline and then William. Ameline was about to take the floor with Sir Martin and William was with his mother-in-law, the Countess. James felt his throat constrict and pulled urgently at his neckcloth. Sir Oliver was talking to Lady Rachael and not troubling to conceal the fact it was James himself they were discussing. Was the tall overpowering man telling the preposterous matron that he would make an unsuitable husband for her daughter?

The Beswethericks would listen to Sir Oliver. James had thought he might receive a sympathetic reception from him as he himself had married a girl notably younger than himself. Life wasn't fair at times, James decided. He had truly thought the girl gliding down the stairs in the sea-green dress with pearls round her throat was one of Ameline's friends; she looked no older than Ameline. How old was Lady Pengarron? He did a quick calculation in his head. According to Ameline she had been seventeen when married, eight years had passed – twenty-five. Sir Oliver had been twice her age at the time of the marriage, which made him now, good lord, forty-two! Even with his colourful past the man could still be taken for James's own age – thirty-six. Life was certainly not fair.

Sir Oliver looked away, and James followed the baronet's gaze. It stopped at Lady Pengarron who was dancing at a sedate pace with Mr John Sarrison in the same set as Sir Martin and Ameline. James had heard Sir Oliver was possessive over his wife, as he was with his land and chattels, but there was more here than that. There was no mistaking the pleasure in those dark unreadable eyes as Lady Pengarron twirled gracefully under the old gentleman's stiffly held arm. When her husband caught her attention, she smiled and waved her hand to him. A surprise indeed. It appeared they were actually in love! It was most unexpected because according to gossip it certainly wasn't the case when they first married and very few married people he knew had any regard for one another, let alone love. Like the self-esteemed coroner, Thomas Cole, and his haughty wife, also in the set, who seemed to be tolerated in genteel company only because of Cole's position.

James wished again he had been in Cornwall for longer than four months. He would have to enquire of Ameline more about the people here, the Pengarrons in particular, if he wasn't going to make a greater fool of himself. It was all so bothersome, he had only come down to this backward county from London to arrange the disposal of an inheritance. He had stayed this long, and at a great deal of inconvenience, because he had fallen in love with Ameline Beswetherick and had had to court her and her family. If he could win Ameline, he would hurriedly set the wedding day and hot-foot with her back to London and never set eye on Cornwall again. And now, just when he was hopeful his suit would be accepted, it seemed Sir Oliver Pengarron was making things difficult for him.

'Are you quite well, Mr Mortreath?' asked Ameline, when the dance ended. 'If I may say so, you look most uncomfortable.'

'I do feel a trifle hot I must confess, Miss Ameline,' he replied, his face lighting up at her concern. 'Did you enjoy your dance with Sir Martin?'

'Yes, thank you, but not with Mr Ralph Harrt, whom I partnered earlier. I believe he dances as he would chase a fox before his hounds. He is not agile on his feet as you are, Mr Mortreath.'

'How kind of you to say so, Miss Ameline.' The remark

gave James encouragement. 'May I have the honour of claiming another dance with you before too long this evening?'

'Indeed you may. I have promised one dance to my brother, Martin, one to my father and one to Mr John Sarrison, although he may soon be danced off his feet in the same way as Mr Alfred. Grandfather has vowed to dance twice with every lady in the room but he looks as if his age and rheumatism will soon have the upper hand of him. Oh, and one dance with Oliver, Sir Oliver that is, but I will save the remainder for you, Mr Mortreath. Have you been introduced to Sir Oliver yet?'

'Yes, yes . . . a . . . a most charming man,' James blustered.

'And Lady Pengarron?'

'Yes, I spoke to her briefly. She seems most charming too.'

'I'm pleased you've accepted her. Some people are beastly about her background, working class, you know, and it does anger me. I believe one should take people as one finds them and she has always been very sweet to me.'

James was relieved he had not made another error about the beautiful Lady Pengarron. He had spoken the truth about finding her charming and would liked to have asked her to dance, but fear of Sir Oliver's reaction had stopped him.

Ameline was smiling at him and James felt another surge of confidence. If she had a regard for him and wished to accept his offer of marriage, then even if Sir Oliver was against him it wouldn't matter.

Ameline's smile died when she became aware that Captain Hezekiah Solomon was looking straight across the hall at her. Her hand flew to clutch James's arm. He misread her action and plunged into part of the speech he had prepared for her father.

'Miss Ameline, I have the intention of asking . . .'

She was not listening to him. Hezekiah Solomon was rapidly making his way over to them.

'What . . . what was that you were saying, Mr Mortreath?' she said shakily, moving abruptly so her back was towards Hezekiah and giving James her full attention.

'I was saying that I intend to speak to your father—'

James was rudely interrupted. 'I am hoping that I may have the pleasure of the next dance with you, Miss Ameline,' Hezekiah said forcefully over her shoulder.

Hardly turning round, Ameline said coolly, 'I'm afraid I have promised the next dance to Mr Mortreath. In fact I have none available for the rest of the evening, Captain Solomon.'

She could feel his eyes burning into the side of her face. They flicked to James Mortreath and back to Ameline. 'As you please, Miss Ameline,' Hezekiah said tonelessly, then bowed with a characteristic flourish and withdrew.

James looked at her shaken face. 'Do you not like him, Captain Solomon?'

'No . . . he . . .' Realising she was still clinging to his arm she pulled her hand away and clenched her fists. 'The next dance is about to begin, Mr Mortreath. Shall we take the floor?'

'I'd be delighted.'

James led Ameline to the set forming closest to them. He felt more conspicuous than usual when Hezekiah Solomon took a position next to Sir Oliver and inclined his cologned white head to the baronet's ear.

Unlike James and Ameline, Kerensa Pengarron was thoroughly enjoying the evening's celebration. She had forgotten her earlier feelings of foreboding due to the fog, and was unaware of the different effects her presence was having on some of Sir Martin's guests.

Chapter 3

Kerensa stood huddled at Oliver's side in the driving rain in Perranbarvah's churchyard. From time to time she glanced anxiously at Ruth and Esther King, two of Pengarron Manor's servants, and sisters of the young fisherman whose burial they were attending. It was two months since the fishing boat tragedy and the fourth time the mourners had gathered to lay a member of the King family to his final rest.

At Kerensa's other side was Matthias Renfree, the son of the Pengarron estate's home farm and stud steward. He was supporting Elizabeth King, the grieving mother of the deceased, Mark King. She sobbed unrestrainedly throughout the solemn words spoken by the parson, the Reverend Joseph Ivey. Matthias was a source of great comfort to Elizabeth, devout as he was, like the Kings, to John Wesley's teaching of the Gospel and Christian way of life. Before the funeral today, Elizabeth had told him, Oliver and Kerensa that she was grateful to the Almighty for giving her back all of her loved ones from the deep.

The Kings were too poor to provide coffins for their dead menfolk and it would have been the loan of the parish coffin for each in turn and burial in nothing more than a shroud but for the thoughtful intervention of Oliver. He'd approached the family through Matthias Renfree, offering to supply a coffin for each of the deceased if and when they were found. Elizabeth King had received the offer with the dignity and spirit with which it was given and her menfolk were lowered into the ground, up above the fishing village where they had all been born, encased in timber from the Pengarron oak plantation.

The first funeral had been for brothers Solomon and Jonathan, who on the day following their deaths were washed up only yards apart on Perranbarvah's beach, not far from the moored boats. The next had been for John, Solomon and Elizabeth's youngest son, whose body was discovered days later trapped among rocks half a mile along the beach. Days later again, Grandfather King's body was found washed ashore further along the coast in Trelynne Cove, his arm flung out with index finger pointing to the sea where many yards away lay Josh. It was said the Kings believed the old fisherman had found his grandson who had vanished unseen from the *Young Maid*.

And then Mark's remains were found floating entangled in wreckage from the *Lowenek* far out at sea. At his funeral today Kerensa noticed there were no Drannocks present. Jenifer, Samuel's distraught widow, the mother of a large family herself, had been ailing for some time and at the previous double funeral had been at the point of collapse. Bartholomew had taken her out of the churchyard and half carried her home.

Kerensa glanced round the graveside taking note of who had turned out to mourn. There was Rosina Blake, a young woman with whom Kerensa had been on friendly terms until Rosina had married Peter Blake, owner of the *Young Maid*. Rosina was well thought of, though her husband was not. She was another devout Methodist and a gentle, caring young woman. She stared down sadly at the grave and shook her head often.

40

Next to Rosina Blake were most of the Trenchard family, whose head, Morley, held a farm tenancy on the Pengarron estate. With him was his elder son, Clem, the man Kerensa had once been going to marry, and his wife, Alice, Kerensa's closest friend. Kerensa would like to have talked to Alice afterwards but she could not with Clem there; knowing that Clem still loved her, Oliver was jealous and suspicious of him. Clem looked at her at the same moment her eyes reached his face. He smiled back weakly, as befitted the occasion, but his face was full of warmth and affection. Before she could reciprocate, as if an instinct had been stirred Oliver moved across her line of vision.

The final prayer was said and the mourners, mostly fisherfolk and a large turn-out of local Methodists, moved off to plod dejectedly back up or down the steep hill that ran outside the churchyard. Kerensa managed a brief smile at Clem before he left with Alice on his arm. Then she turned to speak to Matthias Renfree.

'Ruth and Esther are going to spend another week with Elizabeth,' she told him. 'Will you go with them, Matthias, and see if there's anything they need, please?'

'Aye, m'lady, I'll do that,' Matthias assured her in his quiet, soothing voice. 'Your presence and support has already been very much appreciated. I'll have a quiet word with Matthew. He's been badly shaken up by the tragedy but I'm sure he'll be able to take over from his grandfather and keep the family together. He has a lot of responsibility now with his own young family and Jonathan's motherless brood, but they'll get through with the Lord's help and that of the community.'

When Matthias had gone, Oliver put two firm hands on Kerensa's shoulders. 'Are you all right, my love?' he whispered into her ear.

She turned her head to look up at him and her face quickly became sprinkled with raindrops. They mingled with the tears in her eyes and she was surprised to find herself trembling. 'It's all so terrible, Oliver. Whatever will they do?'

Oliver looked at the mounds of freshly dug wet earth. With the last King buried, and when the ground had settled, he would have a large headstone erected with all their names inscribed on it and the date of their tragic deaths, the twelfth day of April, 1761.

'We'll do what we can to ease their pain and provide for their comfort, Kerensa,' he said dully, 'as much as the Kings and Drannocks feel able to accept. They've lost so much and the parish has lost some of its best characters. While you were talking to Renfree I was having a word with Matthew King and Lowenna, his wife.'

'How is Paul?' Kerensa asked at once, rather fearfully. 'Did you ask them? Did they say if he'll pull through?' Only hours after the terrible accident, Paul King had succumbed to a severe bout of pneumonia.

Oliver smiled and tenderly stroked her cheek. 'His fever has abated at last, my love, don't you worry. Dr Crebo has told the family he has every chance of fully regaining his health.'

Kerensa's slender form sighed. 'Thank the Lord for that, at least. Another funeral would be unbearable.'

'Matthew King has told me something that both he and I find wholly unbearable,' Oliver said, his features hardening. 'Peter Blake will not allow him and Bartholomew Drannock to take over the *Young Maid* when she is repaired. Not only is he denying them the means of their livelihood, the swine is demanding compensation for the damage, too.'

'Oh, Oliver, no! How could he be so cruel?'

'I'm afraid cruelty and unfairness come all too easily to that particular man, as you well know. For all his outward appearance of benevolence, he cares for no one other than his wife and child. King and young Drannock are going to see him again and ask him to reconsider, but if they're unsuccessful at getting him to change his mind, then perhaps I can. I will not leave the situation as it is.'

'What will you do, Oliver?' Kerensa said, hastily taking his hand as if by this she might forbid his plans; she would never forget that Oliver had once almost beaten Peter Blake to his death for harming her. And he could be equally protective over the people of the parish where he was Lord of the Manor.

'I'll take care of it,' he said firmly. 'Do not be concerned, I won't raise a finger to him,' adding mentally, 'unless he gives me just cause.' Oliver knew by the face Kerensa was making that she did not believe him, but before she could extract a promise from him not to lose his temper with Peter Blake he moved on to another concern left by the tragedy. 'Are you still of a mind to call on Jenifer Drannock, my love?'

Kerensa narrowed her eyes at his ploy, but answered, 'Yes. Jenifer probably needs more help than the Kings do. She has no one but Bartholomew to turn to now, the other children are too young to be of much help. Come to that, Bartholomew is very young to be head of the family.'

'You go along now, my dear. I don't want you getting a chill. I'll take some refreshment with the Reverend Ivey and you can call at the parsonage when you're ready to go home.' He gave her his striking smile, said, 'Take your time,' then kissed both her wet cheeks.

The first time Kerensa had entered the Drannock's cottage, set amid the tightly packed cluster of fishermen's cob-built homes, was eight years before when she'd been an unhappy young bride. It had always been a drab, dirty-looking building and in the years since had shown no improvement. Kerensa had visited only twice, because Samuel Drannock had shown his disapproval of her calling and had forbidden her to give Jenifer any more of the gifts she had brought to ease their poverty.

Kerensa wondered how Jenifer would receive her today. She knocked loudly on the battered door. There was no reply. Slowly she lifted the buckled rusty latch, pushed the door open a few inches and called out softly, 'Jenifer, are you there?'

There was still no answer. Kerensa's concern for Jenifer and her children outweighed the fear of a rebuff. She pushed the door open wider, stepped quickly inside and closed the door against the heavy rain.

She was in the kitchen, the only living room of the cottage. It looked empty, bleak and cold. Jenifer Drannock had never aspired to being an efficient housewife and the stark surroundings looked even more untidy and dusty than Kerensa remembered. The room smelled of dampness and stale food. Kerensa rubbed at the top of her arms under her cloak, wistfully noting the cheerless fire sputtering in the hearth, thinking that the vast moorlands of Lancavel Downs in deep winter were more hospitable than this.

With her eyes on a poker and the intention of raking among the charred sticks of driftwood to encourage a blaze, Kerensa stepped over a scattered heap of soiled laundry. She jumped back as a large scruffy grey cat leaped off the back of a chair and hissed at her before its paws hit the cold unplanched floor. The cat glared at her, making her feel even more of an intruder, then made its way to the door with its half-chewed-off tail up in the air. It was then that Kerensa saw the still figure of Jenifer Drannock sitting to the side of the door on a small settle. She was wearing ill-fitting black clothes borrowed from the neighbours and against the dark wood of the high-backed settle only her hands and face were clearly visible. The blank expression on her haggard white face made her seem like a creature from another world.

'Jenifer!' Kerensa blurted out, guilt rushing to her cheeks. 'I . . . I hope you don't mind me walking in like this.'

'Not at all, my dear,' Jenifer replied, her voice dry and vacant. 'It is good of you to come. If you can stay, sit yourself down – if you can find a clean enough chair.' She waved a weary hand in no particular direction. 'I'm sorry, I just haven't had the heart . . .'

'I understand,' Kerensa said gently. 'Would you like me to tidy up a few things for you?' She glanced at the rickety table with its remains of several sparse and unpalatable meals.

'No, it's all right, my dear, thank you. Ruth and Esther King were here a short time ago. They're coming back when they've settled their mother, and seen to Paul. They'll sort out all this mess between them. I feel so sorry for them, losing so many of their family. They'll be kept busy here for quite a while . . . take their minds off the tragedy. You can cheer up that fire if you like, you're shivering in those wet things. People have been kind, they've brought us some extra logs. Pile them on and get warmed through. Here,' Jenifer held out a well-used knitted blanket made up of a few squares. 'Take off your hat and cloak and put this round your shoulders. It's not very big but it will cover a little bit of a thing like you.'

Kerensa stoked up the fire without speaking and when the logs were roaring she cleared laundry off a chair by the table and sat down. 'Wouldn't you be warmer over here by the hearth, Jenifer? It must be draughty by the door and with the window nearly over your head.'

'I'd rather stay here, thank you. Samuel and I used to sit here together so the children could be nearer the fire. We'd cuddle up under a blanket and wear extra clothes to keep warm. Sometimes we'd be so comfortable we'd fall off to sleep and not bother to go to bed. In the summer we'd leave the door open for the fresh air. Samuel would pick up the settle and place it where we could look out over the sea. It's a heavy piece of furniture but he was so strong . . . we'd sit and dream of all the things we'd like to do . . .'

'You were very happy together,' Kerensa said gently.

'Oh yes. I have been very fortunate . . . blessed. Samuel and I fell in love from the very moment he stepped inside my father's chandlery shop. We never lost that wonderful feeling over the years.' Jenifer was smiling at her memories and Kerensa's heart went out to her. 'You know how it is, don't you? You and Sir Oliver share the same kind of love we did.'

Kerensa nodded, touched by the beauty and pain of Jenifer's words. 'You mentioned your father, Jenifer. He must know of the accident. Have you sent word to him? He may wish to help.'

'No, no, my dear. My family disowned me the day I married my Samuel. The Milderns are not of a forgiving nature. They know what has happened, but no one has been to see me or sent any word. To them I married beneath me and must bear the consequences till the day I die.'

46

Kerensa moved to Jenifer and kneeling down beside her took the cold hands from the woman's lap and held them tightly in her own. 'I'm so sorry about Samuel, Jenifer,' she whispered against a lump in her throat. Loving Oliver the way she did, she could feel the agony of Jenifer's loss. 'Please, won't you let me and Oliver help you and the children?'

Jenifer firmly shook her head and stroked the soft, damp, auburn hair from Kerensa's brow with rough, ridged fingers. 'No, no, Kerensa, Samuel wouldn't take charity while he was alive and I won't go against him now. Don't distress yourself over me, it will only be a brief parting for me and Samuel.'

By her deathly pallor and the sunken eyes in Jenifer's face, Kerensa could well believe it. Then there would be six orphaned children to consider. 'Can't you think of it as friendship, not charity, Jenifer?'

Jenifer looked at Kerensa fondly, but shook her head. 'It's best to leave things as they are.'

Thinking back to the day Samuel Drannock had stopped her from helping his family, Kerensa's face coloured a little. What he had told her then always made her feel guilty. 'Is that because of the secret we share?'

'In a way. Samuel was always afraid that Sir Oliver would find out.' Then for a moment Jenifer looked as if she had some energy in her soul as she said, 'And now that Samuel is dead, don't you think it would be worse if he did?'

'Yes, perhaps you are right,' Kerensa replied uncomfortably. 'But I would still like to help you, Jenifer. If you ever change your mind . . .' She glanced round at the scraps of food on the table, bit her bottom lip, then added, 'At least will you accept some eggs and milk for the children? Ruth and Esther can bring them over from the manor, Oliver need never know, and anyway it would be no more than he would expect me to do. He will wonder more if I don't do something for you.'

After a pause Jenifer capitulated. 'You're such a sweet little thing and here's me calling you my dear, or Kerensa, when I should be addressing you by your title or Ma'am.'

'I'd rather no one called me that, or m'lady or Lady Pengarron. I've never felt comfortable with it, it doesn't seem right, what with my background. You've made me feel good calling me Kerensa, it means I really do have your friendship.'

Jenifer gave a short, strange laugh. 'I always said to my Samuel that you look no more than a child, sweet and gentle, not old enough to be married. And now you have children of your own . . .' Breaking off Jenifer looked towards the window. 'Is it still raining?'

Rising, Kerensa pulled open the ill-fitting shutters of the window and studied the streaks of grey painted across the sky. 'It's just about stopped and the sun is breaking through. It should be nice and warm by evening.'

'Samuel liked the warm early summer evenings. He used to say it was the best time of day to be out at sea.' As she talked Jenifer sounded more and more distant. Her eyes became vacant. She looked decades older than her forty years. Her skin was wrinkled and flaking, the flesh mottled with blue and purple patches. Her hair was ravaged of all its natural fairness to a lifeless grey. Kerensa wondered if she had eaten or slept at all in the past two months.

'Jenifer, where are the children?'

'The children? Oh, the little ones are with the neighbours. Cordelia's with the Roskilleys and Charles and Jack with the Laitys. Hannah and Naomi, my older girls, are away at Marazion working for the Sarrison brothers, Mr

48

Alfred and Mr John. They took them both on after the accident. They are very good to my girls. It means I have two less mouths to feed, and there's a little bit of money coming in.'

All you have at the moment, Kerensa thought, unless Bartholomew's been smuggling. 'Has Bartholomew arranged for someone to come in and sit with you?' she asked. 'Should he leave you alone like this?'

'I prefer to be alone, my dear.' Jenifer gave her the faintest of smiles. 'Bartholomew tried to get me to agree to having one of the other women in with me, but I'd rather be alone. He had to go to Marazion, he and Matthew King, to see Mr Blake.' She said no more and as Kerensa knew why the two young fishermen had gone to Marazion, she asked no questions about it.

'Jenifer, will you be all right?'

'Oh yes. You see, I always knew this would happen one day . . . and I'm glad he hasn't been found, I pray to God he never will be.' Jenifer stared into space. 'Samuel would want to stay in the sea, to rest in the deep, not be buried under the earth.'

The door was opened and Ruth and Esther King came in, both carrying aprons. They bobbed Kerensa a curtsy, unfolded the long lengths of crisp white cotton and put them on.

'We'll soon clear this up, m'lady,' Ruth said in a hushed tone, inclining her head of mousy brown hair at the room.

'It's very good of you both,' Kerensa said, 'and I'm greatly relieved to hear Paul is over the worst.'

''Tis thanks to Sir Oliver for sending over the doctor and paying his fees,' Esther asserted, pushing back straight hair the same colour as her sister's under a cap.

'And one of Beatrice's potions,' added Ruth. 'It looked

and smelled ghastly but just one big spoonful and his fever nigh on went at once.'

'I'll call on your mother tomorrow. And Paul when he's well again, if you don't think he'll mind that,' Kerensa said.

'I reckon he'll be tickled, having a lady come to call on him. He's some weak at the moment, m'lady, but is able to sit and sip at a bit of broth.' Ruth was looking around as if she was impatient to get on with the clearing up.

The King sisters were tall like their menfolk and their presence had made the little cottage seem crowded. Kerensa knew it was she who was in the way.

'Jenifer will appreciate your help here today,' she said.

'We'll give the young'uns their tea later on.' As she spoke, Ruth began tentatively to gather up discarded clothing. ''Twill be good to be kept busy at a time like this.'

Esther's hands strayed towards the table and itched to start stacking up the dishes.

'Yes, of course,' Kerensa said, noting their red-rimmed eyes. Before the news of the tragedy, she had never known either of the sisters to cry. Somehow she found it embarrassing. It was time for her to leave. Looking back at Jenifer Drannock, who was now hunched up on the settle and moving her body in a rocking motion, Kerensa thought it a pity this poor woman did not cry too.

Chapter 4

Oliver strode through Marazion's one long straggling street, his head up, ignoring the summer shower of rain blown into the front of his body. Passers-by, hunched over with their eyes down on the muddy road, clung on to their hats, stopping only respectfully to acknowledge the tall imposing owner of the black polished leather boots. Oliver spoke to some, merely nodded to others, as the mood took him.

He called at Araminta Bray's grocery shop. The sharp-chinned bespectacled widow was one of his best customers for the smuggled goods he helped to bring in from various spots along Mount's Bay. Despite the fact that the country was fighting a colonial war with France, on foreign ground, smuggling with the enemy was still active and Oliver kept the shop well stocked and liked to see the neat displays that Mrs Bray made of the tea, coffee, spices, dried fruit and other items he regularly provided. His ventures were mainly with Hezekiah Solomon who had revealed he had a residence on French soil and there passed as a French gentleman. From him Oliver occasionally gleaned useful information which he passed on to the Admiralty; it pleased him to be doing something for the latest war effort.

Oliver took a long, satisfying sniff of the darkened shop's

51

mixture of exotic and homely smells. He handed Mrs Bray an order made up by Kerensa for items he did not smuggle in, then intimated to the shopkeeper that she should be prepared to have her stock replenished in a week's time with the ones he did.

When he turned to go he found a cluster of curious women behind him. They all quickly curtsied and moved back in a semi-circle, a gap at their centre to give him a clear path to the door. They all stared at his handsome face; it was a favourite pastime of the local women of all classes. Oliver included them all in one sweeping glance and abruptly left the premises. Outside he grinned knowingly, confident they would swing back into a huddle and ply Mrs Bray with eager questions as to what business the Lord of the Manor of the next parish had in a woman's domain.

His next stop was a few paces away in a gin shop. He was to arrange there the details of the next smuggling run which was coming into Trelynne Cove. The long mild coastline of Mount's Bay, comfortably sheltered between Land's End and the Lizard, was a haven for smugglers. Oliver had runs operating from Mullion to Mousehole, openly flouting the authorities. He shared the Cornish belief in the right to smuggle in goods to enhance comfort and pocket and only one Customs officer had ever dared to cross him.

A new keen man stationed at Penzance, where the Customs had their headquarters, had forced entry into a house at Marazion and arrested the occupant, one of Oliver's customers. The evidence – bales of silk, brandy and rum and glass for the customer's parlour window – was sitting under the kitchen window. The customer's wife had raced after Oliver and told him of the affront and

Oliver had returned in a rage. He hurled aside the Customs officer's self-made introduction and demanded an explanation during which speech he slipped a silver snuff box into the Customs officer's pocket. He then accused the unfortunate man of stealing it. The Customs officer heeded the warning and admitted he had made a 'mistake'. He kept out of Sir Oliver's way after that.

Oliver bought a full round of drinks in the gin shop, mixing readily with the local men in the clammy smoky room. He accepted a glass of gin from Jake Merrifield of Rose Farm on the Pengarron estate, and amid much hectic betting and riotous cheers won an arm-wrestling match against a swarthy foreign sailor. His ability to mix with and drink alongside these men had earned him their admiration and respect, and loyalty on the runs.

He then moved on to another drinking place, where the beverage and clientele were in complete contrast – a gentleman's coffee shop. Oliver spent an interesting hour discussing the latest political, financial, and royal court news with Sir Martin Beswetherick and James Mortreath. Oliver baited James Mortreath, who was extremely wary of him after the night of Sir Martin's birthday party, without mercy. It put him in just the right mood for his planned encounter with Peter Blake.

After leaving the coffee shop he headed straight for the Blakes' apartments over Angarrack's, the shoemaker's shop, but before entering the building he felt compelled to stand and look across the sea at St Michael's Mount. Rain pelted down at a deep slant, giving the Mount and the castle built on its top, its servants' buildings and tall swaying trees a fairy-tale quality. The scene touched Oliver's deeply rooted French and Celtic ancestry. Monks, soldiers and noble families had all lived on the Mount. It fascinated

Oliver as much as it did Kerensa; she would tell him of the legends she knew and the fantasies she made up of dragons, giants, and maidens locked away in dungeons and awaiting rescue.

Oliver stood there now, forming a tale, with Kerensa as a kidnapped maiden and he as her knightly rescuer – to be told at bedtime of course. He ignored the cold wind and the rain dripping off his hat and coat. The tide was slipping out, revealing more and more of the ancient causeway, laid down for the passage of carts and pedestrians to and from what the sailors and mariners called the Cornish Mount. The ships moored and sheltered at its pier swayed in the wind. If he had had the time, Oliver would have called on the St Aubyns and carried across the talk from the coffee shop but the need to see Peter Blake beckoned more strongly, and Oliver cursed Blake, whom he hated, as an infernal nuisance.

He entered Seth Angarrack's noisy, industrious workshop, the premises rented from Peter Blake, and took the stairs to the rooms above three at a time and rapped on the door with his riding crop.

A woman, hastening on from her middle years to old age, opened the door and gawped at him with her mouth wide open before shrieking, 'What are you doing here? Go away! If you want the master he's out and he won't be back for hours!'

'Then inform your mistress I wish to be received,' Oliver retorted, meeting the woman's hostility and lack of respect with a harsh look. 'She is at home, I take it?' he ended with a snap.

The woman sprang back and began to quiver. 'You're not welcome here, go away, go away!'

'Who is it, Mrs Blight?' came a gentle voice from within.

Mrs Blight did not reply and the light irregular footsteps approaching the door quickened. It was opened wider and a young woman whose appearance matched her voice looked up at the man on her doorstep.

'Sir Oliver!' she said, with the greatest surprise. 'You are the last person I expected to call on us.'

'It is your husband I have called to see, Mistress Blake,' he said in a pleasanter tone. 'According to your servant he is not to be found at home. I wish to see him on a matter of some urgency.'

Rosina Blake smiled in her own peaceful way. 'Perhaps you would care to step inside and talk to me about it, Sir Oliver.'

'That is most gracious of you, ma'am, and I shall not refuse your invitation.' As he stepped over the threshold Mrs Blight leapt further back and rammed her knuckles into her mouth.

'I'll see to His Lordship, Mrs Blight,' Rosina said. 'You may go to your room. If I need anything I'll ring for Kate. Please excuse Mrs Blight's outbursts, Sir Oliver, I do apologise on her behalf,' Rosina went on as she took Oliver's dripping riding coat and tricorn hat. 'She's always been a nervous sort of woman but I'm afraid she's become much worse of late.'

'Perhaps it's her age that makes her so ill-mannered towards your more important visitors, Mistress Blake,' Oliver said, with eyes of ice.

Rosina knew that Oliver knew he really had no right to be offended at such a reception in this household. He looked pointedly at her and she did not lower her eyes. It took only a moment to agree without speech that past events had left no feelings of animosity between themselves.

'Come into the sitting room, Sir Oliver. It's not much of a summer's day today and I have a small fire lit against the chill. You can dry out a little.'

Oliver followed Rosina's lilting movements, thinking it a pity she should have a lame foot but deciding it detracted very little from her pleasant outline. When they were seated in the plush comfortable room, Rosina offered him a dish of tea which Oliver politely declined.

'You are very kind, Mistress Blake,' he said. 'I would have understood if you had slammed the door in my face after the beating I once gave your husband, though he thoroughly deserved it.'

A remark of the kind said to Kerensa about Oliver would have brought her hurtling to her feet and loudly declaring herself in his defence. Rosina Blake stayed in her seat and spoke in her normal voice. 'You did more than just beat Peter, Sir Oliver, you almost killed him. It was all a long time ago, before Peter and I were married, and I would prefer to leave it in the past.'

Pulling back a corner of his full wide mouth Oliver regarded Rosina with an appreciative eye. The same age as Kerensa and also from working-class stock, she had married into the gentry in the same year, meeting Blake by coming to his aid after the aforementioned beating. If one had to marry out of one's class, Oliver decided, you, Rosina Blake, would make a most charming and admirable second choice. He particularly admired Rosina's waist-length corn-coloured hair, which fell like a waterfall about her shoulders when she moved. Obviously in deference to her husband's wish, he mused; a woman in love was like that.

Although chaste until her wedding night, a woman could not be married to a warm, sensuous man such as Peter

Blake without knowing something of the male mind, and Rosina was aware of the interest she aroused in the dark eyes across the room, but she was not offended. Indeed, very few women had looked upon the face of Oliver Pengarron and not found pleasure in his strikingly fine looks and flattery in being the subject of his perusal. Rosina knew he was one half of a very happy and successful marriage, but she wondered if Sir Oliver included fidelity in his perception of what made a good husband.

'If you'd be good enough to tell me why you've called wanting to see Peter,' she said, breaking the silence, 'then perhaps I can be of some help to you.'

'You are not expecting him back home shortly?'

'Not for at least two hours. He's taken our son, Simon Peter, over Trevenner way. You may have heard he's having a house built for us there, close to his half-sister's residence.'

'I have heard and I've seen the builders at work. It will be a splendid dwelling when completed, and you have a fine son to grow up within its walls. Now, to come to the reason for my presence here. It concerns the Perranbarvah fishing tragedy of two months ago. Indeed we were both in the parish churchyard only yesterday paying our last respects to one of the unfortunate victims.'

'It's all so sad,' Rosina said mournfully, unable to repress a shudder. 'I didn't know Samuel Drannock very well but I've known the King family practically all my life, particularly so from the Bible classes up on Lancavel Downs.'

Oliver leaned towards her. 'I'm certain you will agree with me, Mistress Blake, that people in our position must do all we can to help the bereaved families.'

'Yes, of course, I wish we could do more. The collection

of monies raised must have run out by now and unfortunately you can't keep sending food and things, people have their pride and it would be cruel to step on such sensitive feelings.' Rosina brightened and looked at him optimistically. 'You have an idea of some sort how to help, Sir Oliver? Is that why you're here?'

'Precisely. Two of the fishermen involved in the tragedy, Matthew King and Bartholomew Drannock – who incidentally are now left in the position of being the heads of their families – find themselves without the means to pursue their livelihood. One of the boats in the accident, the *Lowenek*, was smashed to pieces, but with so many drowned, one boat would now be sufficient to meet their needs. When the *Young Maid* is repaired it would be an act of Christian charity to give King and Drannock the offer to fish from it rather than let it go to others.' Oliver deliberately smiled. 'I'm certain you will agree.'

'I do agree, Sir Oliver,' Rosina said, 'most certainly I do, and I'm sure Peter had it in mind when he met the two men after Mark King's funeral yesterday. If you enquire from them you will find, no doubt, it has already been settled.'

'If that is so, ma'am, it will take a great weight off my mind and theirs.' Oliver had enquired of the outcome of yesterday's meeting a few hours ago and the angry young fishermen had told him Peter Blake had refused to change his mind about allowing them to fish from the lugger and had restated his intention to seek compensation from them. Oliver intended to help Blake change his decision in favour of Drannock and King. Talking like this to Blake's lovely young wife, who apparently was under some wrong impressions as to her husband's true character, would help it along in a most pleasing manner.

Oliver rose abruptly. The firelight threw his shadow

lengthways across the room and he seemed to fill the confined space. 'I thank you for your hospitality, Mistress Blake. I will be on my way and leave you to the peace of your home.'

'Remember me to Lady Pengarron.' Rosina rang a small silver bell for the maidservant, Kate, to collect Oliver's hat and coat. 'I hope she and your children are in good health.'

'They are. Good day to you, ma'am.'

Oliver rode at once to the site on the east side of the market town where the Blakes' new dwelling was under construction. Leaning forward over Conomor, his proud black stallion, Oliver admired the almost completed three-storey building. He had no wish to live in such a house himself, but had he been on convivial terms with Peter Blake he would have watched each stage of its development with interest.

Narrow in structure, the building boasted a small court-yard in front, a large garden and stable behind, all running in parallel lines. It was half the size of his sister's nearby mansion but Peter Blake was sparing no expense to have a home built according to the latest London designs. The grey bricks making up the main walls were transported from London, the hall was paved in Purbeck stone, the sash windows glazed in crown glass.

Oliver's main interest lay in the woodwork. It was crafted from the finest dark oak, purchased through an agent who had approached the Pengarron plantation. Oliver wondered whether he would have allowed the purchase to go ahead had he known beforehand that the locally ordered consignment of timber was intended for Peter Blake.

By now the rain had tired itself out to a half-hearted drizzle and Oliver swept off his hat to view the doorway and canopy. He concluded that the excellence of the carvings of the portal and overhang were worthy of Pengarron oak. It was a grand house in every way but he doubted if the servants who would be employed in it would welcome the new idea of the kitchen being placed in the basement, causing them much inconvenience as they went about their duties. Replacing his hat, Oliver looked about for his quarry.

There were upwards of a dozen varieties of craftsmen intent upon their industry, and much noise and bustle to sift through. He saw the child first, an attractive boy of seven years who did not resemble either his mother or his father, but in common with them both looked as if he would not grow to much of a height. Simon Peter was being carried on the hefty shoulder of a labourer, chatting away for all he was worth in the indulgent man's ear. Ignoring them and the other building workers, Oliver dismounted. His mouth was set in a grim line. He had located the man he was seeking.

Peter Blake was engaged in a rather mobile discussion with his master builder and surveyor, the one a portly man with a nervous twitch, the other a disdainful-looking character sporting a large Roman nose. They had their backs to Oliver and were unaware of his approach. The rapid change of expression from satisfaction to fear on Blake's face as he looked up and saw Oliver bearing down on him made the craftsmen anxious that he had suddenly discovered a massive blunder in their plans. Blake hastily excused himself.

'Wh-what do you . . . w-want?' he faltered, moving towards Oliver but keeping a good distance between them. 'If you've come to cause trouble, let me . . . let me warn you . . . there . . . there are plenty of people about.'

The distance grew smaller as Oliver kept coming. 'I only want to talk to you – this time, Blake,' he coldly informed him.

'About what?' Blake stepped back towards the master builder and surveyor, the memories of what this big man could do when in a rage forcing him to leave nothing to chance.

'You look like a frightened rabbit, Blake,' Oliver said maliciously, loud enough for as many as possible to hear above the sounds of building work. 'You have my word I will not raise a finger to you, unless of course you give me reason to – as you did once before. I have something to say to you and I suggest we move aside if you don't want these labourers and your son to hear it too. I can assure you, Blake, you wouldn't want your son in particular to hear this.'

'Very well,' Blake hissed between clenched teeth, 'but only a few feet away and from where we can clearly be seen.'

Oliver followed Blake closely until the smaller man stopped in front of a stack of timber, then he went straight into the attack. 'I've just come from your rooms, Blake, where I enjoyed a most pleasant conversation with your charming wife.'

'Rosina? You've been talking to Rosina? Why? What the hell are you up to, Pengarron!' This time Blake advanced towards Oliver, the love and adoration he had for his gentle wife overcoming his fear.

'I arrived on your doorstep to talk to you, but in your absence your wife invited me inside. Such a charming woman, it is beyond me why she married a swine like you.'

'My wife is a true Christian with a forgiving nature,'

Blake said, becoming angrier by the moment. 'Not a hypocrite like you, who only pays lip service to a God you purport to believe in when you attend church. I've regretted a hundred thousand times my actions concerning your wife, but you have made me pay for it a thousand times more!'

'Oh, and why is that?' Oliver asked in a tone of hopeful sarcasm.

'Pain,' Blake answered bitterly. 'You broke my ribs and I am never without pain. I can lift nothing of substance and since he reached the age of two years not even my own son.' His eyes went wistfully to Simon Peter still on the labourer's shoulders.

'Is that so? Well, I'm not as much of a hypocrite as you believe because I cannot in truth say that I'm in the least bit sorry, and I won't bandy words on the Almighty with a confessed atheist. As far as I'm concerned, the likes of you have no right to an opinion on the faith, or lack of it, of others.'

'At least my wife loved me from the start, she took me for what I was and I didn't force her to marry me!' Blake snarled.

That hit a soft spot in Oliver's armour; his face reddened and his nostrils flared. 'And I have never turned up on your doorstep and tried to rape your wife and kill the dog trying to protect her!'

The intimidated expression returned to Blake's face. He wiped a film of rain from his eyes and blinked hard. 'What . . . what did you talk to Rosina about?'

'The recent fishing boat tragedy at Perranbarvah,' Oliver said aggressively, watching for any reaction.

'Why should that concern you? And what connection is there between that and you and I?'

'You've refused Matthew King and Bartholomew Drannock a living from the lugger the *Young Maid*, have you not?'

'What if I have? I'm a businessman and can't afford to allow inefficient fishermen to fish from my boats.'

'King and Drannock are not inefficient. They are among the best in Mount's Bay. The tragedy was an accident due to rapidly changing weather conditions and neither they nor any member of their families were to blame.'

'How would you know that?' Blake asked scornfully. 'And what is your concern anyway?'

'My family have always had the honour and duty of presenting the incumbent to the parish of Perranbarvah and I've always made a point of taking an interest in all that goes on within that parish's boundaries.' Bending his height to bring his face to within an inch of Blake's, Oliver continued acidly, 'As to how I know the tragedy was an accident, I'll have you know, you little weasel, that as a boy and in my youth I went out on the boats many times with Grandfather, Solomon and Jonathan King. I know what good fishermen they were, and a little of the awesomeness of conditions out at sea and how quickly they can change. I am fully satisfied there was no negligence on the part of any of the men in either of the two luggers.'

Oliver chose his next words carefully. 'From the conversation I had with your wife I learned that she believes that when King and Drannock came to see you yesterday you acted very differently from their report of it. Your wife thinks you will allow them to fish from the *Young Maid* when it is repaired. You wouldn't have her believe otherwise, would you? To learn the hard truth of your business affairs?'

Peter Blake did not answer. His face, usually smooth and

63

pale but now purple with rage, shook with the rest of his fashionably clad body.

'Your wife is such a gentle soul,' Oliver went on dangerously, 'sees no evil in anyone – not even you. Now, there will be no suggestion of King and Drannock being refused to fish from the *Young Maid*, will there? No more talk of them paying compensation for the damage done to the lugger. And I would go as far as to suggest that your dear wife would deem it an act of the highest Christian charity if you offered the lugger as an outright gift to the grieving families, to form a partnership. Drannock's very young, so Matthew King would be skipper but the partnership would be equal.' Oliver smiled, but his dark eyes were treacherous. 'Well, what do you say, Blake?'

With an effort he spat, 'I say you are a bastard, Pengarron!'

Oliver smiled with pure joy. 'There are times, Blake, when the weak, the cheated and the downtrodden, if they are to see justice, require the services of a thoroughgoing bastard.' Oliver had no doubt he had won the day, but added for Blake's further discomfort, 'If things don't go quite to my suggestions, Blake, you would be a very foolish man. You see, I would make absolutely sure that your wife became aware of your visits to a certain female you help keep in, shall I say, comfortable circumstances, for services rendered.'

Blake gasped.

'Did you think your indiscretions had gone unnoticed?' Oliver taunted.

Somehow Blake managed to speak. 'We both love our wives, but don't tell me you don't go somewhere for a little extra, Pengarron.'

'You do me an injustice, Blake,' Oliver replied smoothly

before striding away, then threw back over his shoulder, 'I'm not that much of a bastard.'

Chapter 5

Kerensa was in her favourite place, Trelynne Cove. She left Kernick, her chestnut pony, close to the spot where the small cottage she had been born and raised in had once stood. With Bob, her devoted black retriever, at her heels she ran down the remainder of the cliff path, over the scrunching shingle of the beach and on to the coarse dark sand of the shoreline. She glanced up at the hot sun and smiled contentedly. It was late summer, her favourite time of the year, and today the sun was at its best.

Feeling as carefree as in the days of her childhood, when the little isolated, uninhabited cove had been her and her late grandfather's domain, she pulled off her shoes and stockings, discarded her straw hat and ran laughing into the surf of the incoming waves. She shrieked as the cold water bit into her feet and legs, soaking the deep hem of her dress. She felt exhilarated and here, all alone, she could let it out in complete abandonment. Married to an unconventional member of the gentry she had never had to live quite as a lady born into the upper class would be expected to. But it was good to cast off all restrictions with no prying or concerned eyes to judge or chide, or even to indulge her.

Bob barked loudly as he joined in the fun, charging the waves, chasing a bobbing piece of seaweed, allowing Kerensa to splash salt water over him until he was thoroughly soaked. Then shaking out his coat and soaking her in turn he walked loyally at her side as she paddled the length of the shoreline east to west and back again. She tossed pebbles into the sea which he raced after until panting for breath. There was a large outcrop of rocks close to the shoreline which were completely submerged during high tide; they were surrounded only by rock pools now and dog and mistress waded through the blue water and climbed to the summit of the black granite. They sat side by side, the breeze lifting their hair and fanning their faces, watching the sea recede until the shoreline was several feet away.

When Kerensa returned to her shoes and stockings, Bob bounded off to explore and sniff out the semi-circular confines of the cove, curious to find out if anything new had been there to disturb the peace and trespass on their private little world since their last visit. He found a dirty old tobacco pouch lost by a careless smuggler on one of his master's runs and although the contents were gone the piece of rough cloth smelled interesting and the dog lay down to examine it with his broad snout.

Kerensa picked up her footwear in one hand, retrieved her hat in the other and swung it by its red velvet ribbons as she made her way to the smooth granite boulders that edged the cove. She sat on a rock with knees drawn up and used a part of her petticoat untouched by sea water to remove clinging grains of sand and to dry her feet with vigorous rubbing and patting movements, then held them out straight in front of her for inspection. They were soft pink with small patches of purple-blue but with the numbness rubbed away they felt delightfully warm and tingly.

Leaning back against a boulder behind her, Kerensa

closed her eyes to drink in the peacefulness. She opened them again at the sudden noisy flight of a pair of black-headed gulls and kept them open to study her surroundings. The cove had changed little in appearance since the cottage had been pulled down eight years before. Scrubby vegetation had sprung up to cover the building's foundations and she was delighted to see the increase in the wildlife here. Gulls, rock pipits and oyster catchers had grown in number and last year she had seen a seal basking in the sun on an inaccessible ledge further along the cliff under the mythical Mother Clarry's seat. She had stood for an age and watched as the tide had risen slowly until the grey creature with its wide black patches was lazily washed back into the sea and swam off.

Kerensa checked the sun to see how far it had travelled down the sky; good, she had time to climb across the rocks and look out over the sea from a different angle before she would have to leave.

She had hardly moved a step forward when a tall figure loomed up in front of her. Startled, she slipped backwards and for an instant the name Oliver was on her lips but it was 'Bartholomew!' she cried out.

The youth reached out instinctively and caught her arm, saving her from falling and possible injury. They both looked down as her shoes went clattering to the rocks below.

'Lady Pengarron!' Bartholomew Drannock exclaimed. 'I am sorry. Are you all right?'

'Yes . . . yes, Bartholomew. You certainly gave me a fright.'

'Be best if you sit down again for a little while,' he counselled.

Kerensa nodded and he held on gently to her arm until

she was seated again. Then he hopped down, collected her dainty kid shoes and placed them beside her.

'I didn't know anyone but me came down into Trelynne Cove,' she said, looking up at the young dark face and thinking how more and more like Oliver he was becoming. The same black hair and deep dark eyes, the same restlessness and arrogance, and on occasion the same impatient stance.

He was standing in that way now, hands on hips, his guilt at nearly sending her crashing to the rocks fully atoned for in the way he had addressed her and apologised. Before today he had never given her her title, perhaps believing her working-class parentage didn't warrant it.

Staring straight at her he asked in an even tone, 'Do you object to me being here, then?'

'No,' Kerensa replied, meeting his stare without wavering. 'Sir Oliver might. This is his property.'

''Tis yours more than his. You lived in the cove when it belonged to your family, the Trelynnes.'

Kerensa smiled, pleased to find it brought a puzzled frown to the young fisherman's brow. 'Will you please sit down, Bartholomew? I don't have the chance to talk to you very often, but whenever I do it's more like fencing swords than holding a conversation.'

For a few moments he appeared to be thinking, then he sat down very close beside her. 'Are you sure you're not hurt?' he asked rather stiffly.

'Yes, thank you, quite sure. Ah, here comes Bob.'

The black retriever sniffed around Bartholomew, weighing him up as friend or foe to his mistress before settling down protectively at their feet. Kerensa stroked the dog's broad back. 'How's your mother and the children today, Bartholomew?'

He stroked the dog too, his deeply tanned hand moving next to hers until Kerensa took hers away. 'Mother's about the same. The girls are all right of course at the Sarrisons, those old brothers are a kindly pair, the young'uns not too bad. You asked me about my family once before I remember.' He looked directly into her eyes. 'It was after the wreck of the *Amy Christabel*. I told you then that you were pretty.'

'Yes, you did,' Kerensa said, smiling softly at the memory. 'You could only have been about eight or nine, and a most forward child, as I recall.'

'I was nine and I was wrong then.'

'Oh?'

'You're not pretty, you're beautiful, very beautiful.'

Kerensa drew in a deep breath and Bartholomew was satisfied that this time his remark was not to be warded off with indulgent amusement. He knew he was attractive to women, from the village maids to many a woman of mature years. Conquests came easily, but the females concerned meant little or nothing to him. The young woman beside him was a different matter. Kerensa Pengarron was as unattainable as she was beautiful and it was the unattainable and beautiful he seemed fated to desire all his life.

'Thank you for the compliment,' Kerensa said in her soft, lilting voice, then turned her head to the sea.

Bartholomew picked up one of her shoes. Holding it out on his palm he turned his work-roughened hand from side to side while looking at it intently. 'I've always envied and respected Sir Oliver,' he said.

'Have you?' she replied, looking at him now. 'Why is that?'

'To begin with he has you for his wife.'

'Bartho—'

71

Whatever it was that she was going to say was lost as he continued, 'He's strong-minded, knows exactly what he wants and never gives up until he's got it, and of course he's rich and powerful and owns the estate and is the Lord of the Manor hereabouts.'

Kerensa watched the movement of her shoe and smiled to herself. She liked Bartholomew Drannock and if she'd been in the company of any other young man she would have firmly stopped his flow of speech.

'Well, I would certainly say you're strong-minded, Bartholomew,' she said, with little nods of her head. 'Are you happy as a fisherman or is there something else you would like to do with your life?'

Bartholomew studied Kerensa with suspicion; was she really interested in him or merely idly curious? Or even out to make trouble? He had never trusted anyone but his mother and the events of his life so far had given him no cause to think differently. Sweeping his dark eyes from her face and down her delicately curved form he stared at her small bare feet. Surely a lady, if not by birth then by marriage, would not stay here alone beside him in a manner others would think unseemly if it was not genuine interest. His eyes lingered on the way back up until they met her own, and drawing back his lips he gave her the smile that could render a female speechless with admiration.

He wanted to talk more about her beauty but he knew she would not allow too many liberties and he wanted to stay. Apart from his mother, she was the only woman who seemed to be able to hold a reasonable conversation, let alone an intelligent one. Lying with a woman was good, but before and after the relieving of his youthful lust their futile prattle and hints of marriage drove him to distraction.

'I hate to be away from the sea for long, but 'tis a hard

life.' He glanced around the cove. 'Grandfather and Josh King were washed up here.'

'Yes, an estate worker found them. Does it worry you? That you could be lost at sea?'

'No, not really. 'Tis a risk but life's full of them. It's the thanklessness of the job that gets me angry at times. You can never get out of poverty. Most fishermen will never make enough money to buy their boats and the owners take the best part of the profits. The fish buyers get another heavy cut of what's left while we fishermen have more expenses – tackle, nets, the upkeep of the boats to pay for. We get the least reward for the hardest work, while you're safe asleep in your bed.'

'But if you'll forgive a direct question, don't you have part ownership of your own boat now? Isn't that some help to you?'

Bartholomew looked deeply at Kerensa. 'Word's got around, I see.'

Despite her position, in which she should be able to say anything she liked to such as this young man and receive nothing but a respectful answer, Kerensa coloured a little. She respected other people's privacy and the right to run their own lives as they chose. 'Sir Oliver mentioned it to me. We were talking about you and the Kings. I was worried about how you would manage to live without a boat. I wasn't prying, Bartholomew.'

He studied her face. 'Fair enough. Yes, things are better with us owning the *Young Maid* but life's still very hard.'

'Of course,' Kerensa agreed.

'I want to be rich,' Bartholomew said suddenly, raising his voice and holding his head up proudly, 'exceedingly rich. Then my mother can live out the rest of her life as she began it, in comfort and plenty. Did you know she

73

was the daughter of Joshua Mildern, the ship's chandler in Marazion?'

'Yes, I did.'

'He doesn't even acknowledge us.' Bartholomew put her shoe down and fished something out of his breeches pocket, fitfully turning it over between his fingers. 'I can never understand why my mother married my father, she was much too good for him.'

'Didn't you like your father?' Kerensa asked, mesmerised by his fidgeting.

He exhaled deeply and tightened his lips before answering. 'He was a miserable sod. Hard-working and sober I grant you, but too proud for his own good, and ours, and thoroughly boring. I remember when you brought over some clothes for us. A shirt for me, dresses for the girls, something for the little ones. Mother was so pleased we had something decent to wear to church, but what did he go and do? Put a stop to it, just to serve his own rotten sense of pride, didn't matter how any of us felt about it. Mother used to confide in me, she said it did you good as well, giving to others in your new position as Lady of the Manor. He hurt all of us back then.' Bartholomew searched her face. 'You didn't like him, did you?'

Kerensa coloured again, knowing a lie would hurt more than the truth. 'No, not very much.'

A trickle of fear tightened her stomach as she thought of the many different complications if Bartholomew and Oliver ever found out the truth of Samuel's parentage, that Samuel and Oliver had the same father. Samuel had told Kerensa this himself, when he had stopped her gifts to his family, and he had asked her to swear to keep it a secret, pointing out that he hated Oliver as much as he did Sir Daniel Pengarron for siring him and deserting his mother.

Kerensa had not been married to Oliver for long, their relationship had been strained and at the time she had thought it best to keep quiet. She had known Oliver well enough to realise that his honour would have made him want to have some kind of relationship with his half-brother and to provide comfortably for his family. Kerensa had seen Samuel for a stubborn man who meant what he said and there would have been all kinds of troubles and she had not wanted to shoulder the responsibility for that then.

What would Bartholomew think of her keeping the secret? What would he think of his father making them live their lives in poverty when they might have been well off? His reaction wouldn't be the same as Samuel's. Bartholomew desired to be rich, he admired and respected Oliver and probably wouldn't be too proud to accept financial help from him. He would have clashed with his father's views.

Kerensa's worst fear was how Oliver would react if he ever found out the truth and that she had kept it from him for several years. Only she, and Jenifer knew now, and the Reverend Ivey, whom Jenifer had told to ease Kerensa's burden of keeping the secret alone. It was a secret that Kerensa wished she did not know, but one she had been told in order to put right her suspicion that Bartholomew had been fathered and deserted by Oliver.

She had been silent in her thoughts too long. Her eyes returned to Bartholomew's fingers. 'What have you got there?'

He passed it to her, a small piece of wood with a straight line of white marking on it. 'I found it down there on the shoreline. 'Tis a little piece of the *Lowenek*. See,' he pointed, 'there's part of the letter "K". Mother taught me how to read,' he explained.

Kerensa tried to hand it back but he closed her fingers over the fragment of the ill-fated lugger. 'You keep it if you like, it has too many painful memories for me. If my father hadn't wanted to play the hero he would still be alive and my mother would not be a grieving widow.'

'I'm sorry for you,' said Kerensa, offering no pat remarks. She wrapped the piece of driftwood in a handkerchief and burrowed it into a deep pocket of her dress. 'What would you like to do if given the chance one day? Go to sea to a foreign port? Perhaps even become the captain of a large ship?'

'Mmmm, maybe, 'tis a thought that's passed through my mind. Don't matter too much at the moment though, I have my mother and young'uns to care for.' His expression changed, telling Kerensa there would be no more forthcoming, he had said all he was willing to say on his hopes and plans for the future. She had seen that look on Oliver's face, when he wanted to keep something from worrying her, or felt the subject under discussion was not a woman's concern. Oliver would not be moved and Bartholomew, of course, had no reason to be.

'My father was a sailor, on a merchant ship,' she said, trying without success to picture her father's face. 'Anyway, Bartholomew, you've got plenty of time yet to decide on your future. You're how old now? Seventeen? Eighteen?'

'Seventeen, nearly eighteen,' he replied, 'the same age as you were when Sir Oliver forced you to marry him.'

Kerensa's mouth turned into a small circle of shock and she brought up her chin and set her eyes squarely on the young fisherman. 'You would do well not to be outspoken and to exercise some tact,' she retorted primly. 'Your mother would not approve of some of the things you say.'

This brought forth a hearty laugh. 'You're right, she wouldn't, no more than you do.' He put his face close to hers and moved his dark head from side to side. 'I bet Sir Oliver is much the same as me, and gets that look from you more often than not.' He gazed into her eyes until her look of severity slowly melted into a smile and then she was laughing with him.

'I suppose I ought to be used to you by now, Bartholomew Drannock.'

'Things have turned out all right for you though, haven't they?' he asked seriously. 'You are happy in your marriage?'

'Yes, I am,' she replied. 'I have been very fortunate.'

'It's hard to believe you're the mother of two children. You look far too young.'

'Thank you again for the compliment, but I have three children, not two.'

'You look on that other boy as your own, do you?'

'Yes, of course,' Kerensa said emphatically. 'As far as we're concerned, Kane is as much our child as Olivia and Luke are. He has every right to the Pengarron name.'

Bartholomew said thoughtfully, 'He won't inherit the title and estate though, will he?'

'No, that will become Luke's, but Kane will be well provided for, as will Olivia.' Kerensa reached for her shoes and stockings, bringing Bob expectantly to his feet. 'I ought to be going.' She gave Bartholomew a look that conveyed it would be unacceptable for him to stay and watch her put them on.

He nodded but first put both his hands behind his head and retied the piece of old string holding back his long raven hair. Then he gave a brief smile. 'Thanks for the chat.

I suppose we've told each other things we wouldn't tell other people.' He paused. 'Would you mind if I come here again? It won't be very often, I get very little free time. Usually it'll be like today, a Sunday, when we don't put to sea, and I'd come by myself.'

Kerensa smiled warmly at him. 'As far as I'm concerned you are welcome to come here anytime you like. Why do you like to come here, Bartholomew?'

'I like the isolation and at times I have a great need to be by myself.'

She watched his tall energetic figure leap expertly across the rocks then turned to gaze thoughtfully out to sea. Samuel Drannock was somewhere out there, drifting along on the currents or anchored amongst rocks or wreckage. Kerensa hoped for Jenifer's sake his body would never be found. She hoped for her own sake the truth of who had fathered him would never come to light . . . and yet, wasn't that selfish? It would mean the Drannocks would always be poor, dragged down by constant, thankless hard work with no prospects for a better future. Kerensa had often wished she could tell Oliver, but it would have been against Samuel's and Jenifer's wishes, and she felt they had the right to live by their own decisions. With Samuel dead, Jenifer still wished the secret to remain, it gave her peace of a sorts, and how could she go against that? But then again, why should the children suffer?

Kerensa walked slowly back to Kernick. To block out her dilemma over the Drannocks she took her mind back a few years and thought fondly of another young man who used to come to Trelynne Cove. Their meetings had not been by accident. She had waited eagerly for him to come and had run to the top of the cliff to meet him. They had strolled arm in arm across the beach and chased each other over the rocks. They had been very much in love but fate had decreed they would not marry.

It had broken Clem Trenchard's heart when she had gone through with the marriage that had been part of the bargain over Trelynne Cove. It had changed him from a happy young man full of love and hope to one inclined to sullenness and quiet moods. Clem had hoped to win Kerensa back, even after he had married Alice, her maid, and Alice had borne him twin sons. When he realised Kerensa had fallen in love with Oliver his heart had been broken again. He may have bowed out of her life, making himself a good family man, but she was sure there still were moments when he pined for her.

And Kerensa would never forget Clem. Just as the restless sea called to those who lived by it and travelled upon it, a painful tug would catch at her heart for him – a part of it that would always be his. Kerensa stood still and gazed around and wondered if Clem ever came secretly to Trelynne Cove to relive those early memories.

Chapter 6

Clem Trenchard urgently wiped his boots on the rush mat outside miner Jeb Bray's cottage and pushed his sister through the open doorway. Rosie Trenchard tried to shrug him off and nearly lost her balance. She would have fallen into one of the tightly packed groups of people sitting on the floor if Clem had not reached out and caught her. Red-faced with embarrassment, Rosie turned on him.

'Clem, what on earth do—'

'Just get inside,' he hissed.

Rosie obeyed, shaking her head in surrender. At times Clem was hard to understand. Usually Alice, his wife, had a difficult task each week to get him to attend the Bible classes. Today he had been over-eager to get there. He and Rosie had come on their own today and he had rushed her over Lancavel Downs while she had wanted to saunter along and capture the feeling of vastness and majesty that only the moors could give on a sun-drenched day, to breathe in the fresh clean air, grasp the loneliness that touched the soul into half-remembered dreams. The walks provided her with a welcome respite from the noise and eternal busyness of the family farm but Clem's agitation had robbed her of that pleasure today. When she'd tripped in the enforced haste and insisted on sitting on a granite boulder to rub her sore ankle he had trampled a path over a patch of heather and nagged at her until she threatened to turn round and go home. All the rest of the way he had scolded her for making them late.

Another push inside the cottage and Rosie trod on an old man's hand. He grinned understandingly and she smiled back in apology then complained to Clem in forceful tones under her breath, 'Will you stop pushing me, Clem. Whatever will people think?'

Clem spoke straight into her ear, making her shiver and clap a hand there. 'Tell Matthias that Alice can't come today because the twins have gone down with the measles.'

'Why tell him now? Surely it can wait till after? And why can't you tell him yourself? You're acting very strangely these days towards Preacher Renfree. Anyone would think you've had words with him the way you always get me to speak to him for you.' Rosie impatiently pushed her one long plait of fine golden hair from the front of her shoulder to fall in a straight line down her back.

Clem let out an exasperated sigh and swung round to apologise to the woman he had just kicked with the toe of his boot.

' 'Tes all right, Clem, didn't 'urt none,' Lou Hunken said good-naturedly, 'but pushing' 'er through like that towards un went 'elp 'em along, boy. They went see what's in front of their own eyes 'less 'ee comes right out with it an' tell 'em what's what yerself.'

Shrugging his shoulders at Lou Hunken, Clem persisted in badgering his younger sister. 'Tell Matthias that Alice wants him to say a prayer for Philip and David before the class begins. You know how poorly they are.'

'All right, Clem, don't go on so,' Rosie said crossly.

She was standing directly in front of Matthias Renfree,

the stockily built, gentle-eyed young man responsible for holding the Bible classes. He led the people who crowded into the cottage with warmth, sincerity and understanding and was known locally as Preacher Renfree or Young Preacher, although he had never taken holy orders. He had come under some opposition from Sir Martin Beswetherick, the main owner of the Wheal Ember mine where many of the gathering worked. But Matthias had pointed out to the fat baronet that the mine, still producing good-quality ore when most at its age would have been worked out, would be wise to indulge a trouble-free work force rather than risk many of the miners going off to work at a mine sympathetic to Methodism and have them replaced with a bunch of irreligious rabble.

Matthias was standing in front of the hearth, at a distance that offered no harm to Faith Bray's cheap plaster ornaments and her 'pride', a set of matching 'real' brass poker and tongs. His head of nondescript brown hair was bent between his clasped hands and he was making sounds as though he was mumbling to himself.

'He's praying, Clem,' Rosie whispered. 'He could go on for ages and I'm beginning to feel quite daft stuck out here like a sore thumb.'

'Oh, find a place and sit down then,' Clem said irritably.

The other occupants in the cramped room were beginning to follow Matthias Renfree's lead, bowing their heads in prayer, and silence quickly replaced the hum of many voices.

Rosie felt a tug on her skirt and found Rosina Blake pointing to the space she had made beside her by lifting Simon Peter on to her lap. Thankfully Rosie squeezed herself down on the rough rug, one of many spread out on the pressed earth floor. Only the extremely elderly had the privilege of sitting on one of the few hard-backed chairs.

All the men present stood lining the four walls. Clem moved away from Matthias Renfree and joined them, putting his tall lean frame next to Jeb Bray. He glanced at his sister, then his closest friend, shook his blond head and closed his eyes. There was nothing more he could do right now. Clem concentrated on his breathing; a true outdoors man, he hated the weekly crush in the Brays' cottage. Today he found the atmosphere even more stuffy and oppressive. He was uncomfortable and had to keep his head to the side to avoid knocking a picture off the wall.

The classes were meant to be much smaller, about a dozen people, each with its own teacher. But Matthias Renfree was the only local man in this Methodist Society who felt qualified to preside over the meetings and encourage the others to keep the Society's rules of sober and honest living as laid down by churchman John Wesley.

Matthias had tried to persuade Morley Trenchard, Clem's father, to hold a class at his farmhouse, but Morley, shy and simple in outlook, had refused. So had Clem, firmly saying he lacked the religious fervour and application to dedicate himself to a more solid faith. Matthias was unsuccessful, too, with the fishermen from Perranbarvah and the miners of the nearby Wheal Ember mine. So it meant anything upwards of sixty men, women and children jammed into Jeb Bray's little cottage, Jeb being only too willing to make his home available. Matthias, however, was hopeful that the situation would change by the end of the year if the plans he had for a meeting house to be built on the edge of Lancavel Downs came to fruition. It would see the end of all the squeezing in the good people here had endured for several years and the site would be more central for them.

After a formal prayer, Matthias began to read from the Bible. 'The Gospel according to St Luke, Chapter 10, Verse 2. Therefore said he unto them, the harvest truly is great, but the labourers are few: pray ye therefore the Lord of the harvest, that he would send forth labourers into his harvest. Go your ways: behold, I send you forth as lambs among wolves.'

Matthias paused, gazing down at his hands where the fingertips were pressed together before looking up and round the room, his face serious. 'This passage teaches us that every time someone laughs at us, shows us their hatred of our faith, or simply chooses to ignore the Good News we want to share with them, we are reminded that we are indeed called as lambs to be sent out among the wolves of this world . . .'

Clem was not listening to Matthias. He never listened to anyone for long, whether it was his wife, his father, Kenver his crippled brother or even Rosie, his much loved sister. While he worked, he worked hard, his mind fully employed on the task in hand. Other times, with only Charity his dog for company, he wandered off to be alone, to immerse himself in his thoughts of the woman he believed should rightfully be his.

He was thinking of the times they had secretly held hands under her shawl in this very room. Looking about, his eyes fell on Rosina Blake. Clem hated Peter Blake for the same reason Oliver Pengarron did, but he held a grudging regard for Blake for allowing his wife to attend these classes – as she had done in the days when she'd worked as a bal-maiden, sorting ore at the Wheal Ember. Why couldn't his damned high and mighty lordship allow Kerensa the same privilege?

Rosina noticed him looking at her and smiled back.

Clem's face stayed rigid. He rarely smiled. Rosina returned her attention to Matthias's words, her natural beauty shining through as it always did on her peaceful face. 'A woman whose beauty comes from being at peace with God and hence with herself and the world,' Matthias often remarked to him. Clem sometimes wondered if Matthias regretted not asking Rosina to become his wife when he had the opportunity, before she fell in love with Peter Blake.

He looked at Rosie who was listening attentively to the lesson to pass on to the others back at the farm while holding Simon Peter's hand and making funny faces to amuse him. Rosie would make a good mother and Clem believed wholeheartedly that Matthias would make the ideal husband and father for her babies. Renfree was unmarried at the age of thirty and would have the stewardship of Ker-an-Mor, the Pengarron home farm, after his father. Rosie was born to be a farmer's wife and with Matthias she would be the wife of someone with position. She was committed to the Methodist ideals and would be a comfort and support to Matthias. But it was an uphill struggle to manoeuvre the two together. Neither of them showed the least interest in the other. Rosie was a pretty girl with a clear complexion and large blue eyes in a round face, but she stayed solidly with the family at all times. Matthias always dressed as if he was at a funeral, not the sort of figure to turn a girl's eye. No one else would approve but Clem decided to buy a love potion when next at Marazion's market. Perhaps that would get things moving.

Clem noticed his weren't the only eyes that had wandered around the room and stopped at Rosie. A young gangly miner was staring at her with a lovesick look on his pimply face. Clem glared at him; he would have a word with that individual later, nip his interest in the bud. No coarse-mouthed miner was going to snare his sister, and no amount of Bible class attendances was going to make him suitable for her.

When the miner noticed Clem's disapproving stare, he looked away nervously and red-faced. He had witnessed Clem seeing off other young men, including Paul King, who had wanted to court Rosie. Obviously Clem thought no one but a farmer was good enough for her.

Content in her maidenly life and oblivious of the hopes that the two men in the cottage had of altering the situation, Rosie went on happily amusing Simon Peter Blake.

Clem fell back into his private world of self-tortured thoughts of his stolen love, unaware of the shouts and growing commotion outside until the people in the cottage were drawn to their feet. Someone flung the door open and let in the evening sunlight. The sound of a bell's foreboding peel reached his ears. The shouts outside and the stricken faces within spelled out what was happening. People poured out of the meeting and joined the rush to a disaster half a mile away at the mine.

Clem felt an urgent tug on his arm. Jack, the groom from the stables of Pengarron Manor, whispered to him, 'What's happened, Clem?'

'Rock fall,' Clem answered grimly.

'How bad?' Jack looked from one ashen, shocked face to another of the folk huddled close to one of the mine's shafts.

''Tis a long way down, out under the sea. 'Tis reckoned some rotten timber supports gave way, crushing some, suffocating others. Another man lost his life when he fell

87

away from a ladder. Overcome by dizziness, they said, as he fled for his life. 'Tis reckoned at least twenty are dead. They've brought up half a dozen bodies so far, more are missing. We sent the farming and fisher women back home but some of us men have stayed to help out in any way we can. Rosina Blake wanted to stay when her husband came to ride with her and their son back home, but he was against it and the miner's wives told her it was no place for her now. She was upset, but has promised to send bandages and things up here. I've carried a few of the dead to their cottages to be laid out. I asked if I could help down the pit but they only want experienced miners going down there.' Clem had not made the offer lightly but was relieved to have been refused. He was fearful of going underground and found the mine buildings, the clanking from the engine house and the heaps of waste ugly and foreboding.

Jack shuddered as he stared at the black hole a few feet away. 'I wouldn't like to have to go down there. Listen to the sea – sounds wild and powerful from here, like it doesn't give a damn about what's going on under it. Wonder if they can hear it down there, wonder what it sounds like. Don't s'pose they can hear nothing but some awful silence.'

Clem stared at Jack for a moment then pulled his collar up to ward off the biting crosswinds. 'Alice will be upset by this, she worked up here once. 'Tis a good job her family moved on back along or it could be her father or one of her brothers pulled out dead. Can't do nothing for they over there,' he inclined his head in the direction of a group of silent women. 'They're waiting for news of their menfolk.'

The women's faces were set grimly with vacant eyes. Their hands, battered from years of hard work, hammering and sorting the ore at ground level, gripped their shawls about themselves. Young children clung fretfully to their skirts and one young mother sat a little apart, rocking a baby at her breast while softly singing the words of a hymn.

Clem pointed briefly at her. 'She hasn't accepted what's happened yet, can't bring herself to believe it. 'Tis awful, Jack. Her husband's body has been seen, can never be got out, they said. Only been married a twelvemonth. I don't know, some of these people were at the Bible class not so long ago. Were happy enough then, had no idea what was about to happen. How quickly things can change.'

'First Perranbavah, now this,' Jack said softly, with a low whistle between his teeth.

Clem turned his head to Jack. 'Eh? What's that?'

'First the fishing boat tragedy, now this. 'Tis reckoned things, good or bad, but specially bad, do come in threes.'

'Aye, my gran always used to say that.'

'So does old Beatrice at the manor. After the *Lowenek* was torn asunder she said we haven't seen the last of it yet. Looks like she was right. I just hope nothing else happens to tear our lives apart.'

The two men stood with their hands pushed down into pockets. They could think of nothing they could do to help but felt compelled to stay and wait.

A girl ran up to them and clutched Jack by the arm, whirling him around. ''Ere, you! Preacher wants 'ee, 'e's over there by the engine 'ouse.'

Irritated by the girl's action, Jack made to reproach her but instead he just stared. Her long hair was wild and brackenish brown, her eyes the same. They gleamed from a pert pink face that wore a rebellious expression. Her clothes were muddy and she filled them well. She had neither hat nor shawl.

'Are 'ee blamed stupid or somethin'?' she yelled at him.

89

'Come on! Men are dyin' below ground and the preacher wants yer 'elp!'

'What can I do?' Jack muttered, his thin face a blank statement.

'Is 'e bloody daft or somethin'?' she shouted at Clem.

Clem's deep blue eyes widened but he said nothing. The girl blatantly studied him for a moment, she liked the sulky line of his mouth and wanted to kiss and tease it. It would be a hard challenge to take his mind off Lady Pengarron but no man had yet refused her charms. She couldn't do anything about it now because she had been sent on an urgent errand to fetch the youth beside him and he was angering her with his idiotic stare. The next instant she became angered at Clem ignoring her.

'You farmers is all bloody simple-minded,' she screamed, adding another sentence pitted with foul words. They brought anger to Clem's features and a bright redness creeping up Jack's neck. She grabbed Jack's arm again and began to pull him along with her. 'You'll find out what the preacher wants if you ask 'im,' she snarled. 'Come on! Or I'll kick yer arse all the way there!' Without protest Jack allowed himself to be dragged away.

Clem turned to Faith Bray, Jeb's wife, who was tut-tutting at his side. 'Who on earth's she, Mrs Bray, the little wild-cat?'

'That's Heather Bawden, Clem. Like you said, she's a proper little wild-cat. Some d'say she's got an evil spirit in her, right out of Hell. But I believe she's a bit mazed in the head, if you know what I do mean. Poor soul.'

'You mean she's Carn's daughter? I haven't seen her in years. I never would have thought she'd turn out like that. I'm glad my sister Rosie is nothing like her. Carn wasn't at the class earlier. Is he safe, or below ground?'

'Aye, he's below ground, I'm afraid. There's no news of him yet.' Faith Bray sadly shook her head. 'Jeb brought up another body a little while back.'

Clem sighed deeply. 'I'll go see if they want help taking him home.'

Heather Bawden gave Jack an ungainly push towards Matthias Renfree. ''Ere 'e is, Preacher, though I can't see what use 'e's going to be. Dafter than a dog's turd, if you ask me.'

'Thank you, Heather,' Matthias said, frowning as she immediately flounced off with a toss of her head that sent her hair stinging across Jack's face.

'Jack . . . *Jack*.' Matthias had to prod Jack's attention away from staring at the girl.

'Eh? What can I do for you, Matthias?' Jack asked, his face embarrassed and perplexed.

'I take it you've ridden up here?' Matthias would have liked to have explained about Heather's coarse behaviour, asking Jack to make allowances for her, but that would have to wait for some other time.

'Aye,' Jack replied, half turning and glancing at Heather's retreating back. 'I was out exercising Meryn on the pannier tracks when I heard from the fisherfolk going home what had happened. I came here straight away.'

'Good. Would you leave again immediately and ask Sir Oliver's permission for you to ride over to Marazion and ask Dr Crebo to come up here as soon as he possibly can. The mine doctor has been sent for but there's no sign of him yet. He's never been efficient in his duties and I doubt if he'll show up until it's too late for some of these injured men. Ted Trembath was pulled out a while ago with a terrible leg injury that needs urgent attention, and the Lord only knows what we'll have to deal with next.'

'Course I'll go,' Jack returned eagerly, 'but they can't afford a doctor up here, can they?'

'No, but we'll worry about that at a later date. Saving lives is what is important now.'

'I'll go to Marazion straightaway, Matthias. Sir Oliver won't mind when I tell him where I've been and why. 'Spect he'll be up here himself when he hears what's happened.' Jack sped off to the pony and was soon riding over the dried heather and ferns of the downs, his mind only half on his errand of mercy.

Matthias returned to check on the condition of the injured miner, Ted Trembath. Clem had not been needed to carry home the dead miner and was kneeling beside Ted, pressing a bloodied scrap of cloth against his leg above the knee. Ted was the Wheal Ember's underground afternoon core captain. He lay unconscious next to five other injured men and a boy, in a corrugated iron shack cleared out as a makeshift field hospital. Lou Hunken, widow of one of the mine's previous captains killed in a similar accident and living now with her miner son, was wiping dirt, sweat and blood off Ted's craggy face.

'He's lost a lot of blood,' Clem said.

'His leg's stripped clean through to the bone,' Lou Hunken said glumly, 'but I think the break's clean. You've bound un up well and good, Preacher, and Clem's stopped a fresh flow of blood. He'll stand a good chance if only the doctor'll come.'

Snatching a glance out of the doorway and up at the sky, Matthias sighed. 'It'll be getting dark soon. You may as well go home, Clem. Could be hours before anyone else is brought up.'

'I'll keep vigil with you, Matthias,' Clem replied. 'Rosie

will feed Charity for me and send word if I'm needed for either of the boys.'

Matthias raised his eyebrows and looked even more anxious. 'Oh, I hope there's nothing wrong with them.'

'Rosie was going to tell you, Philip and David have gone down with the measles.'

'Oh no. I didn't get the chance to speak to Rosie with all this happening. Are the twins very ill?'

'Alice doesn't seem to be too worried but of course you never know with measles.'

'They should be all right,' Lou Hunken added. 'Your young'uns are strong and healthy with farm life, they'll fare better than the two I lost last year with it.'

On this grim note they all looked back at Ted and fell into a bleak silence.

Two hours later Oliver rode up with Jack by lantern light. Leaving Jack to tie up the horses, Oliver weaved his way through the waiting groups of hushed, shocked mining folk huddled round a fierce bonfire. He stopped to give words of comfort and asked if the two doctors had arrived and where he could find Matthias Renfree. He was told there had been no sign or word of the mine doctor but Dr Crebo had arrived half an hour ago and was treating the casualties in the shack with Matthias's aid.

As Oliver lowered his head to enter the shack, his features hardened at seeing Clem there. A quick glance around the poorly lit shack told him there were eight men and three boys lying injured. A corpse covered with the shawl of a weeping woman was about to be removed.

Oliver ignored Clem, who'd given him a curt nod before turning his head away. Neither man liked the other being there; two things they shared, a mutual love for Kerensa and a mutual loathing of each other.

Oliver spoke to Charles Crebo. 'How are things, Doctor?'

'Not so bad as I feared, Sir Oliver, but tragic all the same,' the surgeon-physician said in a heavy voice, without looking up from a patient on whom he was expertly stitching a badly gashed head wound. He waited for the miner's groans and oaths to die away before going on in precise short sentences. 'Sixteen dead. Twenty-three injured, some severely, some not. Many are missing. Four amputations, two legs on the same patient, he'll probably die; two arms, each on a different patient. Two men comatose, one will certainly die. This patient will recover.'

'There's very little hope of getting any others out alive, sir,' Matthias added. 'Several feet of tunnelling has given way out under the sea. There's tons of rubble to get through and far too little good air for further rescue work. It's badly ventilated at the best of times.'

'Nearly as bad as the accident at the Trewhelah Mine at Porthtowan last year,' Oliver said gravely. 'That, it is said, will shut the mine down about two years early. Let's hope that won't be the case here. Have Sir Martin Beswetherick and the other owners been informed?'

'Yes, sir,' replied Matthias. 'I saw to it straightaway.'

'Good.' Oliver waved his hand at the fug caused by the tallow-dipped rush candles. 'You need more light in here. Jack and I rode over with two lanterns. I'll fetch them and more candles from the miners. I'll replace all that are used so they will have no fear of going without sufficient light down the mine or in their homes in the winter. My elderly servant, Beatrice, would have been of considerable help to you with her herbs and potions. I know you respect her skills, Dr Crebo, but unfortunately she's more or less housebound. The Reverend Ivey will ride over at first daylight, he's too old to risk the moors after dusk. He's pleased you are here, Renfree, to comfort the bereaved.'

'It was good of the Reverend to say that,' Matthias said, 'but we're all doing our best.'

'Yes, I'll agree with that,' Dr Crebo put in. 'People have been good enough to rally round quickly. As soon as the Blakes got back to Marazion they organised a bundle of sheets and bandages for me to bring with me. Tomorrow they're sending over food, extra to their monthly contribution for the miner's children, and the medicines that I'll recommend.'

'Mistress Blake's idea, no doubt,' Oliver remarked, rubbing his chin. Clem grunted in agreement, he also not wanting Peter Blake to take the credit. Oliver looked directly at Clem, and said to Dr Crebo, who had risen to his feet and was wiping his bloodied hands on a piece of cloth, 'Have you enough proper help in here, Doctor?'

'We can manage, thank you, Sir Oliver,' Charles Crebo said almost gaily, lifting his wig to scratch at a troublesome spot. 'This young fellow, Trenchard here, stopped a miner from bleeding to death under my instructions while Renfree and I were vainly trying to resuscitate another. They have both kept their wits about them while others have gone to pieces.'

Clem became aware of the amount of blood on his shirt and breeches and was embarrassed at this unexpected praise. But he looked straight at the baronet to see his reaction and received a small shock. He could have sworn Oliver Pengarron almost smiled at him. But he did not want praise, however faint, from the man he despised more than any other and jerked his head away.

After collecting the bundles of candles the miners wore round their necks to light their way underground then riding the half mile to the cottages to obtain more, there was nothing more Jack could do to help. Knowing few of the Wheal Ember folk, he kept out of the way. The cries of a boy who was having his crushed fingers amputated upset him and he returned to Conomor and Meryn.

He talked to the horses, explaining what had happened up on the cold inhospitable cliff top and why they were there. Conomor's sleek black coat shone in the light of a small bonfire, giving the stallion the warrior-like appearance that appealed to Jack's youthful sense of adventure. He occupied himself by telling a story out loud, urged on by the eerie surge of the invisible sea below, describing danger and doom heroes and wickedness overcome. Conomor became Jack's own horse and Meryn the pony he'd brought with him on his adventure to rescue a beautiful maiden imprisoned in the treacherous clifftop castle of the evil Lord Pendragon. Jack was getting to the heart of the colourful tale when a pair of long clinging arms were thrown about his neck and he was almost toppled to the ground.

'Thought 'twas you,' Heather Bawden purred into his neck.

Thrusting her away, Jack said breathlessly, 'What on earth do 'ee think you're doing of, maid?'

'Can't see no one 'ere but you,' Heather said, pouting her lips and moving up close again, 'so who the 'ell were 'ee talking to?'

'No one,' he replied gruffly. To hide his embarrassment he turned to Conomor and stroked the stallion's strong velvety neck. 'Was just thinking out loud, that's all. The horses like it, it soothes them. What do you want anyway?'

'I wanted to thank 'ee fer goin' fer the doctor. When they pulled out my tas he was nearly done fer, bleedin' buckets,

96

got a proper 'ard bash on the 'ead, poor bugger. The doctor told that tall fair man, you know the one I mean, the good-lookin' one who 'ankers after Lady Pengarron, well, the doctor told un 'ow to stop the bleedin', saved 'is life, I d'reckon.'

'Well, I'm glad to hear he survived all right. Who's your tas?'

'Carn Bawden's 'is name. It was on 'is pitch the accident 'appened, a thousand feet down. 'E's a tributer, works on contract, not like the tut workers. 'E's more skilled, you see,' she ended proudly.

Unaware that he was supposed to be impressed by this information, Jack said, 'Never heard of him, but then I don't know many folk up here. Don't come up this way too often.'

'Don't 'ee now? My name's Heather. What's yours then?'

The screaming from the makeshift hospital started again. The boy who had lost his fingers was terrified and in agony. If he was able to go down the mine again, his days of racing the other boys up the ladders were over. Jack would have pressed his hands over his ears if he hadn't had company.

'Well, what's your bloody name? Or are 'ee too stiff-necked to tell me as you work fer 'is Lordship?'

The screaming stopped; the boy had passed out.

Jack sighed with relief for himself and the boy. He was glad Heather was there to give him something else to think about. 'Jack, that's my name. I'm the groom at Pengarron Manor.' It was his turn to be proud to tell of his occupation.

Heather stood on tiptoe and peered into Jack's face. 'You 'aving me fer a fool?' she asked suspiciously. 'You'm too bloody young to be a groom at an important place like the manor.'

97

'I am then,' Jack retorted, 'and that's the Gospel truth. I was stable boy till I was eighteen, then Barney Taylor, he was the groom, well, his rheumatics finally got the better of him and he took to his bed for good and Sir Oliver didn't take on nobody else but made me the groom in Barney's place. That was two years ago and now I've got two stable boys working under me.'

'Fancy,' Heather said, swaying her broad hips. 'Thought there'd be more'n three of 'ee workin' in a big place like the manor stables.'

'Sometimes someone comes over from Sir Oliver's stud,' Jack said grudgingly.

'This 'is Lordship's 'orse then? The big black un?'

'Aye, he's magnificent, isn't he? I've ridden him occasionally, when His Lordship's not had the time to exercise him.'

'Oh, 'ave you now? What's it called them? Somethin' bloody silly, I d'reckon.'

'It's not silly at all,' Jack returned defensively. 'He's called Conomor.'

'Conomor, a warrior's name, eh? I 'eard 'is master's a warrior in bed.'

Jack was attracted to this wild-looking mine girl and wanted her to stay and talk but he wished she would not use such coarse language. He was not used to it, spending most of the time about the manor where no one spoke like that. He hoped Heather could not make out his blushes. He didn't speak, wondering instead if she really did know that Conomor was the name of an ancient warrior or if she was poking fun at his fantasy tale to the horses.

'Still, Jack, you mayn't be a warrior but you're my 'ero fer gettin' the doc to me tas. I reckon I d'owe 'ee somethin' fer that.'

With swift movements she pressed her curvaceous young body to his and dragging his head down she kissed his mouth fiercely with wet open lips. Before Jack could recover his startled thoughts and feelings she wrenched herself away and disappeared into the darkness as unexpectedly as she'd come out of it.

Jack pressed trembling fingers to his stinging lips. His insides were heaving with a new intense sensation that was almost painful. The terrible reason for his being up close to the bleak looming mine buildings had completely left his mind.

Chapter 7

'I don't think I can face another funeral,' Kerensa confided to Alice Trenchard on Alice's next monthly visit to the rambling Tudor manor house. They were chatting in the comfort of the summer house, a few days after the dead miners had been buried in one communal grave.

'Aye, it's been a grim year so far, and I know what it's like, having lived and worked on a mine face all my life before I came here to work. Beatrice was talking to Rosie and she believes the same as me, that the mine disaster was caused by a scoffer not leaving behind a didjan for the knockers.'

'Could have been. Even if you don't believe in the little people, it doesn't do to offend them. But it's a heavy price for the tinners to pay for not leaving behind a piece of pasty or hevva cake.'

'Well, I hope there won't be the need for another funeral for a very long time,' Alice said. 'As it is, Ben Rosevidney will soon find himself digging new graves over the old ones on the south side of the church. Thank the Lord he won't be digging one for Philip and David now they've got over the measles. They were so poorly and I was so afraid Jessica was going to catch it. I was grateful to the Sampsons on Polcudden Farm offering to take her but I missed her so much. If anything happened to her . . .' Alice shuddered. She dearly loved her eight-year-old twins, tall, strong, blond and robust like Clem. But Jessica, the daughter she had longed for, had replaced Clem as the one she most desired to return her love.

Alice had long accepted that Clem would always love and mourn his loss of Kerensa, but now she had Jessica it didn't matter so much. And nothing could detract from the close friendship she had formed with Kerensa from the days she had lived at the manor as Kerensa's maid. Alice was content with life as a farmer's wife and since the deaths of Clem's mother and grandmother she had presided over the Trenchard household with a firm but fair maternal hand.

'I would love to have had Jessica over here with us, but of course Clem wouldn't have approved,' Kerensa said, knowing Clem would not allow any of his children under the Pengarron roof.

'No, I s'pose not and it's a shame, but it would have meant risking your children getting the measles. There's no children now on Polcudden Farm.'

'Well, that's true, of course. So Jessica hasn't developed any spots then?' Kerensa asked, watching her own daughter at play with her dolls and Bob a few feet away.

'No. You don't think she could still get them, do you?' Alice anxiously dropped her knitting in her lap.

'Probably not, but Beatrice says the illness can lie low for a week or two before the spots appear. But don't worry, Alice, she has plenty more of her coriander seed remedy all ready prepared in case it's needed.'

'Has she? Well, that's a comfort,' Alice said truthfully. She glanced around before she spoke next. 'How is the old mare anyway? She's teaching Rosie all sorts of things when she comes over here to help her with her herbal teas and ointments. Rosie's learning really fast and it comes in very handy at times, both for us and the beasts. Clem doesn't like it, as you can imagine.'

'Beatrice is fine, a bit shaky on her legs these days but still as tough as old boots.' Kerensa frowned. 'Why doesn't Clem like Rosie coming over here? I know he doesn't think it right that our children mix. I suppose I can understand that although I don't agree with it, but Rosie?'

'Don't be offended, Kerensa,' Alice said, looking at her knitting. 'He fears she may not be safe from Sir Oliver's . . . how shall I put this?'

'Charms?' Kerensa suggested and laughed.

'Yes, something like that,' Alice replied, eyeing Kerensa curiously. 'I thought that would upset you a bit.'

'Half the men in the county are afraid their womenfolk will fall under Oliver's charms, why should Clem be any different? And Oliver does turn the head of many a young girl.' Kerensa leaned forward and whispered in a wicked tone, 'Has it crossed your mind that you may not be safe when you come over here, Alice?'

Alice laughed heartily with her friend. 'I suppose Clem takes me for granted. Perhaps I should hint that . . . No, I'd better not, he wouldn't take it kindly, being Sir Oliver.'

'He doesn't mind you coming over here to see me, does he?' Kerensa asked, concerned.

'Not really, he knows it wouldn't be fair to curb our friendship. He, um, likes to hear about you.'

'Does he?'

There was an awkward moment of silence. Kerensa thought it best to get back to the measles. 'I had a good look at my three for spots when I put them to bed last night. I saw no sign of any but as usual Kane and Luke were covered in scratches and bruises from the mischief they get up to.'

Alice retrieved two dropped stitches of her knitting, glad the conversation had turned back. 'You mean from the mischief Luke gets Kane into.'

Kerensa chuckled, 'Yes, and Luke was most put out by me looking for spots. He said he had no intention of catching the measles, that it was not dignified to have me fussing over him and he is far too old for that sort of thing. Can you imagine it, Alice? Luke saying things like that at six years old! Whatever will he be like at sixteen, or twenty-six?'

'Like his father, without a doubt,' Alice said firmly, pausing in her knitting to nestle more comfortably into her chair. She let herself relax; she enjoyed this time spent away from the eternal bustle of farm life and made the most of it. She trusted Rosie to look after Jessica for a short while and the twins would be working with Clem and their grandfather.

'I expect you're right about that, Alice,' Kerensa sighed. 'Oliver encourages both the boys to be rather on the wild side and while he sees Olivia as sweet and ladylike, he likes her to be independent too.' She stood up and took a bunch of red roses out of the vase sitting on a small round table made of local serpentine. 'These are for you to take home, Alice,' she said, laying them down carefully.

Alice thanked her and, as all young mothers do, they chatted on about their families. Alice asked why Olivia was repeatedly smacking one of her dolls and wagging a disciplinary finger at it.

'Oh, that's supposed to be Luke,' Kerensa explained.

'He's upset her by not letting her join him and Kane in his game of soldiers, British against the French, in the orchards. He has his games all planned with great care. Bob is not allowed to go anywhere near them because he gets too excited and once knocked over a really splendid fort the boys had built. Michael and Conan, the stable boys, are roped in if they're not too busy and Jake joins in as a general sometimes, with the other gardeners as infantry men. In fact everyone if they're not female has joined in with Luke's games at one time or another. Nathan has, Oliver of course, who enjoys them as much as the boys, Matthias Renfree once or twice when he's been here, and even the Reverend Ivey.'

'Matthias Renfree?' Alice raised her eyebrows. 'I wouldn't have thought he'd approve of war games.'

'He's very patriotic, Alice. He plays the part of a military surgeon.'

'How about the Reverend Ivey? I suppose he plays the clergyman from the nearest church.'

'No, actually the Reverend likes to be the old King, who's said to have loved to take his armies into battle.'

'Fancy that, the Reverend Ivey wanting to be a king. You never know about people, do you? Young Luke wants to be a soldier when he grows up, I take it?'

'Oh yes, he talks of nothing else. He wants to join the same regiment as his father, the 32nd Regiment of Foot.'

'Well,' said Alice, sipping from a glass of elderberry and mint cordial, 'sounds like Luke will make a good soldier and God help the French or anyone else who might be the enemy when the time comes. I suppose it's him who usually wins and Kane who ends up killed or wounded.'

'Usually,' Kerensa nodded, picking up Alice's knitting to admire it and see how far the garment had progressed, 'but not always. I fear that like most men Luke sees war as romantic or heroic, he enjoys being stretched out with strips of rag stained with berry juice and pretending to be dying in agony. Once, he even got Michael and Conan to carry him into my sitting room to, as Luke told them to say, "present the body to the grieving mother". I was horrified! Oliver just laughed. I think he was even proud of the boy's adventurous spirit.'

'Makes you shudder just to think of it,' Alice said thoughtfully. 'My boys can be just as gruesome about their games and I'm afraid on the odd occasion they let Jessica play with them she's just as wild. I've just had a thought,' she added, putting her hand on Kerensa's arm. 'If old Beatrice was allowed to join in Luke's games she would make a good neighbourhood witch!'

'I 'eard that!' came a rasping voice from a distance.

Alice burst out laughing. 'Oh dear.'

Kerensa hid her smiles behind her hand as Olivia rushed off to help Beatrice shuffle and grunt her way into view.

'Missus Mouth-it-all's 'ere again, I see,' she screeched. 'Makin' fun of an ole woman. I'll tell 'ee one thing, Alice Trenchard, if I wus a real witch I'd turn you into a big fat toad!'

'Alice didn't mean any harm, Beatrice,' Kerensa said quickly, although she knew that Alice and Beatrice, the manor's oldest servant, enjoyed this bickering at each other.

Olivia enjoyed their interchanges too and she tugged at Beatrice's dirty apron while encouraging the old woman to go on. 'Turn Alice into a kitten, Bea, go on, go on, I've always wanted a kitten but Father won't let me. Make one the same colour as Alice's curls, go on, go on.'

Beatrice, who never paid much attention to personal

hygiene and whose presence was usually accompanied by more than one dreadful smell, screwed up her ugly face and winked at Olivia. 'I'd reckon she would better make a brown cow all fattened up ready fer the market, my 'an'some.'

'I think we've had enough of this conversation,' Kerensa said in a tone that defied argument. She knew her daughter could be just as outspoken as her friend and Olivia looked as though she was bursting to say something more. Instead she made a disappointed face at her mother and looked cheekily at Alice, obviously picturing in her mind the creature she had next wanted to have her turned into.

Beatrice studied Alice from short-sighted eyes. 'I've left a basket in the kitchen fer yer little sister-in-law, if ye'll git up off yer lazy backside drekkly an' take it 'ome to 'er,' she said haughtily. 'Rosie'll know what t'do with it.'

'It'll be my pleasure,' Alice replied, smiling back with mock graciousness.

'And there's a parcel beside it thee can drop off to Ricketty Jim, went put 'ee out none, ye'll 'ave to past un on yer way back. 'E's usually to be found on Trecath-en's boundary. 'Tis a nice bit of bacon fat fer 'im, 'e do like a nice bit of bacon fat.'

'Don't worry, Beatrice, I'll give it to him and make sure I'll tell him it's from you. Ricketty Jim's not starving, you know, I send up something to the rover every day by one of my menfolk.'

Beatrice sniffed heavily and swiped at a drip of phlegm hanging from her nose. Alice looked away in disgust. 'Don't 'ee ruddy ferget!' Beatrice instructed her. 'I'll be off then, m'dear,' she then told Kerensa, having always addressed her mistress in these terms, and the old crone shuffled off.

'No guesses where she's going,' Alice said, looking warily round to make sure Beatrice was out of earshot.

'I know,' piped up Olivia, 'off to the stables to hit the gin bottle.'

'Olivia!' Kerensa exclaimed. 'I won't have you saying things like that.'

'Sorry,' Olivia said, quite unconcerned, and went back to her dolls.

Alice pursed her lips and moved them to the side of her face as she watched the little red-haired girl at play. 'If you ask me, they're all getting more like their father.'

'Not Kane so much,' Kerensa said. 'Although he has his moments, he's usually happy to go along with whatever Luke gets up to, but he does insist that Olivia goes riding with them.'

'I've often thought how good it is that the two boys get along so well and how much Kane dotes on the little maid there. I hope they'll always get along with each other in later years. Kane could even be yours with that lovely auburn hair the same colour as yours and Olivia's. How old is he now? Ten years, isn't it?

'Well, ten at the end of November. It's the time of year I rescued him and brought him home and that's when we count his birthday. Oliver says Kane was the best thing I ever brought home from the market,' Kerensa said fondly. 'Dear Kane, he hates the colour of his hair. Oliver used to say he looked like that field mouse he used to carry about, but I think he has a calm and gentle face.'

'He's got a gentle nature, too, despite the terrible start he's had in life,' Alice said wholeheartedly. 'Does he still get those nightmares?'

'Yes, I'm afraid so, but not so often as he's got older. He never remembers what's in them but I imagine they're

108

about his early days spent in that brothel or perhaps the fight I had to put up to get him away from his dreadful father.'

'Well, he's got a good home, a good mother and father now, and he absolutely adores you, Kerensa. It don't bear thinking about what might have happened if you hadn't come across him when you did. And if you ask me he's going to be a fine-looking young man. He'll give Luke and my boys a run for the maids later on, what with those big sad eyes of his, you wait and see.' Alice smiled warmly at Kerensa, she knew how protective her friend was over the boy brought up as the Pengarron's own son.

'It's a shame Clem won't allow Philip and David to come over here to play with my boys,' Kerensa said with real regret, 'and little Jessica and Olivia would enjoy each other's company so much.'

'Well, you know the same as me what Clem's views are on the matter. He can be every bit as stubborn as Sir Oliver if he's a mind to be. Anyway, Kerensa, think of it, your boys and mine, they'd probably start a feud between the next Pengarron and Trenchard generation.'

'But they should have the chance to see if they'll get along or not. It's mainly Clem who has any ill feeling and that's only against Oliver. I do understand his reasons but I wish he'd change his mind. I get very little chance to see your children.'

Kerensa thought back over painful memories of Clem's anguish when he learned they couldn't be married and the clashes he'd had with Oliver. She wondered if Clem would change his mind if she approached him herself, but the opportunity to talk to Clem alone was rare.

'Well, things aren't likely to change, I'm afraid,' Alice sighed. 'Men must have their pride.'

Olivia ran up and dropped a doll into Kerensa's lap and asked her to tie up the fiddly fastenings on its dress. Then she showed Alice the latest addition Oliver had brought home to the overflowing nursery.

Alice admired the doll, lifted Olivia up on her lap and cuddled her, then leaned over to Kerensa as if she was about to divulge a secret. 'You'll never guess what Clem is up to now.'

'Tell me,' Kerensa returned eagerly. She liked to hear about Clem.

'Believe it or not he's trying to get Rosie and Matthias Renfree together.'

'With marriage in mind, you mean? Rosie and Matthias.' Kerensa looked up at the domed roof of the summer house and pondered this. 'Yes, I do believe they would make a good couple. At least Rosie wouldn't have to change her whole way of life like we had to.'

'You try telling her that,' Alice chuckled. 'Clem's getting more and more frustrated with both of them, they don't show the slightest interest in each other.'

'You'll have to help them along, Alice, try your hand at matchmaking.'

'I've already tried, Kerensa, but I've had no luck yet. Kenver's had a go at throwing them together but Father reckons we should leave things alone. Oh well, if it's meant to be . . . Perhaps I should ask Beatrice if she's got a potion, eh? She's got one for everything else.' Alice winked and grinned at Olivia who was listening closely from her perch on Alice's comfortable lap.

'I'll ask Beatrice for a potion for you, Alice,' Olivia offered, wriggling down.

'Thank you, my handsome, but I think we'd better leave it for today.' Alice kissed the top of her head. 'But you can do something else for me because I have to go home to my own little girl now. Will you be a dear and run along to the kitchen and fetch my red cloak for me, please? You'll find it over the back of a chair. And will you bring the basket for Rosie? She's going to pick some herbs and wild salad for Beatrice, now the poor old dear can't get about so much. Can you manage all that? Oh, and you'll find one of my triggy-apples in the kitchen, specially made just for you.'

'Is there one for Luke and Kane too? They love toffee,' Olivia asked, her little oval-shaped face bright at the prospect of the treat.

'Yes, of course there is,' Alice laughed merrily. 'If I forgot them I'd probably find myself caught up in a battle of some sort.'

'Aren't you forgetting something, Alice?' Kerensa asked.

'What? Oh! Ricketty Jim's bacon scraps.'

'I'll put them in the basket,' Olivia said, and ran off obligingly.

Alice got to her feet and watched her. 'She moves as gracefully as you, Kerensa. Why couldn't I keep my figure like you?' she said, pretending to be vexed.

Kerensa put an arm round her friend's shoulders and kissed her cheek. 'You're no more than a bit cuddly, Alice Trenchard,' she laughed. 'Well, I'd better go up and get ready for our visitor.'

'Oh? Captain Solomon, is it?'

'Not this time. It's a young lady. Miss Ameline Beswetherick from Tolwithrick, Sir Martin's eldest grand-daughter. She's had a proposal of marriage and needs time away from home to make up her mind whether to accept it or not. She's quite a pleasant girl, a year older than Rosie. Brought up a lady of course but, unlike her mother Lady Rachael, very prim and proper.'

'Mmmm, she sounds fascinating. What's the man concerned like?'

'His name is James Mortreath and he's a very distant relative of Oliver's. He's in his mid-thirties, a lawyer by profession. He's been very successful in London and is very rich. He's rather quiet and serious. He asked Ameline to marry him ages ago but she keeps the poor man on tenterhooks. He's been up and back from London several times while waiting for her answer. I quite like him. I think he'd be good for Ameline but Oliver deliberately makes him feel uncomfortable, though I don't know why. It makes me cross, I think it's really childish of him.'

'Well, you know what Beatrice says.'

'Yes, how could I forget – men never grow up, they only get worse.'

'And worse!'

The two young women laughed together. At that moment Luke Pengarron appeared dragging a loudly protesting Kane along by his torn shirt.

'Mama, will you do something about him!' Luke demanded. 'Kane is supposed to be dead but he won't lie down!'

Alice quickly summed up the situation. 'Give young Master Luke a clip round the ear,' she advised Kerensa, as one mother to another.

Chapter 8

Rosie Trenchard was seething mad. She had just wasted the best part of two hours taking a so-called important message from Clem to Ker-an-Mor Farm for Matthias Renfree. She had had to wait around to see him, only to be told, eventually, that he was up at the manor house going over the estate's accounts with Sir Oliver. To make matters worse, when she left a message for Matthias, it seemed he already knew its content: that the widow Trewerggie, over Trevenner way, was anxious to learn about how the Methodist Society looked upon God and salvation with a view to joining it and wanted the young preacher to call on her. How Clem knew about it and why he was concerned about the spiritual affairs of a woman he professed not to have spoken to until market day was beyond Rosie.

She had lost all patience with Clem and was beginning to believe that the long periods he drew apart from the rest of the family had left him a little 'touched'. She made up her mind to speak to their father about his behaviour.

Since her mother and gran had died she and Alice were rushed off their feet now they were the only women on the farm. Between them they cleaned the farmhouse, cooked, laundered, scrubbed, attended to the dairy, fowls, pigs, goats and garden, drew the water, hoed the weeds in the fields and helped with the harvesting. They prepared for winter by salting and smoking meat and fish and making preserves of all kinds. If they got a minute to sit down, there was always a mountain of darning to finish. Then there was Kenver, her disabled brother; he needed a certain amount of attention every day and Alice was glad of a hand with three boisterous children to rear. Rosie had very little spare time and she was outraged at having this precious commodity wasted by carrying unwanted messages for a half-mad brother.

'The next time you have a message for Preacher Renfree, or anyone else in the whole parish, Clem Trenchard,' she spoke crossly as she approached the boundary between Ker-an-Mor and Trecath-en Farms on her way home, 'you can do it yourself!'

So as not to have an entirely wasted journey Rosie looked about for berries, plants and the wild herbs Beatrice couldn't cultivate in her garden patch. In return for Rosie's help, Beatrice was teaching her how to make and bottle many useful potions, poultices, and ointments. The ugly, gin-sodden old woman gave her tiny bottles of her preparations, like oil of rosemary and sage to make her golden hair shine. Clem snorted at this arrangement, infuriating Rosie by asking if she was going into apprenticeship as the next neighbourhood witch.

Rosie came to the hawthorn boundary of the two farms where the ground fell sharply into a valley on both sides leading down to a river. She climbed over the stile on to her father's land and looked about for Ricketty Jim. He had been there on her way to Ker-an-Mor Farm, boiling river water over a small twig fire. He had received the little packet of tea Rosie had given to him with many polite thank yous.

'Your brother been free-trading, has he, Rosie?' he'd asked, sprinkling the green tea leaves on to the bubbling water. 'I'd ask you to share a dish with me but I've only got the one crock.'

'That's all right,' Rosie answered, edging towards the stile. Ricketty Jim, whose name came about because of his bent shaky legs, was long-bearded and his fly-away hair was greying but his sharp brown eyes suggested he was younger than he looked. Although Rosie liked to talk to him, and he was a conversational man, she felt it wasn't right to spend time alone with him.

Ricketty Jim had turned up in the parish on a summer morning some three years ago. He was shabbily dressed with an old sack of a few belongings, obviously a rover, but he asked for no charity and would put in a hard day's work on the local farms and ask for no more than a good meal in return. He informed the folk curious about him that he came from the north of the county and preferred to live under the stars, usually moving on every two or three months, and that he was likely to leave a parish as suddenly as he'd arrived in it. While he was in Perranbarvah he made his camp where Rosie had seen him. The Trenchards didn't mind him squatting on their land and other folk soon grew to respect him and took his presence among them for granted, seeking him out for interesting discussions and to listen to his entertaining story-telling.

Rosie could see no sign of him now. Under the hedge by the stile on Trecath-en's side of the valley was one of his favourite spots but he had obviously moved on to another. As always, there was no sign that he had ever been there.

Rosie moved down the valley in careful side steps making for the path at its bottom that led straight home. The ground was rough and uneven all the way down to the cheerful river that ran alongside the path and needed careful negotiation through thick clumps of tall sharp thistles. There were no suitable plants for Beatrice's needs here but Rosie knew she would find a wealth of them down by the river.

Afterwards, Rosie couldn't recall the reason why she lost her footing and fell. She may have been deep in thought about leaves or wild flowers, or where Ricketty Jim had gone, or it may have been her anger with Clem. But she had felt her ankle go in one agonising movement and she was falling, rolling over and over the fierce thistles with the bottom of the valley rushing up to meet her.

When she finally came to a halt, the breath knocked out of her, her hat had come off, her faded blue dress torn from her petticoat. It was several minutes before she could pull herself up to a sitting position but the effort ended with her hunching her upper body over her knees. Her head was spinning and she was horrified to think that somehow she was badly injured.

She moved her arms and legs one by one, a little at a time, overwhelmed with relief to find all in working order apart from the wrenched ankle. It throbbed painfully and was badly swollen. Rosie groaned in anguish when she realised the shoe of her injured foot was missing. She must find that shoe, it was half of the only good pair she owned and there was plenty of wear left in them. She would have to search for the shoe when she was sure the rest of her was not hurt.

To ensure there was no neck injury, she moved her head gingerly from side to side and round in a circle. Then she listened for sounds and gulped with relief at hearing the birds chirping and the gurgles of the river on its progress to the sea. Next she looked up and down the valley; her vision was clearing but tears were threatening to fall as a result of shock and she took a deep breath to forestall them. Grazes and scratches were now beginning to sting; the skin of one elbow had been skimmed off and blood was staining her sleeve. Investigating inside her shift and under her petticoat, she discovered bruises on both shoulders, legs and knees.

Rosie wished Ricketty Jim hadn't chosen today to wander off, he would almost certainly have seen her fall and could have helped her home. When her breath was a little recovered, she decided to try and hobble for home but even the lightest of pressure on her wrenched ankle made her scream in pain and sink back to the ground. She felt sick, her head swam and her ears buzzed.

When she could think reasonably again she knew there were only two courses open to her. She could either crawl home on her hands and knees or wait for Clem or her father to come looking for her. It made sense to wait for help and this did not worry her overmuch. She was not far from the farm, there was a bright warm autumn sun in a clear sky and she should be discovered before darkness fell.

Rosie had been cradling her swollen foot for over an hour when the snorting of a horse at the top of the valley gave her a rush of hope mixed with tearful emotion. She hoped the rider would see her and raised a feeble hand. She expected to see Matthias Renfree who called regularly to see Kenver, or perhaps Adam, Matthias's father, calling on estate business, or Nathan O'Flynn, the estate's gamekeeper, who occasionally paid the family a visit. The horse was a magnificent thoroughbred, as black as night. Its rider dismounted and lowered his great height in front of her.

'Well, Miss Trenchard,' Oliver said, his voice softened in the way one employs to comfort the shocked and injured. 'It seems you have met with an accident. Where are you hurt?'

Now that her immediate ordeal had come to an end, tears sprang to her eyes and she wanted to cry. 'My . . . my ankle,' she sniffed.

Very gently he took her hands away from her foot and studied the swollen tissue round the ankle bone. 'This is a bad injury, Rosie, you must be in a lot of pain. Did you fall far?'

She nodded, afraid to speak, knowing her tearfulness would turn into a flood.

Sensitive to her feelings, Oliver asked questions that required only a nod or shake of her head. 'Have you been here a long time like this, Rosie?'

She nodded again.

'I see you have lost a shoe. I noticed your basket near the top of the valley. Will you be all right for a moment if I go back for them?'

Once more Rosie nodded to him.

Oliver put a hand lightly on her shoulder. 'I won't be gone for very long, Rosie, and then I'll take you home.'

When he had gone Rosie wiped the moisture from her eyes. She was more composed when he returned. 'I found your hat too,' he said, giving it to her, its blue ribbon torn.

Rosie took it but did not put it on. 'Thank you, sir.' She found she was able to speak almost normally.

'Beatrice will have a salve to soothe that,' Oliver pointed to her raw elbow, adding with a smile, 'and your ankle, but you'll know all about that, won't you? I understand she is teaching you some of her secrets.'

'Yes, sir,' Rosie answered shyly. She had never been this close to Sir Oliver before, their class and his height had kept them at a suitable distance. Now he was just in front of her, their eyes on the same level, and he had even touched her. Drawing the undivided attention of a man so handsome and masculine had come only in her maidenly dreams before now. Her predicament forgotten, she hoped that she didn't sound as flustered as she felt. 'C-comfrey, the . . . healing plant . . . for . . . for strains and bruises. I . . . I have some at home.'

'Good. It won't take long to ride to the farmhouse on Conomor. I'll lift you up on his back.'

Rosie's heart fluttered as Oliver eased her up to sit side-saddle and swung himself up behind her.

'Are you ready, Rosie?'

'Yes, sir. I . . . I'll be glad to get home.'

He glanced down at her swollen ankle. 'Try to keep your foot away from Conomor's side.'

'Yes, sir, thank you.'

He stretched round her to take the reins and Rosie felt the strong warmth of his muscular body. It swept a thrill through her and she was not displeased the motion of the horse's movements caused her to sway often against him. A thought occurred to her. She said, 'You called me Miss Trenchard. You were the first to ever call me that, in Trelynne Cove, after the wreck of the *Amy Christabel*. Do you remember, sir?'

'I remember, Rosie,' he smiled as she turned slightly to look at him. 'You were a little girl then, the years since have been kind to you.'

Rosie looked rapidly away, her face aflame. Her heart leapt heavily in her chest. She didn't know if it was permissible for an ordinary girl like herself to speak to a baronet unless he spoke first but she couldn't help herself even though she was nervous. 'I still have the locket Clem found for me. You told me it has a real diamond in it.'

'So I did. You are old enough to wear it now.'

There was no impatient or haughty intonation in his voice so she carried on. 'Well, that may be so, sir, but I don't suppose I shall ever go anywhere grand enough for that.'

'You can wear it on your wedding day, Rosie. Without doubt that occasion will not be too far in the future.'

Rosie looked down at the moving ground. 'There's no prospect of that at the moment.'

They had reached the farmyard and a flock of noisy geese hissed at them. Oliver dismounted and taking the basket, hat and shoe from Rosie he put them on the wall beside the kitchen where at least a dozen untamed cats dozed in the early evening sun. Two white pigs grunted in the sty, a variety of hens scratched in the earth, a few ducks loitered on a little muddy pool and a rough-looking billy goat tied to an old hawthorn tree was trying to reach and eat some of Alice's washing.

'The place looks deserted apart from the animal life,' Oliver said. 'Where do you suppose everyone is?'

'Father and Clem will be back from the fields soon,' Rosie said, feeling even shyer of him now she was home, 'but Alice should be in the kitchen.'

'I'll carry you into the house.'

Oliver had Rosie in his arms as Clem came round the side of the cow shed, Charity at his heels.

'Rosie!' He dropped the bucket he was carrying, startling Charity, and rushed over to them. 'What's happened? I was just about to come looking for you.'

'I fell down the valley,' Rosie explained to her horrified

brother, knowing his horror had more to do with the man holding her than with her recent plight. 'Ricketty Jim has gone off and I was sitting there helpless for ages until Sir Oliver found me.'

Thrusting out his arms, Clem said coldly to Oliver, 'Thank you for your help but I'll take her now.'

Oliver knew how grudgingly the other man's gratitude was given. With a sardonic smile he passed his sister to him. 'Her ankle needs urgent attention.'

'I'll see to it.'

'Thank you, sir,' Rosie said meekly. 'I'm very grateful to you.'

'I am only too glad to have been able to help you, Rosie,' Oliver said graciously.

Clem moved abruptly and carried Rosie into the farmhouse kitchen. Rosie was angered and ashamed at the rudeness shown to the man who had so kindly come to her rescue. She was pleased when Sir Oliver bent his dark head and followed them through the door, and she dug Clem in the ribs as he scowled.

Kenver Trenchard, who was sitting in a corner of the room writing on a scrap of precious paper given to him by Matthias Renfree, looked up and an expression of shocked surprise swept over his face at the unexpected trio of people.

'My Lord!' he addressed Oliver. 'Good evening to you.'

'Good evening to you, Kenver,' Oliver replied, walking further into the spotlessly clean kitchen that smelled pleasantly of roasting mutton.

Kenver waited for an explanation as Clem gently sat Rosie on a chair by a window but no one spoke. He watched his brother fetch a footstool for his sister and carefully place one of her legs upon it. 'Would someone mind telling me what's happened, please. Clem?'

The three had brought an uneasy atmosphere into the room and Kenver knew he would be correct in his assumption that Clem was its creator.

'I had a fall, Ken, sprained my ankle,' Rosie spoke for herself. 'Sir Oliver found me and kindly brought me home.'

''Tis a good job you did then, sir,' Kenver said, returning his attention respectfully to Oliver, 'or the poor maid would still be there now. Clem was about to go and look for her but it'd be a while yet afore he'd have found her. Where did she fall exactly?'

'I came across her at the bottom of the valley. From the look of things your sister fell almost from the top,' Oliver replied. 'She was fortunate not to have sustained a more serious injury than a twisted ankle.'

Kenver went on, 'I'm sure we're all very grateful to you, sir. We were getting worried about Rosie being away for so long. She'd gone over to your farm with a message for Matthias Renfree, you see.'

Oliver looked at Clem to see if he looked as grateful as his more likeable, articulate brother. Clem's face was set sulky, not unexpectedly so, but he said, 'I'm grateful to you,' then clamped his mouth shut.

Rosie was increasingly angered at Clem's lack of manners. He never called the baronet 'sir' or 'My Lord', and it seemed even more rude with him standing in their farmhouse as her rescuer. She knew her father would be angry if he was there.

'Rosie must have had a wasted journey then, I've only just parted with Renfree to ride over here. Anyway, she is home safe and sound except for her ankle,' Oliver said, his voice and demeanour giving no indication whether he was perturbed by Clem's behaviour. 'However, it is time something was done about it.'

'I'll get some cold water for your ankle, Rosie.' Clem snatched up an enamelled bowl and went outside.

'We'll have to beg your forgiveness for Clem's lack of manners,' Kenver said apologetically, but added on a lighter note, 'I'm afraid they don't improve with age. Will you take a seat, sir?'

'Yes, I think I will, for a few moments,' Oliver replied, sitting on a chair close to the young chair-bound man. 'I rode over this way to see Ricketty Jim. I have some work for him on Ker-an-Mor if he's interested. He's a good worker, I'd offer him permanent work but he wouldn't take it. I'll catch up with him another time.'

It was several years since Oliver had seen Kenver, he couldn't recall seeing him once since he had married Kerensa. Oliver called occasionally on Morley, as he did on all his tenants, but Kenver was never about, either busy in his small bedroom-cum-workshop where he made furniture and crafted ornaments, or taking a rest. Kenver needed a short sleep every few hours. Crippled from birth from the waist down, he tired quickly but it did not impair the excellence of his work, some of which had found its way into some of the wealthier local homes. Rosie or Alice would take the finished articles to sell on market day at Marazion and both Oliver and Kerensa had each brought home a piece that had caught their fancy.

Kenver was now twenty-three and claimed the Trenchard fine blond hair and deep blue eyes. His hair was not tied back and it rested on the front of his green striped waistcoat. Oliver had a great respect for Kenver Trenchard. He could have resigned himself to a life of bitterness and idleness, but he was a gifted man and used his abilities to their capacity with honesty and humour. Oliver wondered if he had a talent for a musical instrument and resolved to

123

mention it at a later date, but for now he leaned over Kenver's useless legs and glanced at his scrap of paper.

'What are you writing, Kenver, more poetry?'

''Tis just a few lines that's been running through my head all day, sir.' He handed the paper to Oliver. 'As you can see I'm in need of a word to rhyme with cavalcade.'

Rosie rubbed her leg above the injured ankle to ease the pain, watching the two men with a keen eye as they conversed. Alice entered with the bowl of water with Jessica trailing behind her. She clucked around Rosie having heard the tale from Clem on her way through the yard. Adding her thanks to Oliver she offered him a dish of tea. Oliver accepted, not because he was thirsty, but because he knew it would annoy Clem.

'Your husband not joining us, Alice?' Oliver asked casually, a bit too casually and Alice went pink.

'He's rescuing my washing from the billy goat, he'll be in drekkly.'

'I see,' Oliver replied, amused. Was Clem really doing such an unmasculine thing as bringing in the washing, or was Alice making an excuse for more bad manners on Clem's part?

An unreadable look passed between Alice and Sir Oliver and Rosie was at a loss as to what it meant. She did not know that her sister-in-law and the baronet shared a friendship, of sorts. It went back to the days before Alice married Clem; Oliver had come across her and Clem quarreling in the manor grounds when, not knowing that he had made Alice pregnant, Clem had finished his dalliance with her. Alice had been left sick and distraught and Oliver had taken her home to the manor on his big black horse. At the time Oliver's marriage to Kerensa had been strained and she was away at the Beswetherick's. In their loneliness

124

Oliver and Alice had talked throughout the night and a lasting closeness formed between them.

Oliver looked down at the scrap of paper. 'Serenade would be appropriate at the end of the next line, Kenver,' he said, returning the poetry. He was impressed with what he had read.

Jessica Trenchard was as fair as her father but had inherited Alice's bouncy curls giving her a cherubic appearance. She stood before Oliver and stared at him in the disconcerting way of the child. He returned her stare with paternal amusement. Jessica was approaching her fourth birthday, four years younger than his own daughter. Pretty and small for her age, she was dressed in a frock he recognised as an old one of Olivia's and too large for her.

'You're a big man,' Jessica said, resting her tiny sharp elbows on his knees.

'Jessica, come away and don't bother Sir Oliver,' Alice chided her.

'It's all right, Alice,' Oliver said, and he lifted Jessica up to stand on his knees.

Jessica giggled, her face lighting up like the sun coming out. 'What's your name?' she asked, twisting her thin red lips to the side.

'Oliver,' he told her, smiling back and patting her curls.

'Oli-ver. Ollie's quicker.'

'Oh, I don't allow anyone to call me that,' he said, his eyes twinkling at her.

Jessica next peered closely into his face. 'Your eyes are black, like night-time. Are you old?'

Alice drew in her lips and frowned at her daughter as she attended to Rosie's ankle but Oliver was happy with the child's chatter. 'Some people would think me rather old, others would not,' he said, tweaking her button nose.

125

'As old as my father?'

'I'm a few years older than him and your mother. Now, Jessica, it is my turn to ask you a question. Where are your brothers, Philip and David?'

'Oh, they,' she made a face, 'they've done their jobs and are out playing catch round by the barn. Won't let me play, they never let me play, but I can beat them at anything!'

Oliver laughed. 'It's much the same at my house, young lady. I have two sons and a little girl like you and she gets left out of their games.'

'Why don't you bring your maid over here to play with me?' Jessica asked, intent on rearranging his neckcloth.

Oliver raised his eyebrows. 'Perhaps one day I will.'

'Why don't you get another maid?' Jessica said, now winding her arms round his neck and leaping up and down on his legs with boundless energy. 'Mother says she can't have any more maids. It's not fair, I won't never get someone to play with.'

Oliver held Jessica under the arms to prevent her falling off between jumps.

Coming in with an armful of washing, Clem's face was a picture of horror when he saw his daughter bouncing on the knees of the man he so despised. Bundling the washing into Alice's arms, he wrenched Jessica away. Jessica did not notice Clem's rage and wrapped herself round him, kissing his cheek again and again. Clem held her tightly, as though he had snatched her from danger. He watched in tight-lipped silence as Alice put the washing on a chair then passed one of the only two sets of cups and saucers owned in the Trenchard household to his enemy.

'Thank you, Alice,' Oliver said, then, quite unruffled, speaking to Clem, 'I congratulate you on your daughter,

Trenchard. She is most charming, like her mother and aunt.'

There was an arctic silence. Alice and Rosie hid their embarrassed faces as they set about wrapping wet cloths round the swollen ankle. Kenver coughed and looked down at his writing, his mind as blank in knowing what the right thing would be to say now as it was for the next line of his poetry. Oliver drank his tea, slowly, seemingly oblivious of the atmosphere Clem had created but in reality enjoying it. If it wasn't for the respect he held for the others of the household he would have baited Clem further.

The appearance of Morley Trenchard broke the silence and there was a rush of voices to tell the tale of Rosie's misfortune once more. He removed his hat in respectful acknowledgement of Oliver's presence in his home – usually he took it off only when saying grace at the meal table. Morley settled down with an enormous mug of tea to talk over farming methods with Oliver who congratulated him on the hard work he had put in to make his farm prosper; he made no reference to Clem's contribution. Kenver listened. Alice folded the washing. Rosie rubbed at her aching leg. Clem stood stiffly, and Jessica, growing bored with the 'grown-up' talk, wriggled free from him and ran outside.

Morley was honoured to have the Lord of the Manor and his landlord as a guest in his home. It would have been an enjoyable occasion if not for Clem's attitude, but while he regretted that, Morley understood his son's feelings towards the man who had stolen his bride. They were two fine men, his son and Sir Oliver Pengarron. It was a great pity they could never be on better terms.

Oliver was about to take his leave when Jessica reappeared carrying the farm's one tame cat. Heading straight for Oliver she promptly dropped the fat ginger animal into his lap, saying in her squeaky soft voice, 'I got Scrap in to see you, Oli-ver.'

Oliver sprang up as if the cat was made of hot coals. 'Ugh! I can't abide cats!' Scrap protested as she hit the floor heavily and darted outside. Jessica, frightened and confused, ran to Clem and clung to his legs. 'I'm sorry,' Oliver said thickly. 'If you'll excuse me I really must be going.'

As the door closed behind Oliver, Alice looked about her in shock. 'What on earth happened? Why did he rush out like that?'

'Didn't you know?' Clem laughed with real hilarity and this being rare everyone looked at him. 'He's can't bear cats near him, his eyes go all runny and he breaks out in a rash!' He picked Jessica up and hugged her.

With an irritated click of her tongue Alice followed Oliver outside. He was at the well splashing water from a bucket over his eyes.

'I'm sorry about that,' she said, passing him the kitchen cloth she had in her hand. 'If I'd have known . . .'

'Well, it gave your husband the first hearty laugh he's had in many a year,' Oliver said philosophically, taking the cloth and wiping his hands and face. 'I hope I didn't upset Jessica.'

'She'll be all right when she knows you're not cross with her. I'll have to explain that she must call you Sir Oliver, not just Oliver, that wouldn't do at all,' Alice ended on a chiding note. Then her full face broke into a smile, her hazel eyes held a rather wicked appeal and she twisted one of her curls in front of her ears in a way that was both demure and secretive.

'What is it?' Oliver asked, suddenly uncomfortable after the exposure of one of his weaknesses.

'I'm sorry,' she replied, lifting a hand to hide a smile, 'but it was funny.'

The special friendship made Oliver smile too and he gave her back the cloth, momentarily holding her hand. 'Yes, I suppose it was funny. Let me know if Rosie has any problems with her ankle and I'll get Dr Crebo to look at it. Good day to you, Alice.'

Alice marched back to the kitchen to find Clem laughing with tears running down his face while repeatedly kissing Jessica. 'Sir Oliver is not cross with you, Jessica. Cats make his eyes go all watery if he touches them, that's all,' she said soothingly. Morley and Kenver were laughing too and she shook her head, fixing all three men with a sober stare.

Rosie had a smile on her face but her thoughts were not on the recent discomfiture of the rider on the black horse she could see trotting out of the farmyard. Instead, she was recalling how good it had felt to ride home so closely to him.

Chapter 9

Mrs Tregonning, the Reverend Joseph Ivey's plump, fussy housekeeper, was surprised at the identity of the young man calling at the parsonage door. She bid him wipe his feet, take off his hat and step inside the hall. She eyed his boots critically, grudgingly approved them then waddled to the elderly parson's study to ask if he would receive the visitor.

''Scuse me, Reverend, but Bartholomew Drannock's turned up wanting to see you,' she breathed heavily, her flushed face pressed round the study door. 'Says he can't come back today if you don't see him right away.'

The Reverend put down his quill to ponder on this. A moment later, he said, 'Then you'd better ask him to come in, Mrs Tregonning.'

Mrs Tregonning wasn't so sure the Reverend should allow himself to be disturbed. 'What about your sermon, then?'

'In my experience, Mrs Tregonning,' he said, with a light smile that took years off his kindly face, 'the interruption of a laboured sermon can bring forth the very ingredient one needs to write one of excellence.'

'Very well, Reverend,' she said, disappearing from the door but continuing to speak, 'as you please, I'm sure you know best. I'll show him in, hope it's not bad news about his dear mother, poor soul . . .'

As the housekeeper's voice faded the Reverend speedily tidied up his desk to show no signs of his mental and spiritual labour, then he rose and took up a position in the middle of the room. He always did this when welcoming a caller, expected or not, not wanting them to believe they were a nuisance or wasting his valuable time. He wanted his flock to feel able to unburden themselves of their troubles or if they had joyful news not to dampen their pleasure. For the finishing touch he created a flexible stance and loosened his features, ready to rearrange them the instant he knew why the caller was here.

Mrs Tregonning ushered Bartholomew into the study with an air of total disinterest. It belied her true character, but this was necessary if the parishioners were to feel they could speak to the Reverend in complete confidence.

Reverend Ivey held out his hand, automatically adopting a fatherly expression as he attempted to read the youth's eyes.

Bartholomew glanced around the room which smelled faintly of the lavender water the Reverend drank to ward off headaches. He wanted to be sure no other person was there before shaking hands.

'Thank you for seeing me at once,' he said quietly. 'It's difficult to find spare time to see you and I want to discuss something that can't wait.'

'There's no need for concern, Bartholomew. Please sit yourself down. Can I offer you some refreshment?'

'Not for me, thank you.' Bartholomew chose the chair opposite the desk and waited for the parson to be seated. 'I've come about my mother.'

'I rather thought it might be about your mother. Has her condition worsened?'

'She's wasting away before my eyes, Reverend,' he

answered, sorrow etched deeply in his face. 'Since Father died she's lost the will to live. She just sits on his side of the settle beyond the door and stares at nothing. It's all I can do to get her to eat a crumb. I know you've tried your best to help, Reverend, organising the village women and Mrs Tregonning here to clean the cottage and cook meals for the little ones. But it can't go on for ever. The children need a woman to look after them properly and I'm hardly of an age to get married. I'm getting desperate to know what to do. I realise you must get a lot of people looking for help following the mine accident and you must be very busy, but I was hoping you might be able to get through to Mother somehow. Encourage her to get out and about, be more her old self again.'

The Reverend sighed soft and slow. 'I will go down to see her later in the day, Bartholomew, and of course I will do my best to lift her spirits, but I feel she needs help from a higher level than we can provide for her now.'

'God, you mean,' Bartholomew said blandly, his eyes alighting on a Bible.

'Yes, I do. Your mother needs to be held constantly before God in prayer. The more prayer, the more chance there will be of her breaking out of her despair.'

'You really believe that, don't you?' Bartholomew said, eyeing the parson suspiciously while tapping the Bible. 'And what it says in here? I know what's written in it, my mother used to teach me to read it.'

'Of course. Why are you surprised? I am a minister of God.'

'The few other clergymen I've come across are ministers only unto themselves, their greed and their perversions. I had not expected to find one who really believed in what he preaches. Perhaps if more of them were like you then people wouldn't need to form a new sort of church outside the church.'

'By that I take it you are referring to the people that are called Methodists, but John Wesley has no desire to start another church. Do you not approve of the Bible classes on Lancavel Downs, Bartholomew?'

'I don't feel the need to pursue the clamour for a new ideology and I sometimes wonder if it's the Wesleys or Matthias Renfree people follow rather than God.'

The Reverend Ivey pursed his wafer-thin lips and rubbed at the back of his wispy grey hair. 'Yes, the early apostles were concerned that some of the people were following them and not God. I find your views interesting, Bartholomew. However, do you not think it unfair to form an opinion on what any individual or group of people do, believe or follow if you don't participate in the proceedings or know all about them?'

'I do, and that is why I have only thoughts and not opinions on religious matters, and my thoughts I share only with my mother,' the young fisherman answered as if rising to a challenge.

'I see. Do you believe in God? You never come to church now.'

'I went into the church once, alone, a long time ago . . . to see if God was there.'

'And was He?' the Reverend prompted gently.

Bartholomew leaned back and stared at the array of theological books on a shelf behind the parson's head. 'I felt this strange kind of inner peace, if that was God . . . I've had the same feeling out at sea, up on the cliffs . . . If He is anywhere at all, He's everywhere.'

'You are right in that.' The Reverend felt there was no need to say any more.

Bartholomew suddenly jumped up from his chair. 'Damn it, Reverend, my mother should not have to live in a hovel!' he cried angrily. 'She deserves better. She may not have been gentry but she was a lady, she deserved far more than a life of poverty as a fishwife. I want her to have the sort of life she was born to, plenty of food, good clothes on her back, wine on the table, a big comfortable house. Look at her, Reverend, just look at her, she's like a shrivelled-up body with the maggots already chewing on her!' He threw up his hands, crossed the room and stared out of the window.

The Reverend Ivey went to him. 'You love your mother very much, Bartholomew, but aren't you forgetting something?'

'What?' asked Bartholomew, without turning round.

'Your mother loved your father very much too. She probably would not have lived her life in any other way if it had meant being without him.'

Bartholomew tightened his mouth. He had no more to say.

The Reverend knew when it was time to talk about something else. 'I am pleased that at least you have the means to earn a living. I understand that Peter Blake has given you and Matthew King the *Young Maid* as an unconditional gift.'

'Aye,' Bartholomew snickered, 'it must have half-killed him to make such a gesture. Elizabeth King believes it must be due to the kindness of that lovely wife of his.'

'Rosina? Yes, it is the kind of gesture that gentle soul would encourage her husband to make.'

Bartholomew turned to face the Reverend. His face was strangely alive, mocking, his eyes dark and challenging.

'Matthew'd reckon it was the hand of God. Paul says the hand of fate. Do you know what I believe, Reverend?' He went on, not waiting for a reply. 'I believe it is more likely to have something to do with the heavy hand of Sir Oliver Pengarron.'

At first the Reverend shook his head but changed his mind and brought his head up and down like a puppet on a slow string. He picked up a book resting on the cushion of the window seat and squeezed its top corner between finger and thumb, studied its title without consciously taking it in then dropped it back in its place. Bartholomew waited expectantly.

'There may be some truth in what you say. The information was brought to me that Sir Oliver paid Peter Blake an unwelcome call on the day following Mark King's funeral. Beforehand he called at the Blakes' rooms and was granted entrance by Mistress Blake. He may have said something . . . I know him to be a man who seeks justice,' the parson cleared his throat and pulled at the wrinkled folds of skin under his chin, 'not necessarily by conventional means. Well, at the least it will be easier for you, your brothers and the Kings to make a reasonable living without dues to pay on your boat.'

'I'm grateful for that,' Bartholomew said briefly.

'I have one idea to help your mother,' the Reverend said. 'She usually appears a little brighter after Lady Pengarron has called on her. Perhaps Jenifer's help may come more fully from that quarter.'

'Yes, Lady Pengarron.' Bartholomew allowed a smile to touch the edges of his wide mouth at the memory of their meeting in Trelynne Cove. 'If anyone can help my mother, she can. She's done everything she can to bring Mother back into the land of the living, so to speak, she even invited all of us to have Sunday dinner at the manor. She thought Mother sitting at a well-set table again would spur her on to wanting to do the best for the little ones, but Mother refused. Lady Pengarron stressed that Sir Oliver wouldn't mind, that it could be a time when he wasn't there if it'd make her feel more comfortable about it.'

'That was a shame, an outing of that kind could have been a turning point for her. I hope the refusal was not purely out of embarrassment.'

'Might have been, but I doubt it. Mother won't go outside the door for any reason. She could have been afraid the littl'uns would have felt out of place with the Pengarron children. The youngest one, that Master Luke, is a holy terror and Cordelia's got nothing good to wear like their maid . . . I'd like to have gone though . . .'

The Reverend felt compassion for the youth's disappointment and dilemma. 'I'll have a quiet word with Lady Pengarron, to see what else we can come up with.' Privately he held little hope of reviving Jenifer's spirit.

He showed Bartholomew to the door and then went back to his sermon, writing with enthusiasm on an idea that the interview with the youth had given him.

Bartholomew walked down the steep hill to the village, where Matthew King was waiting for him. To supplement their earnings they were about to go smuggling in their rowing boat. Under cover of fishing for bait they were to meet a French fishing boat out in deeper waters and take from it a quantity of tobacco. This would be sold to the Sarrison brothers who, not having the haughty authority of their class to haggle over the cost, would give a handsome price. It would stave off hunger pangs for a few weeks but it was done at the risk of being apprehended by the Revenue men and under the mutual loathing they held for the

Frenchmen. There was also the risk of falling foul of privateering by French boats out in the Channel. It was just these kinds of risk that Bartholomew needed to make him momentarily forget his heavy responsibilities.

In the course of the same morning Oliver was in the stable yard of the manor talking to Nathan O'Flynn, his game keeper and head forester. They were resting idly against a stall door smoking their pipes while Oliver waited for Conomor to be saddled.

'When I've taken leave of the parsonage I shall be spending nine or ten days away on business. Adam Renfree has been informed and I've left instructions on my desk.' Oliver took Nathan's empty tobacco pouch from his large flat hand and filled it with tobacco from his own.

'Very well, m'lord. I don't foresee any problems,' Nathan said, puffing away contentedly. 'Thank you for the baccy.'

'Good, that's settled.' With that Oliver shouted across the stable yard. 'Get a move on, will you, Jack! I want to leave before this time next week, if you please!'

'I went be long now, sir!' came a hasty voice from within the stable.

'What's the matter with the lad nowadays?' Nathan mused aloud. 'He's as clumsy as a one-footed ox, so he is. You'd think he was in love or something.'

Oliver chuckled knowingly.

The thickset Irishman raised his eyebrows. 'He's not, is he? Young Jack, smitten!'

'Can you think of another reason for him to be slicking back his hair and putting on his best shirt and making his way over to Lancavel Downs? I don't think Matthias Renfree realises there is an ulterior motive for Jack's sudden appearance at the Bible classes.'

'A girl, eh? Let me see . . . Rosie Trenchard, she's a pretty little thing. Got young men from all over the place running after her. Michael and Conan, the stable boys, have both made a bid for her, till her brother saw 'em off. Now it's Jack's turn, eh? Make a good match, he and Rosie,' Nathan grinned, 'if he can get past Clem, that is. Reckon he must think only the Sheriff himself is good enough for Rosie.'

Oliver shook his head. 'You're way off the mark, Nat. Jack! Hurry up, damn you! Whoever she is, he's keeping her close in his thoughts but I've a notion he's trying to catch more than a glimpse of Carn Bawden's daughter.'

'What? That little spitfire? Heaven only help the lad. Jack will never handle that one.' Nathan shook his head as he gathered his gun, crib and dogs together.

Oliver stared at the stable door from where Jack and his mount would appear and made a wry promise. 'If he doesn't bring Conomor out in less than ten seconds heaven help him now. I want to see the Reverend Ivey before he thinks of retiring!'

Thus, as one tall, black-haired, unexpected caller left the parsonage, he was replaced a short time afterwards by another to interrupt the writing of the Reverend Ivey's sermon.

Quill in hand, inspiration on his face, the parson's hand stayed over the paper as Mrs Tregonning announced, 'Sir Oliver for you, Reverend.'

'It looks as if I have broken the flow of something important, Joseph,' Oliver said, as the Reverend stood up to shake hands.

'Nothing important, Oliver, I assure you. Bartholomew Drannock has not long left here. During our conversation he gave me an idea for my next Sunday's sermon. I shall not forget what he said, he is a most intelligent young man.'

'How odd, he is the very person I have come to see you about.'

'Oh, has it anything to do with his mother, Jenifer?' the Reverend asked, as they seated themselves comfortably over a glass of mead. 'Bartholomew is very concerned about her, her condition is steadily worsening. I told the boy just before he left that the only person who may be able to lift her out of her despair is Kerensa.'

'Kerensa will do what she can to help the poor woman, but the reason why I'm here,' said Oliver, attempting to read an upsidedown sentence of the sermon to try and make out what the Drannock boy might have said, 'has nothing to do with Jenifer or Drannock's tragic death, but with the boy himself.'

The parson did not want to talk about Bartholomew Drannock. 'When you came in, Oliver, I was worried you were bringing more sad tidings. It is a month since the last funeral at which I officiated and I hope the last for a very, very long time. In fact on Sunday I have the happy occasion of baptising the infant grandson of Daniel Berryman of Orchard Hill Farm, then in the middle of the week I am to marry the couple who took over Rose Farm. Purely by chance I happened to find out they have never been joined in wedlock and having broached them on the error of their ways they shamefacedly agreed to right their wrong.'

'Yes, I know all that,' Oliver said impatiently, drumming his fingertips on the desk top.

'It is a good thing they have not had any children yet. And how are your dear children? Is Miss Ameline Beswetherick enjoying her stay with you?'

'The children are all well, thank you, and Ameline has

settled in and made herself comfortable.' Oliver glanced pointedly down at his dark blue frock coat and plucked at a nonexistent piece of fluff. The Reverend knew he had to stop the small talk.

'Um . . . you have something in mind for Bartholomew's future?' he asked hopefully.

'His past would be nearer the mark. Since he was a child I've intended to ask questions about the boy's parentage and a conversation I had with Captain Solomon a while ago has prompted me seriously to wonder if there's any Pengarron blood in the boy's family. Captain Solomon pointed out that the boy bears a notable resemblance to me. Have you by any chance heard any mumblings in the parish about his parentage?'

This was what Joseph Ivey had feared, the moment he had lived in dread of. He shifted uncomfortably on his chair, taking a long moment to answer. 'I . . . cannot say that I have not, Oliver.'

Chapter 10

Oliver's dark eyes widened and brightened, his strong features sharpened, his bearing dominated the parson's study.

'I cannot possibly be the boy's father,' he told Reverend Ivey. 'I have wondered if one of my grandfathers had an affair with one of the boy's grandmothers and the resemblance has emerged only now. I have also had the thought that my father may have sired the boy but Jenifer Drannock is not the sort of woman to have given herself freely to a middle-aged married man, even of my father's standing. There could be one explanation, of course. My father may have forced himself upon her. I have no doubt he was capable of such a thing. You usually have your ear to the ground in the parish. Is there anything that you can tell me? I realise of course that it may be difficult for you to speak but rest assured I've never been under any illusion as to my father's true character.'

The Reverend's watery brown eyes could keep no secret from this man. Oliver Pengarron was too perceptive and he had a disconcerting habit of searching a conversant's face.

'Well, I do know something . . .'

'I thought as much. Tell me all,' Oliver commanded, leaning forward, 'all that you know.'

'Well, um . . . your father, Sir Daniel . . .' the Reverend

was obliged to clear his throat noisily, wishing feverishly that Oliver would drop his penetrating stare.

'Yes, my father . . .?'

'Your father, Sir Daniel . . . is . . . was . . . oh dear, this is very difficult. He is not the father of Bartholomew, rather he had an . . . association with Samuel's mother. I . . . ah, know this to be true because I stumbled across them myself at one time. Sir Daniel was very angry, he made me swear never to tell anyone. Samuel's mother married a Newlyn fisherman, Caleb Drannock, and six months later she gave birth to a son. It was in the same year that you were born. As he grew up the child resembled his mother, folk had no reason to believe he was none other than Caleb's son. I believe that was the reason why there has not been the customary gossip, just the odd remark . . . While Samuel was still an infant Caleb Drannock was drowned at sea, his mother returned to live with her family, now all dead, at Perranbarvah. She never married again. The rest you know.'

Very slowly Oliver got up and walked behind his chair. He gripped the back tightly. His face had lost its usual dark colouring. Sparks seem to be darting from his eyes. With the evidence of Bartholomew's looks and manner he had been certain that Pengarron blood flowed, if not in all the Drannock children, at least in Bartholomew. But the closeness of it had utterly shocked him.

'Do you mean to tell me that Samuel Drannock was sired by my own father? Are you telling me that that fisherman was my half-brother? Born when I was born? Growing up not two miles away from me?' His voice was husky, part in rage, part in hurt. 'And all these years I knew nothing about it! Why have you not spoken of this before? Why have you kept silent for so long?'

'I . . . I was not absolutely certain Sir Daniel was responsible for Samuel's birth until Jenifer confided in me a few years ago. Apparently Margaret Drannock confessed it on her death bed. That was how she and Samuel himself came to know.'

'And why did Jenifer suddenly feel the need to confide this astonishing confession to you?'

'You do not expect me to tell you that, do you?' returned the Reverend, rallying briefly to his own cause. 'That is between Jenifer and me.'

Oliver strode abruptly to the window, his silhouette unmistakably similar to Bartholomew's who had stood there a short time before. He looked out at the same scene, the parsonage back garden where autumn leaves were scattered over the neatly cut lawn and beneath the solitary apple tree. And beyond, the silvery shimmer of the sea over the tops of the shabby cottages in the village below.

'I never had any brothers and sisters,' he said numbly, 'they all died in infancy. I'd always yearned for family life. I didn't know what it was like until I married Kerensa and we had the children. Before that I was lonely most of the time, even more so when my closest friend died on the battlefield. And yet all those years, all those years you schooled me as a child, I had a brother . . .'

'I'll pour you a glass of port wine while you take it all in, Oliver,' the Reverend said soothingly.

'Damn your blasted port wine!' Oliver raged, thrusting his arms up in the air with hands held claw-like. 'Don't you understand what this means to me, you old fool? I had a brother out there!' He stabbed one hand at the sea. 'I always wanted a brother, someone I could talk to, share things with. A brother with a family – a sister-in-law, nephews, nieces. Now I find I *did* have a brother! But it's too late. He died just a few months ago. For God's sake, Joseph Ivey, I had a brother. And you knew. You knew. I had the right to know. I had the right, damn you!'

The terrible thunder of his violent outburst shattered the Reverend's composure. He had risen to his feet but fell back heavily in his chair, scattering the notes of his revised sermon and knocking a glass of water on top of the papers. He was blinking rapidly and had to cough several times before he could speak.

'I, I, I . . . um . . . please c-calm yourself . . . I, I implore you, Oliver . . . I . . . I . . .' Water dripped on to his black clerical clothes.

Oliver sped across the room and thumped both fists on the desk. The Reverend jumped at his fury. Then the sparks died out from Oliver's eyes and as though he was suddenly exhausted he slumped down into a chair. It seemed as though something deep inside him, part of his personality, part of the man himself, had died.

After a prolonged heavy silence he gave a shuddering breath. 'I'm sorry, Joseph. Did I frighten you badly?'

The Reverend called on all the years of his experience to cope with the situation. 'No, I . . . no . . . Oliver . . . I'm so sorry about your distress . . . I would like to explain a little more but . . . but I fear it will cause you even more pain. You see, Samuel did not want you to know . . .'

'Go on,' Oliver ordered, but in a subdued voice. 'I want to hear everything you know.'

'Well, he had . . . a strong dislike for you.'

'That wouldn't have mattered,' Oliver said miserably, then laughed ironically. 'I didn't like him. But given the chance to get to know one another better over the years, who knows what may have happened. Now the man is dead and there will never, never be the opportunity.'

The Reverend Ivey was a deeply worried man. 'Oliver, what will you do now, regarding Jenifer, Bartholomew and the children? I strongly advise caution.'

'I don't know, I'll have to think . . . I'd thought originally that if I found out that the Drannocks were my kin today I would think about what to do while I was away, then talk to Kerensa about it. Now I know they're so closely related I don't know what to do. I won't be hurrying down the hill and knocking on their cottage door if that's what concerns you.'

'Good . . . good. I can see it will take time for you to come to terms with all this, Oliver. If you need to talk . . .'

'Yes, of course. Thank you, Joseph. I'm sorry I shouted at you, insulted you.'

'I understand,' the Reverend said, 'and it's better that it was me. It's what I'm here for.'

They lapsed into another heavy silence and eventually Mrs Tregonning tapped on the door and hesitantly entered the room. 'Forgive me for asking,' she said nervously, 'but is everything all right? I mean, nothing awful's happened, has it?'

'Everything is fine, Mrs Tregonning,' the Reverend re-assured her.

She didn't seem the least bit convinced as she looked from one strained male face to the other. 'Shall I bring in some tea, then?'

The Reverend looked enquiringly at Oliver who shook his head.

'I must go,' Oliver said. 'I was going straight from here to attend to business at Penzance, from there on to Launceston and finally up to London for the coronation, but I think I'll go home first. I need to see Kerensa.'

The Reverend paled and wished he had an angel at hand to carry a swift warning to the manor. 'Please, come and see me when you've completed your business and we'll talk this over again.'

When Oliver had left, insisting on seeing himself out, the Reverend turned to Mrs Tregonning who was wringing her plump hands in her huge apron. 'Could you get me a cloth please, Mrs Tregonning,' he said, a shake still in his voice. He moved the wet papers, pulled out his pocket handkerchief and dabbed at the wet smears left on the ancient scratched desk top. He did not look at his housekeeper. 'I seem to have knocked over my glass of water.'

Mrs Tregonning side-stepped the request and broke a rule she had kept the entire time she had spent as the Reverend's housekeeper. 'What on earth was all that shouting about?'

'I really do wish I could tell you, Mrs Tregonning. Before you fetch the cloth will you please pour me a large glass of port wine.'

She stared anxiously at him as she poured the drink, and placed it on his desk. The old parson left it untouched. He was too preoccupied wording a prayer that when Oliver got home and told Kerensa the news that had shocked him her reaction would be the right one.

'Oliver!' Kerensa was greatly surprised at his sudden entry into her sitting room. 'Did you forget something?'

'I had to come back, Kerensa. I needed to see you.' The distress with which he had left the parsonage and galloped recklessly home was unmistakably written on his face.

She rushed into his arms. 'What is it, my dearest? What's happened?'

He held her tightly, crushing her against him so that her

148

face was pressed against his chest. His shirt was wet with sweat and through the linen she felt his skin feverishly hot. She prised her face away and looked up with anxious eyes while ice clamped her stomach and tormented her heart.

Her husband was a strong, capable, confident man. She had never seen him like this before. Something was terribly wrong. It couldn't have anything to do with the children, she had heard them playing in the garden just half an hour ago and now they were safely out for a walk with Cherry their nursemaid, Ameline Beswetherick and her personal maid. There could be nothing wrong with them. Someone must have died. Why else would Oliver be so upset? Kerensa had no living relatives and Oliver had only distant ones; he would not be brought to this by the loss of one of them. Alice was her closest friend. Had something happened to Alice? Was she . . .? Oh, please God, not Clem! But then Oliver would not grieve for Clem.

'What is it, Oliver. Tell me!'

He answered her plea with a long, pained exhalation of breath that warmed her brow. Then at last he spoke. 'Today, my love, I have learned,' he said each word so slowly Kerensa creased her beautiful face and searched his as though to help and hurry him, 'something that has left me very badly shaken. I have just come from Perranbarvah where I called on the Reverend Ivey.'

'The Reverend has . . . has passed away?'

'It is nothing of that nature, my love . . . Kerensa,' Oliver held her at arm's length, 'tell me, has it ever crossed your mind that Bartholomew Drannock bears a likeness to me, his eyes, his hair, his mannerisms?'

So that was it. He knew. The ice seeped into the middle of her heart, spread out and froze solid. 'I . . . um . . . yes . . . I suppose it could be said he is a little like you.'

149

'There's a very good reason for that, my love. I've been curious about Bartholomew for a long time so today I finally made up my mind to ask the Reverend Ivey about it. He told me that Samuel Drannock was my brother, that my father was his father too. It means that Bartholomew and his brothers and sisters are my nephews and nieces, Kerensa. Our children are their cousins—'

Oliver stopped. Kerensa's reaction was not what he had expected. Where was the shock? She did not even seem surprised. And why had her body stiffened? She should be bubbling over with excitement with what he was telling her and yet she was standing like a block of granite. She pulled in her bottom lip and said nothing.

'Did you hear what I said, Kerensa?' His voice began to rise. 'I have just told you that Samuel Drannock was my half-brother!'

'Yes, yes I heard you.' She pulled away and turned from him. 'It took me by surprise, that's all . . . I . . . I . . . the Reverend told you, you say?'

Oliver said bluntly, 'Are you really surprised, Kerensa?'

'What? Yes. Of course I am. It takes some getting used to . . . I . . .'

Another wave of shock coursed through Oliver. 'You knew, didn't you?'

Kerensa did not reply.

'You knew!' Oliver snapped, pulling Kerensa roughly back to face him. 'You knew! God help you, woman, I believe you knew about this before I did!'

Kerensa trembled, her mouth too dry to speak. She felt sick to the core. She had always hated keeping Samuel Drannock's secret from Oliver. She had kept quiet for Samuel's sake then in fear of Oliver's reaction to her keeping it for so long. It hadn't occurred to her that Oliver

150

might become curious himself and ask questions. What a fool she had been. She could only nod weakly at him now.

Oliver could hardly bring himself to believe it. 'How long?' he hissed. 'How long have you known? Answer me!' He shook her once. It was enough to force out an answer.

'When we first married . . . Samuel told me . . . he stopped me from visiting Jenifer and giving food and clothes to her for the children.'

'He told you himself? All that time ago?' he said incredulously. 'So the man stopped you giving charity to his wife, that doesn't explain why he should tell you the truth of his parentage. Why did he do that? What was the reason? What was it?' Oliver was shouting. His face was red, a small vein on his neck prominent and purple from the heat of his fury.

'Let go of me, Oliver.' Kerensa tried to sound calm. 'Let me go and I'll tell you all about it.'

'Indeed you will, Kerensa, or I swear I'll shake the truth out of you.'

He let go of her and she rubbed her arms where he'd gripped her fiercely. She moved out of his reach but he followed her and breathed heavily down on her while she began a shaky explanation.

'On my first visit to Jenifer I . . . I noticed Bartholomew looked a lot like you. He was only a child then but I was quite shocked. Jenifer saw my reaction and told Samuel. They were worried that I might believe Bartholomew was yours . . . your son.'

'And were they correct?' Oliver asked harshly.

Kerensa flinched and looked down at the carpet under their feet, her eyes unconsciously fixed on a crown-shaped motif. 'Yes . . . I . . . I was upset,' she answered with difficulty. 'I was upset because I thought you'd . . . deserted

151

Jenifer . . . It was an easy enough mistake to make at the time, Oliver,' she pleaded. 'I hardly knew you except by your reputation. You went with so many women . . .' Kerensa looked up into his face. 'I know now of course you would never have deserted anyone, leaving them with your child.'

'I suppose I ought to be grateful for that!' Oliver said sarcastically. 'When did Samuel tell you the truth, put you right in your . . . assumption?'

'Well, I . . . I paid Jenifer a visit not long after their last child, Cordelia, was born. When I left, Samuel was waiting by the lychgate to speak to me. We went into the church. That's when he told me about Sir Daniel being his real father. He asked me to keep it a secret from you,' Kerensa proceeded earnestly. 'It was on the same day that Peter Blake attacked me and killed poor Dunstan. I haven't wanted to dwell on anything that happened on that dreadful day. Please, Oliver, try to understand—'

'I understand this!' he snarled. 'You are my wife and you tell me you love me, yet for eight years you have kept this a secret from me. If you had the slightest amount of imagination you would have realised just how important it would be to me.'

'I did what I thought was the best at the time.'

'The best? I can hardly believe you said that. I trusted you, Kerensa, but now I find you've betrayed me.' Oliver clenched his fists and held them tight against his sides. 'It makes me wonder what else you're holding back from me. What other secrets are you harbouring in your pretty little head?'

'There's nothing else, Oliver, believe me. Will you please calm down,' she pleaded, 'you're getting this all out of proportion.'

'Oh, am I indeed! I love you, Kerensa. I always thought I could trust you. I believed there was nothing we did not share, that every part of you was a part of me! Now I find that the only person I've ever been able to trust completely was Arthur Beswetherick. He was my only real friend, the one person in the whole rotten world I've ever been able totally to rely on!'

Oliver was shouting at Kerensa at the top of his voice and his rage was making him shake alarmingly. At first Kerensa had felt nervous at her secret being found out, then guilty, then afraid of losing his love and respect. But now she was angry at his self-pity and it was she who was shouting.

'Shut up! How dare you go on like this! Arthur Beswetherick is dead and in the past, Oliver. And he couldn't possibly have been so perfect, no one is. He must have had faults and weaknesses like every other person who has ever lived. You've put him on a pedestal, turned him into a folk hero. You can't expect anyone to be as perfect as the image you insist in keeping hold of. You don't have to be so angry with me, it was your own father who did the dirty deed in the first place and you don't know the whole truth of the situation concerning Samuel Drannock or you wouldn't carry on so! Many, many times I've wanted to tell you but it would only have caused you pain!'

'How?' Oliver said venomously, furious at her disparagement of the man whose memory he cherished. 'Forget my father and just you tell me how the truth about the Drannocks would have given me pain.'

'Oliver, please,' Kerensa pleaded, taking a gulp of air. She had turned deathly pale and the room swam before her eyes. 'I wish you would not take it this way . . . . this isn't easy.'

'I have no intention of making it easy. Well?'

Kerensa stumbled to the nearest chair, her legs feeling they were about to give way. Oliver followed her, keeping up his piercing glare.

'First of all we must stop this shouting,' she said, her voice quivering. 'It's a good thing Ameline and Cherry and the children have gone for a walk down by the river.'

He lowered his voice but in no way had his rage abated. 'Go on, Kerensa, I'm waiting.'

She stayed silent for a few moments, trying to find the words to relate to her husband what his dead half-brother had told her. When Oliver let out a loud impatient sigh she plunged on.

'Samuel hated the Pengarrons, your father and you. He said nothing could make up for what Sir Daniel had done to his mother. He said he didn't approve of taking charity, particularly from a Pengarron, even me. He was very bitter about it all. He thought you to be selfish and cruel . . . and immoral, criminal even. I begged Samuel to let me tell you the truth, but he only told me because he couldn't bear the thought of me believing there might have been something between you and Jenifer. I told him that I thought the Pengarrons owed him a lot, that he and his family shouldn't have to live in poverty, but that was the way he wanted things to remain. I believe he was as stubborn as you can be. He was a proud man. How could I tell you that Samuel despised you, Oliver?'

'The Reverend Ivey told me as much, it is of no importance,' Oliver said coldly. 'I should have been given the opportunity to talk to Samuel. We should have had the opportunity to get to know each other. Who can say what might have happened. Blood is said to be thicker than water. I never had a family, only a kind but rather distant mother and an amoral father. Most of the Cornish gentry is intermarried yet my own children have no grandparents, no uncles or aunts – save Jenifer Drannock now. Hell to it, Kerensa! I had a brother and you have denied me the chance of ever knowing him. Granted, Samuel Drannock was a miserable, dour man, but he was honest and reliable. If we could have formed any kind of friendship at all he might have been good for me and maybe I might have been good for him! We should have been given that chance. Did that not ever occur to you, Kerensa? Not even once?'

'I just tried not to think about it,' she explained, eyes glittering with unshed tears, hands wrung together. 'Back then I was more concerned with trying to make our marriage work and so many other things were happening. Then we rescued Kane, and because of him we realised how much we were in love. We were so happy, even more so when I became pregnant with Olivia and then Luke soon afterwards . . . Oh, I couldn't see a good reason for bringing it all out in the open. Samuel and Jenifer both wanted it to stay secret and I didn't want anything to threaten the happiness we had found. All I can do now is to say that I'm so sorry, I'm really, really sorry.' She looked at Oliver with all her love plainly in her eyes but he could not see it.

'You certainly will be sorry, Kerensa,' he said slowly and bitterly. 'I can promise you that.'

A peculiar emptiness took over Kerensa's body. 'What on earth do you mean?' she exclaimed, bolting to her feet and clutching his arm. 'Surely we can talk about this and get it settled, Oliver?'

'Talk?' he sneered. 'You should have talked to me eight years ago.' Stalking to the door he angrily threw it open and left the room.

Kerensa was paralysed by his words. Bob ran in, eager to see his mistress, but she did not notice him sitting expectantly with a paw prodding her skirt for attention.

She stood motionless in utter disbelief. Why did this have to happen now? With Samuel dead and Jenifer still refusing help, she thought the danger of the secret being revealed had passed. It was obvious that Jenifer wasn't long for this world and if and when she died, Kerensa had intended to help the Drannock children somehow.

Many times she had been tempted to share Samuel's secret with Oliver. But he was not always an easy man to live with, with his aristocratic ways and fierce male pride coming to the fore in outbreaks of bad temper and impatience. And although they were never directed at her or the children, she had soothed him and calmed the troubled waters. Sometimes, after their moments of exquisite intimacy, she had nearly bared her soul and told him this one burdensome secret that she held from him. But her promise to the dead fisherman and worry over the consequences once the truth was out had always made her keep quiet.

Now it was all out in the open, it was worse than she could have imagined. Oliver's dreadful reaction had stung her in many ways but, worst of all, she could only now understand what she had irrevocably denied him.

'Are 'ee all right, cheeil?'

The rasping voice brought Kerensa out of her trance. 'What? Oh, it's you, Beatrice. I didn't hear you come in.'

The old woman shuffled her flabby body deeper into the room. She wiped her running nose and with her small eyes peered at Kerensa's stricken pale face. 'Sit yerself down, m'dear,' she said. 'I d'reckon you could do with an ear t'listen to 'ee.'

'It's all very simple really, Beatrice,' Kerensa uttered miserably. 'It's all my own fault . . . A long time ago I made a promise I shouldn't have kept.'

Chapter 11

The sea was a myriad of tiny choppy waves, coloured a dull hue by lifeless grey clouds overhead that had not moved all day. Two gulls out on the water were joined by a third and then another, all flying off moments later in the same direction as though they had decided they had business elsewhere and ought to be on their way.

Ameline Beswetherick sat side-saddle on Kernick, Kerensa's pony, her body straight but relaxed, watching white-foamed water smack the perimeter of a solitary jagged stretch of rock several yards offshore. The water swirled in and out of its shapes and crevices, running up channels, making lacy spray, rapidly devouring more and more black granite before subsiding, leaving behind miniature twisting waterfalls to make their own way back into the sea.

Ten minutes passed and the rock was completely submerged, consumed by cold, hungry water. Ameline felt satisfied. She dismounted and with the greatest care led the pony down the winding figure-three of the cliff path that ended in the heart of Trelynne Cove. Kernick was used to the path but Ameline found it necessary to hold on tightly to his bridle and saddle to prevent herself from slipping and sliding onto her bottom. She made it halfway down the path with her dignity intact and jauntily lifted her head and put her gloved hands on her waist to survey her private domain for the afternoon.

Ameline wanted to be alone. She had ordered Conan, her stable boy escort, to stay up on the cliff and forbade him to look over into the cove. He had sullenly obeyed, grumbling that he would get into trouble for letting her out of his sight. Ameline insisted she would take full responsibility should any mishap befall her.

She had ridden to the cove once before, when she had first arrived at the manor, with Kerensa. They had sat side by side on a piece of rock so straight and flat on one edge it could have been sliced away by a giant's axe. And there Kerensa had told Ameline of her life in the cove before her enforced marriage and its stormy first year. And how she and Oliver had fallen in love.

In Ameline's youthful imagination the cove became a place steeped in romance and adventure, the echoes of the violent deaths perpetrated there holding no spectres for her. It was the perfect location for her to return to and dream of love and ponder over her marriage proposal.

She considered herself fortunate to be allowed this time at Pengarron Manor to consider James Mortreath's offer although she knew her parents were becoming impatient with her. They and her grandfather approved of the serious, upright lawyer with his own substantial private means, and were pressing her to take him. They would expect a good reason if she decided to the contrary. But marriage was a lifelong commitment and Ameline could see no reason why she shouldn't take her time making up her mind.

She thought kindly of James Mortreath and she was nearly sure she would agree to become his wife. The fifteen-year age span between them caused her no concern;

many of her contemporaries were married or promised to gentlemen much older and not as presentable. James was considerate, intelligent and, most important to her, neat, clean and unpretentious in dress. She detested the filth some of the gentry indulged in and since the disquieting encounter with Captain Hezekiah Solomon at her grandfather's birthday party she no longer found the perfumed, powdered variety of male a figure of amusement. The sight and smell of such a spectacle now left her chilled to the marrow and she avoided all contact with such men.

James was in no way one of these fops. He was not unattractive and the thought of lying with him was not disagreeable. (This was a thought most contrary to Ameline's disposition but as it was marriage under consideration she thought it permissible.) And James intended to live in London and had intimated she could choose her own house in a secluded and exclusive part of the capital. Ameline had been 'finished' in a ladies' academy in London and she liked the idea of living there. Another point in his favour was his dislike of large, noisy social gatherings. Ameline was enjoying the respite from the long, wearying round of parties and dances her raucous extrovert mother persisted in dragging her to.

Pengarron Manor was blissfully quiet compared to Tolwithrick, but her stay was different to what Ameline had envisaged. The most noticeable thing missing was laughter – yet it had been there when she arrived. As she continued an unsteady descent in a pair of unsuitable high-heeled riding boots, it occurred to Ameline that although she found a feeling of romance in the cove there was none at the manor.

She halted a moment. She had been so entrenched in her own thoughts for her future she had not realised that back in the huge imposing building something was wrong. For nearly all of the two weeks since she'd been there Oliver had absented himself, and when she had asked eager questions about the coronation of the new king, George III, he had given her the details gruffly and not included Kerensa in the conversation. Ameline recalled more than one occasion when Oliver had spoken to Kerensa with unusual sharpness. Kerensa herself was unusually quiet, her voice pitched softer, her words to everyone carefully chosen, and she made no mention of Oliver or any matter relating to him.

Ameline skirted the remains of a gull killed by a bird of prey, holding a handkerchief to her nose in case there was a bad smell. She assumed some boy had killed it; she assumed that anything nasty she came across had suffered at the hands of some awful boy. That made her think of Luke Pengarron, not that he would do such a dreadful thing because she knew he loved animals and birds, but because at times he possessed that sullen look that could proceed to an act of cruelty. She thought of all three Pengarron children and drew in her brows as it struck her that they had become restrained in their behaviour, with Luke in particular inclined to be tetchy and ill-tempered. They ran often to Kerensa with minor complaints or petty quarrels for her to sort out, and if she was not immediately at hand, to Beatrice for comfort and sweetmeats. Ameline wrinkled her nose at the thought of the ageing servant. No one as disgustingly filthy and evil-smelling would be allowed to enter her household when she acquired one.

Ameline did not possess the kind of imagination which would have suggested what the source of the trouble might be and she was unlikely to find out unless she asked some direct questions. But this was not in her nature and there was no tittle-tattle to be overheard at Pengarron Manor. She had brought her own personal maid with her, but Peters considered herself superior to the manor's staff, even to Polly, who once worked at Tolwithrick. She kept herself apart from the others so it was unlikely Ameline would glean anything useful from her.

She reached the end of the path with an ungainly slither and with a start it occurred to her that what she was witnessing in Kerensa was a tightly held-in sadness.

'What is wrong with your mistress?' she asked Kernick. She looked about for something to tie the pony's reins to. There was nothing, but remembering that Kerensa had left them untethered she let them fall from her fingers and told Kernick sternly, 'You are not to wander off.'

She took a few steps then gazed up and down the lonely beach and set her eyes on the restless sea. Although she was there with the intention of thinking about her own future, she was unable to get Kerensa out of her mind. Ameline couldn't believe there was anything amiss with the other young woman's marriage; it was based firmly on a deep, passionate, devoted love. It had to be something else. She would have to keep herself alert, watch and listen carefully but unobtrusively. If she could discover the reason for the uncharacteristic sulky atmosphere in the Pengarron household then perhaps before she left she might be able to help.

Ameline tried not to think about Oliver. From the time she'd begun to butterfly into womanhood, her feelings about men, other than male relatives, and male servants who were nonexistent to her, were uncomfortable and confused. With men like Oliver, who possessed an over-powering male sexuality, she felt utterly ill at ease and was secretly relieved he was not often at home.

She put aside the problem at the manor house and dipped her thoughts back to her own future. She crunched unsteadily towards the rush of the sea, a sharp breeze bending the feathers on her cocked hat. She had decided Trelynne Cove was the ideal place to settle the course her future would take. She allowed her imagination to swirl with possibilities and impossibilities, of undertakings involving many risks and much passion, all safely tucked away in daydreams that could not touch her.

Her train of drifting fantasies was violated by a strong male voice hailing her from behind. Ameline whirled round, angry that Conan had followed her. But it wasn't the stable boy. She watched nervously as a tall young man hurried towards her. He slowed down as he neared her and glaring into her flushed face he did not bother to hide his disappointment.

'I thought you were Kerensa Pengarron. That's her pony back there,' he said accusingly, tossing his dark head backwards.

Ameline thought she should know this young man but she could not place him. She saw by his clothes he was of the working class but did not know whether he was a miner, fisherman or farm labourer. Although there was an edge of refinement in his voice she was offended at the way he addressed her and she deliberately took several moments to speak.

'I am Miss Ameline Beswetherick of Tolwithrick,' she told the young man, keeping her tone clear and superior. 'I am presently staying at Pengarron Manor and Lady Pengarron, as you should refer to her, has kindly loaned me her pony for the day, not that it's any of your business or that you have the right to an explanation!'

The youth was not impressed. 'What are you doing here?' he asked brashly.

Ameline visibly bristled, she wasn't used to subordinates speaking to her in such a disrespectful manner. 'More to the point,' she retorted, 'what are you doing here?'

'I have permission to be here,' he said, his big rough hands moving automatically to rest on his hips as he met her challenge.

'And naturally so have I,' Ameline returned coldly. 'I have told you my name, now perhaps you will have the courtesy to enlighten me as to yours. Oh, and I warn you I have an escort up on the cliff.'

To her consternation he threw back his head and laughed. Then lowering his shoulders, he put his hands above his knees and leaned towards her.

'You bloody gentry!' he said, as if he was about to spit in her face. 'Just who do you think you are? Find yourself born into a bit of money and you think you're better than everyone else, that people like me aren't fit to lick your blasted boots. You and your big words and fine phrases! How dare you speak to me in that bloody damn superior voice and manner. Think yourself a lady, do you? Well, I'll tell you this, Miss full of airs and graces Ameline Beswetherick. I've only met two real ladies in my life. One is my mother, who was born into what the likes of you sneeringly call trade. The other is Kerensa Pengarron, and you're no match for either of them. While you're up there lording it at the manor, just you watch Kerensa closely. She may have been born a peasant in this very cove, but you could learn a few things from her.'

Ameline clasped her fists to her gaping mouth. When the vicious tirade was finally over she gave a small choked cry and ran back to Kernick. Stumbling over the shingle she was crying wretchedly when she reached the pony and in such a state of agitation she could not mount. Her hands and feet were unable to gain purchase and she became frantic in her need to get away from the cove and the angry young man.

But he had followed her and caught both her hands as they scrambled for the reins. Ameline screamed shrilly as he swung her round.

'Shut up that squawking or I'll shake you till your bones rattle,' he threatened loudly.

Ameline stopped, the shock of his words as effective in their intonation as their content.

'You're not going to let me stop you looking round the cove, are you?' he said, slipping into an amiable tone. 'Come on, there's a lot to see, I'll show you around. And don't worry about your escort up there, he's fast asleep by his pony, but you don't need him anyway, I won't hurt you. By the way, my name is Bartholomew Drannock.'

He stalked off leaving her feeling drained and a little faint. She rearranged her hat and dabbed a scrap of lace to her eyes. It did not occur to Ameline that she did not have to obey his command. She didn't wonder why he'd had a change of heart. The only thing that kept running through her mind was that she could have coped with this dreadful dark-eyed, blackhaired young man if he wasn't so incredibly handsome.

While he slowed down and waited for her, Bartholomew compared this sensitive young lady of quality unfavourably to Kerensa. It wasn't the fact that she was not beautiful that annoyed him, it was her ladylike ways. Kerensa would tramp barefoot over the beach, not pick her way slowly and fussily. Kerensa would not be wearing gloves, she would have pulled off her hat to allow the breeze to flow through her hair, she would have laughed with him and been at ease. He'd enjoyed lambasting Ameline, he was enjoying the power he was exercising over her. Now he had a mind to try to seduce her, just for the sport of it.

Bartholomew held out his hand: 'Here, take hold of this.'

Unused to more than a leisurely stroll through the park lands of Tolwithrick, Ameline's passage over the shingle was growing more difficult. As she was disinclined to argue with him, and as she was wearing kid gloves and wouldn't actually have to touch his skin, she complied. She was breathless, her ordinary round face pinched as he closed his long fingers on the gloved hand she put out awkwardly to him.

'Where are we going, Mr Drannock?' she asked, her chest heaving.

Bartholomew suddenly felt a little sorry for her. He smiled as he answered. 'To the end of the beach under Mother Clarry's rock.'

'Oh, Lady Pengarron told me about that,' Ameline said, as they walked on. Bartholomew checked his long strides to match her stumbling steps. She wanted to take the initiative away from him and took the lead in conversation. 'Lady Pengarron said Mother Clarry was supposed to be an evil witch and the smooth, flat rock, high up on the cliff, is reputed to be her seat. She would sit up there on nights bearing a full moon to laugh and gloat over the mischief she had caused. I wonder what she looked like. I should think quite hideous with dirty straggly hair with warts all over her face and a long hooked nose.'

'She looks worse than that, Ameline,' Bartholomew said seriously. 'I saw her myself only the other day perched up on her seat.'

'You saw her . . .?' Ameline stopped walking to read his face. His eyes looked into hers and then the corners of his mouth turned upwards. He was grinning, his eyes gleaming wickedly. And then he was laughing, not unkindly, just a low gentle laugh.

Ameline smiled herself, eventually. 'Yes, I did believe you,' she admitted.

'What an innocent,' he murmured.

She lowered her eyes and they resumed their walk. 'I don't recall giving you permission to call me Ameline.'

'I had no intention of asking you for it.'

'Indeed, and now I suppose you want me to call you Bartholomew.'

'Certainly not. You can call me Mr Drannock.' He was laughing again. She looked wildly about the cove and rested her eyes on the place where she thought Kernick would be. 'Now you don't know whether to go or stay, do you, Ameline?' he said, practically in her ear.

Ameline gave a little shiver despite feeling hot and flustered. 'I don't know what to make of you. I don't know if you're being cruel or lighthearted . . . Perhaps it is better if I leave now.'

She sounded so unhappy Bartholomew found himself pitying her. 'I promise to behave like a perfect gentleman.' He looked at her downcast face. 'Stay, please.'

Realising he was still holding her hand, she blushed violently, wishing she could break the hold of his deep dark eyes. She wriggled her hand free. 'Are we nearly there now? At Mother Clarry's rock?'

'It's not far, only a few yards.'

They walked the rest of the way with Ameline stumbling uncomfortably without his aid.

'Let's sit down,' Bartholomew said, as an order rather than a suggestion.

Ameline obeyed, cautiously lowering herself on to the cleanest looking slab of granite and fussing her skirt into neat folds. He chose a perch not too close but where he could look down on her and placed a foot on another rock.

'Will it be all right to call you Bartholomew now?' she ventured.

'Of course,' he replied, tilting his head up to Mother Clarry's rock. He pointed to it. 'Well, there's the witch's seat. What do you think of it?'

Ameline angled her head and studied the rock carved out of the cliff face by the elements down the ages. 'It's impressive. One could easily imagine a witch sitting up there. It looks very sheer below it. Has anyone ever climbed up to sit on it? It must be very difficult, quite dangerous I should imagine.'

'It is, I've done it often, as man and boy. 'Tis said if you try and fail, the witch will have you in her power for all eternity.'

Ameline looked at him closely. She thought him to be a little younger than herself, perhaps somewhere between man and boy. 'The cove must be very eerie at night with all these tales of witchcraft and hauntings.'

'It is, and during the day when the sea fog comes in thick it feels as though it's trying to stop you from breathing. You can imagine all kinds of terrible things are about to come out of it and do the most gruesome things to you.'

He was smiling with an easy charm and she became aware of why she had felt she ought to have known him when he'd first walked up to her. Bartholomew Drannock looked rather like Oliver.

'You're having a good look at me,' he said. 'Do I remind

169

you of someone or have you never seen a fisherman at such close quarters before?' She blushed again, but not prettily as he was sure Kerensa would have done.

'I'm sorry, I did not mean to stare but you do have a certain look of Sir Oliver about you.' She looked at the sea. 'So you're a fisherman. Living inland as I do I didn't realise how magnificent the sea is. Apart from glimpses when at Marazion, this is only the second time I have really seen it.'

'Aye, it's beautiful and dangerous, its own master, untamable but irresistible.'

'Yes, I agree with that.'

While Ameline gazed at the mesmeric waters, Bartholomew set to thinking. Ameline Beswetherick was not the first person to observe that he resembled Sir Oliver Pengarron. It had happened often over the years. He had caught Kerensa looking at him in that strange sweet way of hers; had she noticed it too? He could easily become convinced there was Pengarron blood in him.

He had wondered if Sir Oliver could be his father although he would never believe his mother lacked the proper morals. Sir Oliver was known as a womaniser before his marriage, but although many a gentleman thought nothing of forcing themselves on village maids with no regard for the consequences, Bartholomew did not consider Sir Oliver to be one of them. On talking to his mother casually about Sir Oliver he'd learned that the baronet had been away with his regiment when he'd been conceived so he could not have sired him. Nevertheless, it might be worth his while to root about a little more. Looking at Ameline it occurred to him she might be of some use to him.

'Do you know what's out there across the sea, Ameline?' he said, turning on his charm to the full.

'We're looking at the English Channel so we must be facing the Channel Islands and France, Bartholomew,' Ameline replied, pleased she knew and didn't appear an idiot.

'I suppose you must have worn some of the French fashions smuggled in through Sir Oliver's ventures.'

'Yes, I daresay I have. It must be a very exciting place to live for the aristocracy but I really think I'd prefer England, particularly London. I'm quite fond of Cornwall but I'd quite like to live in London. Have you ever set foot on foreign parts?'

'Aye, once or twice. 'Tis easy to get into the French ports, they like to think they can get us to bring their spies back over here. Got to be careful, mind. If they think you're cocking a snook at them they'd as soon as cut your throat as look at you, and you don't want anyone to think you're a traitor. I've also sailed the North Sea for herring and I've called in at many other ports around the British Isles like Whitby, Hartlepool and Scarborough. Life away is very different to Cornwall, lived at a much faster pace, exciting as you said, but I find my home calling me back.'

'So you'd like to live in Cornwall all your life?'

'I don't know about that, I want to travel the world.' He presented her with his dazzling smile. 'But right here will do for now. Are you enjoying your stay at the manor, Ameline?'

'Oh yes . . .'

He kept her chatting until the tension slipped away from her shoulders and a becoming brightness turned her eyes from dull to a lustrous grey. He gained her confidence by telling her something of his family and his livelihood from the *Young Maid*. He knew she would feel it impolite and improper to ask him many questions and Ameline did not

171

know he was only imparting the kind of knowledge anyone who knew his family would know. Deeper things were saved for his mother – and, if he got the opportunity, Kerensa.

On their way back he pointed out the spot on the shingle that was sometimes used as a midden by a fully grown dog otter and its mate. Ameline thought it indelicate of him to mention it but she expressed her intention to learn more about nature and her creatures. When they reached Kernick, Bartholomew knew she was pleased to have made his acquaintance and was intrigued by him. He had been careful in his flattery; a plain woman like Ameline would have received little in her time and she would know when it was insincere. He would have to tread carefully. But as he helped her to mount, a thought dawned on her that almost wrecked his plan right at the beginning.

'You are very familiar with Lady Pengarron,' she said, viewing him with a trace of mistrust. 'Does . . . does she meet you here . . . in the cove?' She knew there would be nothing improper on Kerensa's part but she couldn't quite bring herself to trust this handsome youth with his brilliant smile.

'We met here once, purely by chance,' he told her, keeping his voice nonchalant. 'I've known Lady Pengarron for years. She is a friend of my mother's. You can ask her, she used to call on us when I was a child until my father put a stop to it. Now he's dead she calls regularly again. I asked her permission to come here. She gave it gladly and I can assure you Sir Oliver knows.'

His explanation worked. The doubt left her face. Bartholomew thought he could almost like this dull, quiet woman but life was hard and there was no room for sentiment in it. She was certainly destined to marry some boring gentleman, probably much older than herself, who would drain the last spark of life out of her. He might be about to use her but perhaps he could put a little energy and romance into her life at the same time. She might even be grateful to him in her old age.

'Ameline,' he said coyly, 'will you be coming here again?'

She looked all around. 'Yes. I rather think I will. I have yet to see the other side of the beach.'

'You, uh, wouldn't be thinking of coming here . . . say in about four days' time?'

'I might well do that,' she smiled shyly, with eyelashes lowered.

Bartholomew led Kernick up the winding cliff path with Ameline watching his strong broad shoulders from the saddle. When they parted she set the pony at an easy trot. She would not reprimand Conan for falling asleep. She hoped it would encourage him to do it again when next he escorted her here.

She had forgotten the problems at the manor and her marriage proposal. She was intoxicated with new and wonderful sensations of hope and awakening and wanted them to stay with her for ever. She was already planning to wear a more becoming jacket and dress and her prettiest hat for her next ride to the cove. Ameline Beswetherick was attracted to Bartholomew Drannock as a moth was to the fiery dangers of a flame.

Chapter 12

Jack was in the tack room working up a fever while vigorously rubbing beeswax into Conomor's saddle. At intervals he sighed crossly because he had not closed the door properly after him and it was banging in the wind.

''Tis a miserable life these days,' he muttered to himself.

One of Nathan's gun dogs was sleeping fitfully on a bed of straw covered with a cast-off blanket. Jack saw its body jump on the next nerve-jerking bang of the door and it gave a long moan.

'I'll get up and close it for 'ee, Reeth,' he said apologetically to the dog. 'I didn't realise it was bothering you too.'

He shut the door firmly against the cold November rain and knelt down beside Reeth who slowly opened a mournful eye. A week before, Reeth had lost a front paw in an illegal gin-trap set in the oak plantation high on the hill that sheltered the manor house. Nathan had bound the stump and raced with the dog back to the stables and pleaded with Oliver to save him. Oliver had a knack for healing sick animals and after stemming the flow of blood he treated Reeth with a fennel poultice. He prescribed barley water to drink when the dog was able to lap and pronounced that if the infection didn't claim its life it could get along quite reasonably with three paws instead of four.

Nathan watched the treatment with tears flowing unashamedly down his face. He and Polly had been married for seven years and although they hoped and prayed, even resorting to Beatrice's fertility potions, they had not yet conceived a child. Nathan's gun dogs were his 'children' and he swore a terrible revenge on the cruel culprit who had set the trap. So great was his gratitude to Oliver for giving Reeth the chance to live he might well have kissed his master had he been a female. But Oliver's ill temper of the past few weeks forbade even a handshake of thanks.

Everyone took turns to watch over Reeth. Nathan and Polly sat up all through the first night, the dog's mournful hot head cradled lovingly in Nathan's lap. He spent as much time with Reeth as possible. Conan and Michael took turns through the following days. Luke and Kane came together and no high jinks ensued for a change. Kerensa came with Beatrice, with fresh barley water, clean blankets and soft cushions. Olivia came with Cherry and amid floods of tears left her favourite rag doll tucked in under his head. Ruth and Esther tempted his appetite with tender cooked meats. Oliver made inquiries on Reeth's progress but did not check on his condition, being far too preoccupied. And Jack was there as much as the others.

'Life's miserable for you too, isn't it, boy?' Jack stroked the dog's smooth brown and white head. ''Tis miserable for everyone round here lately. Little Miss Olivia'll be along in a minute, she's bringing 'ee a biscuit. Told me she's gonna ask Esther to help her bake it for you herself, bless her heart. She'll be here too, won't let a drop o' rain stop her.'

Jack returned to the saddle. Under his supervision all the equipment in the stables was kept at the highest standard but when Sir Oliver was in one of his bad moods he occasionally found fault. The mood he was in nowadays meant he found them often. He bawled Jack out each time, threatening that if he was not capable of the duties of his post as head groom over Conan and Michael he could soon find himself working under a more able man. His feelings cut to the quick at the injustice, Jack decided to give every item in the tack room a thorough cleaning himself.

The door was firmly shut but Jack thought he heard it banging again until he realised someone was knocking on it and he heard a small voice call his name. Rushing to open it he found Olivia and Ameline on the other side.

'Begging your pardon, Miss Olivia, Miss Ameline, I thought 'twas the wind.' Jack was most surprised to see Ameline Beswetherick there.

Olivia ran to Reeth and gently put her arms round him. Ameline stepped into the tack room quickly to be out of the rain and wrinkled her nose at the strong smells of horses, leather and polish.

'How is the little doggie . . . um . . .?' Ameline called all servants by their surnames but as she had not heard Jack called by any other name she didn't know what his was but she couldn't bring herself to call him Jack. That would be too familiar.

'He's getting better slowly, miss,' he replied, embarrassed by her presence.

'See, Ameline,' Olivia clapped her hands excitedly. 'Reeth ate the biscuit. I told you he would. Father will be pleased.'

'Oh . . . excellent,' Ameline said, gingerly moving forward to view the dog with a precautionary gloved hand held to her face.

'He won't bite you, Ameline,' Olivia said crossly. 'He is ill, you know.'

'Don't be rude, Olivia!' Ameline retaliated.

'He knows you bake a good biscuit, Miss Olivia,' Jack said indulgently.

'Come away, Olivia.' Ameline reached for her hand. 'The doggie needs his rest and . . . um . . . needs to get on with his work.'

'But I want to stay,' Olivia protested. 'I won't get in Jack's way. I often watch him work.'

'You must learn not to argue with your elders,' Ameline retorted. 'Come along at once, Olivia.'

'Oh, don't be so prissy!' Olivia returned loudly.

Jack turned his head as he felt a big smile coming on.

'You spend too much time in the kitchen sitting on the lap of that repugnant woman!' Ameline stamped off in a huff, leaving behind the threat, 'I shall talk to your mother.'

Olivia ran to Jack and put something in his hand. 'Here's a biscuit for you, Jack,' she said, her little face disclosing she was highly amused at upsetting Ameline. She would doubtless share the moment with her two brothers at the earliest opportunity and they would all laugh at the young lady's affront. 'I'd better go. Don't take any notice of Ameline, she's cross because it's raining and she can't go out riding.'

Jack took a small bite of biscuit and gave the rest to Reeth. Reeth seemed to be perking up, he ate the biscuit quickly but let his head flop down as if all the attention was too much for him. Jack ruffled his ears affectionately and felt all over his lean body for fever. 'You're getting better, boy, and you're getting used to all this pampering.'

He picked up his polishing cloth but was soon interrupted again. Beatrice burst in with a full bottle of gin clasped to her huge drooping bosom as tenderly as a new mother nurses a baby. She shook her ugly head, scattering raindrops over Conomor's saddle and making Jack suck in his breath in irritation. Slamming the door shut, Beatrice heaved her fat flabby body down on the old backless chair she kept against the wall in the tack room for her furtive bibbing. She took a swig of cloudy liquid and hummed to herself.

In a while Jack asked her quietly, 'What's going on, Bea?' his eyes darting round the room as if he feared he might be overheard.

''Ow do 'ee mean, boy?' Beatrice was immediately on the defensive. 'I only come out 'ere for a quick sup. I don't do nobody no 'arm. If 'ee don't like it I'll take meself off somewhere else, I edn't afeared of a drop o' rain.'

'No, what I mean is what's gone wrong between His Lordship and Her Ladyship? They aren't happy no more. Why did they have that awful big row? They've hardly had a cross word since the time Her Ladyship brought young Master Kane home from the market. Something bad must've happened. He's always in a bad temper and she looks so sad all the time. Why's he acting that way, upsetting Her Ladyship?' Although Oliver was responsible for Jack's good position and something of a hero to him, if anything was wrong between his mistress and master, like all the servants he declared Oliver to be the villain of the piece.

All the manor staff were aware of Kerensa and Oliver's violent quarrel, of the cooling off of their once joyful, fulfilling marriage. All were affected by the bleak atmosphere they worked in. Jake Angove, the surly head gardener, had issued loudly, taking no care who heard him. 'Wonder what's up with the proud bugger this time? No need fer un to be upsetting the little missus so. Found her in the rose garden this forenoon. She weren't crying nor nothing. She was just staring into space looking all lost and forlorn, poor little maid.'

'Well, Beatrice,' Jack said louder. 'Do you know anything?'

Beatrice grunted, 'If I did I wooddun say nothin' 'bout it. Tes somethin' more 'n' a mite serious I grant 'ee, but there's nothin' we can do 'bout it. Jus' 'ave t'wait 'n' see, 'ope it'll all blow over, boy. Tedn't good fer the missus to be upset like this though. An' I'll tell 'ee one thing, Jack, I won't stand fer it!' She tapped the gin bottle with a gnarled finger. 'I'll not take too much of this these days. She may 'ave need of me.'

'What for?' Jack wanted to know, spitting on the leather and eyeing the crone. 'Her Ladyship's not ill, is she?'

'Never 'ee do mind.' Beatrice peered at Jack. 'Whad're 'ee all 'et up fer at the moment anyway?'

Jack paused in his work. 'I saddled Conomor for His Lordship's early morning ride. Off to Pengarron Point, his thinking place, I shouldn't wonder. Anyway, he reckoned Conomor's saddle wasn't near enough polished properly, said I've allowed Michael and Conan to get lazy. Got in a proper temper, he did. I thought he was going to kick the stable door down he was so mazed.'

'Umph!' Beatrice snorted. 'If 'e don't sort 'isself out soon, reckon someone will 'ave t'do it fer un.'

'You going to try, Bea?'

'Dunno, I might, might not. Whatever tes, tes too big fer a light tickin' off, I can tell 'ee.'

Jack looked at Reeth, sleeping fitfully and giving the occasional shiver. 'I don't like His Lordship's mood and there's only one person I wish it on at the moment and that's the evil swine who did that to Reeth.'

* * *

Later in the day, when the rain eased off and the heavy black clouds cleared from the sky, Jack rode to the horse stud on Ker-an-Mor Farm with Kane and Luke to look over a newly born foal. As they leaned on the paddock fence, Matthias Renfree joined them to admire the foal.

'He's a real beauty, Preacher,' Jack enthused.

'Aye, Jack,' Matthias agreed. 'He's the finest foal I've seen in many a year. My father reckons he's another Conomor.'

'Yes, he certainly looks as good as Conomor,' Luke observed, climbing up to sit on top of the fence and putting his hat on a pole.

'He's better than Conomor,' Kane added, copying his younger brother's actions. They were sitting side by side, Luke, tall like Oliver, head on the same level as Kane's red one.

'Take some horse to be better than Conomor, Master Kane,' Jack said.

The foal left its mother, a neat black mare with white socks and blaze, to try out its long straight legs in short elegant runs round the paddock. The men and boys watched in admiration until it tired and returned to suckle the mare. They made a charming scene against the backdrop of open fields, a few wind-waving tall trees and a clearing white sky.

'We should have brought Olivia with us,' Kane said regretfully. 'She could paint a lovely picture of them.'

'She can come another time,' Luke said shortly, 'with Mama and Cherry.'

'The foal will need a good rider, too, as good as Sir Oliver,' Matthias said.

'I'm going to ask Father if I can have him,' Luke said confidently. 'He's not to be sold, do you hear, Matthias?'

181

Matthias and Jack exchanged amused grins. 'I don't know what plans Sir Oliver may have for the foal, Master Luke,' Matthias replied, 'but I'd be surprised if he's thinking of selling him. Sir Oliver's really proud to see the stud produce such a fine animal again. Cornwall's not renowned for good horse-breeding.'

'Aye, he'll do well at the Truro, Redruth and Bodmin races,' Jack said. 'I'll look forward to seeing him race at them.'

'Me too,' Luke said.

'Me too,' Kane echoed.

'Well, he might outrun Conomor, if he's his father's son, but although he'd have youth on his side, Conomor has experience. Aye,' Matthias said in a satisfied voice, 'one of the best sights in the Lord's creation is a fine piece of horseflesh.'

'Perhaps Father will give him to Olivia,' Kane said. The foal trotted in front of Kane and after a little encouragement moved in close and allowed the boy to smooth its jet-black neck. The mare looked up but stayed at an unconcerned distance.

'Olivia!' uttered Luke with scorn. 'Waste good horseflesh on a girl! I shall ask Father to give him to you, it's you he came up to, it's you he obviously likes.'

Luke Pengarron was an odd mixture of moods and emotions. He was not jealous of the sturdy well-proportioned foal falling in readily with the rapport that all animals shared with Kane, but he was envious of the closeness between Kane and their sister. That Kane was a Pengarron in name only did not matter to him. All Luke required was that he was at the centre of everyone's attention and he ensured that by whatever means it took.

Matthias led the mare and foal into the warmth of their

stall. Leaving the boys hanging over the stall door to talk knowledgeably about the foal's many fine points, he and Jack strolled to the pump at the end of the stable yard.

'You look worried, Jack,' Matthias remarked. 'Is there anything wrong? You missed the Bible class this week. Have you been ill? Is there anything I can help with?'

'No, Preacher, I haven't been ill and I'm still going to give you a hand to build the meeting house, but you're right, I am worried about something.'

'Would it have anything to do with Heather Bawden, by any chance? Or would you rather I didn't ask?'

'You know I've a liking for Heather, do 'ee?' Jack got busy with the pump handle to cover his embarrassment. 'I thought I'd kept that a secret. No, it's not about her, though I admit things aren't running too smoothly there.' He gulped cold water from the ladle and handed it to Matthias. 'Can I confide in you, Preacher?'

'Yes, of course, please do.'

On the way home Jack rode behind Luke and Kane half-listening to their excited talk about the foal, his heart lighter now he had shared his worries about his master and mistress with Matthias. Matthias was a good listener, hardly saying a word until Jack had relayed the full story, as he and the manor staff knew it, of the blazing quarrel and now strained relationship between Kerensa and Oliver.

Matthias told Jack that he knew as much himself and he was not to worry. He was sure that in time, with prayer and the understanding of those about them, the couple would sort out their differences. Matthias firmly believed that two people so much in love would not allow even the most serious matter to come between them. And after all, no marriage had ever been known not to run into problems.

Jack had nearly asked Matthias for his advice on how to handle his proposed courtship of Heather Bawden. But he thought the Preacher, who never sought the company of women, was unlikely to know anything about them and their peculiar ways. His intellect, faith and compassion made Matthias a good comforter and counsellor. But it would take a different sort of man to advise on affairs of the heart – if Jack could ever pluck up the courage to ask.

Jack did not know that although he felt the burden he had shared had lifted, Matthias was left with a niggling worry. If the estrangement between the Pengarrons continued and became common knowledge, what might Clem Trenchard do?

Luke insisted they take a longer route home on the eastern side of Ker-an-Mor Farm where its land verged on the moorland of Lancavel Downs. He wanted to see the foundations of the new meeting house laid by Matthias and his willing band of helpers. Oliver had given permission for it to be built a few yards on Ker-an-Mor land on a spot well drained and sound underfoot and close to the ancient public right of way that ran along the farm's boundary.

Luke was unimpressed by the foundations and piles of granite slabs waiting to form the four walls, declaring it was no bigger than the servants' outdoor closet. Jack patiently asked him to wait until the meeting place was finished before he offered his final opinion.

Luke gave Jack a look that inferred he was stupid, and urged his horse on to the right of way. His sharp ears had heard the sounds of laughter and he was eager to investigate. It turned out to be a group of Wheal Ember bal-maidens making their way home. Among them was the precocious, wild-haired Heather Bawden.

'Well, look 'ee 'ere,' giggled one girl as she recognised the riders, 'tes yer sweet'eart, 'eather.' She ran up to Jack and fell in step beside Meryn, his mount. 'Jus' look at un. Don't 'e look all important like up there on that fine 'orse?'

Luke had not missed the teasing remarks and he shouted across to Jack, 'Which one is she, Jack? Which one is your sweetheart?'

Jack's face grew crimson as the other bal-maidens joined in the leg-pulling but Luke had only to follow the women's eyes to see which one it was.

'Her?' The boy pointed his riding crop at Heather. 'An admirable choice, she's very pretty. If I was a little older I'd give you a run for your money.' Luke wasn't sure what the term meant, it was one he had overheard, but he knew it would provoke the desired shocked reaction.

'You didn't oughta talk like that, Master Luke,' Jack chided, hoping he sounded authoritative.

'He's his father's son all right,' cackled one of the older women. 'That one with the dark hair 'n' eyes.'

Luke pressed his knees into his pony's sides and man-oeuvred closer to the bal-maidens. He smiled at them graciously but not without a hint of ribaldry and bowed from the saddle with a flourish.

Heather moved up to Luke and stroked his pony's neck then gripped a handful of its flowing brown mane. She looked into the boy's face and gave a saucy curtsy. 'I'll still be 'ere in a few years' time if you're still int'rested, Master Luke.'

Kane was enjoying the bawdy interchange but sensitive to Jack's feelings he did not join in. Trotting up beside his brother he prodded his arm. 'I'll race you home, Luke, and I wager you my new pocket knife I'll beat you by more than the whole length of the carriageway.'

185

Luke never refused a challenge but he had more to say to the buxom bal-maiden. He bent his wiry young body to whisper in her ear. 'What about my brother, Heather? I don't do anything without him.'

Heather smiled at the small, handsome, strong-featured face close to hers and glanced across at the beaming red-haired boy. 'Well, it's like this, Master Luke,' she said jauntily. 'Master Kane is nearly as good-looking as you are and if 'e carries on in the same way I'm sure I can manage if both of you can.'

Fresh cackling broke out and Jack was afraid the matter would get out of hand. He was about to order Luke away when the boy, satisfied with the answer he'd got, gave a bawdy laugh equal to that of Sir Martin Beswetherick's and said heartily, 'How about a kiss to be going on with?'

Jack tried to intervene but the other women put themselves in the way. He was outraged as Heather said, 'A kiss, Master Luke? Now that will cost you a shilling.'

Jack's protests were drowned by peels of riotous laughter but he heard Luke say, 'I haven't got a shilling on me at the moment but if you'll allow me I'll open an account.'

Heather turned her head and planted a long kiss to the side of the boy's lips.

Luke let out a mighty whoop and raced off with a shout over his shoulder, 'You lucky man, Jack!'

Kane bolted after Luke and the two boys quickly disappeared into the distance.

Jack debated whether to chase after his charges or stay and talk to Heather. He knew what he ought to do, but he wanted to do the other, despite his affront at Heather's common behaviour. The girl was smiling sweetly at him and she won his decision.

'Well!' she shrieked at her companions. 'Off with you

then. A maid don't need no company when she's met up with 'er man.'

The other bal-maidens carried on their way over the hard, well-worn ground, giggling and throwing back crude innuendoes.

Jack jumped down beside Heather. Her smile vanished and she stared at him. Jack sighed. He could never tell what mood his 'sweetheart' was in.

'You shouldn't oughta have spoken to Master Luke like that and carried on in that way in front of me and Master Kane and they other women,' he reprimanded her.

'Oh, don't be so stuffy,' she pouted, looking annoyed.

'But that's not the point, he's only a boy and shouldn't hear or be saying things like that. 'Tisn't proper.'

'Trouble with you, Jack,' Heather returned angrily, 'is you take all that preachin' you listen to to 'eart. Be up in that buildin' yonder when tes finished, bleatin' with the rest of the sheep. Be a preacher yerself one day, I shouldn't wonder.'

'Wouldn't hurt you none to listen to some of it,' Jack said peevishly.

'What! All that prayin' 'n' stuff! You won't catch me steppin' over Jeb Bray's threshold or no meetin' 'ouse. Silly old sod called me sister the other night. I don't want nothin' t'do with bein' converted, whatever that means,' Heather hooted. 'You want t'be careful, Jack, it sounds ruddy painful t'me.'

Jack squarely faced the smirking girl. 'You don't half say some awful things, Heather. Don't you ever want to better yourself, be more like a lady?'

The bal-maiden's expression changed to fury. 'If you don't like me just the way I am, Jack, you can git yer arse back on that bloody pony and go to hell!'

187

She made to storm after her friends but Jack grabbed her arm. She twisted and struggled and Jack moved his legs smartly to avoid a kick. 'No, no, please, Heather, I'm sorry. Don't go off in a huff. I have to go myself in a minute anyway to catch up with Master Luke 'n' Master Kane. Please stay, I'm sorry, I didn't mean to offend you.'

Heather forgot her wrath. She stared into Jack's anxious face as if attempting to learn a secret from its sharp lines. 'What the bloody 'ell's yer other name anyway? I only know thee as Jack. Never 'eard nobody call 'ee anythin' but Jack.'

The clouds had been gradually returning, the light dimming and now a mist was making the air chilly and damp. Heather pulled her shawl in tighter and it accentuated her well-rounded figure. Jack tore his eyes away from her bosom and looked into her face. Her gipsy-wild hair, full of thick flowing crinkly waves, was sprinkled with drops of moisture and Jack wanted to touch it.

He gulped in a mouthful of air to help dampen down his ardour and answered her question before she changed mood again and screamed at him. 'I haven't got one,' he said quietly.

'What? Got no name? Why on earth not? Everybody's got a first name and a last name, even we poor mining folk. What's 'appened to yours then? The piskies come and steal it from 'ee?'

Jack looked at the place where he had last seen the two boys and hoped they would not arrive home too far in front of him. 'I was a young'un, an orphan, when Sir Oliver took me on as stable boy. I'd been going round with travelling folk, stealing for a living. My parents had been dead for years and I've always been called only Jack. Sir Oliver says if I ever want a surname to see him about it, he'll arrange something for me.'

Heather fell silent. When she spoke again Jack saw compassion in her lively face. 'Must be awful, not knowin' where you come from, not knowin' who you really are. Don't it bother you none, Jack?'

'No, not really. Pengarron Manor is more than just a work place to me, it's my home. Sir Oliver says for me to always feel it's my home. I have my own little cottage in the grounds,' Jack ended proudly. He looked at Meryn and knew he should mount and be on his way.

'Aren't you the lucky one, a cottage all ready t'take a wife to. You'll need another name when you choose one,' Heather said, eyeing Jack sideways but bouncing straight on to something else. 'Sir Oliver's a mixed up sort of man, isn't 'e? One moment shoutin' and bawlin', the next sayin' kind things like that. Bet 'e's soft as puddin' with 'is children and I know 'e adores that beautiful wife of 'is but I d'reckon 'e's probably 'ell t'live with at times. I want a man like that fer meself, mind you, couldn't be doin' with no milksop.'

Jack started forward. 'I have to be going, Heather. I'd better catch up with Masters Luke and Kane and I have work to be getting on with. I have Michael and Conan, the stable boys, to supervise,' he added, to impress her. 'Heather, will you meet me somewhere later tonight? Say you will, please.'

Heather screwed up her face, pretending to think over his request but really to tease him. 'Reckon I can find an 'our to slip away after my shift. I'll meet 'ee 'ere about 'alf 'our after that, that suit you?'

'Aye!' Jack almost shouted in excitement. ''Tis fine by me, but can you find your way over the moors in the dark?'

'Course I can,' she said scornfully. 'Do it with me eyes shut.'

Jack thought he should kiss Heather and bent his head to do so. But she bounded off with a shrill laugh.

Chapter 13

'Oliver, Ted Trembath is here to see you,' Kerensa said from the doorway of her husband's study.

'Show him in,' Oliver returned dully, without raising his head from his paperwork. It was the longest sentence he'd allowed her in the last few days.

'I would like a word with you first.'

The gentle rustle of her skirts informed him she was standing on the other side of his desk. 'I'm busy,' he said curtly.

'I want to know why you spoke so harshly to poor Jack earlier today. He did nothing wrong. Luke and Kane often ride on home alone, you know that and allow it. Please, Oliver, don't take the ill humour you feel towards me out on other people, it's not fair.' Kerensa had her hands clasped together and had no intention of leaving without an explanation.

'Is a man not to be permitted to remonstrate with his own servants?' Oliver threw down his goose quill, showering ink on his papers, desk and soiled shirt cuffs. He glared at Kerensa with cold eyes above an unshaven face and snapped, 'It is none of your business!'

'I think it—'

'I gave Jack the sharp edge of my tongue because he was idling his time away in the company of a whorish

191

bal-maiden. I don't waste my time and I do not expect my servants to waste theirs. Now, as I have told you, I am very busy. If you insist on wasting any more of my time I shall have less of it to spend with Ted Trembath.'

It took a determined act of will for Kerensa to hold back an angry retort. In its stead she said coolly, 'I'll show Ted in then.' At the door she turned back and asked tartly, 'I take it you're not too busy to have a wash and shave after Ted has gone.'

'See to it,' he growled, sprinkling fine sand to soak up the ink blots.

Kerensa had not wanted to be sharp with Oliver but his apparent loathing of her hurt so much. After he'd stormed out of the manor on the day he had learned that Samuel Drannock was his half-brother she had lived in misery and hope both. Misery over his fury and the pain it had caused him, and hope that while he was away on business and at the coronation he would cool down. But after spending several more days away than he'd planned Oliver had arrived home sullen and unforgiving. Kerensa could hardly believe he resented her so much, not after so many years of sharing a loving marriage. She thought it best to try to act normally and hope he would soon come round, but the weeks had passed with no change and he had not once given her a smile, a kind word, or a kiss. She had often tried to talk to him but he had time only for the children; in fact, she thought gloomily as she went back to Ted Trembath, he had time for anyone in the parish but her.

Ted Trembath declined Kerensa's offer of refreshment and when she closed the study door the miner shambled hesitantly to the front of Oliver's desk. He peered round the room, clearly impressed by all he saw. Oliver told him to sit down. Ted did so and laid his hat carefully on his lap, stealing a quick look out of the nearest window to see what grew in the garden.

'I'll show you over the grounds one day, Ted,' Oliver offered tonelessly.

Ted coloured and cleared his throat apologetically. 'Sorry, m'lord, I didn't mean no disrespect.'

'I know that, Ted. What can I do for you?'

Ted Trembath had known Oliver for years, he had smuggled for him until his youngest brother had been tragically killed on a run. Ted was numbered among the many local working-class men with whom Oliver got along well, but Ted was ill at ease in the powerful man's house.

'Well, first I do thank 'ee for seeing me so prompt. As you can see, because of the accident back along I've got a gammy leg and I'll never climb down a mine shaft again on un, and in any case I'm a brave bit old to be going on as a working miner and would have to give it up soon anyway. With no more than meself to look after now Mother and me brothers are all gone these last years, I've managed to put a small bit by and that's seen me through the accident. Well, the thing is, I'll be leaving the cottage on the Downs soon, so a younger miner can take it, and,' Ted looked down shyly, 'I've a mind to marry Hunk Hunken's widow, Lou. She's a good woman and could do with a man to father her littl'uns. Her oldest boy is about to get married himself and he's taking on her cottage. Well, the reason that I'm here, sir, is the offer you made back along, after young Davey died if you mind it, of finding me a cottage and work on the estate if ever I do need it.'

It was a long speech for the humble miner. He couldn't look Oliver in the eye at its end and rested his sight on the fresh ink blots on the desk and papers. Self-consciously

Oliver placed fresh pieces of paper over the ones he'd ruined. He liked and respected Ted Trembath and the insecurity he was experiencing of late pushed him to give the other man an explanation for the ink blots; something he would never have done before.

'A little accident, Ted,' he said abruptly. 'I do indeed remember my offer of employment and a cottage. You may rest assured it's as good as done. You can help load the sanding carts for the fields or something similar until you learn the ways of the land. It's different to working on a vegetable patch. I'll put you under Adam Renfree on Ker-an-Mor Farm, and please accept my congratulations on your forthcoming marriage.'

Ted gave his hat a little toss in the air and caught it with a wide swing of his arm. 'Thank 'ee, sir, tes most civil of 'ee. Lou will be as grateful as me.'

Oliver was startled at the unexpected acrobatics with the hat and took a few moments to pick up the threads of the conversation. 'Um, when would you like to move off the Downs?'

'As soon as tes possible, if that's all right with you, sir.'

Oliver thought for a moment. 'I'm having the lodge at the end of the carriageway to the manor renovated for Nathan O'Flynn and his wife. They will be able to move in at the end of the month. You and Lou Hunken and her children will find his old cottage, small though it is, larger and more comfortable than the cramped shacks on Lancavel Downs.'

'I do thank 'ee very much, sir. Lou will be some pleased to be able to fetch water from a pump instead of a stream. Tes proper civil of 'ee, there's few men, working-class or gentry, who can be trusted to keep their word like you can. Now I best be going and let you get on.'

Ted headed for the door, stopped, then plucked up the nerve to ask, 'If you don't mind me asking of 'ee, sir, but are you quite well? You seem awful poorly to me.'

Oliver rapidly rearranged his stern expression into what might have been a smile. 'There's no need to be concerned, Ted. I've been away on business and have neglected to freshen up since my return.'

Ted accepted this and after sweeping his eyes over the ornamental mantelpiece, up to the ceiling and along the rows of tightly packed bookshelves, he reiterated his gratitude and left.

Feeling drained of energy, Oliver flopped back against his chair and stared blankly out of the window. There had gone a man who had known tragedy in his life, the death of a beloved brother and the heartbreak of feeling responsible for it. Ted Trembath had never forgiven himself for taking the boy along on the smuggling run. In his grief he had murdered evil Old Tom Trelynne, Kerensa's grandfather, for betraying the smuggling run to the authorities, which had led to Davey Trembath's death. Ted had since lost his mother through insanity and his two other brothers had been killed in separate accidents down the mine. Ted had been left with no one, his livelihood had been threatened by the mere fact he was ageing – not that he was old at thirty-four but too old for an underground miner – then an accident had put paid even to that. Now life had taken an upturn for Ted and he was looking forward to a new life with a new family.

Not so with me, Oliver thought bitterly. I had a new life and a new family after years of loneliness and now it's all gone sour. I've loved and trusted one person more than any other in my life only to find that she betrayed me.

Oliver rubbed his hands over his face to force away his tiredness and tried to lose himself in his paperwork. But he knew it wouldn't work for long. He would feel either an uncontrollable rage in which he had to keep away from Kerensa, or an agony of longing to know his lost brother and the desire to jump in a boat and scour the sea for him.

'Is everything well with Ted Trembath?'

Oliver gave Kerensa no answer. He was watching as she attended the lazy fire in the master bedroom. His gaze drifted and lingered on the gentle contours of her slender body, the delicately moulded form that he knew so well. Her flimsy nightgown concealed little to his experienced eyes.

Rising from the fire she shook her head to loosen the silky hair at the nape of her neck, the movement swirling the glossy length teasingly over the ivory-smooth skin of her bare shoulder where the gown had slipped. Her skin glowed rich and creamy in the firelight. The grey-green of her eyes seemed deeper tonight and so poignantly sad. Oliver stood leaning against his dressing-room door, silent and mesmerised.

Believing he was there only to change his clothes before he went out for the night and that his silence would last until then, as it had so many times before, Kerensa gulped back a sob rising in her throat and sat at her dressing table. She picked up a hairbrush and ran a thumb over the bristles then traced the scroll patterns on its heavy silver back.

Oliver blinked heavily and came out of his stupor. Realising Kerensa had said something to him he had to think hard to recall her exact words. After the loneliness of an afternoon getting nowhere with his paperwork, a late supper he'd picked at alone, he suddenly wanted to be with her. When he spoke he said the words rapidly, moving up behind her in the same way.

'Long ago I promised Ted work on the estate and a cottage when he felt he could no longer go down the mine. I repeated the offer after the last mining accident. That time has come and that's why he was here.' He fought down the desire to take the hairbrush and caress her hair.

Before she lost his attention again, Kerensa jumped up and faced him. 'I hate the way things are between us, Oliver. I've told you so many times how sorry I am. Please, my love, say you forgive me. Can't we go back to the way things were before?'

Oliver had torn off most of his clothes and wore nothing but his breeches; the only barrier between his flesh and hers was the nightgown. The knowledge made his heart pound and when she pressed the flat of her hands on the hot moist skin of his chest he was overpowered by a painful desire for her and pulled her urgently against him.

The first touch of his lips was tender but erupted into a long fierce need for more. Kerensa's body shook with a desperate need for him too. She moved her lips hungrily against his and entwining her arms round his neck she strained into his strong muscular body. Her heart and soul, imprisoned in despair since his furious withdrawal from her, soared. She had been so fearful the depths of his hurt and anger would stretch to their marriage bed. Almost roughly he lifted her off her feet and swung her down on the heavily draped four-poster bed.

The ecstasy of their lovemaking left Kerensa feeling vulnerable and wanting to weep. She lay half over Oliver's body. He was tense and breathing rapidly. His arms were about her but his fingers were interlaced. The significance of this worried her; usually after a time of loving Oliver would tenderly caress her. The clasped hands meant an aloofness, a holding back from her. She wanted to get him talking again but didn't know what to say. Yet again she asked herself why she hadn't had the good sense to realise she ought to have told him about Samuel Drannock years ago?

Oliver was highly conscious of the light weight of her hot damp body on his. In the delicious moments of their coupling he had forgotten the anger he felt towards her, his emptiness, the pain of the loss that could never be regained. He stared sightlessly at the canopy above them. If he did not love Kerensa so very much then her betrayal would not have cut so deeply, leaving this bitter, helpless agony.

More hurt came in his secret acknowledgement that Kerensa was right about his dead friend, Arthur Beswetherick, Sir Martin's youngest son. Oliver had grown, been schooled and matured into manhood side by side with Arthur Beswetherick. Everything they had learned they'd learned together. They had planned to take a suitable bride in the same year, rear large families and grow old together, comfortable in a never-ending companionship.

When Arthur bled to death on the battlefield of Dettingen, Oliver had been left distraught and lonely. The memories of his lost friend came back often to haunt him. The comradeship of two men who took up arms to fight, prepared to die side by side, was unique, unlike that of an ordinary friendship or the affection for a member of one's family. In the lonely years until Kerensa had become his wife he had taken comfort in those memories. Oliver didn't want to admit it but Kerensa had been right in what she'd shouted at him about Arthur Beswetherick. It was time to leave him in the past, but with the way things were he couldn't do it yet.

Agonising thoughts of the lost brother denied to him, of how things might have been between himself and Samuel Drannock, refused to be blocked out. They grew and grew and festered like an open wound. Suddenly he thrust Kerensa away.

'Oliver! What's the—' She was interrupted by a child's cry along the corridor.

'I'll go,' he said tersely, kicking the bedcovers so violently they became untucked and hit the floor.

Kerensa lay frozen as she listened to him hastily pulling on clothes. She remained still as she heard him order Cherry back to bed and go himself to soothe away the terrors of another of Kane's nightmares. The two bedroom doors closed, one after the other. She was shut off. Retrieving the bedcovers, she wrapped them round herself like a cocoon. She knew Oliver would not come back to share them with her again that night.

Across the grounds, Jack left his tiny cottage in his one good suit of clothes. He was proud of his suit. He had bought it secondhand from a market stall and was convinced its good fabric and condition meant it had belonged to a man of means either bored with it or down on his luck. And as luck would have it for Jack, it suited his colouring and was a perfect fit.

He had brushed and combed his lank dark hair and oiled it away from his face where it tended to be unruly, then painstakingly tied it back with a bow. His cleanshaven neck and chin were anointed with the dregs of an intoxicating cologne from a discarded bottle of Captain Solomon's, secretly procured from a rubbish pail and hidden away for use on special occasions.

There was no thought in Jack's mind of seducing Heather. A long chat to get to know each other better and perhaps a kiss or two before going home would do for tonight.

Jack had heard talk about Heather at the Bible classes. She was said to be 'loose', 'free with her favours', and prayers for her soul were given regularly. Jack wasn't sure if he believed the talk. He didn't want to believe it. Matthias Renfree said she 'couldn't help the way she was', the Almighty God would be merciful to her, and the members of the Society were obliged to treat her in the same way. Jack saw himself as Heather's personal saviour, leading her away from a wayward life, helping her to start a new one, living quietly in his cottage as his wife. It was a pleasant, cosy idea. But would Heather agree?

If anyone was abroad under the frosty star-lit sky and saw two lanterns making a haphazard passage over the Downs to meet at the right of way, they might have mistaken the bobbing lights for those being carried by incautious free-traders or, even more frightening, by unrestful spirits. An amused smile might have curled their mouths if they had stayed to make out the figures of a youth on horseback and a girl on foot, moving closer together, until the lanterns became still, one beside the other.

' 'Tis a mite cold tonight, Heather,' Jack said bashfully. 'Thank you for coming to see me.'

Heather put her lantern on the cold hard ground and looked at Jack from the glow of his which he held at face level. 'I thought to stay 'ome an' keep warm by the fire, we've got plenty of peat in, but then I wanted t'find out what yer made of, Jack. Aren't 'ee goin' t'give me a kiss then?'

'Of course. I thought in a m—'

what he was ma
experience. Well
Several month
and ale on a fe
Drannock, Paul
parish. All exce
and they sugges
Bessie's kiddley
two fishermen p
Jack knew was
the company of
used to liquor, J
hadn't gone far
Up on the cli
Jack had liste
enjoyed the ch
recollection of
before he black
accompanime
Paul assured h
and exercised
sure it was true
With Heath
very excited.
wished he cou
woman outsid
to proceed.
Heather lea
Jack felt pa
you've got he
ready? Jack d
on with it'. It
moving abou

leave him in the past, but with the way things were he couldn't do it yet.

Agonising thoughts of the lost brother denied to him, of how things might have been between himself and Samuel Drannock, refused to be blocked out. They grew and grew and festered like an open wound. Suddenly he thrust Kerensa away.

'Oliver! What's the—' She was interrupted by a child's cry along the corridor.

'I'll go,' he said tersely, kicking the bedcovers so violently they became untucked and hit the floor.

Kerensa lay frozen as she listened to him hastily pulling on clothes. She remained still as she heard him order Cherry back to bed and go himself to soothe away the terrors of another of Kane's nightmares. The two bedroom doors closed, one after the other. She was shut off. Retrieving the bedcovers, she wrapped them round herself like a cocoon. She knew Oliver would not come back to share them with her again that night.

Across the grounds, Jack left his tiny cottage in his one good suit of clothes. He was proud of his suit. He had bought it secondhand from a market stall and was convinced its good fabric and condition meant it had belonged to a man of means either bored with it or down on his luck. And as luck would have it for Jack, it suited his colouring and was a perfect fit.

He had brushed and combed his lank dark hair and oiled it away from his face where it tended to be unruly, then painstakingly tied it back with a bow. His cleanshaven neck and chin were anointed with the dregs of an intoxicating cologne from a discarded bottle of Captain Solomon's, secretly procured from a rubbish pail and hidden away for use on special occasions.

There was no thought in Jack's mind of seducing Heather. A long chat to get to know each other better and perhaps a kiss or two before going home would do for tonight.

Jack had heard talk about Heather at the Bible classes. She was said to be 'loose', 'free with her favours', and prayers for her soul were given regularly. Jack wasn't sure if he believed the talk. He didn't want to believe it. Matthias Renfree said she 'couldn't help the way she was', the Almighty God would be merciful to her, and the members of the Society were obliged to treat her in the same way. Jack saw himself as Heather's personal saviour, leading her away from a wayward life, helping her to start a new one, living quietly in his cottage as his wife. It was a pleasant, cosy idea. But would Heather agree?

If anyone was abroad under the frosty star-lit sky and saw two lanterns making a haphazard passage over the Downs to meet at the right of way, they might have mistaken the bobbing lights for those being carried by incautious free-traders or, even more frightening, by unrestful spirits. An amused smile might have curled their mouths if they had stayed to make out the figures of a youth on horseback and a girl on foot, moving closer together, until the lanterns became still, one beside the other.

''Tis a mite cold tonight, Heather,' Jack said bashfully. 'Thank you for coming to see me.'

Heather put her lantern on the cold hard ground and looked at Jack from the glow of his which he held at face level. 'I thought to stay 'ome an' keep warm by the fire, we've got plenty of peat in, but then I wanted t'find out what yer made of, Jack. Aren't 'ee goin' t'give me a kiss then?'

'Of course. I thought in a m—'

Heather had no interest in preliminary small talk and gave Jack a full passionate kiss from her open fleshy lips then pushed him away.

'Come on then,' she purred, 'since you've gone to all this trouble t'get all dressed up and t'smell so sweet fer me . . .'

Jack was still reeling from the shock of the girl's hot mouth on his. 'Wh-what do you want?'

'I mean, *come on*!' She cast off the shabby cloak wrapped over her dress and shawl and spread it over the crackling dead heather and ferns.

'What are you doing, Heather?' Jack whispered nervously at her back, looking about guiltily.

'Put that blasted lantern down an' mind 'ee don't kick over mine,' she hissed. 'I know the Downs well enough but I don't fancy walkin' back in the dark, there's always one soddin' great boulder you ferget. And what are 'ee lookin' about fer, we'm a long way from that damned buildin' goin' up, there's no one 'ere to go on about 'ee bein' saved.'

When Jack didn't move, Heather gave a loud exasperated sigh. 'You gonna stand there like a spare un at a weddin' all ruddy night? Tes too bloody cold to 'ang about in, you'll 'ave un freezin' off!' she ended with a salacious laugh. She sat down on the cloak and straightened out its edges.

Jack looked about one more time and quickly joined her, carefully putting his spluttering lantern next to hers. He was relieved the meagre light didn't allow scrutiny of the colour burning his neck and cheeks. He was wearing the fine linen shirt Ruth and Esther King had made for him last Christmas. Heather tore it at the neck as she yanked the front open.

Jack told himself not to panic. He had not looked for this, but clearly his time had come. Heather wanted to see

201

what he was made of. It was a good job he had some experience. Well, he thought he had.

Several months ago, after drinking too much mead and ale on a feast day, he'd met up with Bartholomew Drannock, Paul King and some other young bloods of the parish. All except Bartholomew and Paul had drifted away and they suggested a walk along the cliff top to Painted Bessie's kiddleywink. Inside the ramshackle ale house the two fishermen plied Jack with cheap gin and the next thing Jack knew was that they were leaving the kiddleywink in the company of three females of dubious character. Unused to liquor, Jack was barely able to follow them but they hadn't gone far.

Up on the cliff top above the sound of the raging surf, Jack had listened enviously as Bartholomew and Paul enjoyed the charms of their women. He had very little recollection of what happened with his own companion before he blacked out, but when he opened his eyes to the accompaniment of a blinding headache Bartholomew and Paul assured him that he had lost his boyhood innocence and exercised his full manly abilities. Jack still couldn't be sure it was true.

With Heather pressing up against him, Jack was getting very excited. They kissed long and enthusiastically. He wished he could remember what had happened with the woman outside Painted Bessie's, then he would know how to proceed.

Heather leaned against him making strange little noises. Jack felt panicky. Bartholomew had told him. 'When you've got her ready, boy, get on with it.' Was Heather ready? Jack decided she must be and it was up to him 'to get on with it'. It was easy enough to pull up her skirt with her moving about so much, but what came next? He tried to force his mouth away from hers to gulp in some much needed air but she roughly pulled him back.

Jack's arousal was so strong his insides felt they were knotting, intricately entwining and about to explode. She helped with the move he made to lie over her. Again he wished he could recall his first intimate experience; he wasn't sure of the exact outlines of a woman's anatomy.

Suddenly Heather cried out. 'You bloody swine! Don't 'ee know anything, you stupid bugger!' Shoving Jack off she scrambled to her feet. 'I thought you knew what t'do, you're nothin' but a useless . . .' A stream of obscenities went up and hit the night sky and echoed amongst the stars as she ripped the cloak out from under Jack's hands and knees. Snatching up her lantern the furious bal-maiden ran off, keeping up the tirade of abuse until it ended with a short scream.

Jack sat shivering in his crumpled suit on the crushed foliage. He felt sick and ashamed. He stayed there staring into the night sky until he could find the strength in his legs to get up.

'What a foul-mouthed, bad-tempered . . . what a spitfire,' he told Meryn, his source of comfort, a confidante who couldn't repeat what she had seen and heard. 'If that's women for you, I give up. Bartholomew and Paul can keep them all.'

Chapter 14

Trecath-en's farmhouse was traditionally heavily decorated every year at Christmastide. There were three more weeks yet to Christmas but Rosie could think of no reason not to look out for the best holly, mistletoe and ivy among the giant trees of the Pengarron oak plantation.

It was not unusual for her to be up in the arc-shaped forest high above and sheltering the manor house. Through all the seasons she walked the grassy rides with their rich habitat of wildlife and abundance of flora. She followed the twists and turns of the stream that fed the river that provided the fresh sparkling water supply of the manor. Along its banks she picked watercress and dropwort leaves for the wild salad Kenver was partial to. She also gathered wild herbs, berries, nuts and leaves in a flat narrow wicker basket for Beatrice.

Rosie had become friendly with Beatrice in her childhood when she'd visited the manor with Alice. When she showed an interest in the old woman's cupboard of mysterious looking bottles and pots Beatrice agreed to teach her how to make teas and infusions from plants and herbs. The smells of thyme, horsetail, yarrow, parsley, mint, raspberry leaf, camomile and fennel and many others filled the air when the cupboard was opened. Rosie quickly learned their cosmetic and medicinal value, and found it useful to know that dock seeds or sorrel leaves could be used as a substitute for tobacco and that lavender oil or buttercup salve would soothe burns. She was even making a little money out of her skills now. Rosina Blake had admired the shine of her golden hair and requested some of Rosie's herbal rinse for her own use and insisted on paying for it. It gave Rosie some independence to be able to buy personal items without having to ask her father for money.

As well as the knowledge she gained, Rosie enjoyed stirring the heavy pots containing the mixtures with their heady smells and clattering about the manor kitchens. She worked with Beatrice when Ruth and Esther King were not about, and knowing of the old woman's slovenly habits, she ensured the kitchen was left meticulously clean. Sometimes while they were busy the children would appear to see what they were doing or Kerensa popped in to chat and share a pot of tea.

Only the other day Sir Oliver had entered the kitchen while they were bottling the gorse wine. He stayed to sniff at Beatrice's bottles and asked after Rosie's sprained ankle. He lingered in an aimless mood and when Kerensa called to him he put a finger to his tensed lips to inform them that he did not want to be found and slipped out through the back door into the yard.

The open canopy of the oak trees allowed the mild winter sun to wink through the leaves. As Rosie looked upwards for the best patches of ivy and white-berried mistletoe, she stumbled against a large fallen tree and stayed to examine its dressing of mosses and fungi, making a mental note of them to ask Beatrice if any were non-poisonous and useful for her potions.

She went on through maturing oaks and the regrowth of thin poles of hazel, hornbeam and alder that the farmers and smallholders used, split and woven, to fence in their livestock. The largest of the standard oak trees provided timber for ships, barn roofs and panelling, and furniture for mansions and big houses all over the world. Leaves fallen from the previous season crackled under her feet; she picked some up and dropped them into the stream, watching them scurry away over the streambed pebbles. After drinking cupped handfuls of the icy flowing water she wrapped her hands inside her shawl until they were warmed and dry.

On entering the forest Rosie had heard sounds of woodsmen but they had lessened and now were silent so she knew she was walking away from them. Knowing that if she did not stray from the course of the stream she would not get lost, she plunged deeper into the trees, putting more distance between herself and the rest of humanity. There were times when she yearned for these occasions to be apart from her family and the never-ending work on the farm. To have time to think for longer than a few minutes before someone interrupted her or another chore beckoned.

Coming to a straight line of seven large, flat, stepping stones across the stream, she hitched up her skirt and hopped nimbly to the other side, taking care not to twist her weak ankle. She followed the stream on this side.

One hour, or was it two, passed and Rosie regretfully decided she would have to turn back; Clem would make a fuss if she was late helping Alice with the supper. It wasn't that he would accuse her of skimping her work and Alice was only too pleased for her to enjoy a little well-deserved freedom. But Clem worried over her. She knew she was very special to him, even more so since their mother and grandmother had died. He was overly possessive and it seemed he wanted her to stay on the farm for ever judging by his hostility towards any young man who showed the slightest interest in her; he'd even threatened to speak to Jack from the manor for simply passing the time of day with her. Rosie had noticed Clem was the same with Jessica, and although his marriage to Alice was no love match on his part, he was over-protective towards her too. Rosie believed it stemmed from his emptiness at losing Kerensa; she was certain her brother had a dread of losing any more of his womenfolk. Dear Clem. Rosie smiled at thought of him; though quiet and sullen, he was eager to please them and got in a bit of a state if he wasn't sure of their whereabouts all the time. She must turn back and follow the stream the way she had come.

Rosie was brought to a sudden standstill. She could hear voices. There were two voices, male voices, but whose were they? She was frightened they belonged to poachers; they'd want to silence her if she was seen. But she thought it better to find out who they were before making a hasty retreat.

Creeping forward in and out of the trees she soon made out the owners of the voices. The mellow lyrical tones belonged to Nathan O'Flynn, the other voice, deeper and cultured, was Sir Oliver Pengarron's. From a hiding place behind a fissured trunk of a mature oak Rosie spied on them.

They were sitting on a log in a small clearing, sharing the pale golden liquid of a wine bottle. Rosie's face suffused a hot red to the roots of her hair. She had tried not to confess to herself that the real purpose of coming all this way was the hope of catching sight of the taller, darker of the two men. And now here he was, only a few feet away. She felt a flush of guilt and slightly giddy. She could clearly hear their

208

words. They were talking over matters concerning the estate and Ker-an-Mor Farm. The tone of their conversation was self-congratulatory.

Sir Oliver was saying, 'It's been said, Nat, that we have advanced in agriculture farther than any other county in the country and this year we have certainly seen more than reasonable yields from both livestock and grain. We organise the breeding of our stock on a scale not thought possible in my father's day.'

'Aye, sir, that's true, and with careful management and coppicing of the oak . . .'

Rosie did not want to hear what Nathan had to say. She hoped he would soon go and leave Sir Oliver alone. Then she wished they would both go and hoped they would never know she had been there spying on them. Oh, she thought wretchedly, I don't know what I want at this moment. What would Nathan O'Flynn think of her presence here? Would he think her search for mistletoe and ivy no more than an excuse? He was nobody's fool. Nor was Sir Oliver. He would know why she was here. What would he do with that knowledge? Laugh at her? Humour her? Be angry with her? If they were left alone together would he take advantage of her? The last thought made her sink down till the men were out of her sight. She huddled against the tree trunk, keeping herself just off the cold forest floor.

As she squatted uncomfortably thinking over the many possible consequences of the situation she had put herself in, Rosie was taken over by a rebellious mood and she was sure of one thing. She wasn't going back yet. She didn't care what Kenver or Alice, her father or even Clem thought. She did her share of the work on the farm and she was twenty-one years old, old enough to make decisions for herself.

She remained crouching, catching odd snatches of their conversation. Matthias Renfree was mentioned and she listened carefully. Why was she interested in anything concerning Matthias? It was all so confusing. Clem and Alice brought up Matthias's name often, referring to his qualities and how he would make a good husband, but she didn't realise they had her in mind as his wife.

Rosie herself thought Matthias would make someone a good husband and she had looked him over once or twice. He wasn't much older at thirty than she was and alongside his religious zeal he owned a surprising sense of humour and enjoyed many a hearty laugh with the Trenchard menfolk. To Alice he even displayed a certain amount of charm, to the twins and Jessica he was like a favourite uncle. But he treated Rosie rather as he did the children and she wondered if he'd noticed yet that she had grown up.

The talking in the clearing had stopped. Rosie eased herself up on stiff legs and peered round the side of the tree. Nathan had left, she had no idea in which direction, and waited awhile to see if he would come back. Sir Oliver reached into a pocket for his tobacco pouch and filled his clay pipe. Rosie liked to look at his hands. They were large and rather elegant and although toughened by the hard manual work he liked to do they were not as rough and calloused as Clem's and her father's were. His long fingers, adorned with only one discreet ruby set in gold on the ring finger of his right hand, were different to those of Matthias Renfree, whose were smaller and stocky like the rest of him.

Thinking again of Matthias reinforced Rosie's feelings of guilt. She should not be wanting a secret meeting alone

with a married man, especially with him being her father's landlord, Matthias's employer, the husband of her sister-in-law's best friend and the man who had broken her brother's heart by stealing his bride. It was so very wrong. No good would come of it. Sir Oliver had not and probably never would live down his reputation as a womaniser. It was probably not safe to be alone with him. But Rosie could not help herself. Taking a deep breath she walked towards him.

Oliver glanced up from lighting his pipe, showing no surprise at seeing her there. He looked stern as she came before him like a child sent for by a headmaster.

He considered her for a moment, then said, 'I was wondering how long you were going to stay hiding behind that tree.'

'You . . . you saw me, sir?'

'It is easy to discern a flash of golden hair against the background of the trees.'

'Did Nathan see me too, do you think? I wouldn't like for him to get the wrong idea.'

'And what idea would that be?' She was acutely embarrassed and Oliver wickedly prolonged it for her, playing the verbal predator he'd enjoyed subjecting Kerensa to in their early days together, before she became wise to him. 'Why should Nathan get the wrong idea about you being here alone Rosie? I have always allowed my tenants to wander freely on estate property if they are prepared to respect it.'

'Oh, I don't know . . . I . . . just thought . . . I was out looking for mistletoe, holly and ivy. I often walk through the woods, gathering wild salad for Kenver or herbs and leaves for Beatrice,' she finished lamely.

'Really? A kind and thoughtful act by a kind and thoughtful girl.' He looked in her basket. 'It's empty,' he said.

211

'Well, there's not much to gather at this time of the year.'

He raised a lazy eyebrow. 'Not much mistletoe, holly and ivy?'

'Well, I . . . I . . . I suppose I was too busy thinking of something.' Rosie wanted the ground to open up under her feet and swallow her. What had she let herself in for?

'About something or someone in particular?'

Rosie's heart thumped and her brain raced for ideas for a suitable answer to this. She stared at the basket and recalled her excuse for carrying it. 'Kenver!' she exclaimed. 'I was wondering what to give Kenver as a Christmas present.'

'Were you now?'

Rosie couldn't tell if his question was asked impatiently, sarcastically, or indifferently. She was sure she had made a big mistake lingering behind the oak tree. She was about to make an excuse to go when he asked her something that made her gasp.

'Would you like a drink, Rosie?' he said, picking up the wine bottle and holding it out to her.

Ought she not flee? Some folk from the Bible classes would say to be offered wine by this man was like being asked to drink with the Devil. How much of the Devil was in Sir Oliver Pengarron?

His dark eyes chained her to the spot. She shook her head and heard herself saying, 'No thank you, sir. I had a drink from the stream just now.'

'As you please. Sit down,' he motioned to the end of the log, 'or do you have to be on your way?'

'I . . . I suppose it won't hurt to sit down for a moment or two.' Rosie sat at what she deemed to be a respectable distance.

'I hope you are taking due care while you're out alone,

212

Rosie. I take it you have heard of the disappearance of one of the bal-maidens from the Wheal Ember mine.'

'Heather Bawden, you mean, sir? She's a wild one, that maid. I was almost too afraid to look at her for fear of what she'd say. Some do say because she's young in the head the small people have taken her away to look after their children. But most folk believe she's run off with a man somewhere. There was a travelling group of actors in Marazion of late, she spent a lot of time hanging round they. Some do believe she's gone off after they, looking for excitement.'

'That may be so, but on the other hand the girl might have been carried off against her will. Other people believe she has been murdered and thrown off a cliff or down a disused mine shaft.'

Rosie gave a shiver. 'Poor maid.' She tapped the back of her heels against the tree trunk, releasing the strong damp smell of its moss covering.

'Is all well at home, Rosie?' Oliver asked amiably. The harsh lines of his face had softened now and he watched her moving feet.

'Yes, sir, the twins are as boisterous as ever. They were some put out at missing seeing you the day you were at the farm and Jessica was ever so sorry for dropping the cat on your lap.'

'Ah, Jessica, your angelic-looking niece. A lovely child.' He smiled at the recollection. 'No harm was done over the episode with the cat and I suspect it was me scurrying out just like a scalded cat myself that your nephews were most sorry at missing.'

Rosie laughed gaily but she was surprised this man of noble birth, wealth and power could laugh at himself. She did not ask how things were at the manor. She was not

213

unaware of the tense and gloomy atmosphere there and anyway it would be improper.

'Clem and Alice are lucky to have three such beautiful and healthy children,' she said, picking up a handful of dead oak leaves and crunching them.

Oliver drew deeply on his pipe. 'What kind of a father is your brother?'

Rosie raised her neat eyebrows. She had not expected this piece of curiosity. She was on the defensive at once.

'Clem's a wonderful father. It may surprise you to know he's doted on the twins from the day Alice brought them home from the manor where they were born and he loves Jessica just as much as Alice does. Jessica was a planned baby, not just the natural happening of they being man and wife.' She grew red at the reference to Jessica's conception but didn't miss the contempt in the short laugh Oliver gave. In retaliation she said, 'Strange isn't it? You and Clem both having three children, two boys and a girl.'

'No,' Oliver said bluntly, surveying the girl with a cold eye. 'I intend to have a much larger family.'

Rosie was sorry the conversation had taken this turn. She knew she ought to go but couldn't bring herself to leave this man's disturbing company.

Oliver remarked, as if he was testing water, 'It hasn't escaped my attention that Matthias Renfree has been calling more often at Trecath-en Farm.'

She grasped the opportunity to speak of someone else. 'Well, he's always been around a lot. He's a very good friend of Clem's of course and he helps Kenver to write his poetry down. He's godfather to Philip and David and takes a lot of interest in them.'

'His calls are more frequent now,' Oliver persisted. 'Does he not call on you particularly, Rosie?'

'On me? Whatever for?' Rosie answered too sharply. 'There's no reason for him to. I go to nearly all the Bible classes. If he calls more it's for Kenver's sake, he can't leave the farm and the preacher holds a prayer meeting for him there sometimes.'

'Well, if I were Matthias Renfree and had a lovely young girl such as yourself in the vicinity I'm certain I would ride over to Trecath-en Farm every single day.'

Rosie couldn't help but flush with pleasure. 'Would you?'

'I would indeed.' He leaned towards her. 'And if I was Matthias Renfree, would I receive a welcome?'

'I . . . I don't know. Matthias Renfree is nice enough but I'm not sure if he's looking for a wife, or if he really wants one.'

Sir Oliver had set Rosie thinking about why Matthias was in fact so often at the farm. He didn't seem to want anything in particular, he just seemed to hang around but if Clem wasn't there he didn't leave until he'd seen him. Was he there to ask Clem's advice on matters of the heart?

'Perhaps it would cross his mind if he were encouraged,' Oliver said. 'You do want to be married one day, don't you?'

'Yes,' she said softly, gazing down at her hands.

'And presumably to be a farmer's wife.'

'Yes.'

'Then you could do no better than Matthias Renfree. He'll be steward of Ker-an-Mor Farm after his father, he's learned and godly and has an agreeable countenance. Don't you agree, Rosie, or are you looking elsewhere?'

Rosie frowned and did not answer.

'Why do you not speak?' Oliver asked, as though he was taunting her.

215

'I . . . I'm sorry, sir,' Rosie faltered, looking up appealingly. 'I don't know what you mean by coun-te-nance.'

'Countenance? It's another word for one's face, Rosie.'

'Oh,' she laughed awkwardly. 'I do have trouble understanding some of the big words the gentry use sometimes.'

'No more than I do with an old man or woman speaking in a broad dialect. Now answer my question.'

Rosie did not believe he was trying to sell her Matthias Renfree as a prospective husband but that he wanted to know what was on her mind where men were concerned. She said, finally, 'I haven't given Preacher Renfree or anyone else much thought.'

'Why is that, Rosie?' he said, putting his head slightly to one side, a glimmer of mischief creasing his eyes. 'A lovely young woman like you must surely attract a good deal of male attention.'

He had changed her from 'lovely young girl' to 'woman' and the word had stronger implications. A rise of panic brought her to her feet; what kind of attention did he have in his mind where she was concerned? Something not wildly different from that of the young miners and fishermen that Clem kept at a determined arm's length? Or was the baronet not remotely interested in her, seeing her as only a menial to be made amusement of or a stupid little fool. Whatever it was, her embarrassment was too painful for her to remain another moment in his company.

'I really must be going,' she blurted out.

'Do you like foxes, Rosie?'

The question seemed to be almost thrown at her.

'Um . . . foxes?'

He took a long swig of wine, emptying the bottle.

'A young dog fox established a new den for himself and his mate in the autumn not far from this clearing. I thought

216

to have a look at them the day after the morrow. He's fairly active during the day, this particular fox. Make your way here in the early afternoon if you would like to see them too.'

Chapter 15

The Reverend Ivey no longer looked forward to his regular
visits to the manor house. He had hoped Oliver's emotional
outburst would have settled down by now. But it appeared
that his overheated reaction to Samuel Drannock being his
half-brother was not a sudden furious storm that would
quickly blow out; nor did he seem inclined to forgive either
him or Kerensa for keeping the secret between them over
the years.

Thoughts of Oliver's blinding rage in his study that day
could still make him tremble. The Reverend had a deep
sympathy for Oliver's feelings but it was too late to wish
things had taken a different course. Samuel Drannock was
dead and nothing could change that.

And nothing could change the fact that he was due
again at the manor in an hour's time and if he didn't
hurry along he would be late. During his prayers in
the church this morning he'd thought to offer up one
requesting that Oliver would not be there but then he'd
felt that it wasn't right to ask for such a thing in a
sanctified place. But as he waited for his manservant,
Ben Rosevidney, to saddle his pony, the Reverend hoped
and hoped Oliver would not be at home. He'd had quite
enough of the baronet's stone-hard face glaring across
his desk at him, and the sharp retorts to his every remark,

which made the Reverend's old heart lurch.

Ben Rosevidney was deaf and dumb and during his many years' employ at the Parsonage he and the Reverend had learned to communicate in signs and facial expressions and right now Ben was eloquently communicating his anxiety at the Reverend's apparent reluctance to get going, pointing often in the direction of the manor. Sighing heavily the Reverend finally mounted his pony; if he was late it would only fuel Oliver's ill humour with him.

Why could Oliver not understand, the Reverend reasoned with himself, that he and Kerensa kept quiet for the best of reasons? He kept his pony at a brisk trot but was ready to slow down if it meant being one minute early. If the truth had emerged before Samuel's death, the Reverend firmly believed, to give himself a crumb of comfort, then the situation could have been even worse. Samuel had despised Oliver. If the fisherman had remained stubborn in his assertion never to accept Oliver as kinsman or take any offers of help or money, Oliver would have been hurt and furious. He was a titled member of the gentry, it would have been unthinkable for him to be snubbed by a poor fisherman. Oliver was used to having his own way. If he couldn't have got in by the front door he would have tried the back, probably by using Jenifer and the children as pawns to achieve his own ends. There would have been a terrible clash because Samuel Drannock had been every bit as stubborn and proud as his half-brother.

And what of Bartholomew, the eldest of the Drannock brood? He resented the poverty his family lived in. He might have been set against his father's wishes. Wilful, obstinate and bearing the Pengarron looks, would he feel he had the right, along with his brothers and sisters, to the Pengarron wealth and privileges? The Reverend had marked the changes in Bartholomew's character over the years. He had not accepted his station in life and since his childhood had made large strides in bettering himself. Most importantly, with his mother's help he strove to speak well and had learned to read and write far better than the basic skills. He was not going to be content to fish the seas all his life, even though the shared gift of the *Young Maid* had improved his prospects considerably.

Thoughts of the fishing lugger brought another frown to add further wrinkles to the parson's intelligent face. Although Peter Blake, on Rosina's behalf, regularly sent food to the children of the Wheal Ember miners, it was out of character for him to give away such a lucrative vessel. Had Oliver had something to do with that? He had a responsibility towards those who could not help themselves but it would also have allowed him further revenge on the man who had once tried to force himself on Kerensa. Oliver Pengarron was a complex and volatile man. Perhaps it was inevitable that, given the necessary circumstances, the contradictory emotions in him would one day fuse together and explode. But with what consequences – and for whom?

The Reverend's main sympathies naturally lay with Kerensa. She said very little, putting on a brave front at home and outside of it. Although the children were unusually tetchy, they hadn't seemed to notice the estrangement of their parents; they had only grasped in their young minds that something somewhere was wrong. Kane was the most perceptive. Aware of Kerensa's lingering sadness he spent more time with her, instinctively knowing when to chat and try to cheer her and when to sit quietly and just keep the mother he adored company. He could not guess the reason for her melancholy; his father was careful to appear his normal self in front of his children.

It was a credit to the loyalty of the manor's staff that no gossip of the rift was abroad in the parish. The Renfrees knew and the Reverend had noticed Matthias watching Clem Trenchard closely. Matthias obviously shared the Reverend's own worst fear. Clem still loved Kerensa deeply and if the news broke, he would not simply accept the situation without employing some kind of action to see Kerensa. The Reverend dared not think of what might happen then.

As he neared the manor's parklands a cold drizzle of rain began to wet his face. Jake Angove and an under-gardener were replacing some fencing and by their gloomy faces and short acknowledgement of his approach he knew the situation had not changed. The Reverend reined in under a cedar tree and examined his pocket watch. He was not running late and he set his pony at a slow walk. If time still remained to his advantage when he reached the manor's front door, he would engage the stable boy in conversation and after that Polly O'Flynn who would undoubtedly open the door to him. Joseph Ivey did not consider himself a coward; in his opinion, in the circumstances everyone would behave in the same way.

Pulling his round black hat down firmly, he rode on, gazing downward, not seeing a group of shabbily dressed men coming up to him until one hailed him.

'Af'noon to 'ee, Rev'run'. We'm just come from the manor 'ouse. Bin askin' if anybody's seen my maid or 'as any idea where she might 'ave gone off to.'

The Reverend looked down sorrowfully on Carn Bawden. 'I'm saddened to hear that Heather has not yet been found. Was anyone there able to be of any assistance to you, Carn?'

'Naw,' Carn Bawden replied, wiping droplets of rain from his eyelashes. 'I d'reckon we'm seen the last of 'er. I b'lieve she's gone off fer good. I'm just out makin' one last round askin' after 'er fer the missus' sake. Jack, the groom up 'ere, 'e wus friendly with Heather like. I wus won'drin' if she told un any of 'er wild fancies. Said 'e reckoned 'e wus with 'er on the night she disappeared. The boy's proper worried about it, 'e wus rather fond of 'er, but anyway I assured un I don't b'lieve 'e 'ad anythin' to do with 'er goin' missin'. Young Jack wouldn't 'urt nobody. No, Rev'run', I'm afraid 'e 'ad more t'fear from 'er than she did 'im.'

'If there's anything I can do for you, Carn, be sure to let me know,' the parson told the weary miner.

'Thank 'ee, Rev'run', but I'd reckon it 'ad t'appen one day. Well, good day to 'ee, we went be keepin' 'ee 'ere in the rain.'

A young girl bored with a life of hardship going off to seek excitement elsewhere was no new occurrence. For Heather Bawden to do so was not surprising, the Reverend Ivey thought, shaking his head at life's foibles.

He became almost exuberant a few minutes later when Michael, who came to stable his pony, told him that Oliver had suddenly left the manor after the midday meal and wasn't expected back that day. Polly showed him into Kerensa's sitting room where she was reading a fairy tale to Olivia, Kane and a very fidgety Luke. It was a simply written tale of 'Jack the Giant Killer'; her reading was much improved and she read it with confidence.

'It seems I have come at an opportune moment, Kerensa,'

223

the Reverend said, beaming a smile at each child as Kerensa paused. 'I have not heard the tale in many a year. Do carry on, I will listen with the children.'

Kane and Olivia, sitting cuddled together on a sofa, parted and moved to make room for him to sit between them and then leaned against his arms, holding his hands. Luke, not to be outdone, left Bob where they had been rolling on the floor and clambered on to the Reverend's lap and began twisting his clerical collar. Kerensa looked doubtful at the arrangement and mouthed the words, 'Are you all right like that?' The Reverend nodded happily and she carried on with the tale.

'. . . and that was how the giant came to his end on St Michael's Mount. Brave Jack had won the day.' Kerensa closed the illustrated silk-bound book and smiled at her audience.

'Did you see how big that giant was in the picture, Reverend?' asked Kane. 'He's nearly as tall as Father.'

'Well, I don't think your father is quite as tall as the giant was,' the Reverend laughed.

'Our Jack is just as brave as Jack the Giant Killer,' Olivia said.

'No he isn't,' Luke said, with a snort. 'He may be good with horses but he's not at all brave.'

'Yes he is,' Olivia argued.

'I tell you he isn't!' Luke insisted. 'He happens to be afraid of women so he'd never be brave enough to kill a giant.'

The superior tone in Luke's voice, reminiscent of his father, made Kerensa as cross with him as his words. 'That's enough, Luke! Don't let me hear you say a thing like that again.'

'Well, it's true. I overheard—'

'Luke!' Kerensa warned as Kane and Olivia tittered. 'You should not listen in on other people's conversations and if you do so accidentally, you should not repeat what they say.'

'Jack is very brave,' Olivia poked her younger brother in the side. 'So there.'

This did not bring forth the tussle the Reverend expected. Instead Luke said loftily, 'Girls know nothing.'

'Can we have the story of St Michael killing the dragon at bedtime?' Kane asked, climbing down from the Reverend and giving his mother a hug.

'You can, my love, but not your brother if he's naughty again just once more today,' Kerensa said firmly, kissing Kane's cheek then giving Luke a chastising stare.

'Don't worry, Mama, I know how to behave myself.' Luke said it very sweetly but to the Reverend it sounded like a challenge. 'May I go outside to play?'

'If you don't get too wet and muddy, certainly you may.' Kerensa spoke each word clearly and precisely and Luke lowered his eyes. The Reverend was relieved she had gained the upper hand. But he wondered if she had bigger battles to face with this child in the future.

He pulled three wrapped squares of Mrs Tregonning's treacle toffee out of his coat pocket and the children eagerly took a piece each. Then Luke and Kane went outside to play knights and giant-killers in the rain and Olivia left to ask Cherry to help her lay out her paints.

'They become more charming every day, Kerensa,' the Reverend said after the noisy clattering of shoes had died away.

Kerensa smiled at him, putting the book on a shelf and clearing toys away from the table next to her chair to make room for a tea tray. 'Mind you, they're not perfect,' she said. 'Luke, as you know, can be the most difficult, but Olivia can be stubborn and temperamental and Kane, well, after his terrible start in life he can become very quiet and withdrawn at times. It's as if he knows something really awful happened to him but he doesn't quite know what. I hope he doesn't have trouble feeling part of the family when he's grown up.'

'Does he still have nightmares, Kerensa?' the Reverend enquired.

'Sometimes he has several in a row, then not for ages. Poor little soul. All children have the occasional nightmare but Kane screams like nothing you hear on earth. It goes right through us. Cherry usually ends up in tears.'

'I'm sure he'll grow out of them,' the Reverend said comfortingly. 'He has plenty of love and attention and Luke and Olivia accept him completely from what I can see. Oliver used to have terrible nightmares, did you know?'

'No, he's never mentioned it, but then I wouldn't expect him to talk about anything that seemed a weakness or a failure.' And the sadness that seemed part of her life overshadowed her again.

The Reverend nodded, then, mindful of Luke's recent behaviour, he said thoughtfully, 'Luke is rather like his father was as a boy.'

'Yes, Luke is a miniature of Oliver,' Kerensa agreed softly.

The fire was a poor one, and fearing Kerensa was feeling the cold, the Reverend tapped the three big logs sitting on the embers with a long brass poker until a blaze flared up to his satisfaction. He felt enough at home in the manor to do such things unselfconsciously. He turned round and clasped his hands together under his coat tails. Kerensa did not look any warmer. She looked at him with tired eyes; her sparkle and youthful vitality had dimmed noticeably.

'Does it worry you at all, my dear? Luke being so much like Oliver?'

'Not at all, Reverend,' she replied with a light smile. 'I love Oliver very much. I know Luke will always be difficult and although he is a little jealous of the special closeness between Kane and Olivia, he's very protective towards them. He has Oliver's stubbornness but he also has his love of animals and sense of fairness.'

'Kerensa,' the Reverend moved up and down on his toes and heels and she knew that his next words would be spoken with great care, 'you mentioned a sense of fairness. My dear, I cannot see that Oliver is being fair to you at the moment.'

She sighed and picked at a flower-bud pattern on the sleeve of her dress. 'Or to you, Reverend.'

'That is not important. It is not I who has to live with him. Is there no improvement in his attitude?'

'No, none, I . . .' Kerensa's eyes sprinkled with tears and she wiped them away with the side of her hand. 'I just cannot get through to him.'

'We will have to hope and pray that time will do what is necessary for Oliver's sense of fairness to return. What I do not understand is why he has not been to see the Drannocks. I thought he would have rushed there straightaway.'

'I was afraid he would,' Kerensa admitted. 'I believe he is hurt deep down inside by Samuel's dislike of him. Probably thinks that Jenifer shares the same feelings and Bartholomew might too if he was told. No matter what the other children may want, Bartholomew's too strong-willed for them to go against him. I think Oliver may be afraid to

227

face their possible rejection. His hurt goes so deep. He's biding his time, I think, waiting for what he hopes will be the right moment. I only pray to God that when the time comes it doesn't make matters worse.'

'I'm not saying this as empty words of comfort, Kerensa, but I rather think Bartholomew would not share his father's views. I have a strong feeling he had only a little love for Samuel.'

Kerensa looked thoughtful. 'Yes, I have spoken to him once or twice this year and he told me as much. He definitely wants more out of life for his family. I sometimes think it would be the best thing if Oliver was to go and see the Drannocks and bring it all out in the open and see what happens. If their reaction was favourable it might be the very thing to bring Oliver back to normal.'

'To heal his wounds and fill the vacuum in his mind,' added the Reverend.

'Yes, and then we might be able to do something for Jenifer.'

'I called on that poor woman yesterday. I fear her condition is worsening,' the Reverend said, rubbing the back of his fingers down his withered throat. 'We may be able to do something for her, as you say, if Oliver was to approach her and if Bartholomew talked her round. Do you think we could suggest to Oliver that he sees them?'

'We must never do that,' Kerensa uttered fearfully. 'Better to let Oliver do what he wants when he wants at the moment.'

'Of course, of course,' nodded the parson, acknowledging Kerensa's hopelessness.

Kerensa went to a window and from the firelight cast on the glass she saw her woeful reflection. It was comforting to have the Reverend Ivey here. There were two other men she knew who would work just as hard to console her if they knew of her heartbreak. She had seen neither one for weeks but even so she could not seek solace in their company. Hezekiah Solomon could be kindness itself to her and right now she would have liked to be the recipient of his excellent wit and charm but he was more Oliver's friend than hers and it would not be right to solicit his sympathy at the expense of Oliver. She thought of Clem Trenchard more often and needed him much more but it would be a dangerous road to walk to turn to him. If only she could meet him by chance when she was out alone.

Kerensa made herself smile at her image on the glass and forced herself to speak in a more cheerful tone. 'My boys will be soaked if they're still out there, not that they'll care, they'll run back inside with muddy feet.'

'I always say that boys and mud go together,' the Reverend grinned.

'Mine certainly do. They do enjoy it when you're here, and Olivia. I hope you don't mind me saying so but I think they look on you as a grandfather.'

'I'm delighted and proud to hear you say that.' The Reverend beamed like the sun, his old heart warmed through.

'Olivia is working on a painting for you,' Kerensa said, in hushed tones. 'The Lord Jesus as a little boy in the carpenter's shop.'

'Is she really? I shall be proud to hang it in a prominent place in the parsonage. Oliver had a love of painting as a boy, I recall, it's a pity he hasn't taken it up again, he would find it relaxing.' The Reverend joined Kerensa at the window. 'Goodness, it's really pouring down. I expect Luke and Kane will be sheltering in the stables or the summer house.'

'I hope they're not bothering Jack, he's so worried about Heather Bawden's disappearance. I must have a talk with him later. Ameline is also out somewhere. She went riding hours ago, it's quite a regular occurrence now. I hope she's found some shelter.'

Always the little mother, the Reverend thought to himself. It was a pity the private side of her life was being slowly destroyed.

'Oliver says I fuss over Jack unnecessarily and he's accused me of trying to mother him,' Kerensa said, as though she had read the Reverend's thoughts. 'Says I should let him grow up. I know Jack's a grown man but he was only a twelve-year-old boy when I came here to live.'

'You carry on as you are, my dear. Jack has no family and no idea who he really is. I dare say he truly appreciates the attention you give him.'

'Oh, I intend to, Oliver doesn't get his own way in everything. But there are other children that I'm concerned about, Reverend. The younger Drannocks, Charles, Jack and little Cordelia. They are showing signs of being neglected. Cordelia is eight years old, a year older than Olivia but much smaller. She's no bigger than Jessica Trenchard and she's only four. I send Ruth and Esther over twice a week to cook and clean the cottage and Mrs King is very good the rest of the time. But it's not the same thing as having a mother's care and love. All Jenifer does is sit in Samuel's seat behind the door. Why, I swear she hasn't taken a step out in the fresh air for over a month.'

'Yes, I know. It's a terrible tragedy for any family when the breadwinner dies, Kerensa. I'll try to have a word with Bartholomew but when he's not working out at sea he's rarely to be found in the village. It's difficult to know what to do about the Drannocks.'

'It seems worse when I think of how different things would be if it wasn't for Samuel's pride,' Kerensa lamented.

Polly brought the tea in and they spent a comfortable hour or two chatting. The rain had stopped by the time the Reverend got up to leave. As he made his way to his pony he was pulled roughly on the coat tails by a shuffling, grunting Beatrice. ''Er's in a bad way, Rev'run', the young missus.'

'Yes, Beatrice, I can see that only too clearly, she is in very low spirits,' he returned, smoothing out his coat tails and imagining Mrs Tregonning's chagrin if she knew that Beatrice had touched them with her dirty fat hands.

''E did never 'ad spoken to the little maid like the way 'e did. I over'eard un, you see, 'eard all that was said between 'em. 'Twas ruddy awful. Went tell nobody, mind.'

'I'm pleased to hear that, Beatrice. Keep an eye on her, will you? Send word to me if you think she needs me.'

'Aye, I'll do that all right.'

The Reverend Ivey hastened on his way to escape the crone's terrible smells.

'Tell 'ee one thing an' that edn't two, Rev'run',' Beatrice said to his back and brought him spinning round. 'Ef 'e don't come round soon an' put things t'rights, 'e may 'ave reason to be more sorry then 'e thinks at the end of it!'

Chapter 16

Rosie told herself many times not to go and look at the foxes with Sir Oliver. It was possible that looking at the wildlife wasn't the only thing on his lordship's mind. She had agreed to meet him alone and although it didn't mean she had given him her consent to anything more it might be seen as an encouragement. It could lead to all sorts of complications; he was married, her father's landlord, of a different class. But he was sophisticated and handsome and being with him spelled romance and adventure. Which ever way she looked at it she knew it wasn't right, but she knew she would go in the end.

Oliver had no doubts about it when he'd abruptly left the manor instead of staying to receive the Reverend Ivey. He was waiting for her on the other side of the stepping stones.

'Have you told anyone you were coming here today?' he asked, his voice strong and confident. He smiled in his striking way and held out a hand to help her to the firm leafy ground in front of him.

'No, I thought the family wouldn't understand,' she replied, both her cheeks lightly burning, 'and if anyone else wanted to come they might disturb the foxes.'

Oliver raised an eyebrow into a sensuous curve. 'The foxes, yes, of course. But your brother would not allow you to go anywhere that involved me in any case, would he?'

'No, sir, he would not.'

Rosie put her hands in under her cloak and wondered what his hand would have felt like round hers in that fleeting moment if she had not been wearing gloves. She was determined to get everything possible out of this time spent alone with him. She was not embarrassed by him now, though still filled with awe, and his teasing no longer disconcerted her.

They quickly reached the clearing where Rosie had spied on him and Nathan. Oliver looked up at the muddy grey sky through the swaying trees. A light wind rustled the remnant of shrivelled brown leaves that clung persistently to the branches.

'The rain held off for most of the day, Rosie,' he said contemplatively, 'otherwise it may have been too wet for you to come along.'

Rosie had followed his eyes upwards. 'I like the sound of the wind in the trees, it's like waves coming into shore.'

'Yes, and the wind can match the sea's every mood and wreak just as much havoc.' He glanced at her feet and remarked, 'I see you had a rather wet and muddy walk.'

Rosie was holding up the bottom of her primrose yellow dress and rough brown cloak well above her shoes, which were saturated and muddied from her long trek. The pattens she wore over her shoes to protect them were practically useless in the long wet grass and mud-laden tracks. She was wearing her Sunday best dress which she had changed into furtively in the barn and had wrapped her cloak tightly about herself so none of her watchful family would know she'd put it on. As it was, Alice had given her a searching look before she left home, wondering why she was so determined to go out for one of her long walks in such cold, miserable weather.

'You're getting just like Clem,' Alice observed, 'always going off by yourself the minute you get the chance.'

Kenver had stared at her shoes. He must have been curious why she was not doing the sensible thing and wearing the new soft leather boots he had made for her. He made no comment, just grinned warmly and whispered, 'Enjoy yourself, sis, but take care.'

'Have we got far to go?' Rosie asked Oliver. 'We haven't got many hours of daylight left.'

'No, not far. The vixen has chosen her earth close to an old hideout I made years ago with a childhood friend. We can watch for signs of them from there. We'll be approaching from the right direction regarding the wind and won't be near to their tracks but we'll have to tread carefully and avoid making any noise.'

Rosie watched her footing as she tramped behind Oliver, surprised that the tall man was so light on his feet. After a few minutes he slowed down and stopped and pointed out a small shack-like building, well camouflaged with overgrowth between two tall trees. Rosie would not have seen it herself.

'There it is,' he whispered.

He led the way, creeping forward to the building which was about eight feet wide and five feet high. Pulling aside a length of thick sacking, green from age and foliage, which was nailed across the top of the opening, he beckoned Rosie into the hideout first then hitched the sacking up to allow in some daylight. Oliver had to keep his head well bent inside the shack.

He grinned at Rosie's amazed face as she took in the interior. 'Arthur Beswetherick, Sir Martin's youngest son, and I were very proud of it,' he informed her, keeping his voice low. 'We worked hard to achieve this.'

'I can see that,' she breathed in admiration.

'Let's sit down and make ourselves comfortable before we get a crick in our necks.'

There were benches built into two sides of the hideout. They were scattered with cushions of silk and satin, now faded, and finely embroidered with pictures of animals, birds, knights and mythical creatures, presumably by the mothers of the boys. Rosie picked one up, wondering if they'd been made specially for the shack or had 'walked' out of larger homes.

''Tis like a grand little house,' Rosie said, 'better than what most folks do have to live in.' She held up the cushion. 'We've got nothing like this in the farmhouse.'

'You would be welcome to take it home, Rosie. For your own room. But your family wouldn't like the idea of where it came from.'

There were paintings on the walls as well as various tools and practical items hanging in neat rows on hooks.

'I sleep in here sometimes even after all these years,' Oliver confided. 'It's quite warm and cosy. If you are cold, my dear, there are blankets in the chest.'

'I am a bit cold,' she confessed, looking at her spoiled shoes, 'and my feet are wet through. I suppose I should have worn my boots,' she added, with an element of pride that she could say she owned such things.

Feeling important she seated herself on a bench that ran the width of the hideout. Oliver lifted a lantern off the chest that doubled as a table and pulled out two woollen blankets. He wrapped one round Rosie's shoulders and placed the other on her lap. Rosie thanked him, caressing the soft thick material and wishing the one on her little narrow bed at home felt the same.

'I daresay you and Mr Beswetherick had a lot of adventures here in the woods,' she said.

'We did,' Oliver replied, unfastening his surtout coat and laying it aside with his hat. 'We kept food, water, toy swords, real guns and all manner of things up here. I still keep provisions here and the toys are under the other bench. There are several places in the walls that can be opened to observe the wildlife, or in the days of our youthful imagination, "the enemy".'

'Sounds wonderful,' Rosie said enviously, peeling off her gloves and putting them on the chest. 'I had no one to grow up and have adventures with, Kenver couldn't play outside of course and Clem always wanted to be by himself.'

'Well, my dear,' Oliver briefly took her hand, 'you can have an adventure now.'

Rosie closed her hand to keep in the warmth he had left on hers, while Oliver reached across her and unlatched a long strip of hinged wood set low down in the wall. Very slowly he lowered it, careful not to make a noise. Rosie looked out into the exposed area of the forest.

He pointed and whispered, 'If we keep quiet long enough the foxes may come out from just there, by that clump of dead ferns. You may not see them at first as a visible shape, but as a slight difference in the scenery before you, as though something is there that wasn't there the last time you looked.'

'I didn't know foxes lived in the heart of the forest,' she said, also whispering.

'Actually, from here we're not too far from the outskirts of the north side of the plantation. They have an endless supply of food round about here, rabbits, hares, mice, worms and carrion. This particular dog fox has a most peculiar bark, it chilled me to the bone when I first heard it. It was rather eerie, like a strange haunting sound one remembers from a troublesome dream.'

'Is he very big? I haven't caught sight of a fox since Clem shot a rogue vixen having a go at the geese and chickens about six months ago.'

'He's quite big for a young fox. I've given him a logical name, Kywarn – dog fox.'

Rosie looked up sharply at a noise above the hideout. 'What was that!' she exclaimed.

'Shush,' Oliver grinned with a finger to his lips. 'A squirrel more than likely.'

'Sorry,' she whispered. 'If it was a squirrel it should be thinking about hibernating.'

'A contrary female squirrel,' he teased her.

They waited, neither speaking. Rosie was warm and comfortable. She had slipped off her soggy shoes and tucked her legs up on the bench and wrapped herself in the blankets. She kept her eyes on the woodland outside. Oliver mainly kept his eyes on her. Rosie knew this and felt a satisfied glow inside.

Oliver suddenly moved closer to the opening; his sharp eyes had seen something. Rosie obeyed his beckoning hand and gingerly moved to his side. More time passed and Rosie's eyes stung with rooting them on the clump of ferns. As would be expected, the larger dog fox emerged to full sight first. He looked directly at the light then cautiously from side to side and sniffed the air thoroughly before disappearing in an instant. He repeated this three times before he felt it was safe to remain outside his earth.

'What a beautiful, beautiful creature,' Rosie breathed.

238

The fox looked in a straight line in their direction. Rosie's heart thumped. Had it heard her? Could it see her? Would it bolt inside and not come to ground again?

The fox sniffed the air again with its sharp pointed nose, paced a few steps in either direction and to the front of its den, then remained still.

Oliver put his arm round Rosie and pulled her closer to him, his warm breath grazing her skin as he whispered into her ear, 'Can you make out the vixen's face through the ferns?'

Rosie peered harder. 'Yes, yes, will she come out?'

The answer was no. The vixen's bright-eyed face vanished and no more was seen of her. They watched the dog fox in a fascinated silence until it moved off in a rapid fluid movement among the trees. After waiting a few more minutes Oliver released his hold on Rosie and lifted the flap of wood back in its place and latched it securely. Rosie sat back on the bench, the feeling of his strong arm still about her. Oliver rejoined her, careful not to bump his head on the low roof.

'Thank you, sir,' she said, her face shining with utter delight.

'Why thank me?'

'For letting me see the foxes with you and for bringing me to this hideout of yours.' She looked about the building. There was even one of his school diplomas on a wall. 'This is obviously a special place to you.'

'It is. I must ask you, Rosie, never to tell anyone else about it. I don't want to find squatters in it or to have my things stolen. Well, what did you think of my fur-coated friend?'

'Like I said, beautiful. I didn't expect his coat to be so dark, he was almost black.'

'There are a few about like him rather than the reddish-brown variety. The vixen is much lighter.'

Rosie looked at the pictures. Some were painted in water colours, others in oils. All were scenes of woodland, moorland or seascapes. 'Did you make these pictures, sir?'

'Some of them, the others were painted by Arthur Beswetherick, the uncle of Miss Ameline who is presently staying at the manor.'

'I met her the last time I was there helping Beatrice. She has some lovely clothes and her hair was done beautifully in the latest style. I know that because her maid was boasting about it. Miss Ameline happened to see me when she was looking for someone to ask one of the stable boys to saddle a pony for her. She spoke quite nicely to me.'

'You sound quite surprised, Rosie.' Oliver looked at her inquisitively. 'Did you expect Miss Ameline to ignore you?'

'Some ladies do, but most treat folk like me as very much beneath them. You're lucky to get a civil word out of some, and some gentlemen.'

Oliver looked at her thoughtfully. 'Yes, I suppose you're right. People in my position ought to think more about life as it is for those less fortunate – what it really must be like to be forced to labour for a meagre living or to starve.'

'But you've always been kind to me,' Rosie said shyly, adding emphatically, 'You're kind to everyone.'

'There's many who wouldn't agree with your sentiments,' he returned philosophically, relaxing his back against the wall of the hideout and putting his booted feet up on the chest.

'I'm sure you're very good and kind to Kerensa – I'm

sorry, I mean Her Ladyship. She says for me to call her by name, I keep saying it as I first knew her.'

Oliver said nothing and Rosie looked away, fearing she had offended him by mentioning Kerensa by her Christian name. She wished she knew more about how she should treat the gentry. She gulped and brought the conversation back to the foxes. 'Would . . . um . . . Miss Ameline like to come up here to watch Kywarn and his mate, sir?'

'Not Ameline,' he said with a laugh, and Rosie was reassured she had not committed a breach of etiquette as far as he was concerned. 'She's far too refined.'

'How about Kerensa? I'm sure she would.'

Oliver tapped the chest with the toe of his boot, making it rock. 'Yes . . .' His voice grew low. 'Kerensa would . . .'

'You must bring her up here sometime, she would enjoy it.'

'Yes . . . I suppose I must . . . I don't know why it hasn't occurred to me before.'

'Probably because you're deep.' It was a word she had heard Beatrice use to describe Oliver and it was out before she knew it.

'Deep?' Oliver sounded amused. 'Have you been thinking about me, Rosie?'

'A bit,' she confessed, keeping her face turned away.

'I'm flattered that an old man can find a place in your thoughts, my dear,' Oliver said in indulgent tones.

'You're not old,' Rosie said vehemently, turning back. Her cheeks glowed hotly and her blue eyes looked into his with a new confidence.

'I shall be forty-three on the eve of Christmas,' he said, giving her a pleasant grin and a steady look. 'That's a few years older than the average working span of a miner and makes me old enough to be your father.'

'You don't look nowhere near that age and anyway forty-three's not old. You're the kind of man who will never grow old.'

'I suppose I should thank you for that.' Oliver moved closer. He put his strong dark features a bare inch from Rosie's face. 'Is that the kind of man you would like, Rosie? The kind of man you want?'

After the smallest pause, she murmured, 'Yes . . . I think it is.' She stared at him, but although he was very close she could not read his thoughts. Not even Kerensa could easily do that. What would he do? What did she want him to do? She was frightened of him, not afraid he would hurt her, but of something she didn't understand about him, but she didn't want him to move away and she didn't want to leave.

His hand came up and delicately touched a strand of hair behind her ear. 'I prefer your hair to Ameline's, it's soft and natural.'

Rosie was totally mesmerised. She looked back into his dark eyes without blinking.

He moved his hand behind her and lowered the blanket from her shoulders. She wore her hair in one long plait. He ran his hand down to its tip and wound it round and round his index finger then up and over his hand until the silky length was at the nape of her neck. With a gentle tug he tilted her head back and slid his other hand under her chin. His fingers were resting on the sides of her neck and he brushed her ear lobe tantalisingly with his thumb. Then with the hand gripping her hair he pulled her to him.

Rosie closed her eyes. She had never been kissed before and he gently coaxed her trembling lips apart with his. The kiss went on and on. She was overcome by a strange weakness and leaned into his body. When she felt she could no longer breathe and had no care if she ever did again, he moved his mouth away. Running a gentle finger along her lower lip he gave it several tiny tender kisses that made her body tingle and her head wonderfully dizzy.

She let out a low moan. He lowered her down on the bench and put cushions under her head.

Sometimes when Oliver wanted to make love desperately his body gave a tremendous shudder. In her innocence Rosie misread it for him feeling cold and she rubbed her hands in circular movements over his back and arms to warm him. Encouraged by her stroking, he kissed her passionately and caressed her with his fingertips, years of practice and expertise enabling him to know what Rosie liked and when to proceed. He had not wanted another woman since his wedding night, not even in the early days of his marriage before he had fallen in love with his seventeen-year-old bride. But now he uncompromisingly wanted Rosie Trenchard.

Without her realising it he had released her stays, pushed his hand inside the opening of her dress and rested it on her bare stomach. She pulled her muscles in so tightly he felt the edges of her rib cage and after a few moments he looked at her to see if she was breathing.

Rosie's hair had fallen loose from her plait, her face was flushed. She looked like a little girl awakened from a long dreamy slumber. A little girl, an innocent, trusting little girl – and it hit Oliver with an awesome force that he was about to utterly destroy that innocence. To embark on an affair with her would almost certainly forbid her making a good marriage, would destroy her faith in her superiors and lay her future in ruins.

Was he going to emulate his cruel, amoral father? Before his marriage he had lived by his own moral code, entertaining himself only with society women of a similar mind or the higher class professional. He had never violated a village girl, and now here he was in the throes of seducing a tenant's young daughter, perhaps to leave her with a child to grow up as another Samuel Drannock . . .

Horrific pictures flashed through his mind. Rosie seduced and betrayed. Morley Trenchard, never to respect and trust him again. Alice, no longer his friend. A pregnant Rosie, offered marriage by Matthias Renfree, cuckolded before his wedding night and bringing up another man's child. Rosie and Matthias leaving the estate, Adam Renfree too. And even more hate heaped on him by Clem; although he disliked and distrusted Clem, at that moment Oliver did not want him to suffer any more heartbreak on his account. Then came a vision of Kerensa's beautiful, precious face. He could never reach the level of love and self-giving with anyone in the way he did with her, the woman he adored. There was a rift between them; was he going to risk making it deeper, perhaps unbridgeable, permanent? Could he give Kerensa more pain, that much pain?

Rosie lay quiet, horribly perplexed by his stillness and the mortified look on his face. The passion he had inflamed in her was gone, fear and shame taking its place. It was a relief when the hand that had grown heavy and was now hurting her was taken away. As quickly as her shaking hands allowed she relaced her stays and pulled the blankets protectively about her. Gently, he raised her to sit beside him but he held her in a loose, fatherly embrace to stop her shivering.

'I'm sorry, Rosie . . . I had no right to bring you here . . . no right to try to make love to you. It's a good thing that I love Kerensa so very much . . . or . . . You did not mean anything like this to happen, did you?'

'No,' she said miserably, her face buried in her hands. 'I don't really know what I wanted to happen. From the time I got to know you when I visited the manor as a child I've been fascinated by you. I just wanted to spend some time with you, that's all . . .'

'Dear God, Rosie!' Oliver gasped and shuddered. 'I very nearly ruined you today.'

'It wasn't your fault, sir,' Rosie said, using his title to restore their previous standing. 'I shouldn't have wanted to come, I should have known better.'

'It most certainly was all my fault,' he stressed. 'I have every reason not to behave in such an irresponsible manner. Marry Matthias Renfree, Rosie, be like Kerensa and Alice and let your husband be the only man in your life. You'll never regret it, Matthias is a good man.'

'That may be so,' she said rather bitterly, 'but it doesn't mean he wants to marry me, he hardly notices me.'

Oliver lightly kissed her forehead. 'If he doesn't one day soon then he is the biggest fool on God's earth.'

Rosie pulled away and arranged her hair back into its neat plait. With a weak smile, she said, 'Thank you for showing me the foxes, sir. I'll never forget them. You really ought to bring Kerensa here to see them, specially next spring when more than likely there will be a litter of cubs as well.'

Oliver looked vacantly across the hideout at a picture he had painted of a raging storm sweeping into Trelynne Cove. 'I'll do that, Rosie . . . one day.'

Rosie wanted to be alone but she allowed him to escort her back to the stepping stones. The ground was slippery from a sudden heavy shower of rain they had not heard in their intimate moments in the hideout. She crossed the stream and walked on carefully until she knew she was nearly out of his sight. Instinct made her turn round and Oliver was still there, watching her, and some of Rosie's guilt and shame melted at this show of courtesy and concern. He raised his hand in a small wave, like a salute to a friend.

Oliver returned to the hideout with the hope in his heart that the adverse aspects of the afternoon Rosie had spent with him would not stay in her mind for too long. His eyes found the painting of Trelynne Cove. In his mind's eye he saw a poignant vision of Kerensa walking along the beach holding hands with Clem Trenchard as they must have done in the days of their betrothal. It was strange, he thought, how all the females closest to Clem were drawn to him. It was no wonder Clem hated him so much. He had taken Kerensa away and then she had fallen in love with him. Alice had turned to him for comfort in her moments of despair. Even Clem's small daughter wasn't shy of him and had climbed up on his lap. And now Rosie.

Oliver next fancied he saw Kerensa alone in the picture, standing on the rocks lost and distressed. He wanted desperately to be with Kerensa at that moment. If only he could go and take her in his arms, sweep away the sorrow in those hauntingly deep grey-green eyes. He knew he was responsible for that sorrow and felt guilty at her wretchedness yet at that moment he also envied her. Kerensa was content with herself deep down, never having known the inner turmoils he had suffered throughout his life. Despite his years, experiences, position and wealth he had been torn apart at the innermost part of his being. He was wracked with pain at Kerensa withholding the secret of

Samuel Drannock's true identity from him but what tortured him even more was his reaction to it.

He needed time to think. Time for a deep search inside himself. Time to be alone and make what would be a painful journey. Suddenly, Oliver knew what he had to do. In the not too distant future, when he had made suitable arrangements, he would go away. Far away from Cornwall, the estate and his wife.

Chapter 17

Ted Trembath and Lou Hunken were married on New Year's Eve. After a quiet ceremony, attended by half a dozen people in St Piran's, Perranbarvah's parish church, the wedding party gathered with a greater number for a celebration held in a barn on Ker-an-Mor Farm. Many turned up out of affection for the amiable ex-miner and his widow bride, quite a few more tagged along in hope of devouring foodstuffs, ale and rum laid on generously by Oliver.

Adam Renfree made sure the liquor flowed freely and despite Matthias's attempts to hide away the jugs of ale under bales of hay at the back of the barn, the party was in a merry mood by late afternoon.

'Bring 'em back out, boy!' Adam yelled at his son. ''Twas a bloody damned miserable Christmas and we've a right to make up for it now.'

'Marriage is a holy sacrament,' Matthias argued, to no effect, 'not an excuse to get shamelessly drunk. And please stop that swearing, Father, there's ladies present.'

'Where? What ladies? I can't see no one here who hasn't heard it all before. Look around 'ee, son. Some of these women here are drunker than the men.' Adam swept his bloodshot eyes round the barn until they alighted on a group set apart from the others. They were smiling pleasantly and tapping their feet to the music. ''Cept for your ruddy Methodies over there, of course,' he added disparagingly.

'They're enjoying themselves without drinking and doing anything to spoil other people's enjoyment. Lou's not drinking, nor's Ted, and they're not miserable.'

'Course Ted's not drinking,' Adam said, nodding at the bridegroom who was bouncing his youngest stepchild on his knee. 'He's saving his energies for later on. A man who's stayed unmarried as long as he has will need a clear head to satisfy a comely widow like Lou.'

'Really, Father!' Matthias complained in exasperation.

'Ahh, get on with 'ee, boy, a little bit of that would do you a power of good. Ted'n right for a man to be going without, don't know how you put up with it.'

'Must you bring that subject into everything you ever say? And there is nothing wrong with a man being chaste. There's plenty against being morally loose!'

Adam was unrepentant. 'Yah! Nature's nature and that's the end of it. I'll see about lighting some lanterns, be getting dark drekkly.'

Matthias knew he would never win with his father. Adam was a law unto himself. Inclined to fits of hot temper, he liberally added a variety of swear words to every other sentence. He even swore in front of Sir Oliver, who rarely uttered an oath himself and disapproved of it in others. But he seemed to be oblivious to his farm steward's bad language. Matthias had given up trying to convert his father; Adam was extremely antagonistic to any form of church or Christian fellowship and Matthias had decided the task was best left in the hands of the Almighty.

'Don't worry, Matthias,' Clem Trenchard said in his friend's ear. 'Your father can hold his drink.' Clem had no interest in weddings but he had joined Alice, Rosie and the children in the hope that the occasion would provide him with an opportunity to get his sister to notice Matthias. He was also hoping Kerensa would be there.

'That's not the point,' Matthias responded soberly. 'He's dependent on the bottle now.'

'Are you sure?'

'Yes, but never mind that now, we're here to celebrate a wedding.'

Clem made a quick movement forward. Matthias turned and saw the reason why. Kerensa had entered the barn with her three children. She was smiling and gaily greeted everyone. As she approached the two men, Adam's voice reached them loudly as he concluded a ribald joke.

'I'm very sorry, m'lady,' Matthias apologised.

'It's all right, Matthias. It's only Adam being Adam and I don't think the children heard, they're too busy looking about,' Kerensa said brightly.

She looked beautiful, though pale and a little thin, and had dressed plainly so as not to detract from the bride. Clem stared at her and wanted to ask if she was ill but it would be improper – improper to ask after the welfare of the woman who should be his wife! Was she ailing? Alice had not mentioned anything of the kind, but she had been unusually reticent in mentioning Kerensa of late.

She turned to Clem and smiled lightly under his gaze. She was obviously pleased to see him. 'Hello, Clem, it's good to see you here, and all the family.'

'Hello, Kerensa, it's good to see you too. It's been a long time.' He always called her Kerensa. How could he call her anything else, the girl he had nearly married, the woman he loved?

Kerensa gave a small nod and Matthias thought he

detected regret in that gesture. She moved away and seeing Alice sitting on a bench greeted her, kissed her and sat down beside her. The Trenchard children instantly rushed to their mother like chicks to a broody hen. The six children eyed each other, it was one of the few times they had all been together. Kerensa had not overdressed her children either and apart from the obvious superior quality of their clothes they melted in quite easily with the other children, as was their mother's intention.

As their mothers chatted about the wedding, Kane attached himself to Philip and David. Olivia admired Jessica's blue flounced silk dress, making no mention of its once being one of her own. She retied the new bow Alice had proudly added at the back and was allowed to take Jessica by the hand and lead her across the yard to see the growing foal at the stud. Luke was invited to play with the other boys but refused, going off by himself.

Clem tried to keep Rosie by his side and make sure Matthias was at the other. He glanced often at Kerensa, longing to ask her to dance with him. It seemed such a long, long time ago that they had danced together as two very young betrothed people in love. It hurt and angered him now that it was improper for him even to speak to her unless she spoke first and then only for a few moments. And he was becoming irritated at the inexplicable way Matthias was watching him rather than making eyes at his sister.

Clem put his arm round Rosie and hugged her, hoping she was enjoying the party. She seemed so unhappy these days and had to be coaxed away from the sanctuary of the farmhouse, even to the wedding today. For a brief time she had been different, exhilarated somehow and secretive. The family suspected she was meeting someone and although Clem knew it wasn't Matthias he would have been pleased to see her happy and in love. He knew only too well the painful loneliness of losing the one you loved. If there had indeed been a man in Rosie's life, he was there no longer and his dear sister was miserable, and as Clem looked into the beautiful face of the young woman at his wife's side he knew that she was miserable too.

Kerensa smiled and laughed a lot. She appeared to be enjoying herself and joined in many of the dances and at one point got up to sing with Nathan O'Flynn, who had his own brand of fine Celtic voice, a love song in honour of the bride and groom. But there was not the usual sparkle in her eyes or healthy glow to her cheeks. Although she spoke to many, her expression was far away. It was one he recognised well, it looked back at him if ever he saw himself in the mirror.

Rosie and Matthias seemed at last to be holding a conversation of mutual interest and Clem excused himself to stand alone. His feelings for Kerensa were mixed. He didn't want her to be sad but she was rightfully his and he didn't want her to be happy with the man he hated. He helped himself to a tankard of ale. It was almost knocked out of his hand by a rushing child.

'Hey, hold on there,' he called out good-humouredly, grabbing the child to stop him falling to the ground. 'Oh, 'tis you, young Kane. You're in a hurry.'

Kane, slightly breathless, looked up from his permanently startled-looking brown eyes. He grinned when he realised whom he'd ploughed into. 'Sorry, Clem, I'm playing hide and seek with Philip and David. Where can I hide?' The red-topped head bobbed from side to side, searching up and down the barn, and returned to look hopefully at Clem for suggestions.

Clem liked Kane Pengarron. He had been interested in Kane from the time Kerensa had brought him, as a badly ill-treated infant about to be sold by his terrible father in the marketplace, to live at the manor. News soon after that of Kerensa's first pregnancy had hurt Clem but when the child turned out to be a girl he'd felt rather smug knowing that Oliver Pengarron longed for a son and heir. But, according to Alice, Pengarron had not minded at all that his firstborn was a girl, and the following year when his son was born Clem had harboured an instinctive dislike for the dark-eyed, black-haired child. He was fond of Olivia, so like Kerensa, and having met Kane on various fair days and at Marazion market had become friendly with the boy.

He bent to whisper in Kane's ear. 'If I sit down on a bale of hay you can hide behind me. My boys will never think to find you there.'

'Good idea, Clem,' Kane said enthusiastically.

Philip and David ran into the barn soon afterwards. They searched the faces of the people there and on finding their father ducked in and out of the dancers to reach him. To join in Kane's game, Clem pretended not to notice them but he was quickly forced to.

'Tas, Tas, come outside!' they shouted in unison, tugging at Clem's coat.

'What's up?' Clem said, rising hastily, leaving his tankard on the bale. Kane peeped over from his hiding place.

The Trenchard twins were not the kind of children to play silly practical jokes and from the urgency on their faces there was obviously something amiss. Philip looked at his brother before speaking.

''Tis Master Luke, he's hurting Jessica and won't let her go, she's crying.'

'What!' their father exploded.

'We wanted to fight him, Tas,' David added, 'but Miss Olivia said to fetch someone.'

Kane was now standing on the bale looking straight at Clem. Alice and Kerensa, sensing trouble, moved quickly to the male gathering.

Alice took Clem's arm. 'What's going on, Clem?'

'I'll make him pay!' Clem hissed, pushing off Alice's hand and storming outside.

The twins followed on his heels, leaving Kane, his eyes even more startled, to explain to the two worried mothers the cause of Clem's abrupt departure.

Clem was furious as he ran to the stud stables. Jessica was a tough child used to pitching in with her brothers' squabbles; if she was crying then Luke Pengarron must be really hurting her, and he hated the thought of a true Pengarron even touching his daughter. He found her wailing; the tall, broad-shouldered boy was clutching her by both arms. Olivia was trying to reason with Luke and pull him away. His face red with fury, Clem wrenched Luke away from Jessica and keeping a grip on him by the back of his coat held him up in the air kicking and screaming.

'Let me go, you bloody swine!' Luke screamed in rage.

'I'll thrash the skin off your backside first, you little runt,' Clem snarled, 'terrorising a little maid younger than your self. And mind your language.'

Quick and agile, Kane reached Clem first out of all those rushing from the barn. 'Please, Clem,' he pleaded, tugging at the waistband of Clem's breeches, 'put Luke down, he'll say he's sorry.'

'Sorry! Him!' Clem snorted. 'There's too much of his rotten father in him for that! I'll be the one to make sure he's sorry.'

A crowd was gathering. Alice shouted at Clem to release Luke as Jessica ran to her. Rosie gasped and threw her hands to her face. Kerensa, her face ashen, moved forward to where Clem could clearly see her.

In precise words, she said, 'Please put Luke down, Clem.' Clem made no move and she added purposefully, 'He's my son too.'

Clem sharply dropped his arm, making Luke's feet hit the ground with a thud, but he held on tightly to the boy's coat. He spoke to Kerensa as if they were the only two people there.

'It's hard to think of this child as yours. I see too much of his father in him.'

The music had stopped. All went quiet. Then a voice came through the crisp air like a whiplash.

'Just what the hell do you think you are doing with my son, Trenchard?' Oliver angrily pushed his way through the crowd. 'Release him at once or I'll swear I'll break your neck.'

Glaring at his adversary, Clem opened his fingers slowly and Luke was free. No one dared to move or speak.

Luke straightened his coat then walked haughtily to his father's side.

'Your son,' Clem said harshly, 'your beloved well-brought-up son who should know better but obviously never will was bullying my daughter.'

Oliver shot a hard look at Kerensa. 'Is this true?'

There was no mistaking Kerensa's distress as she nodded and answered quietly, 'I'm afraid it is.'

'I was not!' Luke spoke up angrily. 'We were playing a game and she,' he stabbed a finger in Jessica's direction, 'wouldn't—'

'Be quiet, Luke!' Oliver commanded, fixing his eyes on

256

Clem's face. 'I will deal with my children's misdemeanours, Trenchard. If you ever lay a hand on one of them again I'll not only break your neck but every bone in your body as well.'

'You just be sure your son never comes near my daughter again, not ever,' Clem growled back, 'Or it'll be his neck you'll have to watch out for.'

'Why you—' Oliver sprang forward with clenched fists raised.

'Sir!' Adam Renfree stepped smartly between the two warring men, his elbows out, prodding their ribs. 'Tes Ted's wedding day, sir.'

Clem was ready for a fight and Oliver, in his present state of mind, wanted more than anything to give him one, but Adam's words struck home and the two men reluctantly drew back from each other.

'Take your family home, Trenchard,' Oliver snarled.

'We're not ready to go yet,' Clem returned obstinately.

'You will do as I say!' Oliver exploded. 'See to it, Adam!' It was unthinkable that he should be disobeyed on his own property. With a short but sincere apology to the Trembaths he looked stonily for a moment at his culprit son then stalked off.

'We'll have to leave, Clem,' an acutely embarrassed Alice said from his side. 'For Ted and Lou's sake, not ours.'

'Get the children into the wagon,' Clem told her, only just holding his anger back. 'I'll go find Rosie, she's run off somewhere.' He kissed little Jessica and shooed the disappointed twins after their mother.

Satisfied his employer's orders were to be carried out, Adam gave Clem a reproachful look for disturbing the party then called to the fiddler and other musicians to begin playing again. The crowd of spectators dispersed, eager to get back to the food, drink and dancing, although some were disappointed there wasn't going to be a brawl, reckoning it added to the enjoyment of any social gathering.

Clem was left in the yard with Kerensa and her children. She looked as if she had turned to stone. It was the love he cherished so deeply for her that decided him to leave without further battle.

'Are you all right?' he asked her gently.

Luke glared at him. How dare this farmer speak intimately to his mother and without using her title? He turned to stare at Kerensa to see how she would answer. She merely nodded her head slightly and putting out a hand each to Kane and Olivia she walked away with them to the farmhouse. Luke and Clem were left to scowl at each other.

'You are a very horrid man,' Luke hissed.

'And you are a troublemaker and a spoiled brat,' Clem retorted.

Luke made to go but turned back. 'Are you still in love with my mother?'

Clem reeled, shocked at the question. 'Why do you say that?'

Luke looked at Clem with contempt. 'I know all about it, how my mother left you to marry my father, and all over Trelynne Cove.'

At that moment Clem felt he could hate the son as much as the father. 'Then you,' he said coldly, 'know too much.'

Rosie had run off from the stud, embarrassed and ashamed. She stopped well away from the buildings and put her burning cheeks in her hands. She felt emotionally wrung out. The hatred between the brother she loved and the man she had so very nearly had an affair with left her with a terrible debilitating weakness down to the depths of her

258

soul. It was rapidly growing dark and she wanted to hide for ever in its consuming coldness.

'Rosie?'

It was Matthias. She could not bring herself to turn round and face him.

'There is no need for you to feel badly over what happened,' he said softly.

'How could they behave like that?' she whispered bitterly.

'The enmity between Clem and Sir Oliver goes back a long way.'

'I can understand Clem hating Sir Oliver but why should Sir Oliver dislike Clem so much?' Rosie said harshly. 'He has Kerensa and everything he wants.'

'Fear,' Matthias said simply.

'Fear? But why? Fear of what, for goodness sake?'

'Fear at the back of his mind that Clem could even now take Kerensa back from him.'

Matthias moved in closer behind her and Rosie leaned back to rest her head against his shoulder.

Oliver was mounted on Conomor ready to leave the farm when he was confronted by Alice. Her face was serious and her arms folded in a no-nonsense manner.

'Are you looking for me?' he asked defensively.

'No,' she said tartly. 'Jessica dropped her doll, I'm looking for it. But I'll take the opportunity of having a few words now we're alone and face to face.'

'If you're concerned about Luke I'll make sure he's punished.'

'No, Kerensa will see to that as any good mother would. What I would like to know is what that was all about.'

'I'm sorry if you don't approve, Alice,' he said stiffly, tightening his grip on the reins, 'but I will not allow anyone to treat a child of mine in the manner your husband was employing.'

'You know I'm not talking about the clash between you and Clem,' Alice said stoutly. 'That was only to be expected.'

Oliver jumped down beside her. 'What are you talking about, woman?'

'Don't you "woman" me. We're friends, you and I, Oliver Pengarron, and friends notice things others miss. I mean the way you spoke to Kerensa just then.'

Oliver folded his arms also. 'God damn it, I simply asked her a question, Alice!'

'There's no need to blaspheme either. You spoke to her very harshly and it's not the first time you've done so lately in my hearing. Kerensa is very unhappy, she's tried to hide it from me but I know her too well. I was her maid at the beginning of your marriage, don't forget, I know what you can be like. Please don't get angry with me, but I have to know. Is there some sort of trouble between you and her?'

His sternness died away and he put out a hand and rubbed Alice's arm. 'I wish I could say you're imagining it, Alice, but . . . I wish I could tell you.'

'We've confided in each other before,' she reminded him.

'I know, but this is different, it's something I have to work out by myself, in my own time. Believe me, it's the best way. But I do value your friendship, Alice.'

Alice waited for Oliver to remount, then said, 'Don't be too hard on Kerensa, I beg you, Oliver. I have a feeling she's far from well and couldn't take a lot more upset. Whatever is wrong between you, don't forget that she loves you.'

'I know.'

She watched as he was quickly eaten up by the darkness. She was uneasy and her round face contorted into a deep frown. She had chewed over many times what the reason could be for Kerensa's unhappiness. It was no good talking to Rosie. She was apparently suffering the emotional upheaval of a broken romance and had lost interest in everything, even refusing Beatrice's requests to go over to the manor kitchens and help her with her herbs and potions.

The most obvious reason for Kerensa's unhappiness was that she had discovered Oliver was having an affair. The whole parish had waited expectantly for it to happen. He had never gone long without looking for the favours of a female before he married and women had never stopped throwing themselves at him since. But if Oliver was having, or had had, an affair, Kerensa would be the one showing hostility, not Oliver.

Alice found Jessica's doll lying forlornly on the ground at the scene of the incident, its dress dirtied by someone's careless foot.

'He knows now . . . your father,' she said, rubbing at the dirt with stiff fingers. Clem wasn't blind, he would have seen how things stood between Oliver and Kerensa.

Whatever the trouble was, Alice's worst fears were the same as Matthias's. What would Clem do? She had not asked Matthias the reason for his more frequent visits to Trecath-en Farm but she was certain it had nothing to do with her pining sister-in-law.

After giving Morley and Kenver a brief explanation as to why they were home early, and leaving a subdued Alice to fill in the details, Clem headed out of the farmyard with Charity dutifully at his side. He had a lot to think about. There was enough light from the stars to tramp the familiar track to the bottom of Trecath-en valley and sit under the clump of elm trees at the river's edge.

Kerensa was miserable and now he knew why. Oliver Pengarron had made it plain that at least on his part there was animosity between them. He had not spared her feelings in front of Ted Trembath's wedding guests. He was proud and haughty and Clem despised him for it. His heart ached for Kerensa. Pengarron was a man who could make others suffer. He had better not hurt her, or he'll have me to contend with, Clem vowed angrily.

He gazed up through the still black branches at the winking stars. What had happened? What had changed Oliver Pengarron from a man who openly adored his wife to one who treated her with shameless rudeness in public? There had been no gossip that trouble was brewing. Like Alice, Clem's first assumption was that Oliver was having an affair; it was the easiest thing to believe but Clem grudgingly thought it unlikely.

The stars, silvery and twinkling, gave him no clue. He closed his eyes to dig deeper into his mind, unaware of the gurgling river and intense cold penetrating his bones. If the situation was really bad then Kerensa would turn to him, he was confident of that. It was what he had waited for for eight long years, and he wallowed in the warm, beautiful memories of the times he had held her, comforted her, tenderly kissed her and of the time he had nearly totally possessed her.

Charity, who had been lying across his boots, jumped up at a sudden scurrying sound along the river bank and Clem, disturbed from his memories, opened his eyes and sat up straight. As the bitch sniffed about, Clem thought dolefully that the Pengarrons had probably only had a row like all married folk do. Oliver was a proud man who thought nothing of speaking his mind in public and causing others embarrassment. It was probably no more than that; he was foolish to think of winning Kerensa back. Still, he would look out for her, try to meet her alone, and if she needed him . . .

Kerensa arrived home a long time before Oliver. She suspected he had ridden straight from Ker-an-Mor Farm to Pengarron Point and she would have followed him, intent on a confrontation, but the children were too unsettled to be left. By the time she had helped Cherry to put the children to bed she felt too depressed and weary to face him. She wished despondently that he was not entertaining at home tonight but would stay out all night as he so often did.

Olivia wanted to keep Kerensa in her bedroom, imploring her to read more stories than usual and to look again and again at her paintings. When at last she was coaxed to lie down and be tucked in, Kerensa promised to return a short time later and read her another story if she was still awake.

Kerensa was thankful to have no problems with Kane when she moved on to the room he shared with Luke. Kane was always eager to please her and the moment he saw how fraught she was he settled down, with Bob dozing across the foot of his bed. She did not expect to be so fortunate with Luke and she was not.

He was teeming with unspent energy and frequently interrupted the story Kerensa read, making silly remarks and fidgeting persistently. She was used to his forthright questions made blatantly to shock but she was totally unprepared for the question he threw at her when she thankfully closed the book.

'Mama, did you love Clem Trenchard very much?'

'What? Luke!'

Kane sat up and threw a pillow at his brother. 'Don't talk to Mama about that now, Luke, can't you see she's tired?'

White-faced, Kerensa turned and sank down slowly on Luke's bed. 'How do you know about that, the pair of you?'

'We overheard some people talking in the marketplace so we asked Beatrice about it. We could tell by her reaction it was true.' Luke tried to sound matter-of-fact but he was a little frightened by his mother's colour and reaction and he clutched her hand.

'Yes, Luke, I did love Clem Trenchard,' she replied. 'At one time I was going to marry him.'

'Did you love him more than Father?' Luke sounded vexed.

'No, Luke. I love your father more than anyone else.'

'Even more than Kane and Olivia and me?'

'I love you all as much as your father but in different ways,' Kerensa said, getting a grip on herself and kissing his hot forehead. 'You have nothing to fear where . . . other people are concerned. I'll tell you both, and Olivia, all about the past when the time is right.'

'I don't know how you could love that Clem Trenchard.' Luke's face darkened. 'He's a horrid man, I don't like him.'

Kerensa stroked his hair. 'If you're thinking about what happened this afternoon, my love, don't forget you were being really unkind to his little daughter.'

Kane got out of bed and put his arm round Kerensa's shoulders. She cuddled him, drawing comfort from him. He said firmly to Luke, 'You were wrong to frighten Jessica, Luke. Just think how Papa would have felt if it was one the twins hurting Olivia.'

Luke looked ashamed but warded it off with a rude noise. 'Well, everyone knows that you like that man.'

'Let's forget that now,' Kerensa broke in before her sons quarrelled over Clem. That was the last thing she wanted. 'You bullied a little girl and must take your punishment like a man, Luke. Your father will talk to you tomorrow. Just remember that I love you all and you are the most important things in my life.'

'Unless you have another baby,' Kane said thoughtfully, putting his chin on her shoulder.

Kerensa started. 'If ever that happens then I shall love him as much as I do the rest of you.'

'Or her,' Luke said, losing interest in the whole subject but ensuring he had the last word.

Chapter 18

Polly O'Flynn was putting the finishing touches to Kerensa's hair when Oliver strode ungraciously into the master bedroom. He addressed neither woman and promptly disappeared into his dressing room. When he had washed, shaved and dressed he came back into the room, tall and handsome in clothes of blue, the colour that suited him so well. His waistcoat and breeches were of aquamarine, his dresscoat, lavishly embroidered in gold and black silks, was a deep midnight blue that matched the wide satin ribbon tying back his luxurious hair. Polly had gone and he stood still, irritably surveying Kerensa as she struggled to clasp a crystal necklace.

Three impatient strides and he reached her and all but snatched the necklace from her clumsy fingers. 'You only had to ask me or that woman to do it for you.'

'Polly was needed downstairs and in your present mood you are best not spoken to.'

'What mood?'

Kerensa got up from her dressing table and stepped away but Oliver caught her shoulders and whirled her round, making her shudder. It would have angered her if she had not been so weary.

'What mood?'

'Please, Oliver, you know what I'm talking about. Let's

not argue now. I want this to be a pleasant evening for Ameline's sake. She's going home soon and Martin's sent word that James is coming to supper with him.'

'James Mortreath, eh? This will be entertaining, and Hezekiah has just arrived too.' He smiled without humour; to Kerensa, a dangerous sign.

'What are you planning to do, Oliver?' She scanned his face, afraid of what she would read there. 'You won't be unkind to James, will you?' She wanted to remind him that James Mortreath was his kinsman, even if distantly related, but could say nothing while the existence and death of a much closer one still lay between them.

'Only planning to entertain the fellow, my dear.' There was a trace of maliciousness in his voice. He pulled her close to him. 'Then later . . .'

Kerensa turned her head and his kiss landed on the side of her neck. Gripping her tighter he ran his lips down her neck and along her shoulder. Kerensa tried forcefully to get away. Oliver lifted his head and gave her a small humiliating shake.

'Are you refusing me?'

Chills rose from the base of Kerensa's spine. He was challenging her to say no to his lovemaking and she had sensed of late he was deliberately looking for this – something else to hold against her. It was the one thing she hoped would not change, their moments of the deepest intimacy that no one else could share. She tried to make light of it.

'Of course not but it's really time we were going down. I would like to have a few minutes with Hezekiah before Martin and James arrive.'

* * *

Hezekiah's clothes were as sparkling as his conversation and Kerensa was warmed by his superb wit and interest in the children's welfare. She had always liked Hezekiah. He had always treated her kindly. She found him an intriguing man. Small-boned, over-perfumed and rather effeminate, he appeared to be one of nature's weaklings, but those who knew him sensed his strength and those who sailed with him appreciated his excellent seamanship. He could manoeuvre his ketch *Free Spirit* among the most dangerous rocks and outrun the most determined Revenue cutter.

No one knew much about Hezekiah, not even Oliver. He never talked of the past and skilfully warded off any query on the subject but Kerensa did manage to find out after many years that he was a partner in Oliver and Sir Martin's smuggling enterprises. The evidence had been under her nose all the time but his flamboyant dress and manner were hardly those of an adventurous free-trader.

He cast his deep blue eyes appreciatively over Kerensa's gown. 'I see you have chosen to wear blue like Oliver tonight. How well you complement each other,' he smiled.

'Thank you, Hezekiah.' She smiled back and returned the courtesy. Hezekiah liked to be complimented on his clothes. 'You look more handsome than ever. Sea-green and silver are most definitely your colours.'

'You are too kind.' He made one of his customary bows, pulling delicately at the froth of intricately patterned white lace protruding at his wrists. 'When are we to be graced with the charming company of Miss Ameline?'

'I'll go up and hurry her along.' It was a relief to have an opportunity to leave the winter parlour. Oliver had been making subtly disdainful remarks at her expense, addressing her with exaggerated terms of endearment and causing Hezekiah to cast curious glances at them both.

Hezekiah looked at Oliver. He did not speak but there was a question on his ageless face that Oliver could not ignore.

'What is it, Hezekiah? Do you want another drink?'

Hezekiah held up his sherry glass and swirled the nearly full contents in reply. 'I would like to know what the trouble is between you and Kerensa.'

'It's none of your business,' Oliver said shortly.

'Oh? As serious as that, is it?'

'What does that mean?'

'Serious enough for you to speak to a close friend as you would a disobedient servant.'

Oliver sighed and pulled a wry face. 'I apologise to you, Hezekiah. I've something on my mind.'

'Try taking me into your confidence, it might help,' Hezekiah offered.

Oliver sipped from his sherry glass, his expression thoughtful. Then he spoke as if he didn't want to but felt compelled to. 'It concerns Bartholomew Drannock.'

The other man's eyes flickered with interest. Bartholomew Drannock? The young fisherman whom I brought to your attention? Have you found out something interesting about him?'

'Yes,' Oliver said sharply. 'I have found out . . . learned from questioning the Reverend Ivey that the youth is indeed of Pengarron stock.'

'I see, but that comes as no real surprise to me or to you. Please do go on, Oliver. You have me intrigued.'

Oliver wearily sat down and looked straight at his friend. 'It seems that my father also sired the boy's father, Samuel Drannock, thereby making him my half-brother and Bartholomew and his brothers and sisters my nephews and nieces.'

'And this has upset Kerensa? It wasn't your fault.' Hezekiah frowned. 'It does not fit her character to find exception to this.'

'It is not Kerensa who is upset, Hezekiah. It is I who have not yet come to terms with the revelation.'

'You take issue to having peasants as relatives? Many a gentleman has one or more turn-of-the-blanket in the world to give proof of his virility. No, it does not ring true to you either.'

'You don't know all the facts, Hezekiah.' Oliver drained his crystal glass in one rapid angry movement. 'I have no care if at this moment I'm related to Peter Blake! My chagrin comes from the fact that since the early days of our marriage Kerensa has known and seen fit to keep it from me.'

Hezekiah remembered the deep sadness in the small delicate face a few minutes ago. If the little dandy-like sea captain could feel a modicum of humanity for anyone it was for Kerensa Pengarron.

He said: 'Presumably she had good reason, Oliver. One would be hard pressed to find such a loving and loyal wife as Kerensa.'

'She had no good reason at all!' Oliver slammed his fist down hard on the arm of his chair. 'She is my wife, Hezekiah. I believed we shared everything, knew all there was to know about each other. She knew I'd always cherished the thought of having a family, she realised how lonely I was in the past.'

'I don't quite understand—'

'Samuel Drannock is dead! Drowned at sea on the very day you remarked on his son's likeness to me! I had a brother, all my life I had a brother and now he's dead. A brother and a sister-in-law, Hezekiah, nephews and nieces,

271

who need not have had to live in miserable poverty. I could have done something for them, saw they ate good food, had sufficient clothes on their backs, given the children a good education. If Drannock had not allowed me to set him up as a gentleman I could have at least bought him his own boat. He told Kerensa he would never take anything from me, but who can truly say if he would always have felt that way? What man doesn't want to improve the lot of his family, given the chance? But thanks to the misguided feelings of the Reverend Ivey and my dear wife, Samuel Drannock will never have that chance and I have been denied the chance to know him as my kinsman for ever.'

'What has Bartholomew Drannock to say about this?' Hezekiah asked carefully.

'He doesn't know yet. I cannot bring myself to approach him or his mother right now and haven't made up my mind when or how to.'

'You will inform him, though?'

'Oh yes, there is no doubt of that.'

'And all this accounts for your lack of affection towards Kerensa tonight,' Hezekiah said as though he was talking to himself.

Springing up Oliver paced the floor. 'I shall never forgive her betrayal,' he said heatedly.

'I think betrayal is too strong a word, Oliver,' Hezekiah responded, risking Oliver's wrath. 'Why exactly did Kerensa say nothing to you?'

'She says she was afraid of the way I would take the news,' Oliver replied with a dismissive wave of his hand.

Hezekiah knew he was on dangerous ground but pressed on. 'Do you not think she may have been right? From your reaction now—'

'My reaction, as you call it, is because of her betrayal not because I am related to the family of a poor fisherman!' Oliver snapped. Voices from the great hall saved further angry exclamations. 'Ah, Martin and Mortreath are here at last. When the women are finally ready we will dine and enjoy a good evening's entertainment, I can guarantee you that, Hezekiah. I have lost one relative and gained another but Mortreath in no way measures up to what I desire in a kinsman.'

Oliver left the room to welcome the new arrivals. Hezekiah smiled to himself. He was going to enjoy the evening's 'entertainment' but was James Mortreath? There was another reason for the smile. If there was a chink in the perfect marriage, and if it grew to a chasm, perhaps Kerensa would need a shoulder to cry on . . .

Kerensa had never seen Ameline look so lovely. She was wearing an elegant gown of deep rose silk and a necklace of rubies circled her throat. Peters, her personal maid, had brushed her light-brown hair until it gleamed and arranged it in a simple but fashionable style.

'You will take James's breath away,' Kerensa exclaimed, squeezing her hand. 'Will you give him his answer tonight?'

'I don't think so,' Ameline answered coyly, marvelling herself at her reflection in the full-length mirror.

'Oh, Ameline, the poor man will be distraught.'

'At least my mother won't be here to embarrass either of us. I know I shouldn't say it but I'm rather pleased she and Father were committed to one of Grandmama's soirees tonight.'

'Well then, come on, Miss Beswetherick,' Kerensa laughed, 'let's go downstairs and dazzle the menfolk. We have two apiece tonight.' Something caught Kerensa's eye. 'What's that mark on your neck, Ameline?'

Ameline's hand flew to the blemish in question. 'It's nothing,' she said, blushing fiercely.

'It's unlikely to be an insect bite at this time of year,' Kerensa went on. 'I hope you're not going down with a fever of some kind. Have you any marks elsewhere?'

As she got closer to Ameline the light from the candles was adequate to reveal the cause of the vivid red mark. No insect was responsible. It was obviously made by another's lips. Kerensa's heart jumped and guilt rose to meet it that in her own preoccupations she had taken little notice of Ameline's movements – she had no idea where the girl went on her frequent riding excursions. Could she have been meeting someone?

'I scratched myself,' Ameline would have her believe.

'Oh, I see. What have you been doing with yourself lately? I have been neglecting you, haven't I, and I am sorry, Ameline. I haven't been out riding with you for quite a while.'

'That's perfectly all right, Kerensa, don't concern yourself,' Ameline said quickly. 'I don't expect you to nursemaid me. You have your house and family to care for, not to mention all the people who come begging your help in the parish. I have been content to be on my own and think about my future.'

'Where do you usually ride?' Kerensa asked searchingly. 'I will have to join you on your last outings before you leave.'

'Oh, along the cliff tops mainly, not too close to the edge of course.' Ameline tried to sound offhand while fussing unnecessarily with the floral posy on her gown. 'Sometimes on the outskirts of the oak plantation, other times around the parklands. I have had plenty of time to think. There, I am ready to go down now.'

Kerensa stood in front of the bedroom door so Ameline could not escape her questions. 'Do you ever go to Trelynne Cove?'

Ameline hesitated for just a moment.

'Occasionally.'

'And when you're out do you ever see anyone, anyone at all?'

'I've seen the gamekeeper once or twice, and the farmhands of course.'

'Anyone else?' Kerensa was not going to give up.

Ameline was no good at keeping secrets. 'There was a young fisherman in the cove . . .'

'That would be Bartholomew Drannock,' Kerensa said, watching for Ameline's reaction.

Her face lit up to a gentle beauty as she blushed a deeper red. 'I think that is what he said his name was. He told me you have given him your permission to be there.'

'That's right, I did. What did you think of him? He's rather handsome, isn't he?'

'Is he?' Ameline returned to her dressing table, picked up a powder puff and dabbed at her burning face.

Knots churned in Kerensa's stomach. This was something more to add to her worries. How was she going to get through this evening – and what lay beyond it? 'Hurry up, Ameline,' she said like a bossy mother, 'or the men will see in the New Year without us.'

Kerensa had not mentioned to Ameline that the fourth man downstairs was Hezekiah Solomon and a shock like an ice floe invaded her as he came forward and proffered an exquisitely manicured white hand. He bowed with a flourish. 'A pleasure of infinite proportions to see you again, Miss Ameline.'

'Good evening, Captain Solomon,' she replied tightly, moving quickly on to James Mortreath who was already tugging at his neckcloth as if he was choking. 'James,' she had not called him James before but hoped the intimacy would deflect the small frightening sea captain's interest away from her, 'how lovely to have your company tonight.'

'Miss – Ameline,' James said, his face glowing with delight that she had addressed him in such a friendly, forthright way. 'I would—'

He was rudely interrupted by Sir Martin. 'Damn me, Mortreath, move along, will you? I want to give my favourite granddaughter a great big hug.'

With that done he alighted on Kerensa and did the same. 'Well, my little pretty one, you look just as you always do, ravishing and good enough to eat. I do declare though, you feel a little more cuddly. Why's that I wonder?'

Kerensa shot a quick look at Oliver but thankfully he was talking to Hezekiah and Ameline, although much to her annoyance pointedly ignoring James.

'It's time to eat, Martin,' she said, knowing his interest in good food would out-rival anything else on his mind.

The massive, rectangular oak table in the main dining room was polished until the Carolean candelabras, the cutlery, the bowls of seasonal floral decorations and the many drinking glasses could be clearly seen reflected along its length. Oliver had ordered Polly to set the table from end to end. It seemed ridiculous to Kerensa to have six people spread out so far apart but it would mean risking a biting remark and humiliation from Oliver if she recommended the company be seated closer together.

Only Sir Martin ate generous quantities of the delicious foodstuffs painstakingly prepared by Ruth and Esther King. Kerensa had hardly any appetite and ate nothing after the baked trout. James's throat was too constricted to swallow and he suffered purgatory under Oliver's constant and thinly veiled attacks on him. Unable to control the shake in his hands he dropped cranberry sauce on his neckcloth and breeches. He choked on each apology and his tortured mind swung between trying to reason out why his host held such an illogical dislike for him, the agony of wanting to get Ameline alone, and the fear that after all his painful weeks of waiting, not to mention having to endure this dreadful evening, she would turn him down.

Ameline fidgeted and picked at her food. Hezekiah was sitting next to her, although a long way away due to the extent of the table's length, and his presence spoiled the meal for her. Tonight she had wanted to exert the power of being a woman with more than one man interested in her over James Mortreath. She did not intend to be unkind, just to enjoy her feminine desirability, but Hezekiah Solomon had robbed her of her confidence.

Hezekiah never ate much and only took minute helpings of the food. But he kept asking Ameline to pass the condiments, the sauces, the custards, the nuts and fruit, and while he did not actually engage her in conversation he kept drawing her in by including her in many of his low glances.

Kerensa also came into the span of his attention. She returned his every smile while laughing diplomatically at Sir Martin's bawdy jokes and doing her best to ease James's discomfort by warding off Oliver's open sarcasm. Oliver had no interest in eating but gave much attention to the excellent variety of wines from his well-stocked cellar.

At the end of the meal he bid the gentleman rise to toast the King and Queen. He remained on his feet while his guests reseated themselves and drank to everything and everyone who came into his mind. He even started on national events.

'This year we saw crowned a new king, the third in succession, although not quite father and son, to be called George. At the beginning of June the King was betrothed to Princess Charlotte of Mecklenburg-Strelitz, a dainty, pale-skinned lady of seventeen years – the same age my dear Kerensa was when I took her to wife.'

Everyone looked at Kerensa and murmured little nothings with accompanying smiles but she had the awful feeling she was being put up for public examination. Heads turned back expectantly to Oliver.

'The marriage was solemnised exactly three months later and a fortnight after came the coronation which Sir Martin and I attended.'

'Oh, I do wish I had been there,' Ameline interjected. 'It is said the dear Queen's tiara and train for the wedding were so heavy—' She stopped short, not because of the impatient sigh cast by Oliver but because she had brought herself under Hezekiah's disconcerting gaze again.

Oliver unnecessarily cleared his throat and Ameline looked meekly at her hands. Kerensa would have liked to have got up and dug him in the ribs. James wished he had the courage to remonstrate with him – and ask him to hurry along and finish. Hezekiah smiled graciously at Kerensa, as if he wanted to give her moral support, then turned his eyes back to Ameline. Sir Martin, oblivious of all the tension, started eating again.

'The coronation was a muddled rather unenjoyable affair, with people rushing off to fetch – of all the things to forget – the chairs of state,' Oliver continued. 'The banquet, because there was insufficient light in the hall, was eaten in semi-darkness, and,' he looked severely at

278

Kerensa, 'I do hate important things being kept in the dark.'

Kerensa's insides froze but she kept her wits together and smiled back at him with all the calm and warmth she could muster. Again came that look of understanding from Hezekiah and she took refuge by keeping eye contact with him.

Oliver suddenly seemed impatient with what he was saying and quickly rattled off his next words.

'The King apparently did not marry the lady of his own choice, a certain lady of the court and quite eligible for a royal match. But he bowed to duty. As we all must. As we all ought to! But at least the marriage, although dull, is said to be a happy one – and something must be said for that!'

Kerensa had heard something about the King herself. That he was a devoutly religious man and kindly to his wife and probably wouldn't approve of her husband's present behaviour.

'The colonial war we've been engaged in on land in Germany and on the ocean with objectives in Asia and America I'm delighted to report is going well for us. We're running down France's navy and have taken a station off that country at Pondicherry. It seems to me there is little risk of our own country being invaded, as some people fear. I must say I envy all those fighting for King and country!'

As if he had run out of steam Oliver sat down but before anyone could say a word he resumed his speech. Kerensa knew he had the intention of keeping them seated at the table for as long as it suited him. After remarking that the nation was becoming increasingly industrialised he moved on to topics closer to home. He proposed a toast to the members of the parish of Perranbarvah who had died in the last year.

'We saw the demise of forty-eight inhabitants in all, sadly not many through the natural causes of old age. Many died as the result of a fishing boat tragedy,' he looked at Kerensa with hostile eyes, 'a most painful occurrence. Then there was the mine accident, in which many were lost, a case of blood poisoning, two women lost in childbed, five children lost through the measles, a fall by a roof thatcher, the drowning of a swimmer and a suspected case of murder through suffocation. Other local events of tragedy include the foundering of two ships in Mount's Bay with the loss of all hands . . .'

Kerensa's face was flushed and she signalled to Polly, who was clearing away dishes from the sideboard, to fetch her a fan. When the fan was in her hands and put rigorously to use Sir Martin motioned Polly to place the still laden food dishes around him so he could partake of a second supper.

'. . . A storm lashed the coast on the night of January the thirty-first, giving the year its violent start, and Martha Trewint was delivered of quads at the same moment the thatched roof of her cottage was torn off.' Would Oliver never finish? James wondered desperately. 'The infants all survived and were aptly named Tempest, Gale, Blaze and Glory. Peter Blake's new residence was completed and the family moved in, but he is still an outcast of the gentry and deservedly so. No one was brought to book for free-trading despite one of its busiest years. The Reverend Ivey baptised twenty-four infants and conducted eleven marriages but no one in the parish was confirmed. Heather Bawden disappeared, Mrs Tregonning announced her intention of retiring from Reverend Ivey's employ to live with her widowed cousin at Mousehole . . .'

Oliver went on and on and Kerensa thought she would

either be sick or faint. Hezekiah saved the day by plunging in on a pause.

'And of course we remember Martin on celebrating his three score and ten and I would like to take the liberty of toasting your health, Oliver, and that of Kerensa, our beautiful and perfect hostess tonight, and good health, much wealth and prosperity to the future Pengarron generation.'

Glasses were sipped from, 'hear hears' were said, and after a murmured 'thank you' Oliver finally shut up. Sir Martin noisily picked his teeth and looked about for something to spit in.

Afraid that Oliver would start all over again, Kerensa got up quickly, desperate to get away into a cooler, less hostile atmosphere, and invited Ameline to join her in the comfort of the winter parlour. She avoided going near Oliver as the gentlemen rose to see the ladies from the table, because at that moment she wanted to slap his face with all her might.

James was distressed enough to blurt out, improper or not, another invitation to Ameline to converse with him somewhere alone. Together, Kerensa and Ameline looked at Sir Martin for approval and both did not bother to suppress sighs of relief when he nodded from a bowl of cold egg and nutmeg custard. Kerensa showed the couple into her sitting room and fled to the children's bedroom.

Ameline was so relieved to be out of sight of Hezekiah and the range of his overpowering colognes she even shut the door after Kerensa.

'Would you mind if I loosened my neckcloth for a few moments, Ameline?' James said, afraid he would choke if he did not.

'Please do, Mr Mortreath, that was the most unpleasant meal table I have ever sat at. I can understand you becoming a little overheated.' Then in two understatements she said, 'Sir Oliver has been in a strange mood all evening and Captain Solomon has a disconcerting way of staring at people.'

James was very disappointed with her 'Mr Mortreath'. 'I rather thought it was James now.'

'Oh, yes . . . James . . .'

She left it to him to proceed and James, who had had enough of being bludgeoned for the evening, decided to get straight to the point.

'Have you made up your mind whether to accept or reject my marriage proposal, Ameline?'

Ameline walked to the window, twisting a ring on her finger, then paced back to stand in front of the fireplace. James's eyes shone hopefully as he followed her path but he had missed her agitated hands.

'No,' she said firmly. 'I beg your forgiveness, James, I need a little more time . . . to be sure of something . . .'

'How much more time? Days, weeks, months?' James could not hide his despair.

'Only a few more days.' Ameline smiled to lift his spirits. 'I am to leave the manor shortly. When I arrive home I promise I will have your answer.'

A little later the new year of 1762 was seen in with little ceremony. Only Sir Martin and Hezekiah Solomon enjoyed the celebration and felt that the year held any promise. Kerensa and Ameline cringed at Oliver's thinly disguised fury when James declined to play cards. Kerensa had never learnt to play and Ameline was poor at it, which meant there was no fourth player to make up the table. James was wretched and greatly desired to return to Marazion where he was to stay the night with Sir Martin. But the elderly baronet was just warming up to the occasion and after yet more food and brandy he entertained them with accounts of all the New Year parties he could remember. Ameline excused herself an hour later and scurried away, escaping the ordeal at last. Kerensa would have done the same but she felt sorry for James in his misery and she stayed down to chat quietly with him. She knew that if only Ameline had accepted him, nothing else Oliver could have thrown at him tonight would have mattered.

When Sir Martin's carriage finally left with James and Hezekiah who wanted to catch the morning tide, Kerensa hoped that Oliver would stay downstairs for a nightcap and she could feign sleep when he came to bed. But he climbed the stairs with her, step by step, and stayed at her side as she made a last check on the sleeping children. He did not bother to use his dressing room; pulling off his clothes and shoes he threw them in a careless heap on the bedroom floor. Kerensa joined him in bed, keeping to the edge while wearily brushing her hair.

'Have you decided how Luke is to be punished?' she asked cautiously.

Oliver looked at her in surprise. 'I took it for granted you would have seen to that when you arrived home after the wedding.'

Kerensa felt tears pricking behind her eyes. If he took her to task with his cruel tongue over this then nothing would stop them. 'I . . . I wasn't sure what to do. I thought perhaps you wanted to deal with it yourself.'

'I suppose we ought not be too lenient with the little fellow this time,' Oliver said, his tone thankfully genial. 'It has never been a tradition of the Pengarrons to torment little girls.'

'What will you do?'

'I've told Luke and Kane they can have a race for the

283

ownership of the black foal. He can be confined to the gardens for a week. The restraint will be hard for him.' Oliver laughed heartily. 'It's difficult to believe he's so young at times, only two years older than that little sweeting Jessica Trenchard.'

'Yes, Jessica is a sweet child, I wish I had more opportunity to see her.' A thought occurred to Kerensa. 'Doesn't Olivia wish to have the foal?'

He was immediately vexed. 'Do you think I would leave my little girl out of anything? I asked Olivia if she wanted to take part in the race and she very firmly said she did not. She's too attached to Gipsy, her own pony, and is happy for Luke and Kane to fight it out between themselves, so to speak.'

'When will they have the race?' Kerensa asked, laying aside the brush and burying herself under the bedcovers, hoping Oliver would take the hint and allow her to go straight to sleep.

'When the foal is trained and ready to be ridden will be soon enough.' Oliver abruptly changed tack. 'Why are you so far away from me?' He leaned across the bed and pulled her into his arms. She stiffened, but surprisingly he did not take exception to this. 'You're very tired, aren't you? It doesn't matter, there's always another time.'

She expected him to let her go, to turn his back or leave the bedroom. But he held her, very gently, nothing more. And it gave her hope.

Chapter 19

Kerensa awoke to find herself alone. Her hopes that Oliver at last saw her in a better light were dashed by his sulky face over the breakfast table and his surly response to her every remark. She was further dismayed to learn he intended to spend all day at home.

He bluntly refused to ride with Adam Renfree to Ker-an-Mor Farm and look into the urgent problem of the theft of several sacks of winter feed. He dealt swiftly with Luke's noisy demand that he watch him and Kane practise the race for the foal by telling his errant son that his punishment for his misdeed the day before meant he was not to leave the grounds of the house and was in no position to make demands. Luke threw a tantrum. Oliver spanked him and carried him screaming upstairs to his room where he was to remain until lunchtime and be denied any company in his confinement. Then Oliver went straight back to Kerensa's side.

Everywhere she went he was on her heels. In the kitchen, out in the gardens and even in her sitting room as she worked on a piece of delicate embroidery on a petticoat for Olivia.

'Tes like 'e's afeared to let 'ee out of 'is sight,' Beatrice rasped.

And always he stared at her, hardly speaking. Sometimes

a hard accusing stare, then softening, and his great dark eyes looked as if they longed to tell her something.

At length she could bear it no longer. Throwing down her needlework, she said abruptly, 'I feel restless. I think I'll go for a long ride.'

'I'll come with you,' he said. 'With Ameline lying abed you will be glad of the company.'

'It's all right,' Kerensa muttered. 'You must have something more important to do.'

'There is nothing else that I want to do – unless you would like to come upstairs with me,' he said dangerously.

'No!' Kerensa's snap was out before she knew it and she put a hand to her mouth. She was out of her depth again; Oliver was beginning to succeed in totally undermining her.

'Why?' he growled. 'Don't you want me today either?'

'It's not that,' she choked, her words forming too quickly, forcing her to clear her throat. 'You know I always enjoy us being together. I simply don't want to now. I . . . I feel I must have some fresh air.'

'You change and get ready,' he ordered tersely. 'I'll get Jack to saddle up.'

A tap on the door was followed by the appearance of Polly. 'Pardon me, m'lady, m'lord. The Reverend Ivey is here to see you, sir.'

Kerensa did not wait for Oliver to finish the business the Reverend Ivey had with him. She set off immediately for Perranbarvah.

Bartholomew Drannock ambled down the last stretch of the steep hill that led to Perranbarvah's little fishing harbour and slowly made his way towards two tall fishermen who, like many others, were seeing to the maintenance of their boats.

Paul King saw him and called to his brother across the boat. 'Here he comes at last, Matt!'

'Reckon I could've gone to Marazion and back twenty-odd times in the time it's took he,' said Matthew King, looking up from the length of sail he was scrutinising for holes or tears, a grin on his broad, whiskered face.

Bartholomew was within earshot but he was so wrapped up in his own thoughts he was oblivious of the banter.

'I believe his mind's on some maid or other,' jested Matthew, his giant frame rocking with laughter.

Bartholomew's two younger brothers, Charles and Jack, on their way to help with the work on the lugger after selling dead fish for manure, filed in behind him, snickering. But Bartholomew did not hear them either.

'It'll take some maid to catch he, I d'reckon,' Paul bawled out, signalling to Charles and Jack to join in the fun. 'Be easier to land a two-hundred-pound shark with a pilchard.'

'What?' Bartholomew said dazedly, coming out of his trance.

'Tes a maid all right,' Dan Laity, a neighbour and cousin to the Kings threw in. 'Can't 'ee see the starry-eyed look on his face?'

Bartholomew swelled up and grinned. He was proud of his prowess with the females and his reputation as the local cock of the walk among the fishermen. His brothers were proud of him too. Charles at eleven years old was beginning to understand the true meaning of the jests and innuendoes that passed around the moored boats when the womenfolk were not around and listened carefully, telling Jack what he

287

thought they meant. Jack, nearing ten years, was more interested in play and bird watching.

'Good, was she, boy?' Paul shouted down from the boat.

'Let me put it this way.' Bartholomew breathed in a lungful of the sharp salty air and looked round at the expectant faces. He toyed with the idea of launching into a lurid account of a past conquest, but mindful of the respect owed to the older and religious fishermen and the presence of his younger brothers, he disappointed the indecently minded minority by saying simply, 'Yes.'

Amid a variety of laughs and murmurs the men returned to their work. Bartholomew, still grinning broadly, leapt aboard the *Young Maid*. He had been to Marazion to buy supplies from a ship's chandler and had used the two-mile walk there and back to think deeply.

The King brothers had been correct in their playful assumption that he'd been thinking of a 'maid' but they would never have guessed at Ameline Beswetherick.

Bartholomew put the packages containing candles, length of rope, pot of pitch and block of fish salt down in the lugger and looked about for a bundle of horsehair brushes. It was now his job to give the *Young Maid* a fresh coat of pitch and after that he, Matthew and Paul would launch their rowing boat and indulge in some free-trading. After that again he would walk to the outskirts of the manor's parklands, and there underneath a sycamore tree he would leave two marbled pebbles, a sign to Ameline that he would meet her in Trelynne Cove in two days' time.

Bartholomew had had no success in gaining any information from Ameline to fuel his suspicion that there was Pengarron blood in his family. He had soon given up this course. She was unwilling to talk about the Pengarrons or their history. She didn't speak much about any other subject either and he concluded that she knew little of life unless it concerned how to dress, how to act and react in genteel society, and how one day to be mistress of her own household.

He had warmed to the girl during their meetings in Trelynne Cove. With all the pretensions of her class put aside after their first meeting he discovered an awkward and shy, yet quite intelligent, caring being. It was a long time before he had put his arms about her and held her close, and he did so many times before her natural rigidity gave way and he felt her soft feminine body as it really was. It was only on their last meeting, three days ago, that he had actually kissed her. He had not taken any liberties but had asked her if he might do so. They were sitting side by side on her pony's blanket on the very same boulder of black granite where he had sat with Kerensa the summer before.

He kept the first kiss short and simple, barely touching her lips. Then she turned her head away again. Bartholomew waited patiently. Every time they had met he had reassured her she was not to worry about them being seen. As a fisherman he lived by his senses as much as by brute strength and fortitude. If anyone was about he was sure he would know and he knew Trelynne Cove well enough to be able to disappear rapidly among the rocks.

After what he judged was a suitable length of time he said softly. 'Am I to be satisfied with just one kiss, Ameline?'

He gently took her face in both hands and turned it to him and kissed her as before, slightly increasing the light pressure of his full sensuous mouth until he felt a tenuous response. It was delicious and he wanted more. He hadn't meant to mark Ameline's neck, to leave evidence of their tender, innocent passion. It horrified him. It was so inappropriate on this girl's slim white neck. He had decided he would never attempt to seduce her, he liked her too much to take advantage of her. Ameline was blissfully happy. He knew she found their meetings exciting and romantic. Was she hoping things would develop in some way?

They had been tender, special moments, those last ones in the little cove, nothing like he had expected or experienced before. Bartholomew could not get them out of his mind and he wondered deep in his heart how he would feel when that quiet, well-bred young lady could meet him no longer. They had arranged to meet one more time before she left to return to Tolwithrick.

'You got someone coming to see 'ee, boy,' Matthew called out as Bartholomew bent his long legs to apply the first stroke of pitch to the bottom of the lugger. ''Tes a lady.'

'What!' he exclaimed, banging his shoulder on the hull of the boat as he sprang up and splashing pitch on the pebbly ground. He was shocked to think Ameline had actually come down into the fishing village to see him. It wasn't her, however. Dropping the brush and rubbing his hands on his breeches he walked rapidly to meet Kerensa.

'Have you come to see Mother again?' he asked, full of curiosity, then glancing at the other fishermen dotted around them, 'Or someone else?'

'No, it's you I want to speak to, Bartholomew,' Kerensa informed him. 'Can we go somewhere?'

'Yes, of course.' Bartholomew was quietly delighted. He was always pleased to be in Kerensa's company and he felt important to be singled out for a private discussion with her. The ordinary folk of the parish had long stopped thinking of Kerensa as 'the little maid from Trelynne

Cove'; they held her in as much esteem as they would a lady of genteel birth.

They drew aside from the curious fishermen and walked over the crunching pebbles of the beach with a stinging salty wind straining at their faces.

Kerensa looked at him critically. Because he so much resembled Oliver she felt even angrier over her suspicions that he'd been dallying with Ameline. She went straight in on the attack, her voice like sharded glass. 'Have you been down to Trelynne Cove of late?'

He frowned, he was puzzled but became immediately defensive. 'Yes, you said it was all right. Have I done something wrong?'

'Yes, I rather think you have. Have you met a young lady there? A young lady staying at the manor house, Miss Ameline Beswetherick?'

His delight at seeing Kerensa died. 'I've met her once or twice. Why? Has she made a complaint about me being there? Is that what this is all about?'

The water in the bay was coloured in soft greens and blues. It lapped calmly onto the shore in slow, majestic sweeps of lightly frothing waves, as though it was taking care to disturb as few of the smooth dull pebbles as possible. But Kerensa knew it was not going to stay gentle and lazy for much longer. There was a hint of the sweep and swell getting stronger, the waters whipping out a deeper dip a few feet down the shoreline and making a longer slope of the beach. She took her eyes from the sea and stared at the uncertain youth.

'Why are you so agitated, Bartholomew?'

'I'm not!' he said crossly.

'You are,' Kerensa corrected him sternly, 'and it only serves to convince me that certain suspicions I have about you are true.'

'What suspicions?' he demanded, kicking at the pebbles. 'I haven't been landing contraband in there. Is that what she's been saying?'

'Last night I noticed a mark on Ameline's neck, the kind of mark made by lips in contact with the flesh. Many things lead me to believe you are responsible for making that mark. I know of your reputation with women and I don't give a damn about what you do with others but Ameline is my guest, she's my responsibility while she's under my roof. She's very young for her age and innocent of what experienced men like you can do to her. I want you to leave her alone.'

Bartholomew hated to be told what to do. Adopting the Pengarron stance of hands on hips he said angrily, 'And what if I don't choose to?'

'So you don't deny it was you?'

'No, why should I? I haven't done anything to her that she didn't want me to. If she wants to meet me I consider it none of your damned business!'

Kerensa was furious. All the hurt and frustration she had suffered at Oliver's cruel behaviour broke to the surface and found an outlet in lashing the youth before her.

'Well, I'm making it my business whether you like it or not! I will make sure you don't have the chance to see her again or do anything else to her.'

His dark eyes flashed. 'If I want her I'll take her and you won't be able to do a thing about it!'

'Don't you be so sure about that, Bartholomew Drannock! Ameline will listen to me and there are other steps I can take to stop her from seeing you, I can assure you of that.'

'Like telling Sir Oliver, I suppose,' he taunted, his mouth curling to a snarl.

'I don't need to do that, I can assure you of that too!'

'I don't think you really do believe you can stop me and Ameline meeting. I think you're bluffing.' He lowered his head and spoke straight at her. 'Of course, if you want to make sure of it, you can always take her place.'

Kerensa's hand flew sharply across his cheek. 'I should have you whipped for that!'

Bartholomew's head was hurled sideways but he turned straight back to meet the rage in her face with a supercilious smile. 'Do it again,' he said, between his teeth. 'I like it.'

Kerensa shrieked. She slapped his other cheek with all her might. Then beating her fists against his chest she pushed him over heavily on to the shingle. Before he could recover from the shock she wrenched his head back by a vicious handful of his long black hair.

'It's time you grew up, young man! You're not half as unlikeable as you would have people believe. I can see straight through you. You're trying to emulate Sir Oliver but you're making a very poor job of it. Those who know him will tell you you're no match for him. He had qualities at half your age you can't even dream of. It's time you stopped playing the brave young hero and looked after your mother and your brothers and sisters properly. I forbid you to set foot on Pengarron land again until you can at least try to be truly like its present owner!'

When it was over Kerensa was out of breath. She let go of Bartholomew's hair; the scrap of red sailcloth that held it back was in her hand. He let his head fall forward, unable to look her in the eye. Kerensa moved away from him, her chest heaving and tears searing her eyes.

The tide was on its way in, the waves sweeping and lifting the shingle towards her feet. Kerensa could not stop shivering. Tears gathered at her eyes but refused to give way and bring relief. The wind tugged at her hat and she swept it off and pulled at the tip of its one lone decorative feather. She stood still for several long moments, unaware that Bartholomew had come to stand beside her until he gently nudged her arm.

'I didn't know you had such a hot temper,' he said. 'That was quite a speech.'

'What?' she said numbly. 'Oh . . . I surprised myself.'

'You're very loyal to Sir Oliver.' His eyes were set grimly on a distant pinnacle of rock under the cliff face just above sea level.

'Yes.'

'There's something wrong, isn't there? You're not just angry with me.'

'Why do you say that?'

'Well, you're right about me, although I hate to admit it. It is time I took stock of myself and looked after Mother and the young'uns. I was extremely rude to you and deserved what I received in return, but there must be another reason for you getting in such a rage.'

Kerensa did not speak, words would not form inside her head.

'You can't talk about it . . . I'm very sorry. If there's anything I can do to help . . . You've been so good to me and my family.'

She managed a barely audible, 'Thank you,' then said, 'You're frightened, aren't you, Bartholomew?'

He took a long time to answer. 'Yes. My mother is dying before my eyes and I don't know how I'm going to cope with Charles, Jack and Cordelia after she's gone. I feel so helpless. You seem to know me so well, better than anyone apart from my mother and she can't help me.'

'Bartholomew.' Kerensa reached out and slipped her

small cold hand inside his and felt the gentle response of his warm calloused skin. 'Would you let me help you? If you like we could do it secretly, no one need know except us. I have a bit of money put by and I will never need it. Forget your pride and let me help you for your own sake as much as for Jenifer and the children.'

He looked at her uncertainly and Kerensa went on quietly but earnestly, 'I don't believe any of us have the right to refuse help on behalf of others if it means only hardship, suffering and poverty for them. It's the way I felt about Samuel all those years ago. Say yes, Bartholomew, I beg you. There, I haven't so much pride that I can't beg. Let me take away the worst of your worries for you.' She handed him the piece of sailcloth. 'What do you say?'

He tied back his hair, then said, 'Thank you. There is nothing else I can say.'

Kerensa found herself in Marazion. After the emotional meeting with Bartholomew she could not bear to ride home. If Oliver was finished with the Reverend Ivey and had ridden after her he was more likely to seek her out on the cliff rides they used to enjoy together, or at Trelynne Cove. So she urged Kernick on to the market town hoping he would not turn up there.

Leaving Kernick with Ned Angove, the blacksmith, she meandered down the long street, hoping to be anonymous among the people. It had grown very cold and with her cloak pulled in tight and her head bowed she hoped no one would recognise her. There was no market today and few people were about but she was stopped by Sarah Harrt, the coroner's wife, who subjected her to an unwelcome twenty minutes of useless gossip. She also met Rosina Blake rushing home out of the cold with Simon Peter. Rosina was very concerned about Kerensa, who looked unwell, and implored her to go with her and her son to the rooms they still kept for convenient use over the shoemaker's. But Kerensa firmly declined a dish of tea by the fire and Rosina reluctantly bid her a blessed New Year and went on her way.

Kerensa wandered in and out of the shops and for no particular reason bought a half-dozen yeast buns in a baker's shop. As she left the shop a spit of freezing rain began to fall and as it gained momentum people disappeared as if by magic. Kerensa hugged her bag of buns under her cloak and ran over the increasingly muddy ground on her way to collect Kernick. It would be wonderfully warm in the smithy and she intended to ask Ned for a secluded corner to take refuge in until the rain stopped. Ned's wife continually presented him with huge mugs of steaming hot black tea and Kerensa saw a cosy picture of herself drinking tea with them while sharing the yeast buns. Perhaps it would be just the thing to warm her soul and give her strength to face Oliver again.

She rounded the corner of the Commercial Inn and was brought to a jarring halt. A cold blast of terror coursed through her veins. A filthy, ugly man was barring her progress, a man she had hoped she would never see again for the rest of her life.

'What are you doing here?' she gasped.

'Thought t'ave seen the last of me, did 'ee, pretty lady?'

'Get out of my way!' Kerensa screamed, fighting to control her trembling.

'Now that's no way to speak to an' ol' friend, me 'an'some,' the man grinned.

'Friend! If my husband knew you were here he would probably kill you!'

'Now that's not very nice of 'ee, sweet'eart, an' you oughta be nice to me.'

Kerensa whirled round and stormed off the way she had come, her face white with shock.

''Ow's that son of mine?' the man called after her with a malicious laugh.

She froze. He tramped round and faced her. 'Deaf, are 'ee? 'Ow's my little boy keepin'?'

'What do you care, you vile creature!' Kerensa hurled at him, shaking with fear, anger and disgust.

''E's my son, ain't 'e?'

'No! Kane is my son, mine and Sir Oliver's. You signed a legal document to that effect and didn't even say goodbye to him, remember? How dare you come here now! Don't you dare to ever come near him!'

Kane's sailor father put his head on one side and rubbed at the wet matted mess of his beard with his finger and thumb. Water was dripping off his greasy bald head and making him squint. You are hideous, thought Kerensa fleetingly.

'I can't really say I want to see the little bleeder,' the sailor said, a tone of menace coming into his voice, 'but'll cost 'ee plenty to keep me away from un. I bet e's all well set up, livin' like a little lord in the manor house. Be a bit of a bleddy fright fer un to see 'is real father, don't 'ee think, my pretty?'

Kerensa kept her head held high. 'Kane knows his origins, you can't hurt him that way, you wretched beast.'

'Oh, can't I now? Are 'ee sure about that? If yer thinks of me as a vile creature an' wretched beast, what will 'e think, eh? What will yer other young'uns think? Bit diff'rent to the 'an'some Sir Oliver, ain't I? An' who knows, mebbe the boy might fancy life at sea, seein' the world an' that, eh?'

Kerensa fully understood the thinly veiled threat. 'All right, you despicable swine, what is it you want?' she got out, as though she was being strangled.

'Well now, let me see. A pretty lady like yerself would be most enjoyable in the sack.' He sniggered at her violent shudder. 'Not partial to the idea, eh? Don't 'ee find me a fine figure of a man, then? Or do 'ee want to keep it all fer Sir Oliver? No, a nice bit of money is what I want, then I can buy meself the favours of the local 'ores an' 'ave a drop o' drink.'

'How much?' she asked, unable to conceal her contempt.

'Reckon my silence is worth at least . . . five 'undred guineas.'

'What? Don't be so foolish! I can't get hold of that kind of money. If I asked my husband for it he would want to know what it was for, he'd come after you and you'd be in more trouble than you've ever dreamed of.'

The sailor's ugly face fell and he swore heartily. 'Fair 'nough. I'll take what you've got in your purse fer now and you can bring me fifty guineas 'ere tomorrow. Don't 'ee tell me you can't manage that,' he scowled.

Kerensa's heart gave a panicky jerk. Fifty guineas would halve the amount she wanted to give to Bartholomew. 'Here!' she shouted, throwing her purse at his feet. 'There are two sovereigns in there. I'll bring as much as I can tomorrow, here, where we're standing now. I'm not meeting you in an alleyway, it will have to be out in the open. It had better be the last time I hear from you or I promise I will tell my husband and you can face the consequences!'

She darted forward to get away from him but the sailor snatched the bag of buns out of her hands. This was the final insult. With her whole world seemingly crashing down around her and her brutalised emotions refusing to give

298

vent in tears she ran blindly to the blacksmith's shop. A scream tore from her heart as a hand on her arm pulled her into a doorway.

Chapter 20

'It's all right, Kerensa, it's me.'

'Oh, Clem, Clem!'

And then suddenly she was crying. She threw herself into his arms and sobbed wretched tears. She clung to him, clawing at his coat, her body heaving as all the fears, frustrations and pain she had endured for so long swelled up and flowed through her, to rip out at the surface in scalding bitter-sweet tears.

Clem held her very close. 'What is it, my precious love,' he murmured soothingly, slipping back easily into terms of endearment for her.

'Oh, Clem, hold me, please don't let me go,' she sobbed, her words muffled in his coat.

'I'll hold you for ever if you want me to, my love,' he said tenderly, raising her face and smoothing her hair from her wet eyes. 'But we can't stay here in this doorway, someone might see us. An acquaintance of mine lives here and is away visiting his folk at Lamorna. I've been looking in on the place for him. Let's go inside.'

Clem had been about to leave for home when he saw Kerensa running wildly through the rain. He unlocked the solid wooden door again, ushered her into a gloomy room, then looked up and down the road to see if anyone was watching.

'I don't think anyone saw us,' he said. Without a moment's hesitation he took Kerensa back in his arms and rocked her slowly in a natural rhythm until she had grown quite calm.

Her frightened eyes had taken in some aspects of the small square room. The ceiling was low, barely above Clem's head. Ragged mats were on the floor and a loose window creaked in the wind. There was a strong smell of dampness and camphor oil. On the mantelshelf was a row of pottery figures, one had an ugly leering face which reminded Kerensa of the sailor. She turned quickly away, pressing closer to Clem and finding comfort in his familiar lean body.

'You'll get a fever in this wet cloak,' he said, lifting it up at her shoulders. 'Take it off and I'll find something to wrap round you.'

Cold and wet through, Kerensa's numb fingers were barely capable of removing the cloak and Clem did it for her. He smiled, the same boyish grin that she knew from long years ago, and Kerensa smiled back.

'This should help,' he said, engulfing her in a grey blanket he took from the back of a settle. 'Now tell me, my love, what's upset you so much?'

This was the moment he had prayed for, the time when she would turn to him. Now he could comfort her, hold her, show her his love was as strong as the moment he had first declared it. He would not let her down.

She sat on a rickety chair beside the empty hearth and wiped at her tear-streaked face with the back of a hand. 'Coming through the town a sailor suddenly appeared in front of me. Oh, Clem, it was Kane's father, his real father!' A fresh sob caught in her throat and she buried her face in her hands.

Crouching in front of her and clasping her hands in his, he asked, angry in her defence, 'What did he do? Did he hurt you?'

'He didn't hurt me but he insulted me with his filthy remarks,' she replied angrily, gazing into his summer-blue eyes. 'And he stole a bag of yeast buns I'd bought.' That sounded rather ludicrous after all she had been through and she laughed.

'That's better,' Clem said. 'I hope the greedy swine chokes on them. Did he threaten you?'

'Not me personally, Clem, but he threatened to kidnap Kane and take him away to sea!' And she got panicky again.

'It's all right, my love, you're quite safe with me. I'd go after him but I don't want to leave you alone.'

'No, Clem, no. Don't leave me, right now I can't think of anyone I would rather be with more than you.'

'Even him?'

Kerensa knew whom Clem meant. 'Especially Oliver. In his present state of mind he would probably kill the sailor and be hanged for it.'

'I could easily do that myself. Let's leave the subject of the sailor for a minute. There's much more than him upsetting you, isn't there? What's going on, Kerensa?' Clem's handsome fair features were creased in concern for her. 'I'd have to be dead not to notice there was something wrong between you and him at Ted's wedding yesterday. I detest your husband, you know that, but you love him and I don't want you to be unhappy. Tell me what's wrong, my love, I may be able to help.'

'There's nothing you can do, Clem,' she stated. He moved closer and with the end of the blanket she carefully dried his rain-spattered face. 'But it will help me to confide in you.'

He tenderly kissed her chilled hands and tear-wet face. 'I'm listening.'

A heavy weight seemed to be lifted from her shoulders as the tale of her woes left her lips. Even the worst of them didn't seem quite so terrible. Except for the Reverend Ivey there was no one else she could confide in like this, and she found she could tell Clem more than the old parson. He didn't interrupt or change his expression except that his eyes became a much deeper blue. Kerensa looked into those wonderful soulful eyes and couldn't remember moving and putting herself back into Clem's arms. She only knew she was there, warm and comfortable, his body strong and capable, and she was safe.

'Was I wrong, Clem? Was I so very wrong not to tell Oliver what I knew about Samuel?'

Clem stirred, unwilling to have the spell broken, having her close to him again, keeping her secure in the confines of his love. He thought back over what she had told him.

'I don't know, my love. I hate him for treating you so cruelly and yet I can understand how he must be feeling – up to a point. If Samuel had been dead for many years it probably wouldn't have seemed so bad, but with him only being drowned a few short weeks before he was told, well . . .'

'You'd feel cheated?'

'Perhaps,' he said carefully, not wanting to tear at her vulnerable feelings.

'It's what Oliver says. I'm beginning to think he'll never forgive me, Clem. One moment he's the same as he's always been, then he gets moody towards me. Just lately he's got worse. Except for the children anyone can be at the nasty end of his tongue.'

Clem ruffled the silky hair at the crown of her head and kissed it there. 'He can't keep it up for ever, Kerensa. No one can love you and stay angry with you indefinitely.'

'That would be true if it was you, Clem,' she muttered in her misery.

He lifted her chin and smiled at her. 'It will be with him too, you'll see.' It was an effort to say it, but his love was too deep not to offer her a crumb of comfort.

'I hope you're right,' she said lamely, trying to return his smile. 'Talking of the children just now, I really am sorry about Luke's bad behaviour yesterday. Please believe me when I say I'm not making excuses for him but he's been very unsettled lately. I think he senses Oliver's ill humour.'

Clem let out a puff of breath. 'Oh, I'm not really bothered about that. I suppose I did overreact a little. The thing is he looks so much like his father. Alice tore me off a fair strip all the way home and so did Rosie and Father, and Kenver wholeheartedly agreed with them. I began to feel such a rat. They all pointed out if it had been Kane or some other boy rather than Luke I wouldn't have got so angry. I suppose at six years old he's not much more than a baby. I was thinking of riding over to the manor to apologise.'

Kerensa looked deep into his eyes. With a knowing smile, she said, 'You weren't really thinking of doing that, Clem.'

He admitted, with a sheepish grin, 'No, I wasn't.'

'My dearest Clem, I'm surrounded everywhere by stupid male pride. Oliver, Luke, Bartholomew Drannock, and even you,' she lovingly stroked his hair, 'my dearest Clem.'

'I still love you, Kerensa.' There was no doubt of that in his eyes, his voice, his arms.

305

'And I still love you.' Her words caressed his heart.

'I know you do and it's wonderful to hear you say it. It's what's kept me going all these years, knowing you keep a part of your heart specially for me.'

The rain stopped suddenly, leaving a sulky yellow-grey sky. The wind dropped and the window stopped creaking. They were content for a while to be alone together again. She had grown pleasantly sleepy when he spoke again.

'Kerensa, why did you mention Bartholomew Drannock just now? He doesn't know yet about Sir Daniel being his grandfather so how are you involved with him? Something to do with his mother? I know you call regularly on her.'

Kerensa sighed wearily, reluctant to be reminded of her problems again. 'It's not that. Before I rode here today I first went over to Perranbarvah to give young Master Drannock a piece of my mind over a guest who's staying at the manor, Miss Ameline Beswetherick.'

'Oh, yes? I saw her once, looks as though a handful of dust would choke her.'

'Ameline is rather delicate but she's very sweet, very naive and innocent. I found out she and Bartholomew have been meeting in Trelynne Cove. I had reason to fear Bartholomew would try to seduce her and I had to put a stop to it.'

'Bet he didn't take kindly to that!' Clem exclaimed. 'You have had an awful time today, my love. What did he say? I hope he didn't upset you.'

'He didn't like it at all,' Kerensa replied calmly, 'but I got the upper hand of him so I have no more worries on that score.'

'Good, I'm glad of that, but we still have that sailor to contend with. I won't let him get away with blackmailing you and having you live in fear of him kidnapping Kane. I have an idea how to deal with him. Will you leave it to me, Kerensa?'

'Depends what you're thinking of doing,' she said uncertainly. 'I don't want you getting into any kind of trouble.'

Trust me, will you do that? I can't help with your other problems except to be always here for you, but I can do something about this one and your husband need never know about it.'

'I don't know, Clem,' she bit her bottom lip, 'it will mean keeping another secret from Oliver.'

'Damn his pride! This is different. Don't forget the thrashing he gave Peter Blake for hurting you. The sailor wouldn't get off so lightly.'

Kerensa was torn, but she said, 'What have you in mind? Shall I meet him as arranged?'

'No, I want you to promise to stay at home all day tomorrow. You're not to worry. I'll see to everything. This time he won't come back to haunt you.'

She felt his strength but was still unsure. 'You're not going to—'

'Of course not, you know I'd never harm anyone.' He kissed her forehead and stroked her cheek with his thumb. 'Can you come here the day after tomorrow? I'll tell you then what's happened. Now, let's forget other people for a little while longer, we'll have to leave here soon.'

'There's something else, Clem . . .' she faltered, 'something more I haven't told you . . . something even Oliver doesn't know.'

Instinctively, Clem held her closer, 'What is it, my love?'

On unsteady feet, Clem was shown into the captain's cabin of the ketch, *Free Spirit*. The captain was in residence, seated at his small, immaculately tidy table, and after dismissing the first mate he viewed the handsome young farmer with cold interest.

'I thank you for seeing me, Cap'n Solomon,' Clem said. He returned the other's icy gaze and understood why so many folk were afraid of Hezekiah Solomon. His heavy scent made Clem want to cough.

'You are fortunate to find me here, Trenchard. I thought to put to sea on the morning tide but I decided to wait until I have accomplished a little business I have in mind. What can I do for you? You are surely not contemplating leaving your family for a life at sea?'

'I'll get straight to the point, Cap'n Solomon,' Clem said boldly. 'Lady Pengarron is in trouble, and unbeknown to her I've come to you because I believe you are the best one to help her out of it.'

Hezekiah was fascinated to meet this tall blond man, so cruelly pushed aside when Kerensa was forced to marry his friend. If Kerensa was in trouble and needed a pair of comforting arms round her, with Oliver acting so coldly it followed she would turn to Clem Trenchard. Hezekiah wanted Kerensa himself. He had no scruples about making love to a friend's wife, even if it meant losing that friend or, better still, killing him in a duel, but up until now he had not tried to win Kerensa. There were two strong reasons: Kerensa would tell Oliver, and Oliver was the only man he was afraid of. Now there was some hope. He would never refuse to help Kerensa, but if he could help her where Clem Trenchard could not, and if Oliver prolonged the cold treatment, then perhaps . . .

'Well,' he said slowly in his melodic voice, 'you had better tell me what ails the dear lady.'

'A sailor, the disgusting swine who is supposed to be the

308

real father of Kane, has turned up in Marazion again. He's demanding money to stay away from the boy and Lady Pengarron fears that if His Lordship was told he would become so enraged he'd kill the sailor and pay for it with his own life on the gallows. She doesn't want him to know, you understand.'

'I understand perfectly, Trenchard. I agree with Her Ladyship. It would be better if that particular piece of human flotsam remained at sea permanently. Do you understand me?'

Clem fancied the ship moved and spread his feet for balance. 'I believe I do, Cap'n Solomon,' he answered, narrowing his eyes. 'It would be too bad for Her Ladyship to be bothered by that scum ever again.'

'Then it is as good as done. Have you any idea where this . . . problem might be found at this moment?'

'Aye, as a matter of fact I do. I scouted round the town after I saw Her Ladyship safely on her way home. He can be found fully legless in the gin shop next to the watch-maker's.'

Hezekiah's white hair gleamed in the light of a lantern lit to offset the afternoon's gloom. He patted a few strands above his temple and the scent of cologne grew unbearably stronger, threatening to cut off Clem's air supply. Clem could hardly wait to leave, the cabin seemed no bigger than an outdoor closet. He found it claustrophobic and pre-ferred the smells of dung and sweating bodies to the unnatural aromas wafting up his nostrils courtesy of the sea captain.

'I shall attend to it, Trenchard,' Hezekiah said, with a twisted smile that chilled the marrow of Clem's bones. 'Lady Pengarron can be told I will be taking him on board my ship to answer a charge of violence made against him in a foreign port – the murder of another British sailor, for instance.'

Clem frowned. 'I don't think she will want the child to grow up and perhaps learn his real father was hanged as a murderer. 'Tis bad enough his mother was a prostitute.'

Hezekiah considered this. 'Robbery by violent means then. It is also a hanging offence. Later it can be divulged he met with an unfortunate accident at sea and was never brought to justice. Knowing he is finally out of the way for good will surely ease her torment.'

Clem's body gave a small involuntary shudder as the sea captain's eyes turned to slits and glowed strangely, rather like a snake's.

'I thank you, Cap'n Solomon,' he said quickly, wanting to get back on the firm ground of St Michael's Mount again.

'Indeed, I thank you, Trenchard, it will be a pleasure to come to the assistance of such a charming lady.'

As he left, Clem felt uneasy. He didn't like having to ask this strange individual to help Kerensa, and he didn't like the thought of her mixing socially with him either.

When he had seen Clem off his vessel, Hezekiah reached down to his soft fawn-coloured kid boot and pulled from its confines a thin jewel-handled stiletto blade. Almost reverently, he stroked the cold, hard steel.

Ameline was sitting before her dressing-table mirrors attempting a more natural arrangement of her hair in the hope of pleasing Bartholomew on their next rendezvous. A small sound made her look anxiously at the window for signs of raindrops. If the weather turned wet again she feared Kerensa would not allow her to go riding and she would miss her last opportunity to see Bartholomew.

She thought again about his kiss. She felt he had been

rather rough with her, his hands had gripped her uncomfortably and the touch of his lips on her neck had hurt and left a mark. She had looked for such marks on the necks of Kerensa and Polly O'Flynn. They were married, and were presumably kissed often by their husbands, but she found none and could not think of a reason for Bartholomew leaving one on her. She would tell him he must not do it again. It was a most unseemly blemish for a lady to acquire and if anyone but him had been responsible it would have brought an end to their meetings.

Ameline was fascinated by Bartholomew. When she was with him she gave no thought to James Mortreath. Bartholomew could offer her nothing that James could, but he was handsome, kind in his own way and charming in his attempt to speak well and use perfect manners. He talked often of his intention of becoming a wealthy man, of becoming important, respected, to have his company sought after. He was so earnest she could easily believe he had the inner strength to make it happen.

Of course she could not bear to become the wife of a poor fisherman, to exchange her genteel life for one of hard work and squalor. But she was powerfully drawn to Bartholomew and her head was full of romantic notions; if he happened to propose on their next meeting, if he would agree to wait a few years to see if his dreams came true . . . Even if her family could not overlook his low background, Oliver would understand. He had married out of his class, and she would always have a friend in Kerensa. They would convince her father and grandfather— she heard a step outside the door, a step lighter than Kerensa's.

Ameline dropped a handful of hairpins. 'Olivia, is that you?'

But Olivia had been taken over to Tolwithrick by Cherry

to attend the birthday party of one of her many younger sisters. In fact there were few people about the manor today. Angered that Kerensa had ridden off without him, Oliver had postponed Luke's punishment and taken him and Kane over to Ker-an-Mor Farm. Ameline had given Peters, her maid, permission to visit an acquaintance on the staff of Sir Martin's house. It was Polly's afternoon off, the King sisters were at the fishing village attending to a very ill woman and Beatrice was drunk in the tack room. Kerensa was at home, but having returned in a somewhat distressed condition from Marazion she had retired alone to her bed-chamber, giving strict orders she was not to be disturbed.

A feeling of acute unease brought Ameline to her feet. Her spine stiffened as the handle of her bedroom door was slowly turned.

'Who's there?' Her voice came out as an unrecognisable squeak.

The door was opened fully. Ameline's eyes enlarged in their sockets, her throat constricted to choking point.

'I . . . I thought you would be at sea . . .'

'I have delayed leaving until a later tide,' Hezekiah Solomon poured through his teeth.

His smile did nothing to lessen her horror. Ameline lurched backwards until her back hit a bedpost. She could not tear herself away from his steely-blue snake's eyes.

'What . . . what do . . . do you want? Why are you here?'

'I've come to keep you company, Ameline.'

'I . . . I have plenty of company, Captain Solomon. Kerensa—'

'Is fast asleep. I crept into the house unseen. There is no one about. No one knows that I am here.'

Ameline watched petrified as he slipped off his brocaded frockcoat and took meticulous care to fold it and place it over the chair she had vacated. Seemingly from out of nowhere he produced a thin stiletto blade and after testing the point on a fingertip in front of her stricken eyes he placed it on her jewellery case. As he came towards her, soundless as a cat, there was not a hint of expression on his ageless face.

Ameline had drifted off into a short dreamless sleep. When she awoke Hezekiah had not moved but lay still with his arm, hot and moist, under her shoulders. She had not struggled or pleaded with him, she had been too scared, but he had not hurt her. His touch had been light and silky and he had patiently coaxed her young, inexperienced body until it was entirely relaxed and responsive. His expertise had magnified her terror, giving her shame, making her hate herself; it hadn't been a natural loving gentleness but something pitiless and calculated to add to his own pleasure. There had been no pain and his body was smooth, light and strangely soft and warm. She felt strangely elated now, wanting to laugh, cry, shout, and sing. He had forced himself upon her and made himself her first lover, and yet, cruelly somehow, she felt he had taken her to the heights of fulfilment.

With a liberal-minded mother like Rachael she had not been brought up to think that the act of physical union was something a woman had to endure, but surely the first time was usually uncomfortable. Ameline knew now that Bartholomew Drannock had offered her no more than the selfish gropings of a lusty youth. With him it would have been clumsy, painful and far more degrading than what she had just experienced.

She raised herself on an elbow and looked down into Hezekiah's face. He was over fifty, or so she thought, but

313

there was hardly a wrinkle in his smooth, perfumed skin. If he had asked her at that moment, Ameline would have agreed to marry him, even become his mistress. Although he would undoubtedly have slit her throat if she had resisted him earlier, now, she would willingly have departed with him on the next tide. For one mad moment her mind and body surged with the desire to warm his ice-cold heart with the fire of her love. Hezekiah turned his head and looked back at her and his eyes deepened into shards of kaleidoscopic colours. She could see pure evil there. She gulped and shuddered. He returned his gaze to the canopy above them; Ameline was dismissed.

He made no attempt to stop her fleeing to the tiny connecting room where some of her clothes were kept and where Peters slept. Numbly she dressed herself. When she returned to the bedroom Hezekiah had gone, and with him the jewelled stiletto. The bedcovers were smoothed down without a crease. She sat back at her dressing table and trying not to think she proceeded to arrange her hair in its usual style.

Then for over an hour she cried her heart out. She had known terror, numbness, hysteria and a kind of madness, all in a very short time. But at the end of her distressed weeping her mind was clear and she knew exactly what she would do. She would return at once to Tolwithrick and ask her father to send for the one man she knew she could trust, and perhaps one day, as he deserved, she would truly return his love and devotion. With him she would be able to leave Cornwall and she would never return and risk facing the man who had so coldly violated her, the man she hated with all her being, whom she could never bring to justice for his heinous crime for fear of retribution and the risk of losing the man she now wanted to spend the rest of her life with. Ameline intended to tell the comfortable, serious, uncomplicated James Mortreath she would be honoured to accept his proposal of marriage.

When Hezekiah Solomon returned to his ship, after spending the evening at a brothel, there was someone waiting for him on board.

'You have a passenger, Hezekiah, I was going to seek a berth on any ship going across the Channel but as you have delayed setting sail . . .' Oliver leaned against an overhead beam, his over-generous height preventing him, as it did Clem only hours before, from standing fully upright. A packed canvas bag sat on Hezekiah's table.

'You really mean to sail with me, Oliver?'

'I do. Now the festive season's over I'm leaving Cornwall for a while.'

'I see. For how long?' Hezekiah wanted to question him further but Oliver's gaunt expression spoke of an intention to keep his reason to himself.

'That remains to be seen. I've made all the necessary arrangements at home, the Renfrees and O'Flynn, and Angove the head gardener and even Jack are all capable men, they'll see to everything between them in my absence. I've taken the liberty of opening a cask of your boot-legged brandy. Will you join me?' Oliver gave a shudder that made Hezekiah raise his silky eyebrows. He explained, 'I've not long since seen a sight so hideous that it will haunt me throughout the rest of the night.'

'Oh? What was that?' Hezekiah asked, taking a glass of his own brandy and warming the bowl in his delicate hands.

'A body. A man's body, at least I think it was a man's. It was badly slashed and cut up, and apparently left in the gutter for hours in the belief it was an animal. I am told there were parts of it everywhere. I've seen men killed on the battlefield, but this . . . ugh! Some believe him to be a sailor – not one of your ship, I hope.'

Hezekiah smiled. It had been a very good day. 'Have no fears, my crew are all safely on board to a man. Drink up, my friend, and put it out of your mind. It will be good to have the company of a gentleman on the journey, but I can delay leaving port if you'd like time to reconsider your plans.'

'No!' Oliver said adamantly. 'My mind is made up.'

'Then let us raise our glasses to the Channel Islands.'

Oliver looked blankly into his glass. 'Yes . . . but that won't be the end of my journey.'

Chapter 21

Nothing could thaw the deathly coldness Kerensa felt inside. She pushed Charity away without realising she had done it, unaware of the dog's hurt looks before it moved away and flopped down in front of the hearth. She crumpled the dampened folds of her cloak between tensed hands. She sighed over and over. She flicked the tips of her nails together, making tiny clicking sounds that set Clem's nerves on edge and made Charity blink every time.

Clem watched her anxiously. 'Kerensa, is there anything I can get you?' he asked gently, hoping to counter her vacant stare. 'Shall I make up a fire?'

It was ages before she answered and he was about to repeat the question when she whispered, 'No, thank you, Clem. You've got a tidy blaze going already. Won't people wonder why there's smoke coming out of the chimney of this house?'

'No, the neighbours are used to me calling here when Mr Barbary goes on a long visit to Lamorna. I've been doing this for years, keeping an eye on the place for the old boy. I usually light the fire if it's been cold and damp for several days to keep the house aired out.'

'Where did you meet him, this Mr Barbary?'

'At the Bible classes. When he said he was afraid of

317

having a break-in with the house standing empty for long periods at a time, I offered to look in on it from time to time. You know me, my little sweet,' he smiled, 'if I get the chance to spend some time alone I take it. It's even better with you here.'

'It's a nice little house,' Kerensa moved her eyes round the four white-washed walls, 'in reasonably good repair except for that creaking window.' She settled her gaze on its small square panes. Raindrops were sliding down to merge with others and form links like strands of diamonds. 'I take it Mr Barbary is comfortably off.'

'Kerensa, my dearest love.' Clem moved to her side on the settle. He took her hands from her lap, peeled off her gloves and rubbed her stiff fingers. 'You have no real interest in who lives here or in what circumstances. What is it, what's happened? You're in a worse state than you were a couple of days ago.'

In a pitiful whimper, she replied, 'He's gone, Clem.'

He eased her against him and wrapped her in his arms in the same way he did with Jessica when she was upset or in pain. 'Who's gone, my love?'

'Oliver . . . he's left me . . . and the children.'

Clem was relieved she couldn't see the shock on his face. This was the last thing he had expected.

'Left you?' But surely not for good, Kerensa, he'd never leave you for good, he'll be back. He's probably gone away to one of his business meetings.'

'No, he hasn't, it's not like that. I knew he'd been trying to tell me something just before I rode to Perranbarvah to see Bartholomew. He came back from Ker-an-Mor later in the day and found me lying abed and Ameline packing up to leave. He was very quiet and after the children were in

318

bed he told me he was going away. He said he was sorry that we hadn't spent the day together because it would be the last day for a long time. I pleaded with him to stay, at least not to go until we had worked things out between us, but he insisted he had to go away before he could do that. Far away from Cornwall. Far away from me! From everything until he's sorted it all out in his mind about us and Samuel Drannock. He refused to tell me where he was going or when he's coming back.' She swung round and clung to Clem with considerable force, digging her nails into his neck. 'What will I do, Clem? He might stay away for months, years. He might never come back! What will I do?'

He fought to control her clawing hands and held her tightly until her trembling ceased. She cried with her heart breaking and he whispered in her ear, 'You've done the only thing you need to do. You've turned to me, my love. You'll always have me, I'll never let you down.'

She looked up with frightened eyes. 'Oh, Clem, why didn't I marry you when I should have done! I loved you and yet I treated you so badly. Now I'm paying for it.'

'No, Kerensa, that's not how I see it is. It cuts me to the quick to admit it but you love Pengarron more than you could ever love me and despite everything I'm sure he loves you very much too. I don't want it to be that way . . . because I want you all to myself. I know it's selfish of me but I can't stop loving you.'

'And I'll always love you, Clem,' she said softly, then her ravaged feelings came to the fore and she said resentfully, 'You would never leave me. Why did he have to go? Why is he making me suffer like this? Must I be punished for ever? It's not fair, I tell you it just isn't fair!'

'Don't, Kerensa,' Clem pleaded, 'don't get bitter.'

'I'm sorry,' she whimpered, and went limp in his arms.

Clem stroked her hair and held her close. 'I have one comfort for you, my love. I promise that you'll never be bothered with the sailor again. You can at least live in peace that Kane will be safe for ever from any threat from him.'

'What did you do, Clem?' Kerensa murmured against his chest, and although she trusted Clem she became tense again.

'Well, after you left me the day before yesterday I went to see Cap'n Solomon.'

'Hezekiah? Why him? I thought he had sailed on the early-morning tide.'

'He changed his mind apparently. I'd noticed his ship moored up at the Mount before I brought you in here out of the rain. I went aboard the *Free Spirit* and asked him to help us.'

'What did he say?' she asked, looking anxiously at him now. 'Did he do something?'

'We talked, and he was only too happy to help. He said he happened to know the sailor was wanted for a hanging offence, somewhere abroad he said it was, it's of no matter where. He assured me he'd take the sailor back to see justice done. You can forget all about him.'

Kerensa sighed, then said in a small voice. 'If Hezekiah didn't sail until later perhaps Oliver sailed with him. He didn't take Conomor when he left.'

'You think he's gone across the Channel then?'

'He could have. I thought perhaps he'd just gone off somewhere close by to think. I sent Jack over to Mullion to look around our cottage there but the caretaker had seen no sign of him. If he's gone overseas, it suggests he'll be gone for a long time.'

'I'll wait with you, Kerensa,' Clem said softly.

She traced a finger down his cheek, 'Yes, I know you will.'

They looked into each other's eyes. Clem smiled. It was the same gentle smile that had looked at her every day of their betrothal long years ago. It made her feel special, so loved and cherished. If she had married Clem he would never have let hurt and resentment overshadow his love for her. His love would have grown only stronger over the years.

She smiled back then kissed his cheek. He returned it. She kissed his other cheek then ran a fingertip over his lips. He looked deeper into her, searching her eyes. Her lips sought his and kissed them lightly. He held her closer and tried to put her face against his shoulder but Kerensa kissed him again.

'What are you doing, Kerensa?' he whispered.

'You like me kissing you, don't you?'

'Of course I do.'

'Then don't talk,' she smiled.

Clem kissed her gently, relishing the feel of her soft mouth under his but when it ended, Kerensa clung to him.

'I want you, Clem,' she said huskily, kissing him fervently. 'I want you . . .'

'Do you know what you're doing, Kerensa?' and now his voice was husky as he held her face away from his.

'I love you, I always have and at this moment I need you. Please, Clem, don't hold back from me.'

He could no more resist her plea than he could stop breathing. He allowed himself to be overwhelmed by the sensations of her body pressing into his. It had been so long since he had kissed her like this, so long since he had held her and felt that at last she could be his.

Disengaging herself, Kerensa stood up from the settle and untied the ribbons at the neck of her cloak. Clem watched trance-like as the black voluminous cloth fluttered to the floor in slow folding movements.

Clem lowered his arms to allow her to push off his coat, then she took his hands and led him across the room to the other door. He opened the door, and together they crossed the threshold of Mr Barbary's bedroom. The room was cold but rather than allow the heat from the fire to filter through, Kerensa closed the door against the rest of the world.

Moving to either side of the small narrow bed they discarded their clothes and lay side by side under Mr Barbary's sheet and blankets. Kerensa was shivering but did not notice the cold. Taking Clem's hand she moved into his arms. He gasped at the sensation of her skin against his and was lost the next moment as she lay over his chest and kissed him with hungry passion.

He loosened all restraining pins from her hair, then slowly and gently he turned until he lay over her. He clasped both her hands on the pillow above her head. He was aware of every sensitive part of her body, it screamed at him to give her release and fulfilment.

But tears suddenly stung his eyes as he knew with a deep painful ache that he could not possess her. He couldn't bring himself to perform the act of love that would meet their long-time need, that would claim her as his own. Not after what she had told him two days ago. Not when he was so fully aware of the outward curve of her gently rounded stomach – and the presence of another man's baby living and growing between them.

The tension and desire left Kerensa when she realised Clem had stopped returning her love. She read the pain in his eyes and pulling her hands from his she tenderly wiped away his tears. Then they cried together. They held on to each other, their nakedness no embarrassment or barrier to their special need for closeness and comfort. They stroked each other, not intimately as in the way of wakening a physical response or in the natural winding down after the deep emotional release of lovemaking, but to give reassurance and affection.

'I hate to see you hurt like this,' Clem said, his voice carrying fragments of his anguished emotions.

'Why, Clem?' she whispered. 'Why did you stop?'

'I couldn't go through with it, not with your body showing the beginning of the new life you're bearing. It's not my baby. It reminded me you're another man's wife, and that you love him more than me. Kerensa,' he moved to look at her full in the face, 'I know you love me and in your distress it was all too easy to turn to me, to make love with me and block out your pain. Tell me this, my love, how would you be feeling now if we had made love? Could you look me in the face without the horror coming to you of what we'd done.'

A different kind of horror showed on her face. 'Oh Clem, don't think I was using you.'

'You didn't mean to, my love, but don't you see? We would never be in this situation now if things weren't desperately wrong between you and Pengarron. You didn't come to me because you've fallen out of love with him or can't live without me. It hurts me to know how much you love him and you don't love him any the less because of his wretched behaviour. If we had made love, if you didn't hate yourself now it would happen tonight, tomorrow or next week and you might have found yourself hating me for being so weak and selfish. It's been hard living these last years without you, but knowing you could never meet me face to face again without feeling a sense of shame . . .' He could say no more.

'I'm so sorry, Clem,' Kerensa said miserably, pulling his head to rest on her shoulder. 'I never meant to hurt you again, please forgive me.'

Several minutes later, he said, 'There's nothing to forgive, Kerensa. The only hurt I feel is yours at losing Pengarron for the moment. You see, I've been thinking.'

'And?' she said, as he raised himself to look down on her.

'Kerensa, you and I weren't meant to be lovers. A long time ago we very nearly were, but it wasn't to be then and it isn't to be now.' Clem used a fingertip to run gentle little circles on her flushed, puzzled face and eased away the strands of auburn-red hair on her brow and temples. 'We have a special love, my little sweet, you and I. We have a part of each other that no one else can touch or take away. It's a love we can share on a higher plane of life to the physical act of love that would only destroy it. Do you understand what I'm trying to say, Kerensa?'

'Yes, I think so,' she found a simple smile from somewhere and used his favourite form of endearment for her, 'my little sweet. A different kind of love to that of husband and wife, brother and sister and even lovers.'

'Most of the time people need to fit their feelings into neat little compartments, parent to child, friend to enemy. But we have something completely different, something really unique, quite wonderful.' He fell silent for a while, then asked, 'Do you feel any better now, Kerensa, my love?'

She stroked his hair, twisting its silky fineness round her fingers. 'Yes, a little . . . It was beautiful, what you said, I

324

shall never forget it. Does it make you feel better, Clem? You looked so pained a little while ago. I thought I'd broken your heart again.'

He smiled so deeply his eyes shone with their deepest summer blue. 'Since I've thought it through I seem to have come out of this better than you. I was still cherishing the hopeless dream that you belonged to me and I had the right to claim you as totally mine. Now I know I was wrong. Stealing one afternoon of lovemaking won't make you mine and it would turn all we meant to each other sordid!'

'You're a wise man, Clem, wiser and stronger than I am,' Kerensa said.

'No harm has been done,' and Clem chuckled, adding, 'though no one would believe very little happened to see us like this.'

'Not to mention what Mr Barbary would say if he came home at this very minute.'

'He's a nice old boy and wouldn't jump to hasty conclusions.'

'Clem!' Kerensa couldn't help giggling, 'What else could he think? Our clothes are on the floor and we're lying in his bed with nothing on!'

Clem couldn't help himself from lifting the sheet and looking lingeringly down her body from head to toes. 'You are so very, very beautiful, Kerensa,' he said appreciatively.

'You're rather beautiful yourself, Clem Trenchard,' Kerensa murmured, adding not at all coyly, 'I have noticed.'

They kissed, for the sheer pleasure of the contact of their lips, then Clem suggested they go back into the other room.

'I'll cheer up the fire and leave you to get dressed. You, um, you wouldn't tidy up the bed, would you? I'm not very good at that sort of thing.'

'I'll join you in a little while,' she told him with an amused face.

As they entered the snug living room in turn Charity looked up, but having been deserted by them earlier she decided to ignore them now. She replaced her head on the hearth and went back to sleep.

'Charity is vexed with us,' Kerensa observed, 'just as Bob was with me for not allowing him to come with me today.'

Clem stroked Charity's back. 'You warm enough, Kerensa?'

'Yes, I'm fine,' she replied, resuming her place on the settle.

'You didn't tell him about the baby, did you, Kerensa. If you had I'm sure he would have stayed.'

'I wanted to, Clem. I very nearly did, but I didn't want him to stay and feel trapped. This is something he has to do and maybe when he comes back . . .'

'He'll come back,' Clem said at once. 'He wouldn't leave you and your children and his responsibilities for ever.'

'Yes . . . I believe Oliver will come back, but it will be agony wondering what he'll be like towards me when he does. There have always been depths to him that I've never been able to fathom. What if he comes back hating me, never to forgive me?'

'It won't come to that, I'm sure. But will you be able to forgive him?'

'I think so. You see, I do understand a little of what he's going through. I just want things to get back to normal.'

'They will, I'm sure, it just takes time.'

'Dear Clem,' she said wanly, 'you're trying to say the right thing but you know so little of what Oliver is really like. I'll just have to wait and hope.'

326

'You have me to wait and hope with you, my love,' Clem said, sitting beside her on the settle. 'Do you have to go home yet? I can stay another couple of hours. Father won't be pleased, but no one questions me going off on my own and I can make up my work on the farm tomorrow.'

'I can stay. I told Polly I needed to see a few people and then wanted some time to myself.'

'That's good,' he smiled, sitting beside her and putting a strong arm round her shoulders. 'We rarely get any time to be alone and I'd just like to hold you for a while longer.'

Kerensa leaned into him, closing her eyes as he held her tightly. 'Right now, Clem, I could stay like this for ever.'

Chapter 22

Rosie Trenchard climbed up Trecath-en's valley with her niece, Jessica, holding on tightly to her hand. Jessica had small legs but she climbed just as fast. They were on their way to get the twins away from Ricketty Jim; Philip and David had been sent to take bread and goat's milk up to the rover and as usual had lingered too long.

'Why couldn't I take the food up to Ricketty Jim's?' Jessica asked for the umpteenth time.

'Because you're too young to come this far all by yourself,' Rosie answered patiently, yet again.

''Tisn't fair, they get all the adventures,' Jessica pouted. 'And Mother said we're not to stop 'cos they'll be late doing their jobs. But I like talking to Ricketty Jim, he says some funny things.'

'Never mind, Jessica, perhaps when your mother comes this way next time she'll take you with her and you can have a long chat with him then.'

'Mother's always too busy,' Jessica complained. 'Why not you, Aunty Rosie, why don't you bring me?'

'Because I'm busy too, Jessica,' Rosie replied, pushing up the hood that had fallen away from the child's golden curls.

Jessica crossly pushed it back off. 'Why not? You won't

go anywhere these days, you're always moody, what you need is a man to cheer you up.'

'Jessica! What a thing to say!' Rosie felt angry, her family did nothing but badger her these days, telling her to get out more, urging her to take up any invitation she was offered. All she wanted was to be left quietly in her own little world with only her private thoughts for company; she didn't want to be with anyone else, let alone a man, and that meant any man. And now even her little niece was harassing her, repeating things she heard others say. 'Don't speak to me like that again, Jessica,' she warned, 'or I'll tell your mother.'

'But it was Mother who said it first,' Jessica wailed. To her mind the threat of punishment for what she'd repeated was unfair.

'Let's just forget it then,' Rosie said wearily, taking Jessica's hand again and pulling her away from a clump of dead thistles and back on to the worn path.

Rosie stared downheartedly at the ground. Why couldn't she just be left alone? If she wanted to be quiet and even miserable, didn't she have the right to be, for goodness sake? She would say nothing to Alice. She'd told her often to mind her own business but Alice only said she was trying to help, that what was a family for if not to rally round when one of its members needed help? Rosie's pleas that she didn't want or need any help fell on deaf ears.

Mostly Rosie's thoughts were filled with daydreams and memories of her childhood. They brought her no pain or misery. But just sometimes she would allow herself to think of that afternoon spent alone with one special man in a forest, of the events shared with him. She had not seen him since the awful clash on the Trembaths' wedding day. A few weeks ago he had mysteriously gone away but it hadn't lessened the bitter-sweet memories she had of him. Alice reckoned she needed a man 'to cheer her'. What she meant was a husband. But what man would do after a young woman had had an encounter with Sir Oliver Pengarron?

Ricketty Jim was full of apologies for keeping Philip and David talking, or rather listening to him. 'I'm awful sorry, Rosie, it seems I like the sound of my own voice too much and you've had a needless long, wet, muddy walk.'

'Well, it's used up some of this little miss's energy,' Rosie said, eyeing her recalcitrant niece.

Jessica had straightaway made herself at home under the awning that was Ricketty Jim's home, squeezing in between her brothers. 'Out of there, young lady,' Rosie ordered, bending down to look in, 'and you two boys can come out as well.'

'Jim was telling us some wonderful stories,' David said enthusiastically, 'about kings called pharaohs and chieftains and sheiks.'

'You can tell me all about them on the way back, David,' Rosie said, trying not to sound impatient. The longer it took her to get the children back home, the longer it would be before she finished her own jobs.

'Jim said the Pengarron boys came over to speak to him the other day,' Philip said, scowling as he appeared in the open. 'Jim said that Master Luke was rude to him. I said I wasn't surprised, I hate him! He's nothing but a bighead, thinks he's so wonderful!'

'Now mind what you say about other folk, young Philip,' Ricketty Jim cautioned.

'Well, 'tis what you said!' Philip said heatedly.

'I only said he was rather rude to me. He hasn't got your good manners,' the rover replied soothingly, 'and there's no need to copy him.'

Rosie knew Philip was jealous of other children talking to Ricketty Jim, he considered the man 'belonged' to him and his twin, but Rosie was sympathetic to Philip's point of view over Luke Pengarron. Once, when she had been up at the manor kitchens, Luke had muttered, 'I see the peasants are about again,' and she had been offended.

'Well, never mind him,' Rosie told Philip. 'We must be getting back or half the morning will be gone.'

'Is Uncle Matthias at the farm?' David asked.

'No, why should he be?' she replied, getting annoyed.

'Well, he's there all the time these days, spends more time with us than at Ker-an-Mor.'

'Yes, and constantly hanging around and getting in the way,' Rosie said sharply.

At this Ricketty Jim looked at Rosie curiously. 'I'll walk down to the farm with you, Rosie,' he said. 'Clem's asked me to make some dung pots for him today.'

Ricketty Jim chatted all the way to the farmyard carrying a delighted Jessica on his shoulders but Rosie shut herself off and let the children talk to him. A little while ago the rover had shaved off his beard and tidied his hair which revealed a not unpleasant face round his large brown eyes and his age possibly not above forty. With only his bent legs and rolling walk to his disadvantage, some of the unmarried local females had begun to show an interest in him. But not Rosie. As she made for the well to draw water for the kitchen, she wished the world was devoid of all men.

In the six weeks since Oliver Pengarron had suddenly absented himself, Matthias Renfree had kept a close watch on Clem and called more often at Trecath-en Farm. He was worried that now the rift between his master and mistress had taken this turn for the worse, Kerensa would look to

Clem for comfort and Clem would no doubt try to rekindle the old feelings of love they had once shared. Matthias had no evidence that anything furtive was going on. Clem wandered off frequently with Charity trotting at his heels, but it was something he had always done. Kerensa for the most part stayed close to home – she was showing signs of being with child – and Alice Trenchard had increased her visits to the manor. After Miss Ameline Beswetherick's wedding day, too, Lady Rachael had stayed for a long period at the house. There had been little opportunity for Clem and Kerensa to meet privately even if they'd wanted to. But if that happened, Matthias hoped he could appeal to Clem's better sense, remind him that he had a wife and family.

Since Matthias had appointed himself watchdog over them both, his first concern was what excuse to offer for his frequent presence at the Trenchard's farm. Morley had inadvertently come to his aid. He had asked in that quiet disinterested way of his, 'Come again to see Rosie, have 'ee, boy?'

'Yes, that's right,' Matthias had answered, latching on eagerly to the convenient excuse.

After that, however, whenever he dropped in, Rosie was called from her chores or the tiny cramped room she slept in. Matthias was seated next to her at the supper table and sometimes the family drew aside and left them alone together. But when Philip and David began grinning at him and muttering about another wedding feast and Alice's face took on a certain knowing look, the look females reserve for manipulating an unmarried man into wedlock, Matthias grew alarmed.

He took a long ride over the moorland of Lancavel Downs to think it over. It dawned on him how unfair he was being to Rosie, lovely sweet Rosie. Matthias was shocked as another realisation surged through his brain.

Lovely sweet Rosie – not Clem's little sister any more as he had always thought of her. She was a young woman now and must be all of twenty-one years old. Most girls were married at her age. Rosie was a comely young woman and must have had lots of offers, many men had beaten a path to her door despite Clem's over-protectiveness.

'No, she's more than comely,' Matthias told a bird skimming on the wing, 'she's quite beautiful and very sweet and the most pleasant company.'

He smiled manfully as he summed up Rosie's attributes and recognised he liked her far more than as just a member of 'his flock', as he thought of the folk who attended the Bible classes.

But how does she see me? he wondered. As a man, her brother's friend, a likely suitor, a possible husband, or only as 'Preacher Renfree'? Morley, Clem, Alice, Kenver and the twins obviously saw him as Rosie's suitor. But did she? He didn't think so, and suddenly he wanted her to; he wanted to see her eyes light up when she saw him, see her blush and smile when he looked at her. How did a man attract a woman? He really had no idea.

He could not talk about Rosie to his father. Adam wasn't a sensitive man, seeing women only as a vessel for his lust or a provider of meals. Matthias could hardly ask Clem or Morley, they would think him an idiot, and Kenver probably had little idea how to advise him.

Then came the dark brooding face of Sir Oliver. Matthias gave an ironic laugh. There was a man who would certainly know all there was to know about women and the wooing of them – and their conquest. But he was away, and even if he hadn't been absent, Matthias wasn't sure he

334

could have brought himself to confide in his master, although Sir Oliver always gave a sympathetic ear to requests for help. Jack? He was too young. Jake Angove, too old. Nathan O'Flynn – of course! Nathan! He had been successful in courting Polly although a confirmed bachelor in his late twenties. He would ask Nathan what the best approach was.

Nathan advised Matthias to give Rosie flowers, the perfect gift to give to any woman on any occasion, but especially for the kindling of a romance. But what flowers grew in this wild-weathered month of February, the month known as the gateway to the year? Matthias knew that like most country girls Rosie preferred wild flowers. Perhaps the right bouquet could lead him through the gateway to a new life.

The eventual bunch of flowers and leaves was a resplendent host of mainly subdued colours gathered with the greatest of care from the roadside, grassy banks and coastline. Fluffy yellow lamb's tails mingled with the vanilla-scented flowers of winter heliotrope, white and purple scurvy grass, male ferns, coltsfoot, chickweed, strawberry leaves, and alexander – a tall bushy plant with pale yellow flowers. Cautiously set in the middle were a few prickly teasles and budding golden gorse.

Matthias set off with the bouquet tied firmly with a length of bright purple ribbon, the effect finished off with a delicate bow at the front. The ribbon had been left, long forgotten, in Ker-an-Mor's farmhouse parlour by Kerensa.

As he crossed over from Ker-an-Mor to Trecath-en farmland he was pleased he had got thus far without anyone seeing him. He sighed with relief that Ricketty Jim was not to be found about his ditch home. Ricketty Jim, who swore he had seen the spirit of an ancient Guise Dancer moaning up in the branches of a hawthorn tree on Twelfth Night this year, never missed a body walking or riding, even if you tried to slip by him. With his gossipy disposition he would have wanted to know whom the flowers were for and might have spread the information around. Matthias didn't want it known that the 'young preacher' was calling on the 'young maid of Trecath-en Farm' all spruced up and armed with a great big bunch of flowers. Then, on another thought that threatened to upset Matthias's fragile confidence, what if it spurred the rover on to make a play for Rosie? Some women seemed to find him attractive. Matthias decided he didn't like Ricketty Jim living this close to Rosie.

A little further on Matthias could see Clem, with one of the twins alongside him, driving a team of docile oxen as they ploughed up the next field. Morley and the other twin were following in their wake removing rocks of granite that the plough had churned up and carrying them to the edge of the field to be used later for walls. Matthias passed them unseen – the last thing he wanted was the Trenchard menfolk making fun of him.

As he closed in on the farm itself he slowed his horse down from its canter to a plodding walk that matched his wilting spirits. All his bravado had disappeared by the time he reached the yard, and he made up his mind to give the flowers casually to Alice.

He prayed fervently that Rosie would be nowhere about today. But the good Lord must have decided he was capable of going forth without divine help, for there was the object of his romantic desire drawing water from the well in the middle of the yard. Matthias dismounted, braved the walk through a gaggle of hissing geese and endeavoured to look serious. His face was fiery red.

'Good morning to you, Rosie.' He peered nonchalantly up at the sky.

'And to you, Preacher,' she replied evenly, only looking at him briefly out of a moody face.

There it was, 'Preacher' again. Did the girl see him only as a disciple of God, perhaps like a monk, unmasculine and unapproachable. He must make the point at the Bible classes that many of the apostles had been married, even St Peter.

'Busy are you, then?' He hoped his voice sounded natural.

'Aye, I am. Alice and I are doing the big wash.'

'Um . . . seen any sign of Ricketty Jim today?'

'Aye, he prepared some dung pots for Clem then took himself off. Wanted to see him, did you?'

'No, not particularly . . . I . . . I was just wondering how he fared during the storm the other night.'

'He was all right. If the weather's rough he comes and stays in the barn. We invited him inside but he says he couldn't bear to spend a minute under a proper roof.'

Good, Matthias thought, smiling tightly, he'll probably never think of getting married then.

Rosie had stopped turning the stiff iron handle and was staring at him. Matthias gulped.

'Is . . . is there something wrong?'

She reached for the pail to take it off the giant hook. 'Pretty flowers,' she remarked slowly.

To his horror Matthias saw he was actually holding them. He had intended to take off the ribbon and hide it in his pocket and leave the flowers hitched on his saddle.

'They're yours!' he blurted out, his cheeks on fire. 'I mean, they're for you . . . if you'd like them.'

Rosie straightened up sharply and stared at him with disbelief written plainly all over her face. 'For me?'

'I only thought . . .' Matthias was stumped, stupefied. What happened next was up to Rosie. He had made it plain by his gift that he had intentions towards her. Now, how would she react? He held his breath. A proverb raced to mind – fools rush in where angels fear to tread.

Rush? He pondered on the word as Rosie lifted the heavy pail to the ground. Before this moment he had never given her the slightest idea he saw her as anything other than a little girl. He should have tried to find out how Rosie felt about him first, before making this declaration to her. Matthias frowned, all the family had thought he was interested in Rosie because of his more frequent visits. Couldn't one of them have hinted that he might be interested in her? Then this wouldn't be so difficult and embarrassing now.

Completely taken aback, Rosie said, 'I'll find a crock to put them in, Preacher.'

He had been staring anxiously at her pale face trying to read her reaction. 'Eh?'

'Thank you,' she nodded at his hand, 'for the flowers.'

'Oh! Yes, of course.'

Matthias stepped forward with the flowers in his extended hand. Rosie accepted them and a smile brightened up her face. There, it was done.

Then disaster. Rosie shrieked as he knocked over the pail and bitterly cold water splashed over her feet and lower legs, leaving the hem of her rough woollen skirt dripping on to her shoes. He apologised profusely. 'I'm sorry, I'll fetch some more water and bring it into the house. I should have lifted the pail down off the hook for you in the first place, I'm so sorry.' Then he added hastily, 'You go inside and dry off.'

Rosie changed hurriedly out of her wet skirt and stockings and sat shivering on her little bed. She pictured her gift of flowers as she'd left them lying on the kitchen table. She'd been given what she considered the most romantic gesture in the world, and the bouquet of flowers had obviously been picked and made up with much care. Then she thought of Matthias. She was still shocked. Matthias Renfree, giving her flowers, declaring with them that he had an interest in her. It was all so much to take in.

How long had Matthias been interested in her? She must be the reason he had been calling so often at the farm these days. But he hadn't shown any particular interest in her. But then Rosie recalled the times he had sat next to her at the table, how Alice always called to her to come and greet Matthias when he dropped in. Rosie had thought it had been out of politeness because he was a man with some standing in the parish. She looked out of her tiny bedroom window down into the yard. There was no one by the well now.

If Clem or Morley had been about, if anyone had witnessed the fiasco, Matthias would have died of shame. Feeling exceedingly foolish he drew another pail of water and carried it into the kitchen with more care than was necessary. Rosie was not there, her shoes were in the hearth and presumably she had gone to change into a dry skirt and hose. Thankfully Kenver could be heard in the next room busy about his crafts. Only Alice and Jessica were in the kitchen. Jessica was putting her rag doll to sleep beside the curled-up purring fat body of Scrap, the cat, in a wooden toy cradle made by her Uncle Kenver. Alice was arranging the flowers in a tall clay pot crafted by the same hand. She greeted Matthias with a cheery smile.

'Hello, Preacher,' she said pleasantly. 'This was very kind of you.'

'Is Rosie cross with me, Alice?' he asked worriedly.

'Cross? For giving her these lovely flowers? Why on earth should she be cross? If I was her I'd be over the moon with delight.'

'Well, she might not want me making such gestures, she hasn't been very friendly lately, but what I really mean is, is she upset that I tipped water all over her feet?'

'Well, it did rather spoil the moment,' Alice smiled, 'but it was an accident. Rosie'll understand and it's just the thing she needs to bring her out of her sulky moods, a bit of romance.'

'I hope so. Oh, Alice, I hope so.' He felt a little shaky and sat down without waiting to be invited.

'That's right, make yourself comfortable.' Alice sniffed at the vanilla fragrance of a heliotrope blossom and looked at it thoughtfully. 'You really took Rosie by surprise.'

'Oh dear, I didn't mean to, I just wanted to . . .'

'Don't you worry now, you've made your feelings plain and that's the hardest part over with. The family will be fair pleased, particularly Clem. He's been trying to shove the two of you together for over a year but it was a devil of a job to get either of you to notice one another. Now, at least you've noticed her.'

Matthias lifted Jessica up on his knee to stop her staring at him. She didn't understand the conversation her mother and Uncle Matthias were having but he looked a bit excited today and she wanted to know why. He kept ducking his head from her so she began earnestly to rearrange his tidily combed dark brown hair and this he happily succumbed to.

'Do you think she likes me, Alice?' he asked, peering anxiously under Jessica's armpit. 'Do you think she'll mind me calling on her?'

'I don't see why not. It's high time the maid got married.'

Alice gave the embarrassed young man an old-fashioned look.

'And it's high time I got married, Alice?'

Alice slipped the last flower into place and carried the heavy pot over to a huge oak dresser, yet another piece of her brother-in-law's excellent craftsmanship, made from timber scraps Oliver had had sent over to him. She poured a mug of steaming tea for Matthias and herself from the never-empty pot on the brick oven, then sat herself at the head of the table. Glancing at the door that shut off the staircase she listened for Rosie's returning. There was no sound from upstairs. She turned to Matthias.

'I love Rosie like she's my own sister. Clem absolutely adores her, you know that.'

He nodded and Jessica stubbornly yanked back his head.

'Jessica, don't be so rough, my handsome,' Alice checked her daughter, then went on to Matthias, 'No one could make a better husband for Rosie than you, Matthias.'

With 'Preacher' now dropped, he recognised that Alice was speaking as surrogate mother of his intended bride. He opened his mouth to respond but Alice held up her hand to silence him.

'Hear me out,' she ordered kindly. 'You'll not find a better wife than Rosie, brought up as she is on a well-run farm. She's a good Christian girl and will support you in this ministry you've taken upon yourself, but,' and Alice emphasised the 'but', 'are you sure, Matthias, that you have room in your life for a wife? Most of the time these last years you've been almost totally absorbed with God's work, as you call it. A wife could be more of a hindrance than a help to you if you're not prepared to put time and effort into a marriage. Have you thought of that? I wouldn't like to see Rosie hurt.'

Matthias did not have the opportunity to reply. Rosie lifted the latch of the stairway door and joined them. Her face gave nothing away as she made for the teapot. Pouring herself a mug of the almost black liquid she sat down on a stool in front of the hearth.

Alice smiled maternally at her. 'Nice and dry now, m'dear?'

Rosie nodded.

Then Alice cast a glance at Matthias. Jessica had climbed down off his lap and returned to her doll and he swept his hair back in an attempt to tidy it again. It made him look younger and rather vulnerable. He was gazing at Rosie with the side of his face cupped in a hand. Alice looked satisfied. He was smitten all right. She could think of no reason why Rosie should reject Matthias. After all Clem's proddings and machinations, it looked like all that was needed now was to allow nature to take its course.

Chapter 23

Bartholomew sat across the room from Kerensa. He looked all round her sitting room and Kerensa fancied he was thinking that his mother should have lived in similar surroundings. The tall windows were opened wide and the heady scents of spring flowers refreshingly invaded the room on the warm tingling-fresh air. His eyes flicked from pictures to portraits, ornaments to vases of flowers, mantelpiece to curtains, carpets to ceiling, furniture to the sewing she'd put aside.

'I'd be happy to show you over the house when we've discussed the reason for your visit, Bartholomew,' she said, bringing him out of his reverie.

'I'd like to see over it very much,' he replied. 'It's something I've always wanted to do, but I don't want you getting tired climbing lots of stairs and walking along long corridors.'

'Because I'm going to have a baby?' Kerensa smiled.

'Aye,' he lowered his head shyly, his blunt, selfish attitude showing its decline since the time she'd slapped his face on Perranbarvah's beach, 'but I didn't like to mention it.'

'I can manage, don't you worry, but if I tire I'll ask Polly to show you what you might miss.'

'I'm going to live in a house like this one day,'

Bartholomew declared, looking up at the high ornate plaster ceiling and spreading his big hands to encapsulate the whole building.

'I'm sure you will, Bartholomew,' Kerensa told him sincerely.

''Tis not just a dream,' he emphasised. 'One day it will be a reality and I shall invite you and Sir Oliver to dine with me – if you will do me the honour.'

'I will look forward to it.'

The dark Pengarron eyes were bright and alive. Kerensa thought he should be captured in just this way on canvas and the portrait deservedly hung in its place beside the one painted of Oliver three years ago to mark his fortieth birthday.

'If someone wants something badly enough they usually find a way to achieve it. Of course, how you go about it is a different matter altogether.'

Bartholomew smiled mysteriously. 'You need have no worry on that score. You see, fate has been kind to the Drannocks at last.' He paused to gain maximum pleasure before he relieved Kerensa of her burning curiosity. 'I've come into some money – rather, I've come into a lot of money, an inheritance, in fact!'

Kerensa resisted the impulse to fly across the room and take Bartholomew by both hands and dance him round the room but she could not hide the excitement in her voice.

'Oh Bartholomew! I'm so pleased for you, that's really wonderful news. I could cry with happiness for you.'

'Well, I have cried,' he said proudly, 'and I'm not ashamed to admit it.'

'Having money isn't everything in the world, of course, but life can be wretched without it and it does take away a lot of worries. And how, when, did this happen? If I'm allowed to ask.'

'Of course you may ask. I want you to know the whole story. 'Tis only right and proper, after your kindness and generosity to us, that outside the family you should be the first to know.'

Laughing with utter delight, Kerensa said, 'And I was so afraid you'd come today with bad news and now I feel I'm bursting with energy. Why don't you tell me all about your good fortune while we look over the house.' She held out her hands and he jumped up to help her to her feet.

As they climbed the principal staircase, Bartholomew took in each Pengarron face that stared back at him from the portraits high up on the ascending walls. Their clothes changed with each generation and century, but it was their eyes that claimed his attention. Even in the females they spoke of their highborn place, their assurance and dignity of belonging to an old aristocratic Cornish family. Bartholomew felt that he knew them.

In the long gallery that overlooked the stairs and great hall they stood in front of the portrait of Oliver. First impression showed a contented man, but closer observation revealed a light in his eyes that betrayed a restless spirit. Beside it was a radiant portrait of Kerensa.

'There is a more recent one of us all together in the library,' Kerensa said. 'It was painted out in the gardens, the only place Luke promised to keep still enough for the sittings.'

Bartholomew studied the ones in front of him. 'You look beautiful and serene but Sir Oliver looks restless, happy enough I suppose, but as though he wanted to be on his way.'

Kerensa was not surprised at the accuracy with which

Bartholomew had summed up Oliver's mood at the time. Her heart ached at how things had changed. Oliver had always been over-energetic and inclined to impatience but the contentment on his face had been replaced with hurt and resentment. He had been away for three months now and she couldn't bear to think of how she missed and needed him.

Moving quickly on and passing by the portrait of Sir Daniel, Bartholomew's grandfather, she said, 'Tell me how you've come by this inheritance of yours, Bartholomew.'

'I've received a letter from a lawyer in Marazion, who in turn had received one from a lawyer in Portsmouth,' he began, offering her his arm in a natural movement. 'I don't know all the details yet but it seems a sailor uncle of my father's, Obadiah Drannock, many years ago married a wealthy merchant's daughter in Portsmouth. Over the years he made a sizeable fortune as a merchant himself in cottons, silks and other fine goods. There was no issue from the marriage and after his wife died he willed his wealth and business interests to my father and his heirs. About a month ago he died an old man, and with my father dead too all of his fortune comes to me.'

Kerensa let out a long soft sigh. 'I can hardly take it in. Wishing no ill will to your late great-uncle, it's a pity the money wasn't available many years ago when you were growing up. And it's a pity your father didn't live to enjoy it.'

'Aye, Father's been gone nearly a year now,' Bartholomew said thoughtfully, angling his head for a closer view of a dour sixteenth-century Pengarron who shared a blank expression he'd seen often on his father's face. 'Doubt if all the money in the world would have cheered him up though. 'Tis Mother who would have had the benefit. Sir Samuel Pengarron,' he read the name plate under the imposing picture. 'Strange . . .'

Pulling at his arm Kerensa moved him on and said quickly, 'Will you take advice on how to use the money? You don't want to waste it or have it stolen or have someone dupe you out of it. I mean, you're not used to a large amount of money and you don't know how to run a business. Will you go to Portsmouth? Will you sell your share of the *Young Maid*? What does Jenifer say about this? Are the children excited? Goodness, I feel so elated. Would you like some tea?'

Her joy was infectious and he laughed heartily. 'I've never heard you go on like this before. Reminded me of Mrs Tregonning. No, I don't want any tea, thank you, but I think you are in need of some. We've seen most of the rooms on this floor, I think we ought to go back down.'

Back in Kerensa's sitting room, without being asked to Bartholomew rang the tinkling silver bell on the small round table at Kerensa's side and resumed his seat.

'I will take advice,' he said seriously. 'I thought to ask the Reverend Ivey.'

'That would be the best idea,' Kerensa said approvingly.

Polly appeared and Kerensa ordered the tea, insisting Bartholomew join her, and as an afterthought asked for a plate of cakes and biscuits. Polly was relieved, she had had a hard task trying to get her young mistress to eat since the master had so mysteriously gone off.

Bartholomew finished off all the cakes and biscuits after Kerensa had taken her own meagre helpings. He also drank the teapot dry and the one after that. Then assuring Kerensa his hunger and thirst were fully satisfied, he spoke of his immediate plans.

'I'm to receive one thousand pounds by the end of the

week. I can't imagine what so much money will look like, 'tis enough to set up several families for life. I've decided to buy Mother and the young'uns a house in Marazion. There's one for sale close to Dr Crebo so he'll be close at hand when he's needed. Mrs Parkin, the woman I hired with the money you lent me to look after us and the cottage, has agreed to live in as housekeeper. Naomi and Hannah will leave the service of the Sarrisons at once. The old brothers have been good to them but there's no need for them to skivvy for anyone any longer and Mother will be glad to have them with her to nurse her rather than strangers.'

'I agree, Jenifer deserves the best of everything,' Kerensa stated, becoming serious, 'and thank God she will receive it in her present condition.'

'Mother won't last the year out, we've accepted that, but 'tis a blessing her last days will end in comfort and dignity. I thought it would be a devil of a job to get her to leave the cottage but she says as long as she can look out over the sea where Father died and rests, she'll die content. I've made another decision too, to hand over my share of the *Young Maid* to the Kings. I haven't really had the heart to fish from the boat that cost my father his life. The Kings can prosper from our good fortune too.'

Kerensa gave a satisfied smile. 'You've matured a good deal in the last months, Bartholomew. You deserve your good fortune. I'm very proud of you.'

'Thank you. The strange thing is, I can't stop myself from wondering what Sir Oliver would think, though there's no reason for him to take any interest in me.'

'I think he would be very pleased for you and impressed by your good common sense at such a young age.' A sudden strong thought made Kerensa doubt the existence of Bartholomew's great-uncle Obadiah and caused her to swivel in her chair and look out of the window. For one terrified moment she feared Bartholomew would read her mind.

'Are you all right?' he asked, half rising from his chair. 'Shall I ring for Polly?'

'No, no,' she stressed, turning back and waving a hand in front of her face to hide what she felt was glaringly displayed for him to see. 'I was just wondering where the children have got to,' she lied.

'When I arrived, your two boys were sliding down the banister of the stairs. Your little maid was shouting at them to stop.'

'That sounds very much as usual.' Kerensa was glad she could smile.

'It must be hard going for you. Three active children, another soon to bear, and Sir Oliver away,' Bartholomew said slowly.

'I am fine, Bartholomew. It's near seven years since Luke was born, it's a big gap, things are different this time, that's all.'

'How much longer till you expect the birthing? I know it's indelicate to ask but I'm concerned for you.'

'I confess I'm not sure. Dr Crebo reckons about ten weeks and Beatrice is in agreement.'

'That settles it then,' Bartholomew said knowledgeably. 'When Beatrice says a baby's due, that's when it comes.'

Kerensa was amused. 'I didn't know you were such an expert on childbearing, Bartholomew.'

'Well, I'm the eldest child of a family of six,' he grinned at her. 'I know a thing or two about it . . . I suppose Sir Oliver would like another son.'

'I don't expect him to mind either way.' She wanted

desperately to drop the subject. She was uneasy about Oliver not knowing about the baby and as each day passed she became a little more fearful about it. Every time there was a knock at the door, every time it was opened, at every sound of a horse or carriage approaching the house she desperately hoped it was Oliver come home in time for the birth of his child and a new beginning for all of them.

Bartholomew was as curious about Oliver's sudden departure as was the rest of the parish. 'Be back soon, will he?'

A shadow dulled Kerensa's eyes. 'I have no idea when he's coming back.'

He saw the subtle change in her deep grey-green eyes. 'I'm sorry, I had no right to ask such a personal question.'

'It's all right.' Kerensa tried to sound cheerful. 'Women in my condition are susceptible to sudden changes of mood, as you probably know. It's been good to have someone to talk to, I haven't had many visitors of late.'

'May I call again, later in the week? I can repay the hundred pounds you lent me.'

'There's no need,' Kerensa protested.

'There's every need,' Bartholomew said darkly.

'Yes, of course,' she smiled knowingly, 'you have your pride, I'm sorry.'

When he left the manor house an hour later Bartholomew had a lot to think about. As his boots crunched over the gravelled carriageway he resolved that when he returned to give Kerensa her hundred pounds he would not be on foot, he would be on the back of one of the finest Pengarron stud horses. Kerensa remained the main subject of his thoughts. He longed to know why she was so unhappy, what had got into Sir Oliver to make him take off so suddenly and without saying when he intended to come back. It would be uncharacteristic of him to stay away for the birth of his child. Not every husband stayed at home for his wife's confinement but Sir Oliver had defied convention and horrified Dr Crebo, Beatrice, and the local midwives by insisting on staying in the childbed room when Miss Olivia and Master Luke were born. Bartholomew suspected that Sir Oliver did not know another child was soon due to join the family. Why hadn't he been told?

Another concern was over what would happen to Sir Oliver's well-organised smuggling runs if his absence continued. The runs still took place regularly under the supervision of Daniel Berryman, the tenant farmer of Orchard Hill Farm, but Sir Oliver's presence was required to ensure that the authorities continued to overlook the operations. If the men decided in his absence to arrange landings in the coves and creeks themselves, it would be a more risky business. The authorities could only be guaranteed to overlook Sir Oliver's activities, and that was because of his position and well known short temper as much as his generous bribes. An arrest was required every so often to satisfy higher-up officials and the more conscientious Revenue men stationed at Penzance. There had been good pickings recently from a wreck at Loe Bar and that might keep folk content for a while, but it would be a bad thing all round if the Lord of the Manor stayed away for too long.

In the following week Kerensa had another visitor. Hezekiah Solomon was shown into her empty sitting room while Polly sped off to fetch her mistress from the kitchens.

Hezekiah checked his appearance in the oval gilt-edged mirror above the mantelpiece. He took an ivory comb from a waistcoat pocket and drew it through his pure white hair, poking and fiddling with the fragrant arrangement until it suited his high standard of perfection. He had dressed with his usual fastidiousness and had been careful not to be over-liberal with cologne.

He wanted Kerensa very much, the desire irrevocably set in his mind from the moment he first saw her on her wedding day. Seducing a man's wife was one of Hezekiah's more pleasing pastimes. Few women had failed to succumb to his flattery and mysteriousness over the years and taking girls like Ameline Beswetherick was exquisite delight; virgins were hard to come by. But Kerensa was his greatest challenge, would be his greatest conquest.

Subtle enquiries at a high-class brothel brought Hezekiah up to date on the local speculation about Oliver's long unexplained absence. It was said he had run off with a wanton female from his past, or he had gone insane. Others believed he was on the run after committing some terrible crime. As inaccurate and laughable as the gossip was, it pleased Hezekiah, especially the talk of Oliver running off with another woman. If he could artfully put the idea into Kerensa's mind, it might well help his cause . . .

He would have to pursue his campaign with the utmost delicacy. Kerensa loved Oliver passionately and would not readily be unfaithful to him. Hezekiah would take his time, offer first a brotherly shoulder and gradually win her over. He licked his lips, his eyes glowed like a serpent's as he dwelled on the prospect of lying with Kerensa. Oliver was a sensuous man, she would know how to please a man after nine years of marriage to him. Oliver, no doubt, employed a delicate touch; so did he. Even when he forced a woman he never hurt her in the intimate moments; that could come later . . .

'It's good to see you, Hezekiah.'

He had not heard her come into the room. Kerensa was standing behind an armchair, her hands resting on its back, the soft smooth hands he wanted to glide over his flesh lying one on top of the other. With irritation he saw Olivia was there too. He abhorred children.

'I felt I could hardly not call upon you, Kerensa, even with Oliver still away,' he said, his smile softening his hard white features.

'I would be hurt if I thought you could not call on us at any time,' Kerensa said.

She was as beautiful as ever but the sparkle, the exciting energy she had formerly exuded had left her. She was a lover without its mate. Hezekiah wanted to put that right.

She wore a dress of slate-blue and grey, the subdued colours adding to her paleness. Given the opportunity he would revive her youthful energy, her verve for life – for a short while anyway. He knew it would only be the one time with Kerensa; guilt or similar illogical feeling would over-whelm her, forbidding a repeat performance. But once would be sufficient . . .

'Will you be staying for dinner, Captain Solomon?'

Olivia had asked the question but she instinctively backed away from him. Hezekiah was sure the child was afraid of him; he would play on her fear to rid her from the room. He advanced on her as he answered.

'If I am invited I shall be honoured to stay, my dear.'

Staring back with her eyes doubled in size Olivia retreated to Kerensa's side and clutched her skirt. 'May . . . may I go and finish my painting for Father, please, Mama?'

'Of course you can, cherub,' Kerensa said. 'I'm sure Captain Solomon will excuse you. Run along and ask Cherry to help you tie your apron.'

Olivia disappeared in a flash. Hezekiah looked into Kerensa's eyes.

'A painting for Oliver? Let us hope it will not be too long before he is back at home to see and enjoy it.' It was a good beginning to rub salt into her wounds, then he could offer the salve to soothe them.

'The children miss him very much,' she said sadly. 'We all do. Have you any idea at all, Hezekiah, when he will be back?'

'No, I'm sorry, none at all,' Hezekiah answered, sounding wistful.

'But he sailed with you, I know that much now. Did he say nothing to give you even the smallest clue?'

'You know Oliver only too well. If he does not wish to disclose something, nothing will persuade him to do so.' This was a truthful statement. Oliver had said nothing of his reasons for making the journey other than that he needed to get away from Cornwall, or of his intended destination or length of absence.

Kerensa sighed and smiled weakly. 'I suppose he'll come back when he's done whatever it is he's so set on doing. I just hope and pray it will not be much longer.'

'It is a pity, my dear, that he left no word of his intentions. But how are you coping, Kerensa? The estate must be of great concern to you. There is no need for me to sail for a long while yet, in fact I am free to stay in Cornwall indefinitely, so if I can be of any assistance to you I offer it gladly.'

'Thank you, Hezekiah. I have no real worries over the estate. Adam and Matthias Renfree, Nathan O'Flynn and the others are more than able to run everything efficiently and they keep me well-informed. I've heard of no complaints from the tenants, although Adam is being over-protective. Oliver allowed me to get involved in some estate business but Adam won't hear of it, he's very set in his ways where women are concerned. It's the children I'm worried about. They can't understand their father going away so suddenly and I don't know how to explain it to them. The boys, Luke in particular, are so restless . . .'

Kerensa picked at the material of the chair all the way along its top as she spoke, watching her taut fingers absent-mindedly, then she looked up. 'Hezekiah, there is one way you can be of help to me.'

This was perfect for Hezekiah's seduction ploy. Kerensa would see him in a favourable light, a woman's gratitude was of immense help in getting closer to her.

'You only have to name it and it shall be done,' he said huskily, with a flourish of beringed hands. 'May I suggest we sit awhile and discuss it?'

Kerensa found herself relaxing. She enjoyed Hezekiah's company and thought she understood him a little better than most other people did.

'Forgive me my lack of manners. Please sit down, Hezekiah, I'm a poor hostess today, and I do hope you will stay for dinner.'

'I shall be delighted to stay and dine with you, Kerensa.'

Hezekiah glanced from chair to chair to decide which one would give him the most advantageous position as Kerensa moved round the back of the chair to sit down. When his eyes alighted on her again he let out an involuntary gasp of horror.

'You . . . you're with child!'

His reaction shocked Kerensa and she instinctively wrapped her arms protectively round her swollen middle.

'I had no idea!' he uttered, feeling sick to the core. The

sight of a pregnant woman filled him with revulsion and it took an immense effort to hide it from Kerensa.

'What's the matter, Hezekiah?' she asked rather sharply.

'It's nothing . . . nothing, Kerensa . . . really, believe me. I'm just shocked . . . that Oliver could leave you in this way.'

The quickly thought-out excuse satisfied Kerensa and looking more at ease she lowered herself into the armchair.

Quietly, she said, 'Oliver doesn't know.'

'About . . . ?' He couldn't bring himself to mention her condition and pointed at her middle.

'No, Hezekiah, Oliver doesn't know we are to have another child.'

Kerensa sounded rather cold and Hezekiah knew she was finding his attitude distressing. Resolutely he told himself to be calm.

'Forgive me, Kerensa. I've been so concerned at Oliver's behaviour towards you these past months,' he lied, pulling and prodding at his elaborate clothes in an unconscious attempt to help himself into a calmer state of mind. 'I have had to stand by helpless while your marriage has foundered like a hapless ship. I must ask you this, why did you not tell him he was to become a father again? It might well have brought him to his senses.' Hezekiah was furious. With his plan of seduction foiled he felt no desire to be tactful. 'I may as well tell you, I know all about the Drannock boy.'

'I see. Oliver told you Samuel Drannock was his half-brother?'

'Yes, I know the whole story.'

'I didn't tell Oliver about the baby because I hoped he'd get things clear in his mind first. I didn't know he planned to go away and when I did find out I didn't want him to feel trapped and resent me all the more. If I'd known he was intending to go off I would have told him a long time before.' Tears filled Kerensa's eyes and ran in tiny sparkling droplets down her pale cheeks. 'Now when he comes back he'll be able to accuse me rightfully of keeping another secret from him.'

And not the only one, Hezekiah thought. What would Oliver think of Clem Trenchard coming to see me about your eldest child's real father trying to blackmail you?

He said, 'It would have been better if you had told him, Kerensa. You need him now, don't you?'

'More than ever,' she said from graven lips. 'I only wish I knew where he was, then I'd beg him to come back to me.'

Hezekiah watched her cry softly. A short time before he would have hoped for this, then he could have put his arms about her, held her close, comforted her. Once a woman was in your arms the next step was so much easier, and she would have felt so good to hold. But all he could do now was to watch her shaking body and grow steadily more frustrated. He looked at her with cold detachment. What was this feeling, so strong and powerful, called love? It turned men and women into fools! Why did people desire it so much? It was as dangerous and destructive as it was supposed to be wonderful. Here, in this wretched, beautiful young woman was the clear evidence of it.

In a grim voice Hezekiah suggested she lie down and rest and he rang the bell for Polly to come to her. He left without enquiring what it was she had been about to ask his assistance for. He rode from the manor with a boiling rage seething inside him and his mind went straight to the cold shiny blade nestled inside his riding boot.

Chapter 24

Adam Renfree called at the manor each morning to advise Kerensa on the activities of the estate. He hovered over her like a worried maiden aunt, puzzled by the rift between the young woman he still looked on as a 'dear little maid' and his master, a man he admired and respected. To Adam it was all such a shame, such a great pity. What had got into the pair of them? What could have happened to turn their idyllic life together sour?

Before he began his latest visit Adam stopped in the stable yard to discuss with Nathan the increase in poaching on the estate since Oliver's absence. He took no notice of Jack saddling Kernick outside the pony's stall, thinking he was going to exercise it, but he stopped in mid-sentence when he saw Kerensa waddling across the yard. She was dressed for riding.

He stalked over to her. 'You didn't oughta be thinking of riding in your condition, ma'am.'

'I'm not going far, Adam,' Kerensa retorted, not looking at his severe face and hoping to get away without any fuss. 'I feel restless today, I must get out for a while.'

She was almost pleading with him but Adam felt he had a duty to stop her. Jack fastened the last strap of the pony's tack and looked up uncomfortably. It was obvious he had tried and failed to forestall his mistress.

'Then I offer you my arm, ma'am, and we'll take a stroll round the grounds.' Adam barred her way to Kernick. 'If you have a fall and hurt yourself His Lordship will never forgive me, went forgive myself neither. I'm sorry, but I insist—'

'I'll take Jack with me.' Kerensa glared at him. 'I will be perfectly all right in his company and I'm not prepared to argue about it, Adam.' She looked round the side of his shoulder. 'Jack, saddle up for yourself without delay.'

'Well,' Adam pushed his fingers underneath his cap and scratched his head. 'I s'pose it went hurt if Jack goes with 'ee, just for an hour or so round the grounds.' He added crossly, 'I'm not happy about it, mind.'

Kerensa stubbornly set her face, turned aside and was confronted by Nathan. She was vexed with herself for blushing as she read in his broad bushy-eyebrowed face that he shared the opinion of the other two men. He said nothing and this made her feel more cross and guilty; it would have been easier to argue him down.

Adam took Jack roughly by the arm and hissed, 'Watch over her carefully, boy.'

Kerensa wanted to go further than the grounds and chose a route along the twisting country lanes that had begun life as wide detours to avoid puddles and quagmires, when the ground was common pasture land centuries ago, and now ran between Orchard Hill and Polcudden Farms. Seeing that she wished to be alone, Jack dropped back a few paces on Meryn but did not take his eyes off her back. They next rode the narrow rutted cart track at the edge of Rose Farm and Jack hoped she would soon want to return home, agonising over how much longer he should bite his tongue and remain silent.

Kerensa was beginning to feel lighthearted; the cobwebs of the long weeks spent cooped up in the manor dissolved from her mind and colour seeped into her cheeks. Tall tapering foxgloves grew proudly out of the low hedgerows. Buttercups and daisies vied with each other to fill every available space of the grassy verges and the perimeters of the planted fields. Dandelion clocks danced on a soft breeze. A swallow looking for food in a long-winged graceful flight gave Kerensa a sudden feeling of freedom and she began humming a country song.

When they were in sight of the rowan trees that conveniently marked the ground where Polcudden Farm ended and Trecath-en Farm took over, Jack moved Meryn up to Kerensa's side and spoke anxiously.

'M'lady, don't you think we should be going back now?'

'Pardon?' She turned, having heard his voice as if it was part of a faraway dream.

'We've been out nearly an hour, be nearly two when we get back.'

'It was Adam Renfree who said to stay out for an hour, not me, Jack. You may go back if you wish, I shall carry on.'

'No, no, I'll go on with you, m'lady,' Jack said quickly, worried that her lighthearted mood was blotting out her good sense. 'Whatever you say is fine by me.'

'Good, we'll leave it at that then, shall we?'

They rode on, Jack dropping back as he had before. Five minutes later they rounded a bend in the track which brought them well on to Trecath-en land and there they saw three men approaching on foot.

Kerensa turned round to Jack. 'Who are they, Jack? Do you know them?'

'Can't say I do, m'lady,' Jack replied, gazing at the men through anxious eyes. 'Rovers probably by the look of 'em, probably looking for work on the farms.'

They passed the men, giving a brief nod to each one. One muttered, 'Mornin' to 'ee, lady.' Another looked down on the ground without speaking and spat at Meryn's hooves. The other looked sideways at them through slitted yellowing eyes. All were unkempt and unwashed, their clothes rough and greasy.

Kerensa sank back into her pensive mood and gave them no further thought. But Jack was uneasy. He looked anxiously behind. The three men had stopped and were looking at him and Kerensa with their heads close together as they stood in a huddle.

Kerensa and Jack covered another three hundred yards at walking pace, then again Jack suggested they ought to return home. This time Kerensa passively agreed but not before reining in to peer over the growing wheat, oats and barley of Trecath-en's fields. A few more minutes passed by before they finally began to retrace their steps. Jack was relieved to see no sign of the travellers but he was still uneasy.

When they reached the ground where they had passed the three men Jack brought Meryn to a halt and lifted himself up in the saddle to look intently all around.

'What is it, Jack?' Kerensa asked. 'Is something wrong?'

'I dunno, m'lady. I just have this feeling we're being watched.'

Kerensa swivelled in her saddle as much as her bulging middle allowed. 'I can't see or hear anything unusual.' The nagging ache in her back that had started in the early hours of the morning had steadily increased with the length of the ride. She knew it had been foolish to go riding now she was so big; it was her own fault she was uncomfortable. She longed to rub at the root of the pain but did not want an 'I-told-you-so' look from Jack. Instead she smiled brightly to humour him. 'Come on, let's get home, I'm ravenously hungry and I expect you are too, eh, Jack?'

There was no answer.

'Jack?'

'I can hear voices,' he said at last. 'Could be they men we passed just now. I didn't like the look of 'em.'

'Do you think they may wish us harm?' Kerensa was anxious herself now.

Jack slid off his pony, his eyes searching keenly for anything that would serve as a weapon.

'What are you doing? Shall I get down too, Jack?'

'You stay put, m'lady. 'Tis probably nothing to worry about, could be just one of the farmers, but if they others show up again I want you to ride for the manor as fast as you can.'

They listened fearfully for voices and watched for movement. Jack broke off a thick stem from a hazel bush, picked up a large stone in his other hand and took up a defensive stance.

'What are you going to do, Jack? You must come with me.'

'No, if there's any trouble I'll hold 'em off while you get away. I'll catch you up.'

A short time later Jack said cautiously, ' 'Tis all quiet, I d'reckon we can go on now.'

'I'm sorry, Jack.' Kerensa said humbly.

'What for, m'lady?' he asked, looking at her in genuine surprise.

She massaged the small of her back, no longer worried at revealing her discomfort. 'Because you're worrying about me, aren't you? It's making you jumpy. I should not have insisted on us going so far.'

'All I want is for you to be happy,' Jack said, tossing the stone away.

Jack looked so serious Kerensa was touched by his concern. With a shy grin he reached for Meryn's reins to mount and didn't fully absorb Kerensa's sudden shrill scream.

He was hurtled forward by a searing pain across the back of his shoulder that forced the hazel stem out of his hand. Kerensa screamed again as she was roughly pulled off Kernick to the ground. The attack happened so quickly there was no time for her to flee or for Jack to put up a fight. The three men they had seen on the cart track earlier had crept up on their bellies behind the cover of a stretch of wild hedge.

Kerensa's arms were pinioned cruelly behind her and she was forced to watch as Jack was kicked and punched to the ground. She could hear his bones cracking as two of the assailants laid into him with their fists, their feet and the stick he had dropped. They struck his back, chest, legs and head. She screamed throughout the vicious beating, hearing it echoing back until Jack stopped crying and groaning and lay still.

'Jack! Jack! No! Oh no!'

A heavy slap across her mouth quietened Kerensa to a whimper. Her hat was torn from her head and a cruel hand grasped the back of her neck.

'Leave me be!' she cried, kicking out with her feet.

Her attacker thrust her against Kernick's flank and looked her up and down. 'Yer a plucky one,' he sneered, his watery eyes taking in her heavily swollen middle.

''Ere, yer not thinkin' of doin' nothin' to 'er, are 'ee, Dando?' one of the other men growled before giving Jack one last kick in the gut and leaving his inert body to stain the dusty track a liquid red.

'Naw, t'wouldn't be much fun with 'er like this,' Dando replied gruffly, his evil breath swamping Kerensa's face. She tried unsuccessfully to turn away from him.

'So she's stuffed up, that gonna stop either of 'ee?' the third man sniggered. 'She's some beautiful.'

'You filthy animals, you savages!' Kerensa shrieked at them. 'Keep away from me!'

Dando suddenly let her go and clutching her stomach Kerensa moaned and sank to the ground. She kept her eyes rooted in fear and anger on his coarse ugly face.

'About ready to drop un, are 'ee?' he asked in mocking tones.

'Yes,' she answered defiantly, flinging up her chin, 'and if you lay a finger on me my husband will have all three of you hung!'

'Would 'e now and who might 'e be?' Dando bawled, as he touched Kernick's saddle. 'The Lord Mayor of London, mebbe?'

'He's Sir Oliver Pengarron,' Kerensa got out with a snarl.

'Pengar'n, eh? I've 'eard of 'e, a 'ard bugger 'e be.' Dando pounced on Kerensa and brutally gripped a handful of her hair. 'But 'e's not around at the moment, so I've 'eard. I 'eard too 'e married a comely young wench. I 'eard right, an' yer more 'n' comely, m'dear, yer soft 'n' smellin' purty too.'

'C'mon, Dando,' urged the second thug. 'Get 'er jewel'ry and the 'orses an' let's get the 'ell out of 'ere. I don't want no trouble with that Pengar'n. I saw a piece of gentry beaten to a bloody pulp by 'im a few years back along jus' fer trying to 'ave 'er. 'E's got some awful temper.'

'I edn't afeared of 'e,' Dando spat out, twisting Kerensa's head cruelly to the side. ''E edn't 'ere, is 'e, though I don't know why 'e's gone off fer so long an' left this little beauty all alone.' He caressed the red hair spilling over his hand. 'Besides, if we'm caught we'll be 'ung fer killin' the stable boy anyway.'

An agonised scream ripped deep from Kerensa's throat. 'No!'

'What's up, me 'an'some,' Dando jeered. ''E wus only a servant – or did 'e stuff 'ee up instead of Pengar'n?' He turned to his companions and laughed. 'P'raps that why the bugger went off, eh?'

'You disgusting—'

Kerensa was suddenly forced back on to her feet. Her wedding ring was ripped from her finger and her clothes torn as Dando performed a humiliating search for more jewellery. There was none to be found and he swore profusely.

'Leave 'er be, fer God's sake,' snarled the third robber. He was mounted on Meryn and his mate was up behind him. 'Git on that other bleddy pony and let's git away afore someone sees us.'

A sudden sharp pain made Kerensa stiffen and she groaned heavily. Dando pushed her away and spat on the ground beside her then climbed clumsily on to Kernick's back, making the pony whinny in fear.

'Don't leave me like this!' she appealed to the two other men. 'I think my baby's coming! Please!'

For a moment it looked as if one of them was going to dismount but Dando kicked the pony's rump and it charged off. He looked down at Kerensa. 'I 'ope the brat comes right 'ere on the roadside an' is born dead!'

He galloped after his cronies, sending dust flying over

Kerensa and choking her. Coughing violently, she somehow crawled over to Jack. He lay on his back, his head
turned to one side with his mouth wide open and his tongue
hanging out. She knelt over him and her hands hovered
over his body, not knowing what to do or what to touch
first. Then she smoothed streaks of dusty bloodied hair
away from his battered face and cried tears of hopelessness.

'Oh Jack, what have I done to you? My poor Jack, it's all
my fault. My poor dear Jack. I'm sorry . . . I'm sorry . . .'

Sobbing wretchedly she lowered her head on his chest,
feeling sharp edges of broken rib under her cheek. She
stayed like that till her tears slowed, then raising her head
she pushed back her hair and looked helplessly about.
What should she do now? She could do nothing for Jack.
He was dead.

She hoped she was mistaken about the baby coming but
another strong pain convinced her the birth was not far off.
She breathed in deeply in the way Beatrice had taught her
until the pain passed. From her experience of giving birth
to Olivia and Luke she reckoned she had at least four or five
hours. Long before that she hoped help would come from
someone travelling along the cart track or out looking for
them.

She put her head sorrowfully on Jack's chest again.
Suddenly her body stiffened. There was a faint sound
. . . definitely something . . . The heady knowledge that
she could hear something stirring in Jack's beaten body
brought her fully to her senses.

'You're alive! Jack! Oh Jack!' She gently shook his still
body, desperate for any movement, however small. It came
in a weak flutter of an eyelid. 'Oh, thank God, thank God.'

Her mind now crystal clear, Kerensa knew she had to
get help for Jack. The day was advancing towards the

afternoon and getting warmer but even so Jack could become cold and it would worsen his condition. Taking off her jacket she placed it over him. Carefully she pulled off his neckerchief and dabbed at the blood on his face but it made no difference to his mauled features. She straightened his limp legs, praying it would not make his injuries worse. Then she placed her hat over his head to keep off the sun. She kissed his cheek and whispered in his ear.

'I'm going to get help, Jack, I promise. Just hold on, I'll make sure you'll be all right.'

She got shakily to her feet. She would get help. But from where? There was only one answer. The nearest dwelling was Trecath-en Farm. She would go to Clem.

Chapter 25

It was about half a mile through the fields to Trecath-en's farmhouse. A ten-minute walk in normal circumstances but Kerensa knew it would take her much longer today. She expected to have two or three contractions on the way. There was no need to panic, it wasn't her first baby. When the pains came she would stop and wait for them to subside, then carry on her way. Alice would be there at the farm. She would know what to do. She had had babies of her own. And it would be hours yet. Time enough for Clem to put Jack on the farm cart and take them back to the manor for the birth and to fetch Dr Crebo for them both.

The trek across country was more difficult than Kerensa had counted on. The ground ran downhill and every step she took was heavy and jarred her tender stomach and persistently aching back. She was in shock from the attack, her mouth was dry, she felt sick and black edges round her eyes threatened to cut off her vision. She stumbled over protruding corners of granite rock, slithered over pebbles. She was brought often to her knees, each time finding it more difficult to get back on her feet.

The contractions were closer together and more painful than she had anticipated. Suddenly she could no longer stand but lowering herself onto the short green corn was an agony she'd never known before. She closed her eyes tightly and tried to breathe evenly. Once, she opened her eyes and looked down and saw the pointed whiskery features of a tiny field vole. It turned its head to the side and sniffed the air, its bright, curious eyes seeming to ask what she was doing there. It was the only sign of life she could see and in her desperation she asked it to go and fetch help. But the field vole only scuttled away. She laughed and cried together when she realised what she had done. Now if the little creature had been a dog it might have worked and she cursed herself for not bringing Bob along.

Then fresh hope brought her to her feet again. She had an idea and shouted 'Charity!' as loudly as she could. If Clem was working in the fields then Charity would be with him and, with her sharp ears, would alert Clem. But even though Kerensa shouted until her throat was hoarse and felt fainter as the effort starved her brain of oxygen, no big black retriever came barking and bounding towards her voice.

She tramped on, but not for long. She woke up on the ground sweating and cramped all over and she knew she had fainted. She did not know how long she had lain there, her face pressed to the ground.

'Jack!' she cried out. 'I'm going, Jack, I won't let you down.'

She struggled to her feet in a panic, praying through her tears that the delay had not cost Jack his life.

She dragged herself along, taking one slow, anguished step after another, holding her belly and fighting against the pain. Her whole being consisted now of nothing but pain. Pain in her weakened limbs, the pains of the child making its way out of her body, throbbing pain where Dando had struck her face, and the worst pain of all, the knowledge that if she had not been so stubborn Jack would not be lying, dead or dying, in the dirt.

'Oh Clem,' she gasped, 'where are you? Anybody!'

When she saw the first of the farm buildings, tears poured down her face. She trudged on past the barn and outbuildings and had to skirt round the billy goat on his long tether to avoid it nibbling at her clothes. She was dismayed to find the farmyard deserted. None of Clem's three children was playing or doing a chore there. Even the wild cats that were usually to be found sunning themselves beside the kitchen wall were absent.

She called out in panic. 'Clem! Alice! Anyone! Where are you?'

She reached the open kitchen door at the same moment a fierce pain made her cry out and she fell across the doorstep.

'Who's there? Is that you, Alice? Is everything all right?'

She recognised the voice of Kenver Trenchard but could not answer him. A strange rolling sound came towards her and she imagined that the house was about to collapse about her. She looked into the kitchen and saw an even stranger sight. Kenver was seated in an upright chair with big cart-like wooden wheels attached to either side, the rims of which were covered with strips of leather. Kerensa was so surprised at the sight she uttered a choked cry.

Kenver was even more surprised. 'Kerensa! What's happened to you!' She had never been Lady Pengarron to him, he had not set eyes on her since before her marriage.

Kerensa stayed sprawled on the doorstep, her back leaning heavily against the door. She tried to gain her breath.

'I need help . . . Kenver . . . for Jack . . . we were attacked . . . by thieves up . . . on the edge of . . . the fields. He's lying out there . . . barely alive. Where is everyone? Where's Alice? . . . I need her, Kenver. My baby's coming!'

Kenver wheeled himself closer. He looked grave. 'I'm afraid Alice and Rosie have taken the children to a wedding at Perranbarvah. Clem and Father are cutting furze and logs and won't be back for an hour or so.'

'But Jack needs urgent attention!' Kerensa wailed. 'Isn't there something we can do?'

'I'm afraid not, but they won't be late, they don't leave me alone for long. Your baby won't be born for a while yet, will it?' he asked anxiously, her despair making him feel all the more helpless.

Kerensa rubbed her dirtied hands over her bulge, pain-less and quiet for the moment. 'I'm afraid it's coming quicker than I first thought but not for quite a while, I hope. It's Jack I'm worried about.'

'Well, you won't help Jack by sitting in the doorway,' Kenver said. 'Let me help you inside. Then we'll just have to sit and wait it out together and pray Jack will be all right.'

Although his legs were useless Kenver's arms had great strength and effortlessly he put them under Kerensa's arm-pits and eased her up gently to sit on his lap. She held on thankfully to him as he wheeled his strange moving chair to a window in the corner of the room then helped her into a firm comfortable chair that was piled with colourful patchwork cushions.

'Would you rather lie down, Kerensa? My bed's through the next room so you won't have to climb the stairs.'

'No . . . thank you, Kenver. I'd rather stay here then I can see if someone's coming.'

'I'll, um, fetch you a dish of tea,' he said. 'You look really parched.'

372

'Your mother never had an empty teapot as I remember,' Kerensa remarked, the memory almost making her smile.

'Then I'll get you some water so you can clean up a bit.'

'Thank you, Kenver. You are kind.' She rubbed at fresh tears and sniffed and gulped. Kenver reached round to a pile of laundry airing behind him and took one of Alice's handkerchiefs which he gave to Kerensa. She thanked him and buried her face in it.

'I wish I could do more for you, Kerensa,' Kenver said, and seeing her only as a friend of the family in distress he patted her shoulder and wound her hair back behind her ears.

'I'm just so glad you're here, Kenver. It's a great help.'

'Have you any idea who attacked you?' he asked, as he expertly manoeuvred his chair round the furniture to reach the teapot.

'No . . . none at all,' she sniffed, peering out through the window and willing Clem or Morley to appear.

She took in the contents of the kitchen, noting the new touches Alice had made since Clem's mother had died. Some of the ornaments on the mantelshelf were ones Alice had had in her room when she lived at the manor as Kerensa's maid. The bellows leaning against the wall of the fireplace were on the lefthand side; Florrie Trenchard had always insisted they be kept on the right. On a little shelf beside a chair at the hearth she saw with irony a tinder box that she recognised as belonging to her late grandfather. Clem must have taken it from the cottage in Trelynne Cove after she and Old Tom Trelynne had left it deserted all those years ago. This room could have been her domain, she could have been Clem's wife and shared his life with him here. With painful regret she wished she did not love two men. Even more painful was the fact that the one she needed the most at this moment could be halfway round the world, and might not even care.

'Pity Mother isn't here now,' Kenver said, coming back with a mug of tea. 'She was strong enough to have carried Jack home on her back and if Gran were alive she could have seen to you.'

'Like I said, thank God you're here, Kenver. I feel a bit safer,' Kerensa said, gazing at him with blinking eyes. 'It's years since I was here last. You haven't changed a bit.'

'You have, you've changed a lot, Kerensa,' he said, looking at her closely.

'Have I?'

'Yes. Even with your clothes all torn and your face scratched and dirty I can see you're far more beautiful. Everyone says you are, and now I can see for myself. I'll get that water I promised you and a cloth to wash your face.'

Kerensa gulped at the bitter strong tea and watched him ladle water from a pail behind the door into a small tin bowl. Kenver was an attractive young man, his flawless skin pale from a life spent mostly indoors. His hair was lighter than Clem's, almost white like the twins', his eyes a deep violet blue. If he could stand, Kerensa believed he would be nearly as tall as Clem, and even with his physical disability she thought if ever he chose to leave the farm he would turn many a girl's heart.

Finishing the tea she put the mug on the deep windowsill. Kenver wheeled over and handed her a clean cloth, the one Alice used for washing the children. He kept the bowl of water on his lap.

'When you're ready,' he said encouragingly.

'You always were good to me, Kenver.'

374

'I was a lovestruck boy of fifteen when I last saw you. I believed I loved you as much as Clem did.'

Kerensa hung her head as she dabbed her sore face with the cloth. 'It was one of the cruellest things to happen when . . . when I didn't marry Clem . . . not being able to come to the farm and see you. You do understand . . . with Clem living here . . .'

'Aye, but I knew I'd see you again one day and here you are.'

'A pity it has to be with me in this sorry state and with poor Ja—'

She clutched her stomach and lowered her head to her chest as another contraction came. Kenver took her hands and she gripped his long, cool, sensitive fingers until it must surely hurt.

'Sorry,' she said, a while later.

'It's all right, I did the same for Alice till she went upstairs with Jessica. Are you sure you won't lie down?'

'No, please, I'd rather stay here.' A small look of fear creased her face. 'There . . . there may come a time when I'll have to.'

'Don't worry,' he said soothingly. 'I'm sure I'll manage to do what I have to. One thing about being stuck most of my life in the house with the women is I've overheard a heck of a lot about childbirth and other unmentionable things. Now wash your hands and face, you'll feel a bit better. Then we'll sit quietly and pray for the Lord's protection over Jack.'

There were no clocks in Trecath-en Farm but Kenver reckoned when the sun dropped out of sight behind the barn and cast a long shadow over the yard an hour had passed. He hoped Clem or his father would appear very soon. Kerensa's pains were becoming more frequent and knowing the layout of the farmland he knew Jack would be fully exposed under a scorching sun. He was worried about Kerensa. Her condition was weak and shocked for a woman about to face the final stages of labour and she was constantly falling into a faint. All his life Kenver had had people help and wait on him. Now, all of a sudden, here he was faced with the awesome responsibility of someone else's welfare.

A cheerful whistling from out in the yard brought Kerensa to consciousness, her body rigid. If she'd been able she would have jumped out of the chair. Painfully she stood up and went to the door, blinking in the light. Clem was strolling across the yard, his crib bag held loosely over his shoulder. Kerensa couldn't move or cry out, only stand and watch the tall young man with blond hair coming towards her.

When he saw her the crib bag was thrown aside. He ran, and in an instant she was in his arms, strong, capable, comforting arms to hold and protect her. She was safe now, held in his love. And then she drifted away into a sweet welcoming darkness.

'You've been asleep for nearly an hour,' Clem told Kerensa gently.

'Where am I?' she murmured, gazing about the room where she lay in a small lumpy bed. 'I've not been here before.'

He took her hot moist hands from the green and blue patchwork cover. 'This is the main bedroom of the farm.'

'Where you and Alice sleep?'

'Aye, it was Father's idea to move into the lean-to after Mother died and for us to come in here. I think he wanted some peace and quiet from the rest of us.'

Kerensa smiled at the little bed in the corner where a rag doll she had made herself sat propped up against the pillow. It was Jessica's bed and she could picture the tiny girl with the golden curls cuddling the doll in her sleep. Kerensa wanted to go back to sleep and closed her eyes again. But a terrifying vision of a young man, battered, bleeding and dying on a cart track invaded her mind and she screamed out his name. She struggled to sit up but Clem firmly held her down.

'It's all right, my love. Jack is in the lean-to. Father fetched him in the cart. It's too risky to take either of you back to the manor so Adam Renfree, who arrived here a little while ago, has ridden off to Marazion to fetch Dr Crebo. Adam was worried out of his mind about you, he's been out looking for you, he and many others, but they went to places like Trelynne Cove first.'

'Jack's alive? He's still alive?'

'Yes, my love, he's still alive. Kenver's with him, he's cleaning up some of his wounds with Rosie's concoctions, the stuff Beatrice taught her to make, so they won't go septic.'

'And Jack will be all right, Clem?'

Clem stroked her cheek very tenderly. 'We don't know that for sure yet, my love, but we mustn't give up hope.'

Kerensa became calmer, she raised her arms and put her hands on Clem's shoulders. 'It's so good to see you. I think I rode out this way in the first place with some vague idea of seeing you.'

'You know I'm here whenever you want me.' He softly kissed her flushed cheeks.

'It was such a relief to find Kenver here in that strange contraption of his. It gave me quite a shock but I'm glad it helps him to get about.'

377

'It was his idea, he made it himself.'

'I must have given him a fright myself, turning up like this. Oh, what have I done, Clem,' she said wretchedly. 'It's all my fault Jack got beaten the way he did. If I hadn't insisted on—'

'None of that.' Clem pressed a finger to her lips. 'Jack was hurt trying to protect you. It's all that would have mattered to him.'

'But he's just a boy.'

'No, my little sweet, Jack's a grown man now.'

'He'll always be a boy to me, like one of my own children.'

'And you'll soon be adding another to your family,' Clem said, pressing a hand to her forehead to feel her temperature.

'What?' Memory of her labour rushed back to her. 'But the pains have stopped.'

'No they haven't, you're so worn out you've been sleeping through them. I've felt your middle, it's still contracting and they're getting stronger.'

As if to prove the truth of his words she felt the next pain. Caught unaware, it was sheer agony and she doubled over, fighting to control her breathing and letting out a loud squeal.

'This one is different . . . to my other labours . . .' she panted. 'I wish Alice was here . . . and that . . . I had some of Beatrice's . . . raspberry leaf tea to ease the discomfort . . .'

Clem held her hands as Kenver had done. 'I'll go and have a look in Rosie's box of remedies and see if she's got some in there. Father's gone to get Alice so she'll be here quite soon.'

'No!' Kerensa said fearfully. 'Please don't leave me,

it won't be much longer now.'

'If Father can get Dr Crebo to come straightaway he might feel he'll have to treat Jack first. If Alice is not here in time, well, I've delivered many a calf and lamb.'

Kerensa had sunk back into the same welcome, comfortable darkness. When she opened her eyes her head was turned towards the window and she stared out at the cloudless pale blue sky and waited for the next contraction. None came.

'Kerensa.'

She turned to face Clem.

'That's the second time you've fainted on me today.'

'I'm sorry,' she said wanly, 'you always used to say you had no patience with silly fainting females.'

'In your case you're excused,' he smiled. His shirt sleeves were rolled up to reveal suntanned arms about a bundle of cloth.

'What have you got there?' she asked sleepily.

'This tiny little thing in my arms?'

'Is it – my baby?' Her face broke into a shining smile. 'You have my baby?'

'Aye, and she's as beautiful as her mother.'

'She?'

'A tiny wisp of a thing but I reckon she's fine. Do you want to hold her?'

Kerensa held out her arms, she had no strength left to try to sit up. Clem sat on the bed, handed her the baby, then lifted her and encircled them both in his arms.

'I've never held a newborn baby before. I've always been afraid of them, even my own, but it's different when you help bring one into the world,' he said proudly.

'Just look at her,' Kerensa whispered. 'She was nearly full term but she's smaller than your twins were.'

'And with none of her mother's red hair or . . . his black hair. It's fair like mine. People could talk, you know,' he teased.

Kerensa laughed. 'My father and grandfather were fair.'

'Ah, but who will remember that?'

Clem cupped the tiny warm head in his hand. The baby was quiet, putting her pink tongue in and out of her puckered red mouth as if she was tasting this new thing called air. Her eyes were open but not for long and she nestled into her mother's breast and slept. She was wrapped in a floral patterned petticoat snatched from Alice's drawer and tenderly Clem positioned the fabric to cover the top of her head to keep her warm.

'I did a good job helping this little one into the world but I suppose I should have found something more suitable than this to put her in,' he confessed. 'I just didn't think.'

Kerensa kissed her daughter's forehead and said, 'Now isn't that just like a man! This will do for now.'

Clem gently tilted Kerensa's face to look into her eyes. 'There is a part of you, Kerensa, that belongs to me. A part of you Oliver Pengarron can never have. I helped to bring this child into the world. I was the first person to set eyes on her, the first to hold her and I feel a part of her belongs to me too . . . Have you got a name for her?'

'No, I hadn't given much thought to what the baby I was carrying would be called.'

'Kelynen is nice, Cornish for holly, and right now she's as red as a holly berry.'

'It's a beautiful name,' Kerensa said thoughtfully.

'A beautiful child deserves a beautiful name.'

'Yes,' Kerensa said, sadly. 'I was hoping I wouldn't have to choose alone and she must be called something.'

Chapter 26

Two days later Alice Trenchard, holding the new baby snuggled in close to her body, sat beside Kerensa in the Trenchard farm cart for the journey to take mother and child home. Morley drove the team of two oxen with Nathan O'Flynn and Adam Renfree riding as escort. All three men kept a wary eye open in case of any more trouble. Morley had wanted Kerensa to send for a Pengarron carriage, worried that any other means of conveyance would be uncomfortable for her and the baby. But Kerensa had insisted the farm cart with plenty of straw and a couple of pillows was more than suitable. She nursed a secret fear that a rich man's coach might attract the attention of more highwaymen.

Kerensa cast Alice many a sly look, turning quickly away whenever Alice looked back at her.

'What?' Alice asked eventually.

'Oh, nothing.'

'Must be something. Have I got a dirty mark on my face or something?'

'No.'

'What then?'

'You look different, that's all.'

'Different? In what way different?'

Kerensa pouted her lips, picked up a long straw and bent

it over and over while she considered. 'Well, you're sort of bubbly. More like you were when you lived at the manor.'

'Oh, that sort of different. I suppose I had become rather matronly over the years,' Alice said breezily, 'and I suppose I do feel sort of . . . bubbly today.'

'You've been the same way since the baby was born. If it's going to make such a difference to you perhaps I should come over to the farm next time I want to deliver a baby.'

Alice looked at her friend to see if the remark reminded her that the father of the baby she was holding and any future babies was not around any more, but Kerensa was in a lighthearted mood today.

Alice smiled contentedly, more to herself than to Kerensa.

They reached the part of the rutted track where the attack had occurred and Kerensa looked anxiously about. She shuddered at the pale stains on the ground where she'd been forced to leave Jack lying hurt.

'Don't you worry, m'dear,' Morley called back to her. 'They swine be long gone from hereabouts by now.'

'Aye,' Nathan added from his horse, patting the firearm resting across his saddle, 'and this'll see to any trouble-makers, m'lady.'

'We're ready for anything, m'lady,' Adam said, in a tough voice, 'and Nathan's dogs are running about sniffing everything in sight. You have nothing to worry about.'

'You all right?' Alice asked, squeezing her arm.

Kerensa assured them all that she was and the company fell silent. She didn't regain her earlier light mood until they were travelling over the manor's parklands.

Kerensa watched the way Alice was cooing to her baby even though she was peacefully sleeping.

'I know,' she said triumphantly, clapping a hand down on

Alice's arm, 'you're having another baby yourself. I should have guessed at once. You always gaze wistfully at every new baby in the parish when you're expecting.'

'I am not,' Alice replied in a sing-song voice. 'I just love to hold a newborn babe, that's all, and it's been so good having you to stay for a couple of days. Rosie is very sweet and I love the maid dearly, but she's so quiet these days. It's been a real treat having another woman in the house again.'

'I'm afraid I didn't get much chance to speak to Rosie with my concern over the baby and Jack. How is she? How's the romance going? Is there to be a wedding? Is that why you're so bubbly?'

'I've really no idea what's going on between they two – she and Matthias. She don't give nothing away, there's too much of Clem in her for that, and he's so shy about that sort of thing.' Alice giggled. 'I know I shouldn't laugh but he looks so pained at times.'

Alice wished she could tell Kerensa the true reason for her new-found radiance, but it was too close to her heart, too personal.

It had been a shock when Morley had turned up at the home of the Perranbarvah bride to collect her, Rosie and the children with the astonishing news of the attack on Jack and Kerensa.

On her arrival home Dr Crebo was getting ready to leave. The surgeon-physician had patched up Jack as best he could and he pounced on Alice as the obvious head female of the household, giving her precise instructions on how he was to be nursed. He had little hope of Jack recovering. His injuries were very serious and the main concern was the internal bleeding he had suffered. The doctor wasn't concerned about his fees, he was content in the knowledge that at some point the Pengarron estate would forward the payment, and after warning sternly that on no account was Jack to be moved he'd made to go.

'But Dr Crebo,' Alice hailed him from the door.

'Yes, what is it, Mrs Trenchard?' he replied impatiently. 'I thought I had given you clear instructions.'

'Aren't you going to stay and deliver Lady Pengarron's baby?'

'All safely over and done with,' the doctor beamed. 'Your husband delivered the infant a goodly time before I arrived here. I have examined Her Ladyship and her child and both are well, despite Her Ladyship's terrible ordeal, I'm happy to say. Your husband can pride himself on a task well done.'

Alice sat down. 'Clem delivered the baby?'

The doctor promptly left, leaving Alice in her amazement. Morley had hurried off to do the evening milking, Kenver was watching over Jack and Rosie was keeping the children out of the way outside. Clem, presumably, was upstairs with Kerensa and the baby he had delivered.

What would this mean? With this special and intimate event between him and Kerensa, and with Oliver still away, would it open up a new longing in Clem for the beautiful, desirable, and now so vulnerable young woman lying in her bed? Alice knew Kerensa still held a deep affection for Clem. Would she feel an overwhelming need for him? Alice knew neither Clem nor Kerensa would lightly hurt her, but emotional needs could and often did outweigh the conscience.

'You all right, love?' Clem's voice intruded on her thoughts.

It startled Alice to her feet. 'Dr Crebo's just told me the news. I'll go up to Kerensa. What did you wrap the baby in? I'll turn out something of Jessica's. I still have her baby clothes, I didn't have the heart to give them away even though it's unlikely I'll have another.'

Clem went to her and kissed her forehead. 'I'm glad you're back, I needed you.'

This was so unexpected Alice gasped. He rarely kissed her unless as a prelude to lovemaking and he had never told her he needed her. 'You did? What is it, a boy or a cheeil?'

'A little girl, so tiny she looks like a drop in the ocean.'

Alice looked deeply into her husband's eyes, trying to read what this birth meant to him. Often when she spoke to him he gave her only half his attention but the steady gaze she received back seemed to suggest that this time he was fully with her.

'Has Kerensa chosen a name yet?'

'Aye, Kelynen.'

'That's nice.'

Alice climbed the narrow turning staircase with a heavy heart. Clem had wanted Jessica to be called Kelynen but Alice had insisted on naming their daughter as he had chosen the names of the twins. Clem must have suggested Kelynen to Kerensa. Alice knew Kerensa had deliberately not chosen a name for her baby in the hope that Oliver would be home in time for the birth and they could choose together, and hopefully be brought closer together again. If that had been the case, the baby's first name would not have been Cornish.

That night Alice and Clem made up a bed for themselves in the kitchen where they could easily be called if Kerensa wanted anything and Morley could quickly fetch them if Jack needed extra nursing or took a turn for the worse. They pushed the heavy table aside and Clem laid sacks of clean, fresh-smelling straw in front of the hearth. Alice covered the sacks with a sheet and stood back and frowned.

'How are we both going to fit on that? 'Tis no bigger than Jessica's bed and I've put on a bit of weight in the last few years.' She patted her generous hips and fully expected Clem to say he would sit up all night in a chair.

But Clem laughed and coming up behind her put his arms round her waist and nibbled her ear.

'What are you doing, Clem Trenchard?' she giggled, yet elated inside at this unexpected attention from him.

'We managed in the small bed in the lean-to when you were carrying the twins,' he said, his voice low and sultry as he ran his hands over her hips and bottom, 'and have I ever complained about an extra pound or two around here?'

'But—'

'But what?' He started on the other ear, making her wriggle about.

Alice had nearly said, 'But Kerensa is so beautifully slim.'

Clem turned her round, putting his hands firmly on her waist. Alice liked it when he was attentive, when there was desire in his handsome fair features. Sometimes she couldn't get over the fact that he was her husband; many other women found him attractive and would remark, 'You're some lucky woman to be hitched to someone like he,' and 'What's he like?' – meaning, 'What's he like in bed?' But he was her husband, and right now there was desire in his eyes and the desire was for her. Still, she could not get Kerensa and what she meant to Clem out of her mind.

Clem would not have been surprised if he'd known what was going through her mind. He had not missed the new look of hurt in her eyes when he'd come down from Kerensa and the baby. But Alice need not have worried.

No matter how badly Oliver Pengarron treated Kerensa, or how long he stayed away, she would always love him passionately. Clem could only ever claim a small part of her, and he was content with that. At one time he would have thought it impossible, but time and circumstances had changed, and here he had a woman who loved him, cherished him and who would always be faithful to him. Alice wasn't a dream he would ever have to chase. And now, after nine years of marriage, he realised he needed her, and Alice deserved to be told that no one else could take her place as his wife. They were joined not only by sacred vows, but by their own special kind of love.

So he said softly, 'I love you.'

She could not hide her shock. He had given her a few endearments down the years, but not once had he proclaimed he loved her.

'Do . . . do you?'

'I really do love you,' and he said each word slowly and evenly.

Alice could hardly take it in. He had spoken the words she never thought he'd say to her. Exhilaration filled her soul.

In a voice that sounded as if it was coming from eternity, she said, 'I love you, Clem. I always have.'

'I know you have, my dear, wonderful Alice.'

The depth and tone of his voice chased tantalising tingles down her neck and spine and sent them spinning outwards to tease her flesh. Alice had never spurned Clem's advances and found them quite pleasant. They had never been numerous, never passionate. More of a not-unwelcome duty he sought to perform every few nights.

At a point when Alice was worried Clem's feeling for Kerensa would grow out of control and take him further away from her, he was showing for the first time a real desire for her. He had even declared that he loved her. A burst of joy flowed out from her inner being and engulfed her mind. Whatever part of Clem remained Kerensa's for ever, the rest of him was hers! He could have chosen to turn to drink, to entrench himself in the farm, even to turn to another woman, or women, to make up for losing Kerensa, but he was a strong man, and instead he wanted her, his wife.

Clem moved closer, as if to emphasise he was giving himself to her at last. Nuzzling her neck he tugged open the fastenings down the back of her dress. Alice had wondered what it would be like to be made love to with real ardour. She pressed herself against his strong lean body. For a moment her natural shyness held back the deeper inner needs denied all her married life, then, in a moment of triumph, she swept all her inhibitions away for ever.

They woke at dawn, long before it was time to rise to begin the next day's work, to make love in the same full, lingering way. When all the others were settled the following night, they rushed laughing like newlyweds to lay out the sacks of straw before the hearth.

Alice changed noticeably over those two days. She was livelier and looked years younger. Even Morley, who thought of little apart from his Maker, his work, the weather and his meals, looked up from the supper table to remark on her sudden rosy glow. Only the worry over Jack, whose condition remained stubbornly unchanged, marred her newfound happiness.

'Poor little Jack,' Alice said. 'He hasn't had a good time of it these last few months, what with that maid, Heather Bawden, messing him about and now this.'

'Yes, poor Jack,' sighed Kerensa. 'Strange how we still

think of him as a boy. It's good of you to nurse him, Alice. If he does pull through, he'll be a long time on the mend. I feel so responsible for him, I wish I could bring him back to the manor with me.'

'Well, he's too ill to travel, at least for a while, but there's Clem, Rosie, Kenver and Father and me to take turns tending and sitting with him. Dr Crebo is going to call in regularly and I daresay Beatrice will make her way over somehow to pass on her opinion. Matthias Renfree is holding a meeting to pray for his recovery tonight, so he'll have the best of care from all quarters.' Alice looked Kerensa directly in the face. 'You must come over often to see him, and bring all the children. 'Tis high time yours and mine met properly and played together, even if it means they fight like cats and dogs. What do you say, Kerensa? There's no reason for you to stay away, is there? There's no one to say you can't come . . .' Alice smiled to herself, 'And I think I can get Clem to change his mind.'

After witnessing the change in Alice and Clem's relationship Kerensa was sure Alice could do that. She wasted no time in thought. 'You're right, Alice. We're friends and our children should have the opportunity to become friends too. As soon as mine are used to having the baby in the house I'll get Nathan to ride over with us,' she promised, then grinned, 'Be really interesting to see what will happen with so many strong-willed children playing together.'

She looked soberly at the wild flowers in the fields and on the roadside and it seemed most of them had died in the last two days. There was no one to say she shouldn't ride over to Trecath-en Farm or anywhere else. She was looking forward to seeing Kane, Olivia and Luke, wanting to spend lots of time with them and allay any fears they'd had of losing their mother in the aftermath of the attack. They would be there to greet her and their new little sister, but apart from that her home was an empty and lonely place to return to.

A sudden burst of sounds and voices made Kerensa jump and cry out.

''Tis all right, Kerensa,' Alice said soothingly. 'It's only the children with Cherry and Polly coming to meet you.'

Kerensa wiped her misty eyes as she watched Olivia, Kane and Luke running towards the cart, waving and shouting to her excitedly. Morley stopped the cart and they clambered on to it. Alice told them to watch out for the baby as they all tried to hug their mother at once.

'We've missed you, Mama,' Kane said seriously, then gave Kerensa a bright smile before gazing over Alice's protective arm at his new sister.

Olivia did much the same but Luke eyed Kerensa sulkily. 'You shouldn't have gone off and had the baby somewhere else,' he said accusingly.

'Mama couldn't help it,' Kane said at once, snuggling into Kerensa's side and holding her hand.

'I'm sorry, Luke,' Kerensa said, looking at Alice hopelessly. 'Mama was very silly.'

'Looks like you're going to need all your patience,' Alice commented wrily to Kerensa.

'Where's Jack?' Olivia asked, clutching at Kerensa's other hand. 'Why hasn't he come with you?'

'Jack is too poorly, my love,' Kerensa said softly, running her hands through Olivia's hair to tame the long red length that had fallen out of its ribbons, re-establishing herself as her mother. 'He'll come home when he's better.' Kerensa knew Olivia adored Jack and she would be distraught if he died.

They alighted from the cart at the manor's front door and

Alice gave the baby to Cherry who rushed her away to the nursery, with Olivia close on her heels.

As Morley drove away with Alice sitting up beside him and waving goodbye, Luke said disparagingly, 'That was the most uncomfortable ride I've ever had. Look at the mess those beasts have made on the carriageway.'

Kane looked anxiously at Kerensa, who was leaning on Polly's arm. 'Well, I enjoyed it. Mama is tired, she needs to rest. Let's go and play and we can see her a little later.'

Kane pulled on his brother's arm and without a word Luke stalked off with him, scowling. Kerensa stood at the front of her home feeling quite numb.

'He'll get over it, m'lady,' Polly said, helping Kerensa inside. 'You know what Master Luke is like, he doesn't really mean what he says, and what with you and Jack being attacked and now a new baby to preoccupy you, it'll take him a while to settle down.'

'I know,' Kerensa sighed as she allowed the housekeeper to fuss over her, 'and I can't say I blame him for being upset.'

She had only just settled, half-lying on a sofa and happy to be back in her own surroundings, when Polly appeared.

'There's someone to see you, m'lady,' she said quietly, her face grave.

Kerensa jumped up and started forward. Polly looked at her compassionately and stopped her rushing out of the room. 'It's not Sir Oliver, m'lady. It's a Mr Ralph Harrt.'

Disappointment so quickly on top of her hope left Kerensa feeling weaker than before and she sat down to receive her visitor. Ralph Harrt would not be paying her a social call. He was one of the local magistrates.

Chapter 27

Matthias Renfree sat at the solid oak desk in the agreeable surroundings of the parlour of Ker-an-Mor Farm. He was trying to concentrate on the figures he was noting down from receipts covering the last month's expenditure on the farmhouse and the items bought for the upkeep of the estate and tenants' dwellings. He wrote the word 'plait' instead of 'price' and slapped his pen down in a rare fit of temper.

'You need a drink, boy' – that's what Adam would have said if he had witnessed his son's pique.

'I can understand why people are tempted,' Matthias muttered to himself. A short time ago he would have said confidently, 'Problems are not solved at the bottom of a bottle.'

He knew why he'd written 'plait' instead of 'price'. Rosie Trenchard had that one long plait of silky golden hair running down the middle of her back. Every time he was alone with her he wanted to untie the ribbon at its end and pull apart the soft flowing mass and caress it and . . .

Matthias shuddered. He had always thought himself protected by his faith from the natural urges of the flesh, but of late he was greatly bothered by a sensation about the body that led to a terror it would grow out of control. It was the reason he took pains not to be alone with Rosie for long. The problem was this did not help with the courtship. Apart from his gift of flowers to her, he had done little to suggest to Rosie he was in fact courting her – trying to court her.

Love was supposed to be in the air in spring. Daffodils and primroses had flourished in the gardens, ditches and hedgerows. Fledgling birds had chirped their way out of their eggshells and went on to sing with joyful abandon in the trees. Streams had sparkled in the warm sun and chuckled over their stony beds. Everywhere he had looked, Matthias saw Mother Nature painting her uncompromising colours and warming the earth for the awakening wildlife. But no new dawn of life had begun for him then, and now it was deep into the heart of summer.

He picked up his pen to make the correction but he did no more than twist it aimlessly between his fingers. What was the matter with him? Other men had no trouble turning the woman they loved into their bride. Why was he so different? Men up to thirteen or fourteen years younger than he was were getting married all the time. Men who once had been boys in his Bible classes were marrying and producing families.

He thought often that his father's attitude counted towards his difficulty with forming a romantic attachment with a woman. Adam was scornful of his celibacy, at times taunting the strict moral code he lived by with brutal remarks: 'What you could do with is a bloody good night in a brothel. Tedn't natural for a man to be going without a woman, what's the matter with 'ee?'

Matthias asked himself that same question over and over again. He had hoped Adam would marry his constant companion, Jenna Tregurtha, but Adam wanted only food and bed without responsibility. Matthias longed to have someone else to come home to apart from his foul-mouthed father. But if he couldn't overcome whatever it was that was blocking his courtship of Rosie, that would never happen, and if he didn't do something about it soon he would probably lose her to another man anyway. There were plenty of young eligible men showing an interest in her and Matthias couldn't bank on Clem's attitude to ward them off indefinitely.

He rose from the desk and looked out of the window. His mood was black and he virtually hated the sight of every flower and shrub, every line of shells laid along the edge of the twisting narrow garden paths, and every post of the white-painted fencing that enclosed the flowerbeds that Jenna Tregurtha painstakingly tended in an attempt to lay a claim to belonging here.

Matthias was in pain. A deep, hollow, debilitating pain. He could have cried with sheer longing and frustration. Suddenly, he could bear it not a moment longer. He felt he would rather die than not know before the morning was over whether Rosie Trenchard would have him or not.

Matthias was distressed to find all the family out in the farmyard. Clem and Morley were making repairs to the barn roof. Kenver was in his wheeled chair chipping away at a piece of driftwood. Alice was sitting beside Kenver teaching Jessica how to spin. Philip was passing nails up for the barn while David played with Charity. They were all there except Rosie.

'Hey!' Clem called down to Matthias from his precarious perch after taking nails out of his mouth. 'Anything up? Don't usually see you this early in the day.'

Matthias blushed blood-red. 'I . . . um . . . I think I left my Bible here last time . . . I . . . I need it for the class tonight.'

397

'Your Bible, eh?' Morley snorted on the ladder. 'No one's left a Bible here, have they, Alice?'

Alice hurried across the yard to Matthias's rescue. 'You're welcome here anytime, Matthias, you know that. You can stay for the midday meal with us, I hope?'

'Thank you, Alice,' Matthias said, fussing with his hair, hoping he looked presentable after riding off in such an undignified rush.

'She's in the dairy,' piped up Philip.

'Who is, Philip?' Matthias asked, then immediately regretted the question. He had left himself wide open to the awful humour a man is subjected to when he shows any sort of interest in the fairer sex.

'Aunty Rosie, of course,' Philip replied, huffing with deliberate impatience and giving his twin a pointed 'come-and-join-in' glance. 'Can't be anyone else, can it?'

'Don't be so rude, Philip,' Alice ordered, giving her son's head a light-handed swipe.

'Aye, Aunty Rosie'll be pleased to see you,' David added mischievously, '. . . probably.' He ducked expertly out of his mother's reach.

'Yes, well . . . all right then . . . I . . . um,' Matthias pulled agitatedly at his shirt cuffs, 'I . . . think I'll just slip into the dairy and say good morning to Rosie then.'

'You do that,' Clem chuckled. 'Like David said, she'll be delighted to see you. 'Tis ages since you last spoke to her – must be all of yesterday.'

Matthias felt he had to join in the silly laughter that ensued and backed away, almost knocking Jessica off her feet. 'S-sorry, Jessica.' Patting her curls he rushed off.

'Clem!' Alice scolded, wagging a finger.

Clem blew her a kiss and carried on with his hammering.

Attached to the full length of the kitchen of the farmhouse, with a lean-to roof, was the back kitchen. Alice and Rosie did all the laundry and washing-up in this room, keeping the kitchen with its huge hearth all the more comfortable for visitors. At one end of the back kitchen lay the 'spence', or larder, full of pies, pickles and preserves and the ingredients for making them. At the other end, screened off, was the dairy, and Rosie was busy at work inside it.

She had heard Matthias's voice outside and wondered why he was at the farm again so soon. 'But it won't be to see me,' she muttered.

Matthias Renfree made her livid and she banged jugs and milk cans about. Her emotions had been all over the place since her assignation with Sir Oliver Pengarron. She had felt exhilaration, shame and a sense of adventure on that day. After the upset at the Trembaths' wedding, which had left her feeling a stupid little fool, she had managed to get her feelings into perspective, then out of the blue had come Matthias Renfree with his magnificent bouquet. And then nothing.

She had been stunned and then delighted with his sudden interest. She'd compared Matthias with Sir Oliver and Matthias had come out favourably. He was mature, thoughtful, humorous and as Sir Oliver had said, possessed an agreeable countenance. She'd waited in suspense for Matthias to begin a formal courtship.

Her expectations had quickly received a cruel blow. It seemed his interest in her was no more than a passing whim. She knew he was shy and hadn't expected any more bold gestures but he almost ignored her. She'd sensed him looking at her over the meal table but when she looked back he'd turn away with a red face. Then it seemed he didn't want to spend a minute alone with her.

Rosie felt slighted and these days she was moodier than ever. She knew, deep down, that she had wanted Matthias Renfree's interest in her to be greater than Sir Oliver's, and more lasting. To forget him she had secretly tried to become interested in some other young men. She'd gone on a picnic with a young miner from the Bible class. He had turned up dressed smartly, had held an intelligent conversation in a soft voice and had a gentle laugh, not what was expected from a coarse miner, but when he shyly tried to kiss her she had pushed him away and refused to see him again. Bartholomew Drannock had asked if he could see her. Rosie had considered it. He was very good-looking and hard-working but while he displayed chivalry of a sort, Rosie knew he only wanted to add her to his list of conquests. After that she had gone out only to the Bible classes where she kept close to the family.

Damn you, Matthias Renfree, she thought in a wild, bitter mood, patting butter furiously over the stone sink, I'll marry Ricketty Jim if he asks me and go off with him! I'll make a play for him when he's next in these parts and we'll see how you like that!

Matthias could hear Rosie moving about in the dairy. It was thankfully cool as he stepped inside and he opened the top of his shirt front and shook it away from his skin to ease his feverish sweat. Screwing up his eyes as they adjusted to the darker light he spotted Rosie in a corner across the stone-flagged floor, her arms moving sharply.

He plucked up courage. 'Good morning, Rosie.'

'Oh!' The half-pound of freshly patted butter fell from her hands, slid down her skirt and over her feet with a muted plop. 'Oh no! It took me ages—'

'I'm sorry, Rosie! Here, let me help you.'

Matthias was distraught and snatched up a piece of

cheesecloth. The action knocked over a pitcher of milk and sent pots of scalded cream scattering off a shelf. Cream oozed out of the pots, but worse was yet to come. In her speed to save some of the cream, Rosie slipped on the greasy butter and fell headlong into Matthias. It sent them both crashing to the floor with Rosie across his lap.

The variety of exclamation noises Matthias made were harshly silenced.

'Don't you dare move, Preacher! Don't you dare to move a muscle.'

Matthias obeyed. His heart sank as rapidly as the creamy white milk that dripped onto his head and spread all about them. Rosie would never look kindly on him now, would probably never speak to him again after this latest disaster, and he ached to put his arms round her and keep her close to him in the middle of all this ruined dairy produce.

Rosie pushed herself away and got gingerly to her feet. Turning her back on him she righted the jug and dropped a dishcloth on the shelf to stop the milk from dripping down. She turned again to look down on him sprawled in a pool of milk on the floor. He waited with bated breath for her to explode, but instead she did the worst thing in the world as far as he was concerned. She laughed. She couldn't help herself, he looked so funny. She held her sides and laughed until tears streamed down her face. Matthias wanted to die. For the ground to open up and swallow him, taking him out of her sight for ever. Rosie thought him ridiculous!

He was about to get to his feet when she bent from the waist and wiped milk from his brown hair with the end of her apron.

'You look a sight, Preacher,' she said chirpily.

'I expect I do,' he answered miserably.

'And your face,' she tried not to laugh again, 'it's a cross between guilty, nervous and afraid. Philip and David don't look like that even when they've been caught out doing something really wicked.'

Matthias remained still, he liked her drying his hair. 'I wish you'd call me Matthias, not Preacher, Rosie.'

'It wouldn't feel right after all these years,' Rosie said stubbornly, rubbing at his hair. Was he getting friendly again? Well, if he was, she wasn't going to let him build up her hopes and dash them again.

'Please, Rosie,' he pleaded.

He sounded so sincere she softened a little. 'All right then, I'll try.' She viewed his hair, all fluffed up and giving him a boyish appearance. 'That's almost dry now, but I can't do anything about your, um, breeches.'

He sprang up, wiping his hands down his shirt front. 'It's all right, really, I'll bring over some milk, cream and butter from Ker-an-Mor . . . to make up for this waste.'

'There's no need,' Rosie said, watching his hands. 'Father won't mind, it wasn't done on purpose. You startled me.'

Matthias saw the direction of her eyes and dropped his hands to his sides. 'I'm not usually so clumsy, I'm never like this around other people.'

'Just me?'

'Yes, unfortunately.'

'I see, there's something about me that turns you to jelly and makes you accident-prone.' Rosie didn't find that flattering and went to the stone sink to get more cloths. She started vigorously cleaning up the mess.

'Let me help you, Rosie, it's the least I can do.' Matthias was unsure of her mood and thought his only hope was to keep her talking.

'I'd rather you didn't.'

'I am sorry, Rosie. I hope you're not angry with me.'

'No, I'm not angry,' she said, carefully picking up pieces of broken crock and putting them in her apron.

'Cross then?' he persisted, bending down to help her and very nearly cracking his head on hers.

'Not cross either.'

She was beginning to sound exasperated. Matthias ran anxious fingers through his hair. He didn't want to leave Rosie until he had straightened things out with her. And he definitely did not want to rejoin the others and have them laugh at him. Rosie glanced up from her cleaning and saw his desperate face. She softened again.

'Don't worry, I won't tell anyone what really happened.'

'It's not just that, although I would appreciate it, Rosie,' he said glumly. 'If my father got to hear of it he would take me for an idiot.' Straightening up he stood back out of her way.

'There, it's all cleaned up now,' she said a few minutes later. 'Not as bad as it looked.'

'Is the floor still greasy?' he tried to sound calm and caring. 'I wouldn't want you to slip again.'

'Everything's fine, Preacher— Matthias.' She tilted her head to the side, her golden plait swaying like a pendulum. She was curious now to know why he was here, and a little hopeful. 'Did you want to see me about something?'

He hesitated, his mouth gaping open, and the moment was lost.

'No, no . . . that is, I rode over to see if I'd left something here. I just called in to say good morning.'

So that was all! 'Well, the morning is nearly over,' Rosie said tartly, 'I daresay Alice will ask you to eat with us. She'll be calling any moment now. Excuse me, I need to change my skirt.'

It was a painful reminder that once before Rosie had had to change her skirt because of his own peculiar clumsiness.

'Yes, yes, of course, don't let me keep you. I . . . I . . . I'm not really hungry and we're very busy on Ker-an-Mor. Alice did invite me to stay for dinner but please give her my apologies. Besides, I can hardly sit at her table in wet clothes. I must go. I have a lot to get on with.' It all came out in rapid garbled words.

Rosie walked away from him as if she'd lost interest. 'Goodbye then,' she said, and left him alone in the dairy.

All the way to the top of Trecath-en valley Matthias cursed himself. Why was it that he, who could talk so long and eloquently on God and salvation, and offer wise counsel to those many years his senior, could not simply ask a girl to look on him as a suitor? Why did he get embarrassed and tongue-tied and behave like a clumsy oaf? 'You'll lose her!' he angrily warned himself.

Fiercely pulling his nag to a halt he threw back his head at the sky and cried with real anguish, 'Oh God! I can't stand any more of this!'

He rode back to the farmyard at full pelt, jumped off his horse before it stopped moving and burst into the kitchen. The Trenchards, seated round the table, looked up in surprise. Marching straight up to Rosie he hauled her to her feet.

'I'm no good at this courting business, Rosie Trenchard, but I want you to know this very minute that I love you with all my heart and I want you to be my wife and I don't want to live another minute of my life without you. I'm going now but I'll be back at the same time tomorrow for my answer, yes or no.'

He let her go so abruptly Rosie fell back on her chair and was gone before she could catch her breath.

He wanted to gallop off without delay but his nag had walked across the yard and was drinking from the trough. Matthias went over to it and patted its back. He watched the animal drinking with his head bent, breathing in deep lungfuls of air to stop the dizziness in his head. He tried not to think about what he had just done. Better to concentrate only on his breathing and go home. When the nag lifted its head he began to mount, then stopped. Rosie was standing a few feet away. She did not move or speak. She just stood and looked steadily at him.

'Rosie . . .'

He held out a hand to her then dropped it. She put a hand up to her hair and quickly lowered it. They seemed to be standing on the edge of time.

She took a single step towards him.

Instinctively, he did the same.

She ran straight into his receiving arms. He held her close as could be. Although he had never kissed anyone before Matthias found her lips as if it was the most natural thing in the world to do. Warm, dizzy waves of ecstasy joined them together in their first kiss and when it ended it was an experience they both wanted again and again.

When he could find his voice at last, he breathed, 'I can't believe it. Oh Rosie, does this mean I won't have to come back for my answer tomorrow?'

'You can have it now if you like,' she said softly, her head tucked in under his chin.

His shyness and awkwardness were gone now she was in his arms. He moved both hands behind her neck and entwined his fingers in her hair, moving them down gently, down and down until all the glossy mane was loosened from the plait. The ribbon at the end fell away to the dusty ground and her hair was free. And so was Matthias. Free to touch and lift and swirl the glorious crowning beauty of the girl he loved. He looked into her face.

'I've had such a miserable time trying to get close to you and tell you how I feel, but I can say it now. I love you, Rosie, and I'm going to ask you again, in a proper manner this time. Rosie, will you marry me?'

'Yes, Matthias.' She hugged him tightly. 'There's nothing I'd rather do.'

After more kisses, he asked her, 'Had you no idea I was falling in love with you?'

'I couldn't be sure,' she said, smiling into his gentle eyes. 'When you gave me those lovely flowers I hoped it was the beginning of something. But then you became all serious and treated me like a child again.' She took something out of her apron pocket. 'Look, I kept the purple ribbon that was round the flowers and have carried it around with me ever since. I've even dried some of the flowers so I could keep them for ever.'

'I'm sorry I put you through all that. I was afraid,' he admitted.

'I thought p'raps you were. I wanted to give you a bit of encouragement but I was afraid it would frighten you away.'

Matthias was overwhelmed. 'So all the time you were hoping I was interested in you?'

'The thought that you might be took me by surprise at first, but when I got used to it I liked the idea. I knew what that gesture with the flowers must have cost you. I've had a really miserable time too hoping and waiting for you to say something to me, Matthias.'

He kissed a handful of her flowing hair, then her lips, before saying, 'Seems rather silly now, the both of us being afraid and miserable all this time. I'll make it up to you, my own sweet Rosie, and in the future we must say whatever is on our minds. Agreed?'

'Agreed,' Rosie said happily, kissing his chin then pressing her head against his chest. 'I'd rather stay here like this but I daresay the twins will be out in a minute to see what we're doing. Are you coming inside to eat?'

'Yes, all right,' he replied, putting a hand behind himself to tug at his wet breeches. 'The others will think I've fallen in the horse trough. But I'm not going in before one, no, two more kisses first.'

Rosie returned his wonderful passionate kisses then took his arm as they walked back to the farmhouse kitchen.

She said happily, 'If I'd thought a dip in the water trough as well would have got you to propose to me, Matthias Renfree, I would have pushed you in there myself.'

Chapter 28

Kerensa approached the summer house in the manor's grounds carrying a tray set with two tall glasses. One glass contained fresh goat's milk, the other a murky green liquid made up from one of Beatrice's secret herbal recipes. Bob padded along at her side, sniffing the air above his head where the tray hovered and giving Kerensa meaningful looks.

'You wouldn't like the green mixture, Bob,' she said, 'no more than the one who has to drink it does.'

She smiled at the thought. Her situation had eased a little. After nearly three weeks of slow recovery at Trecath-en Farm Jack was back home. The men who had attacked them were safely in custody. Mr Harrt had come to inform her of their apprehension on the day she had brought Kelynen home. The robbers had gone to Penzance and, after getting drunk, they had tried to sell the ponies there the following day. A constable had been suspicious as to why they should have had such good horseflesh and after getting help arrested them. Kerensa had also got her wedding ring back, they'd hadn't got round to selling it. Now they had been tried, convicted and would soon hang. Due to their injuries and confessions from the accused neither Jack nor Kerensa had been forced to attend the trials.

When she stepped inside the summer house with its high

domed roof she shook the hand of a magnificent marble statue of a stern aristocratic-looking Roman senator. It was a superstition of Kerensa's, done from her very first venture here. The summer house had been erected by Sir Henry Pengarron, Oliver's great-grandfather, a man of elaborate tastes, and Kerensa had felt the statue forbade her entry; he was a noble man, she only a working-class girl. Its hand was stretched out as though it was about to begin a speech and she had shaken it in a gesture of friendship. Since then she had felt it tolerated her presence if she performed this simple ceremony. Sometimes she bid it the time of day, but not now. She put the tray on a table and crept up to the figure lying on a padded couch.

'You're going to drink it all up, young man,' she whispered into the figure's ear, 'whether you like it or not.'

The figure did not move so she allowed Bob to lick its face. This did the trick and Jack sat up smiling and pushed the dog away.

'How'd you know I was awake?'

'When your eyes are open, Jack, they're so bright you can see them a mile away.'

With her fingertips Kerensa pushed streaks of hair gently away from Jack's eyes and viewed him critically. 'I have never seen such unruly hair. No matter how many times it's brushed and combed, within minutes it's all over the place again. Jack, you're as untidy as the other boys.'

'Me a boy?' came the scornful reaction. 'I'm only a few years younger than you are.'

'Well, you know what I mean,' she said, handing him the glass of strong-smelling green medicine that Beatrice maintained would restore his vigour. 'I keep forgetting you're quite grown up. Now prove it by drinking this straight down without your usual fuss.'

Jack rose to the challenge and drank the bitter liquid in two courageous gulps then without taking a breath snatched up the goat's milk at once to wash away the taste.

'Ugh!' he complained. 'I sometimes wonder if Beatrice is trying to kill me off.'

Kerensa put a finger to her lips. 'Shh, don't let Beatrice hear you say such a thing or we'll never hear the last of it. She takes great trouble to mix up her herbs and other ingredients to heal the many parts of your body needing treatment.'

'Sorry,' Jack said contritely, 'but it tastes some awful, worse 'n the stuff that doctor man gave me at Trecath-en Farm.'

'Dr Crebo takes Beatrice's mixture for gout himself. Says it works better than anything an apothecary could make up for him.' Kerensa patted Jack's hand and gave him a maternal smile. 'You won't be like this for much longer. As soon as you can keep your balance you'll be able to do light jobs around the stables and by the end of the summer you'll be almost back to normal. It could have been worse, we thought at first you'd been blinded.'

'I know, but I just aren't used to lying about all the time,' Jack said, scratching a troublesome spot above Bob's nose. 'I want to see for myself that Kernick and Meryn are really all right. I want to check 'em over 'n' make sure they footpads did 'em no harm.'

Kerensa sat at the table and pulled at a fold in her skirt. She was still nervous from the attack but it helped to talk about it with Jack who'd shared the same terrifying experience. 'They're fine, according to Clem. He gave them both a good look over when Mr Harrt asked him to bring them back from Penzance market.'

'Begging your pardon, m'lady, Clem's a good farmer but he don't know nothing much about horseflesh.'

'Michael and Conan are quite able to take care of them, Jack, but if you're so concerned, would you like me to ask Adam Renfree to take a look at them? He's been in charge of the stud for over thirty years, he should be able to set your mind at rest.'

'If you would, I'd 'preciate that.' Jack leaned gingerly towards the table and flicked a fly off the rim of one of the glasses. 'You'd think they men would have had more sense than trying to sell the ponies so close to home.'

'Apparently they were so drunk when they were caught, one is thought to have believed himself to be in Truro.'

'All they miles away! P'raps they thought they'd sell the ponies for the races.'

'Well, it's a relief to know they'll all be hung. Apparently they've been found guilty of many other crimes too.'

'Serves 'em right,' Jack said with feeling, his hands going instinctively to the parts of his body injured in the attack. ''Tis probably they who've been murdering and cutting up all they people. We was lucky, they might have cut we up too.'

Kerensa shuddered and reached out to Jack. 'Are you in pain, Jack?'

'Just a little, m'lady, there's always a dull ache somewhere, but 'tis just reaction mostly, that's all. You don't need to fuss over me so, although I must admit I rather enjoy it,' he added.

'And I enjoy it too. Besides, it keeps me busy. Kelynen Ann rarely wakes up between feeds. Olivia is absorbed in her painting, and Luke and Kane are often out in the grounds practising their race for the foal.'

412

'I'm some proud to be asked to give another name to the baby,' Jack said humbly. 'I always liked the name Ann. 'Tis simple but pretty. I keep wondering, though, what His Lordship will say . . .'

'I made a vow on that terrible journey I made to Trecath-en Farm that if you and the baby got through the ordeal all right, you would choose one of her names. Kelynen was my choice, well . . . Anyway, Sir Oliver can choose as many names for her as he wants when he comes home.'

'I'd feel happier if Ann became her last name then. 'Tis a good name to finish off with.'

'Don't worry, Jack, Sir Oliver won't feel it improper for you to have picked a name for his daughter in the cir cumstances. After all,' she said tightly, looking away, 'he was the one who wasn't there.'

Quickly changing the subject, Jack said, 'The children on Trecath-en Farm are like Masters Luke and Kane, always off on their own getting into mischief. I enjoyed watching what they got up to. All the family were good to me during my stay there. Morley used to sit with me and tell me about the time he worked on the estate in his younger days, and till I could see properly Kenver read his poetry to me. I used to watch him at his craftwork, he's some clever. I think it made a change for him to have someone about him who couldn't dash about on their two feet. The things he makes are a wonder to see, all the better when you've feared you'd never see again.'

'How about Clem?' Kerensa asked slowly. 'Did you get on well with him?'

'Aye, I did. He's not near so quiet and moody when you get to know him and I was surprised at how close he and Alice are. They behaved more in the way you'd expect

Rosie and Matthias Renfree to now they're betrothed, and they can be some soppy, 'n' all. Didn't expect the Preacher to come out with all that romantic stuff. You never really know people, do you?'

'No, you don't.' Kerensa felt a glow of warmth for Alice, pleased that her friend was receiving the love and affection she deserved. It seemed after all these years their situations were reversed: Alice had a loving husband now and she did not.

'What I'm meaning is, m'lady, the Trenchards were good to me, but I'm glad to be home. Be even better if everyone was here.'

Kerensa sighed. 'I know what you mean, Jack.'

'I hope you don't mind me saying, but I miss him too, Sir Oliver. I know it must be the hardest for you, but he wouldn't have gone away . . . unless . . . unless . . .' and Jack blushed and faltered.

'Unless he had a good reason?' Kerensa muttered. 'Is that what you're trying to say, Jack?'

'Aye, yes . . . I mean . . .'

'He did have a good reason, Jack.' Then she spoke as if to herself. 'But to stay away for so long, without any word . . .'

'I'm sorry, I didn't mean to upset you, it's just that Sir Oliver is a good man, he wouldn't mean to hurt. I just wish there was some news of him.'

'Don't worry, Jack,' Kerensa said wearily, 'he'll be back. Sir Martin has been making inquiries for me on both sides of the Channel to see if he can come up with anything. I'm sure we'll hear something soon.' Kerensa found it hard in her own heartbreak to have to comfort those around her. She had to display a constant bright outlook, when in fact she was beginning to share the private fears of others, that

Oliver wouldn't have stayed away for so long and without communication unless he was dead. Kerensa knew Jack had another fear – that she wouldn't readily take Oliver back. But while she sometimes resented his actions, she thought of her part in what had provoked them, and her love was so deep she knew she'd have him back at any cost. She just wanted him to come home.

'He'll be surprised to see the little one when he does come home,' Jack said, in a bid to be more cheerful.

'Yes, he will.'

Kerensa stared blankly across the perfectly landscaped gardens, mentally imagining Oliver riding up the long gravelled carriageway that lay beyond the imposing granite manor house. She suddenly wanted to cry but shook herself and took a deep breath, forbidding the tears to appear. The children were becoming used to their new sister; would they get used to not having a father? They asked fewer questions about him now.

'Anyway, Jack,' she smiled bravely, 'at least I have you home again.'

Since the attack on herself and Jack, Kerensa had forbidden the children to ride outside the manor grounds unescorted. Frustrated by his father's prolonged disappearance which delayed the race for the black foal at the stud, Luke was angered by this restriction. He constantly picked away at Kane's better judgement and urged him to ride further afield. That afternoon Kane finally gave way.

'No one will know if we don't go too far,' Luke said perkily. 'Just a mile or two, along the edge of Lancavel Downs where no one is likely to see us.'

'I'm not sure about this, Luke,' Kane argued, regretting his weakness at allowing his younger brother to get the upper hand once again. 'I hope Mama doesn't find out, it wouldn't be fair to give her any more worry.'

'Don't be so soft!' Luke scoffed, prodding Kane in the chest. 'You're no fun, you're always round Mama's skirts. Well, I want to be more like Father.'

'But we're riding over to Trecath-en Farm tomorrow with Mama and Olivia and Nat to play with Jessica, Philip and David again. That will get us out of the grounds and I'm sure Clem will organise a race for us. I bet he's good at that sort of thing.'

Luke was wildly jealous of Kane's fondness for Clem. 'He's only a farmer! The girl squeals if I just look at her and those twins can't talk properly! I probably won't even go.'

'Oh, Luke. Mama will be so upset if you throw another one of your tantrums. You know she's got her heart set on us going and getting on well with all the Trenchards. After all, it's up to us to set a good example.'

They were in the hut set aside for injured and convalescing birds and animals. Luke kicked a crate in bad temper and frightened a jackdaw with a splint on its wing. He was immediately sorry about that but he pushed his brother out of the door. Kane stumbled down the steps and landed on his backside. Luke stood on the top step and scowled down at him.

'If you don't go with me right now, I swear I will never, ever go near that beastly farm again and the next time I see Ricketty Jim I'll give him a good kicking!'

Kane stared at Luke unbelievingly as he stalked off to the stables.

'Well, are you coming or are you going to stare at me like a damned fool idiot?' Luke stopped and taunted.

'I'm coming,' Kane said, getting up and rubbing his hands on his shirt front, 'but this is a foolhardy adventure, and one of these days you could be sorry for the things you do and say.'

As they rode along Kane looked about uneasily, half expecting to see a spy jump out from behind a boulder or hedge and run home to tell their mother they were disobeying her orders. Luke set his sulky mouth in a tight determined line and prodded his knees in his pony's sides.

'We'll race from here,' he said in superior tones a short time later, 'a mile to the new meeting-house building. Agreed, brother?'

'But it's dangerous riding fast over the moors,' Kane protested. 'It's safer to wait until we reach the pannier tracks.'

'There you go again. We've ridden this way many times with Jack, we should know every dip and obstacle by now – at least I do.'

'Oh, very well, but only if you promise to go straight back home afterwards and promise not to try any of those tumbling tricks that circus rider showed us when Mama asked him to perform for us.'

Luke glared at Kane. Their father and Beatrice had filled their heads with the daring, apparently death-defying things he had done as a boy and he'd never once got hurt, at least not badly. If Kane had his way they would never know the thrill of repeating them and making up some new ones of their own before the age of fifty! They'd probably live the lives of two soppy girls!

Making a rude face, he said in a sarcastic sugary-sweet voice, 'Fine by me. Ready?'

Kane counted to five and they both surged forward. Luke moved quickly ahead, but only because Kane had made up his mind to let him win the ultimate race for the pony. He had no heart left in the challenge, not with the father he loved so far away and with the mother he adored heartbroken. Neither of them would be interested in the outcome of the race and so neither was he.

They rode swiftly over grassy tussocks, expertly skirting round huge boulders in natural but strange formations and solitary ones standing or lying mysteriously alone. Banks of tall ferns bent with the wind of their passage. A slow worm scuttled away to safety. Insects disturbed by the ponies' thunder ceased their humming and search for food until they had passed by.

Kane's hat was blown off; he did not stop to retrieve it but slowed his pony down to a walk. His younger brother would be furious with him for giving up the race, but Kane was in no mood for the contest. Luke was out of sight now and Kane lingered along the edge of a narrow fast-running stream to see if it held any wild watercress with its dark green tangy leaves. He loved wild cress piled on top of thickly buttered bread, soaked in vinegar and liberally sprinkled with sea salt. He would eat it late at night with Beatrice, who could be relied on to keep his waywardness a secret; she approved of boys being boys.

There were many unusual and sometimes eerie sounds to be heard on the moors. Rumours of lost souls of those who had stumbled and drowned in the bogs came to mind and folk were apt to look fearfully over their shoulders. All thoughts of watercress and secret suppers vanished as Kane heard a cry like nothing he had heard before. His heart hammering in his chest, he urged his pony forward.

Luke was a good distance away from him but it soon registered in Kane's mind that what he could hear were the terrified high-pitched screams of his brother. Kane spurred his pony on, dreading what had happened.

He found Luke lying face down over a granite boulder

close to the meeting house; his pony could just be seen running a race of its own along the path that led to the Wheal Ember mine. Bringing his mount to a jarring halt Kane hurtled off and raced to his brother who was now babbling incoherently.

Kane recoiled in horror when he saw Luke's injuries. There was a deep gash that seemed to reach right across his head which was running with blood, and his right arm was forced back and upwards at the shoulder at a grotesque angle.

Fearfully Kane moved closer and touched Luke's good shoulder.

'Can you get up, Luke? Can you move at all?'

Luke kept babbling and Kane fought his horror and fear to stop himself from freezing on the spot. With an effort he knelt down to look into Luke's stricken face. Blood from the gash was trickling over his face and dripping off his chin.

Kane wanted to be sick but he knew he had to do something, to take charge of the situation, or his brother might die. His voice was panicky but the words came out clearly.

'I'll get you on my pony, Luke. You're not to worry, you'll be all right, I . . . I promise.'

But the moment he said it he knew it would be foolish to try to move Luke. It would aggravate his terrible injuries and Luke had their father's build, he was tall for his age, and would be too heavy to be lifted safely. Kane tilted Luke's chin a little and tried to get his eyes to focus on him.

'Listen to me, Luke. I'll have to leave you to get help. I won't be gone very long. You're going to be all right. You mustn't worry, don't worry.'

Luke blubbered something, then his eyes rolled and closed.

Kane cried out, 'My God! Don't die, Luke. I'll get help, don't give up! I'm going now!' He didn't take his eyes off his brother's body until he'd leapt on his pony again.

As he rode, as swiftly as he dared, he harshly accused himself. 'It's all your fault! You're the eldest, you should have refused to go along with this silly race. You should have told Mama what Luke was planning.'

It was several seconds before he realised that he could hear more than the wind in his ears or his muttered fears; someone was shouting to him from behind. He reined in and watched in utter relief as three riders picked their way carefully towards him. One was leading Luke's pony.

The fact that the three riders turned out to be the Blake family did not diminish his relief. At that moment he didn't care that his father hated Peter Blake and his mother would not have his name mentioned in the house. The presence of an adult meant the terrible weight of sole responsibility for his brother's fate was lifted from his shoulders. Mr Blake would know what to do.

It was Rosina who spoke to him. 'Simon Peter recognised this pony as belonging to Master Luke. Obviously something is very wrong. Can we help?'

'Luke's had a bad fall,' Kane plunged straight into the facts, 'not far back there. He's lying over a boulder close to the meeting house. Please do something, he's very badly hurt. I'm afraid he'll die!'

'We must have ridden close past him on our way back from the mine. I'll go back with you, Master Kane,' Peter Blake said, taking charge of the situation, 'and see what I can do for your brother.'

Turning to Rosina he handed her the reins of the runaway pony. 'You take the pony and Simon Peter straight to the manor, my dear. I can hardly go there myself at this point, but you can tell them to expect Master Kane and myself along with the injured boy and to send at once for a doctor.'

The company parted, two for the manor, two of them to return to the scene of the accident.

Earlier in the day, in a big house at Marazion, a visitor had been shown into the sick room of Jenifer Drannock. Jenifer showed no surprise or emotion. She invited her visitor to sit at her bedside in its position beside a large window which looked out over St Michael's Mount and the busy shipping on the sea around it.

'I knew you would come to see me, by and by. You have been home first I take it,' she gasped, her voice now weakened out of recognition.

'I have not.'

Jenifer raised her faint eyebrows. 'Then you can tell me, Sir Oliver Pengarron, why you have chosen to come to see me before your family.'

Oliver studied the changes in Jenifer's appearance as keenly as she did his. While she had shrivelled in size and grown as pale as the white nightgown she wore, he was deeply tanned and dressed in the clothes of a working man.

He said, 'I need to straighten out a few things with you before I see Kerensa, to be able to face her with a clean breast. How is she, Jenifer, and my family?'

'Why ask me? I never leave this bed.'

'Because I am certain you have kept yourself informed of their welfare.' He waited patiently for her to answer.

She did not spare him. 'They're missing you terribly.'

Oliver sighed and looked away. 'I've missed them more than I could ever have imagined . . .'

His thoughts drifted away and Jenifer knew he was

oblivious to her blatant scrutiny of him. He had changed much in the months of his absence. The devilish arrogant gleam at the back of his black eyes was gone. The straight back, the firm set of his broad shoulders, the fine handsome lines of his face were still there. But the restlessness was missing, the constant urgency to be on the move, always seeking to be doing something, to have his own way. Yet there was pain in his face; the changes had cost him dearly, Jenifer was sure of that.

'You're wondering where I've been and what I've been doing all this time I've spent away,' he said, his eyes darting back to her. His voice was also different, a tone softer, more mellow, the words delivered just that little bit slower.

'I daresay you'll tell me if you want to,' Jenifer replied. 'Are you wondering what I'm doing here,' she could only manage a slight lift of one weak hand, 'in this grand house in Marazion? It's a far cry from the life I was used to in Perranbarvah. This nightgown I'm wearing is made from the finest Irish linen, it cost more money than I've had to spend on my family in all my married life. What do you think about me living here as the lady of the house, Sir Oliver? How did you know I was here? Or, have you, as I suspect, been keeping an eye on my welfare too?'

Oliver smiled in submission. He would not play verbal games with the dying woman. What he had come to tell her she knew already, she had been with him every step of the way.

'You and my Sam had two things in common,' Jenifer said, 'both satisfied to have only one woman in your life, and like you Sam liked to think he could get one over on another person.'

'Go on, Jenifer Drannock, say it.'

A faint smile softened the deathly hue of Jenifer's face.

'Very well, welcome home to Cornwall . . . Obadiah Drannock of Portsmouth. Welcome home to Cornwall and back from the dead.'

Oliver couldn't help smiling. 'How did you know?'

She looked at him with wisdom in her fading eyes. 'Kerensa has visited me often since you left, she hasn't told me anything about your personal life but I think I've a reasonably good idea of what's been going on. Forgive me if I'm speaking out of turn but I believe there's a huge rift in your perfect marriage. And what other reason could there be for that but the truth of Samuel's parentage coming to light? Samuel and I should never have asked and held Kerensa to that promise. It is never right for a man and wife to keep secrets from each other. It was because of our selfishness that you and Kerensa and your lovely young family have suffered so much.

'Then, of course, once you knew the truth, there was the problem of what to do with your half-brother's family. You could not, of course, allow us to go on living in poverty. I knew at once you were behind this sudden inheritance of Bartholomew's. Samuel had no distant relatives. There have been Drannocks in Newlyn for as long as there have been Pengarrons as lords of the manor. Samuel and I knew his father Caleb's family very well. There was never an Uncle Obadiah, in Portsmouth or elsewhere.'

As she talked Jenifer had grown weaker. Oliver rose and poured her a glass of barley water, holding the bottom of the glass as she sipped.

'Don't tire yourself, Jenifer. As you already know what I came here to tell you I'll leave in a little while so you can rest. I only need to know if Bartholomew and your other children, my nephews and nieces, have been told my father was their grandfather.'

'Not as yet, but they must be told. They have the right to know the truth before they learn it from another source and suffer the same shock you unfortunately did. Bartholomew has always had his suspicions, you know. Many times he has remarked on his resemblance to you. I have been hoping you would return before my time came, but when I felt the time was very near, I would have told them myself. I ask only one thing of you, Sir Oliver, be with me and let us tell them together.'

'I'm glad you've asked me that, Jenifer. It will be the best thing to do.'

'I have a question for you, Sir Oliver. What do my children, Samuel's children, really mean to you? Do you have any objections to acknowledging them publicly as your kith and kin?'

'I have no objections, Jenifer. I will be proud to make the fact known all over Cornwall. And please, no more of this "Sir Oliver". I am your brother-in-law, so just Oliver from now on. I will call again, in a couple of days, and we can talk to the children then, if that is agreeable to you.'

'It is. Will you bring Kerensa with you? She was so pleased with our good fortune. I always enjoy her company when she calls.'

A look of uncertainty showed on his face. 'I will bring her,' Oliver said quietly. 'If she will ever go anywhere with me again.'

'Why should she not?'

'More to the point, why should she? I have treated her extremely badly, she must be deeply hurt.' Oliver bowed his head and looked at his feet.

He looked up again when Jenifer said, 'Kerensa loves you. Have you any doubt she would not go to the ends of the earth for you?' She reached out and placed a trembling hand on his. 'You said you are proud to have my family as part of yours, but have you rid yourself of that other pride? The pride that drove you away from the people that love you the most in all the world?'

Gripping her withered hand, Oliver brought it tenderly to his lips and placed there a gentle kiss.

'Yes, Jenifer, it is all gone. It was a long and painful experience, but I could not come home until I'd endured it to the bitter end.'

Jenifer looked out across the sea. 'He's out there somewhere . . . my Samuel . . . When our little business is done I can die in peace and take my place with him. My only regret is that he never purged himself of that useless destructive pride as you have done.'

Chapter 29

Kerensa was half sitting, half lying on a sofa in her sitting room. Her chest rose and fell softly as she dozed.

'Kerensa . . .'

Oliver barely whispered her name, but it was enough to make her draw in her features and move slightly. Her glossy auburn-red hair was splayed out on the cushions behind her head. Her beautiful face was tinted a soft satiny pink. She looked child-like and vulnerable and although all conscious thought was lost to her there was sorrow etched in every breathtaking line of her face, the face that was so dear and which he had missed so much.

He wanted nothing more than to take her in his arms and swear on his life that he would never leave her again, but he stayed by the door. He felt strangely shy in his own house, as if he was something of an intruder and she had more right to be here than he did. He felt awkward about letting her know he was there. He had put that sorrow on her face; what right had he to walk back into her life and hope all could be as it was before?

'Kerensa . . .'

She woke with a small start and looked down at her side and murmured something. He only caught the end of what she said, '. . . heard your father calling my name,' and assumed she was half awake and dreaming she was talking to one of the children.

He took a deep breath, tears misted his eyes and he could only speak in a whisper.

'You were not dreaming, Kerensa, my love.'

Her head spun round. 'Oliver! Is it really you!'

He tried to answer but the words choked in his throat. Kerensa stared at him, too afraid even to blink lest he disappear like an apparition.

'Have . . . have you come back to me?'

Her eyes were startled and full of fear. Oliver could not bear to see her like this.

'If you will have me, Kerensa.'

The next moment he was kneeling before her – not the words and actions of a man torn by arrogance and pride.

'I have waited so long for this moment.' Tears of joy and emotion sparkled in her eyes and she let them gather and fall unchecked.

Oliver grasped her hand and placed his head on her lap, then lifted it again swiftly. He had looked straight into the face of a wide-awake pouting baby.

'What . . . who . . . ?'

Taking the baby more fully into her arms, Kerensa smiled with real happiness for the first time in months.

'Kelynen Ann Pengarron, meet your father.'

Oliver was stunned. 'You mean . . . I'm her . . . she's my . . . ? It was her you were talking to.' Then he was horrified. 'Dear God, are you telling me that I left you to bear this child alone!'

Kerensa laughed and said fondly, 'I fed her not five minutes ago and we both dropped off to sleep. She's a good baby, the children adore her.'

The horror had not left Oliver's face. 'How will you ever forgive me, Kerensa?'

'There is nothing to forgive.' She leaned forward and kissed his shocked face. 'Have you forgiven me, Oliver?'

'There was nothing to forgive you for, my precious love. I have such a lot to tell you, a lot to explain.' Oliver looked intently at his newest child. 'She's beautiful, like you are. You must have a lot to tell me too. I've been longing to see you again and Olivia, Kane and Luke. Are they well? Have they missed me? Will they be glad to have me back?'

'They'll be as happy as I am.' Kerensa stroked his hair and he kissed her hand, reaching up to kiss her cheeks and lips and then the baby's head. His touch, his lips, the weight of his arms as they rested lightly on her lap reassured her he was really there and it wasn't just a wonderful dream. She took in his deep suntan, his calloused hands, the working-class clothes he wore. It spoke of at least some of his activities since he'd been away from her, but explanations could wait till later.

'Would you like to hold Kelynen?' she asked proudly.

'Yes, I want to hold her. I want to hold you. And all of my family. But she will do for now.'

He took the baby into the crook of his arm, she looked engulfed against his big strong body. He kissed her tenderly, doing the same to Kerensa before standing up and studying his daughter again.

'I hope you did not have a difficult confinement. You must tell me all about it, I want to feel as though I'd been there.'

'It was an unusual event,' Kerensa said in understatement.

'Kelynen. You have given her a Cornish name, like yours. I like it, it sounds so right for her – and Ann, simple but lovely. How came you by these names, Kerensa?'

Kerensa stood up and linked her arm through his. She

wondered how he would feel when all the facts of Kelynen's birth were revealed.

'One was from a suggestion from someone, the other I asked another person to choose . . . It's a long story, Oliver,' she said carefully, smoothing a hand over Kelynen's delicate head. 'She's different from the others – see, she has neither your colouring nor mine, but she has your dark eyes.'

Oliver slipped an arm round Kerensa's waist and could not conceal his relief and joy. 'This is the best homecoming I could possibly have, knowing that you still love and want me, and a new little daughter. She's a little sweeting, have you had her baptised?'

'I have delayed in having her baptised in the hope you would come home and give her names after Kelynen of your own choosing.'

Oliver gazed in wonderment into Kelynen's clear dark eyes. His thoughts drifted to a foreign country and then nearer home to Marazion.

'There are two particular names that come immediately to mind. Michelle and Jenifer – Kelynen Michelle Jenifer Ann,' he said humbly. 'What do you think, Kerensa. Are they acceptable to you?'

'Yes, of course,' Kerensa replied, marvelling that this moment had come at last, of Oliver being home and choosing their baby's other names. 'Jenifer after Jenifer Drannock, I presume,' and it gave her a clue to the peace he had found. Then looking at him curiously, she added, 'Michelle is a beautiful name, I've never heard it before.'

'It's foreign and the reason why I would like it comes from a long story.' He smiled. 'We must—'

Urgent noises at the double doors drew their attention away from their baby and a host of people rushed into the room. Polly was at the head of the group with Rosina Blake behind her and then came Olivia holding on to Simon Peter's hand. The two sets of people stared at each other in surprise.

'Father!' Olivia rushed to her father and clung to his legs.

'Sir!' Polly dropped a rapid curtsy with her mouth agape.

Simon Peter walked further into the room and stood expectantly at Olivia's side, rising up on his tiptoes to get a better view of the baby. Then Rosina came forward, her surprised expression fading at the seriousness of her errand here.

'We've come about your son Luke,' she spoke to both Kerensa and Oliver. 'I'm afraid he's had an accident, out on the edge of Lancavel Downs close to the meeting house. I believe he's quite badly hurt. Master Kane has taken my husband back to the spot where it happened, they should not be long behind us.'

'Oh no!' Kerensa gasped. 'They were told not to go out of the grounds.'

'Polly, run and tell Jack to fetch Dr Crebo here without delay,' Oliver ordered, handing Kelynen back to Kerensa. 'I'll go and meet Blake and my sons.'

'Begging your pardon, sir,' Polly said hastily, 'but Jack was attacked back along, he won't be fit to ride for weeks.'

'What?' Oliver snatched a worried look at Kerensa. He had a lot to catch up on. What other dreadful things had he left her to cope with alone? 'Then get Michael or Conan to go instead.' Turning to Rosina, he said, 'I thank you for coming to tell us, Mistress Blake. Please, stay with my wife until your husband arrives.'

With a quick kiss on the top of Olivia's head and a hug for Kerensa he darted after Polly out of the room.

Oliver and Conomor rode out of the stable yard at

breakneck speed. Horse and rider were pleased to see one another again. The black stallion needed no urging after the months of gentle exercise he had received instead of the regular long gallops he was used to from the only man who could truly master him.

Oliver took in none of the familiar sights that he had been so eagerly looking forward to seeing again. He galloped through the manor's grounds and parklands with his mind only on his homecoming. He had been sure he would find Kerensa waiting at home with their children for his eventual return, but not of how he would be received. During his anxious journey home he had told himself he had no right to expect her to welcome him with open arms. Even if she still loved him, his long silent absence might have stolen some of that love. But Kerensa's joyful reaction at seeing him suddenly before her had proved she loved him as much as ever. The hopes he had nurtured had been wonderfully fulfilled.

Then had come the mixed feelings at learning he had fathered another child, a child he had known nothing about. He understood why Kerensa had kept it to herself. Because of his harsh treatment of her he had missed Kelynen's birth, forfeited the joy of seeing one of his children enter the world. He had not been there to share the pain and wonder of the experience with Kerensa. And then, just as he had begun to take pleasure at Kelynen's presence, horror had been thrust upon him that another of his children had been in an accident, might be badly hurt. Was he to gain a child only to lose another on the same day?

It was not long before he saw riders coming towards him. Slowing down the restless stallion he was soon face to face with Peter Blake and his two sons. Kane's scalding tears turned to those of shock, then relief, at seeing his father.

'Oh, Father! It's all my fault Luke's hurt. I should never have agreed to race for the pony out of the grounds.'

'It will be all right, son,' Oliver said, leaning over to give the distraught boy a quick hug. 'Don't you worry about it now, let's just get your brother home.'

Peter Blake was nervous; even though in an act of charity he was bringing home Sir Oliver Pengarron's son, he wasn't sure how the other man would react towards him.

'I'll take my son now, Blake,' Oliver said, looking grimly from Luke's unconscious twisted body to him.

'It's his arm,' Blake said gravely. 'It's twisted right back from the shoulder and he has a serious head injury too.'

Oliver thrust out his arms. 'Give him to me. I'll take my son home.'

Blake tried not to fumble as he passed Luke over. Oliver held Luke's twisted arm away from his own body, grimacing at the grotesque position in which it jutted out. A large bloodied gash covered the top half of the dark-featured face that so clearly resembled his own.

Blake looked at the ground and said in his quiet voice, 'I would be grateful if you would tell my wife and son I'll meet them by the lodge at the end of the manor's carriageway.'

Oliver looked at him coldly, but said, 'I asked your wife to stay and comfort mine. You are welcome in my house this day, Blake. I daresay in the circumstances my wife will offer no objections.' Then, softening the harsh lines of his face, he added, 'Thank you for bringing Luke home.'

Oliver kneed Conomor to walk on. Kane fell in beside him, rubbing tears away with a grimy hand. After a moment's hesitation, a much surprised Peter Blake followed them.

'Kane.'

'Yes, Father?'

'Has your mother's instruction that you stay within the manor grounds anything to do with Jack being attacked?'

Kane hung his head, doubly ashamed. 'Yes, Father, he and Mama were attacked by footpads while out riding.'

Another shock hit the pit of Oliver's stomach. 'Your mother was attacked too?'

'Yes, and the baby was coming and Mama had to crawl through the fields of Trecath-en Farm to get help and Clem Trenchard had to deliver her.'

Oliver looked sharply at Kane. His heart felt as though it had received a tremendous blow.

'Clem Trenchard . . .?'

After Luke's injuries were treated, and pray God he would recover, he and Kerensa had a lot of talking to do.

Luke was laid out on clean sheets on the large oak table in the winter parlour. Dr Crebo set to work aided by the light of scores of candles. From his preliminary examination he was confident Luke's life was not in danger. He had suffered a mild concussion and although the wound on the head was deep and required several stitches, Dr Crebo announced that most of the scarring would be hidden behind the hairline and that he had been responsible for the recovery of patients with much worse injuries on not such young hard heads. The pronounced bruising on Luke's face which made the injury look worse than it really was would heal in the course of time but, Dr Crebo said grimly, the condition of the arm and shoulder was much worse.

Kerensa had refused to be forbidden from the room by the doctor and was angered at his presumption that all mothers were needlessly hysterical where sick children were concerned. She stood opposite him holding Luke's good hand, speaking reassuringly to him when he stirred and moaned as the head wound was stitched. But it required Oliver's strength to hold him still when Dr Crebo worked on the arm to try and manoeuvre it back into place.

Beatrice was the only other person there. She laid out her ointments, rolled up bandages, fashioned a sling from a piece of torn-off sheet, but kept her distance. She cried and cried, blubbering copious amounts of foul green phlegm down over her chins. It gave Oliver real moments of panic. Before this he had never seen her cry once.

Kerensa wanted to hold on to Beatrice for comfort but stayed close to the table, passing the doctor cloths to wipe off the mounting sweat from his face. She winced as he grunted with the effort of his labour. She was distraught at Luke's screams of agony and prayed the rum the doctor had forced down his throat would soon work and he'd stay unconscious until his arm was back in place. She felt sick to the stomach.

Oliver's panic turned to ice-cold terror when Beatrice stopped crying and began to wail loud snatches of prayer. In all his life he had never been so afraid. Or felt so guilty. He would never come to terms with the knowledge that it was his pride and neglect that could mean his son living life as a cripple. The boys would never have disobeyed his orders as they had Kerensa's. He could hardly bear to look at Kerensa's face, deathly white, frightened. She had forgiven him for going away and leaving her for so long; could she forgive him for what was happening to Luke? A quick glance and he caught her eye. He saw only love there for him, the need for his strength and comfort. Why did she not hate him for this? At that moment hatred would have been more bearable.

The doctor pulled and heaved on Luke's arm, and the boy thankfully passed out. The sound of bone jarring on bone was clearly audible. 'Ah,' breathed Dr Crebo as if he was confident the arm was about to slide back into place, then he swore as the movement went wide. He sat down to get his breath back. He walked to a window to gulp in much-needed fresh evening air. Then he returned to the table and said, 'This time I will damn well get it in.'

Five minutes later he was still trying. 'I hate putting limbs back into sockets but they usually—'

'For God's sake, Crebo, let me try!' Oliver cried in desperation.

The doctor looked crossly at Oliver as he pulled on the arm. It shot back into the shoulder socket with a sickening click. Luke woke and screamed but it was not as loud as Kerensa's.

Luke groaned and lost consciousness once more. Dr Crebo fell back on a chair and put his face in sweating, trembling hands. Kerensa ran round the table and fell faint into Oliver's arms. Beatrice approached the table and the motionless boy slowly. She took the hand of his good arm and her old head swung from side to side as she scrutinised him. Then she started to strip away the rest of his clothes and began to wash him down, singing a nursery rhyme as she worked. Kerensa was soon able to help her and moments later Luke was carried upstairs.

Beatrice stood at his bedside murmuring, 'Poor little mite . . . poor little mite . . .' until Kerensa could stand it no longer and asked her to go and comfort the other children.

Dr Crebo lifted Luke's eyelids. The boy's pupils were responsive to light.

'He will be all right?' Oliver asked in a shaken voice as the doctor began to pack his things in his bag.

'Yes, Sir Oliver,' he said breathlessly, 'for now. I've

done the tidying up and his arm is in a sling to keep it absolutely still, but . . .'

'But what?' demanded Oliver, glancing fearfully at Kerensa.

Dr Crebo looked sympathetically at the parents as they stood clutching each other. 'I'm pessimistic the arm will heal as before. As you saw for yourselves it was a very bad injury, not just a case of an arm out of its socket. All the pulling and prodding I had to do was necessary but it will have aggravated the condition. It is possible that the boy's arm may prove to be totally useless. But he is alive, be thankful for that.' It was the worst dislocation he had ever had to treat in his long career. He was shaken and went on sharply, 'Now if you'll be good enough to provide me with a glass of brandy.'

'Yes, of course. Thank you, Dr Crebo. You'll find all the refreshment you need laid out in the hall. If you'll excuse us, my wife and I will stay with our son.'

Dr Crebo left Kerensa and Oliver to begin an anguished vigil at Luke's bedside. He stood at an open window in the corridor for a few moments retying his neckcloth neatly before he hastened downstairs. He was astonished to see the Blake family in the hall, in the process of leaving.

'This is a surprise indeed, Mr Blake, Mistress Blake,' he blurted out, his curling eyebrows moving upwards to meet his wig.

'We stayed a while so Simon Peter could keep Master Kane company and take his mind off the accident,' Rosina explained. 'We came across them on the way back from the Wheal Ember mine and my husband brought Master Luke most of the way home.'

'Did he indeed,' replied the doctor, helping himself to the food on an assortment of plates laid out in the centre of the hall. 'Taking your monthly distribution of foodstuffs to the miners's children, I suppose. How fortunate you chose today to make your journey. I take it you were invited into the house by Sir Oliver himself?'

Peter Blake fidgeted uncomfortably under the doctor's inquisitiveness. The last time he had entered the manor was when he had tried to force his amorous attentions on Kerensa. She had barely spoken to him today. Either she would never forgive him or she was too worried over the plight of her son to indulge in polite conversation.

'This has been a day for shocks and surprises,' Charles Crebo remarked to his plate, as if the Blakes had already left. 'First, Sir Oliver turns up out of nowhere as unexpectedly as he went off, second I am called upon to treat a most interesting injury, and then Mr Blake's presence here seems agreeable . . . Now where is that brandy?'

At ten o'clock Kerensa left Luke's bedside for the nursery to feed Kelynen. A few minutes' later Luke stirred and cried out. Oliver dropped to his knees and stroked the boy's sweating brow.

'It's all right, Luke, it's Father. I'm come home to take care of all of you and make everything all right again.'

Luke's eyes flickered and opened slowly, they were dulled with pain and incomprehension. He licked his dry bottom lip and screamed as he tried to move his tender arm and shoulder.

'Keep still, keep still, Luke!' Oliver said loudly to break through the boys delirium. 'You must keep still, try not to move for now.'

Luke opened his mouth and formed a soundless word. It happened again and again until a puff of sound issued from his cracked lips.

'Fa . . . ther.'

'Yes, Luke. I'm staying right here beside you, I promise, and I'll never go away from you again.' Feelings of guilt racked Oliver for leaving his child. If he had not gone away, the race for the foal would have been over long ago.

Luke's eyes grew large and rounded, fear contorted his small swollen face. His head rolled from side to side, his whole body agitated.

'Go back to sleep, son.' Oliver was alarmed but kept it under control. 'Shush now, it's all right, everything is all right now.'

Luke suddenly pierced Oliver's eyes with his own. 'Father . . . I saw . . . I saw . . .' and he could get no more out.

The same pitiful fear-stricken cries went on throughout the night until, unable to face the terror of his nightmares, Luke slipped into a deep state of unconsciousness.

Kerensa slept for an hour as dawn approached but only from sheer exhaustion. She awoke to find Oliver gazing out of the window. His stance was strained and she was afraid he wanted to go away again.

'Oliver!'

She rushed to him and swung him round. He wrapped her in his arms, crushing her to his body. He read her thoughts and kissed her so tenderly she was left in no doubt that her fears were groundless.

'You can trust me, my sweet precious love,' he said, his voice low and husky. 'You have so much to forgive me for, but I swear you can trust me, please believe me.'

'I know, I know,' she choked into his broad chest. 'Luke's accident has unnerved me, that's all.'

He gently pulled her head back to look up at him. 'Are you sure of that, Kerensa?'

439

She nodded, and the hungry demand of his mouth brought an immediate response. With reluctance they pulled apart for they could not stay long from their son's bedside. They whispered, heads together, as they watched over him.

Oliver said, 'When I talked to Kane about the accident he said Luke fell from his pony and landed on a slab of granite. As far as Kane knows there is no reason for Luke to be afraid like this. Something must have happened afterwards.'

Kerensa shuddered and tenderly stroked Luke's hot face.

'Something frightened the poor little soul,' Oliver went on. 'I can't get those awful words of his out of my mind – I saw . . . I saw . . .' He sighed. 'I know it will distress Kane, but I'll have to ask him to show me the scene of the accident and have a good look round out there.'

Daylight flooded into the bedroom on a sudden shaft of the rising sun, illuminating the little boy's bandages with an eerie glow.

'Will you be all right with Luke while I'm gone, my love?' Oliver said, his voice aching. 'Polly will sit with you. I'll be as quick as I can.'

'I'll manage,' Kerensa said, wishing he did not have to go but seeing the sense of it. 'Poor Kane, I'll go to him before you leave.'

Kane hated the thought of going back yet again to that granite boulder stained with his brother's blood but he was glad to be doing something useful instead of aimlessly waiting about. Oliver kept him chatting, hoping to alleviate his tortured feelings of guilt and put them more appropriately on his own shoulders. He reminded Kane that his single-minded brother, who sought to be disobedient so often, was bound to have had an accident sooner or later.

As he listened, Kane ran a hand through his red hair. He knew he had no Pengarron blood in him but had always felt a true member of the family, knowing how special he was to his adoptive parents. And as the eldest child of the family he believed he should take care of the others and in many ways he had tried to take on the responsibility as head of the house in Oliver's absence. He felt a dismal sense of failure over Luke's accident. He looked across at Oliver, feeling better now that his father had discarded his strange peasant costume for his usual clothes.

'Father, I don't want the foal, not ever,' he said vehemently. 'I don't expect Luke will either when . . . when he's well again.'

'Don't worry about that now, son, we'll decide what to do with the foal at a later date.'

Oliver knew at once which boulder Luke had landed on. The bloodstains spattered on it told the whole story. He looked steadily at the boulder. There was a smaller one at a right angle to it, with thick growths of fern and creeping wild plants around it. Leaning over to look beyond the foliage he saw what had terrified his small son.

Chapter 30

Oliver went into one of the manor's smaller bedrooms and found Jack sitting miserably in a cushioned chair staring out at the stable yard below. He put up a hand to stop Jack from rising then carried a chair to the window and joined him.

'I've always enjoyed the view from this window, Jack. If you put your head out far enough you can see for miles and you can make out the course of the stream running right through the oak plantation.'

'Yes, m'lord. I like it here so I can keep an eye on the stables and watch the horses going to 'n' fro. Can't tell you how I felt when I saw you galloping out of the yard yesterday on Conomor. Didn't know the reason then. 'Tis some good to have you back, sir,' Jack said, swallowing hard.

'Thank you, Jack. It's good to be back, and it's good to see you again.'

'It was Her Ladyship's idea for me to sleep in the house and have a room overlooking the stable yard,' Jack said. He didn't feel at all comfortable to be convalescing in the big house, and even less so in his master's presence. He missed his little cottage and its simplicity and spartan furniture. He had spoken of it to Kerensa and hoped she would allow him to return home, but he was still very unsteady on his feet and she just laughed and assured him he was in the plainest room in the house. It didn't seem at all plain to Jack, with velvet curtains, drapes round the large high bed and a canopy above it, furniture here, there and everywhere, and tassels on everything.

It was one of the pictures he disliked the most, of an old woman dressed in black puritan clothes and tiny round spectacles on the end of a pointed nose. Her dark eyes looked at you no matter where in the room you were, and Jack fancied she was a witch and would put a spell on him. He wanted to hide away from her but she seemed to be everywhere.

'I'm pleased that you are here while you are recovering, Jack. How are you today?' Oliver asked. He sounded as fatherly as Kerensa was motherly, and Jack had a horror that his master would get up and plump up his cushions and rearrange the blanket over his lap.

'I'm getting better all the time, sir. Never mind about me.'

'Is there anything I can get for you? Anything you can think of that you would like to while away the time until you are active again?'

'Not really, but . . .' Jack stopped, embarrassed.

'Yes, what is it?' Oliver grinned kindly.

'Well, it's not so much that I want anything,' Jack dared, 'but, if you don't mind, if it's all right, could I possibly have that picture of that old woman taken down, she gives me the creeps.'

Jack's face was as red as beetroot as Oliver got up laughing, lifted the picture off the wall and put it beside the door.

'I'll take it with me when I go,' he said, coming back, 'and I agree with you wholeheartedly, Jack. I have never liked that picture, she always gave me the feeling that when I turned my back she would come out of the picture and I'd find her standing right behind me. Well, you can rest a little easier now.'

'Thank you, sir. 'Tis very good of you. I just can't wait to get back to work. I miss the horses and goodness knows what Michael and Conan are doing with them and what mess they're making of the stables.'

'The horses are well, so I'm told. I'm afraid I haven't had the time to look for myself but Adam Renfree has been supervising them so there is no need for you to worry, and you have trained Michael and Conan to a high standard, don't forget. The stables are lacking your touch, of course, but you'll soon put that right.'

Oliver looked uneasy. He leaned forward on his forearms and gazed, without seeing, at Jack's feet.

Jack curled his toes until they were out of sight. He waited uncomfortably for his master to say something more. He felt he ought to be standing, at a respectful distance, not able to look over the bowed black head.

Oliver looked serious when he raised his head. 'I'm here for two reasons, Jack, three if you count me looking in on you.'

A terrible thought raised Jack's voice a note too high. 'It's not Master Luke is it? He's not—'

'No, Jack. We think Luke is over the worst. He was sleeping quite peacefully a short time ago.'

'I'm some glad to hear that,' Jack said, puffing out his relief. 'Poor little fellow . . .'

'First of all, Jack, I want to thank you for trying to protect Her Ladyship on the day you were attacked. It was a very brave thing that you did and a dreadful experience for you both. It was a shock to learn of it. I feel responsible for what

445

happened, and ashamed.' Oliver spoke as intimately as to a close friend. 'None of these terrible things would have happened if I had been here.'

'You mustn't say that, sir. And I really didn't do anything. Didn't even get a blow on one of 'em before I was laid out on the ground. It was Her Ladyship who got help, and her with the baby coming . . . Has she told you she let me choose the little one's name, Ann?'

Oliver raised his eyebrows and it made Jack blush and look away.

'No, I don't mind, Jack. I have a lot of lost time to make up and these last twenty-four hours have given me one shock after the other. No matter, I shall learn all there is to know when I've had the opportunity to speak to Her Ladyship at length, and eventually you may know where I have been and what I've been doing for the last six months.'

'There's no need for that, sir. You must have had your reasons. You don't have to explain anything to me,' Jack protested loyally.

'It will be necessary, to put an end to all the speculation and wild gossip that doubtless is being circulated in the parish. I feel my servants, many of whom I regard as my friends, deserve a full explanation.' Oliver fiddled with his pocket watch. He opened the casing and glanced at the gold hands inside without registering the time. 'And now, Jack, I fear my other reason for being here will greatly upset you.'

'I've done something wrong, sir?' Jack frowned, letting his feet fly forward.

'No, Jack, be easy on that score. When Luke fell across the boulder yesterday, he saw something, something that very much frightened him. Since then he's had terrible nightmares, so I decided to search about at the scene of the accident myself. I quickly found what had upset him so much. Lying over that boulder, Luke saw a body. It must have been there for some time . . . Jack, I'm sorry to have to tell you this, it was the body of Heather Bawden.'

Jack groaned and raised his hands into fists. 'Oh no. But how? How did she get there?'

'In all probability it happened on the night she disappeared, the same night you met her on the moorland. From the position of her body it appears she stumbled over a smaller block of granite, hitting her head heavily on the boulder Luke was thrown onto. She was lying out of sight of the track, with her cloak and lantern close by.' Oliver put his hand on Jack's shoulder. 'I'm sorry, Jack. I know you had a fondness for the girl.'

Jack was crying, rocking himself back and forth with his arms wrapped about himself. 'She . . . she ran away from me . . . she wanted me to . . . to . . . but I didn't know what to do. She got proper mazed. Shouting and screaming, swearing worse 'n any man I've heard. Then I heard her scream, just once, then silence. That's when she must've . . . fallen over.'

'It wasn't your fault, Jack. I'll see she gets a decent burial.'

'It might have been my fault she died,' Jack sobbed, then abruptly stopped crying. He wiped his eyes with his knuckles and dug his toes into the wooden floor. 'She may not have died right away. She might have lain there all night, too hurt or dazed to cry out for help and I could have saved her, she might have died from the cold . . . in pain . . .'

'I don't believe that to be so,' Oliver stressed, feeling sorry for Jack and wishing he could put things right for him. 'The girl had a terrible head injury. I'm not a physician but

I am sure no one could have survived such a fall. You must not torture yourself.'

Jack considered this, sniffing deeply because he had no handkerchief. 'But why wasn't she found before this?'

Oliver gave the matter thought, then offered, 'It's a little way off the beaten track, by the spring. The body was partially hidden by grasses, heather and ferns, easy to miss unless you knew exactly where to look.'

'Poor Heather, all the time we was working on the meeting house we never knew she was lying only a few yards away. Sir?'

'Yes, Jack?'

'I've . . . I've had nothing to do with women since that night, all I want to do now with the rest of my life is to serve you and Her Ladyship.'

Oliver got up and pressed a firm hand on Jack's shoulder. 'One day you may change your mind, but do whatever pleases you, Jack. You may rest assured you will always have a place here.' He left the room; it was time to leave the young groom alone with his grief.

It was evening. Oliver was out in the stable yard. He had stepped outside for a few moments of cool fresh air and to smoke his pipe. He heard boots on the cobblestones and looked up to see Bob rushing to defend his territory from another retriever. He called to Bob and he reluctantly came back to stand obediently at heel; the other dog was a bitch and Bob had smelled some sport.

Clem Trenchard walked up to Oliver, head up, eyes blazing the intention of not leaving until his business for being there was done. He stopped a few short inches away and ordered Charity to lie down.

Oliver and Clem eyed each other, weighing up the

448

other's mood. Oliver could see Clem had no subservient feelings towards him but he thought that in different circumstances, without the love they both had for Kerensa creating an unbridgeable chasm between them, he could get to like the sulky-faced farmer. Clem took in the changes in the baronet's appearance and pursed his lips. Oliver knew that Clem would never like him for a moment.

'I take it you've heard about my son?' Oliver said shortly.

'That's why I'm here,' Clem replied stonily. 'Alice could n't come because Jessica has a bit of a fever and wouldn't let Alice leave her.'

'Nothing serious, I hope.'

'No, 'tis nought but a child's runny nose but Alice has always run to her. I said I'd come over to see how your boy is. Alice is very worried about him and Kerensa.' Clem said Kerensa's name as if he was challenging Oliver to rebuke him. 'The whole estate's fair buzzing with the news of the accident, and the finding of the girl's body, and,' he looked at Oliver purposefully, 'your return.'

'Does my return not suit you, Trenchard?'

'No, to be honest, but 'tis your place to be here, not gadding off somewhere and allowing your family and servants to fall into all manner of trouble.'

At one time Oliver would have been furious to be spoken to like this, but he nodded and said, 'My father would have had you horse-whipped for saying such things to him.'

'Why not you?' Clem challenged, standing ready, as if to ward off being struck.

'You know that kind of retribution is not my way, Trenchard. A short time ago I would have fought you, cleanly and fairly, but now it doesn't matter. I am back and I have Kerensa. I don't give a tinker's cuss about what you think of me.'

Quite unexpectedly, Clem smiled wryly, but he said, 'Feeling your age, are you?'

'I think age, breeding, maturity, and a pleasant personality win every time over the likes of you, Trenchard.'

Clem did not blanch but just looked steadily back. It seemed neither man was to be provoked. Oliver realised that Clem Trenchard, too, must have undergone changes in his absence.

The dogs crept forward on their bellies and sniffed at each other, wanting to get more friendly.

Oliver pulled out his tobacco pouch. 'You can tell Alice that Luke is sleeping most of the time,' he said. 'Dr Crebo is of the opinion he will pull through but we won't relax until a few more days have passed.'

'Aye, 'tis natural to worry. I hear his arm is pretty bad.'

Oliver filled his pipe, then in an intimidating gesture offered the pouch to Clem. Clem considered refusing, but accepted it as though he was a man of equal standing.

They began to pace the yard, puffing fragrant smoke on the cool breeze. Grass and moss were growing between the cobblestones and Oliver kicked disapprovingly at a weed.

'This is the sort of thing that happens when a man goes away for a while.'

'Aye,' Clem said, 'and it was a long while in your case. The stable boys must be finding it hard with Jack laid up, a lot of responsibility for them.'

Bob and Charity had followed faithfully on their heels but basic instinct soon took over and they sniffed each other and suddenly scurried off.

As they walked, the two men were thinking about each other. Deeply jealous that his baby had been delivered by Clem, Oliver was wondering what effect Kelynen's birth had had on him. Clem was eager to know what sort of reception the baronet had received from Kerensa, and what he thought about all that had happened since his departure.

They moved out of the stable yard and rounded the side of the house. Clem had never been here before and was impressed by the wealth of colour each side of the summer house. Sweet william, gladioli, hydrangea bushes flowering with blue, white, pink and purple crowns. The gardens were immaculate; Jake Angove and the under-gardeners had not slackened in their work.

Clem pointed to the patches of wild flowers growing among some of the more formal flowers. 'They must be Kerensa's touch. I couldn't imagine her living without her wild flowers.'

'You are correct, Trenchard.' Oliver was stung by the familiarity with which Clem spoke of Kerensa. He realised that next to himself and perhaps Alice, Clem knew more about her than anybody. What a fool he had been to risk losing her to him. He vowed he would never run such a risk again.

Clem was watching his face, trying to read his mind. 'So, she's taken you back, has she?'

'That's none of your damned business!' Oliver snarled.

'I can always make it my business,' Clem threatened coolly.

'Don't you be too sure of that, Trenchard,' Oliver hurled back.

'She's a fool to love you, Pengarron. You don't deserve her. I hate you for what you put her through all these months.'

'Again, it's none of your damned business, Trenchard, but I'll tell you this, Kerensa will always love me.'

'Aye, I know, although only God knows why.'

451

Oliver stooped to tap out his pipe on the soil. 'You'll always hate me, won't you?'

'To my grave.'

Oliver looked nonchalantly at his pipe as he cupped the warm bowl in the palm of his hand. 'And for that I don't give a tinker's cuss either.'

Clem nodded and puffed on the air. 'I'd be surprised if you did.'

The men stared at each other again. Challenge lay heavy in the air, only a breath away from physical confrontation.

Then Clem asked evenly, 'How is the baby keeping?'

No man asked after a baby unless it meant something to him. Oliver didn't like the question but in the circumstances he could not begrudge an answer.

'My daughter is very well,' he said, in a tone that forbade further questions.

They fell into an uneasy silence. It dawned on Oliver that it was Clem who had suggested Kelynen's name. Oliver hated the very thought of it and resolved he would never call his daughter by that name.

Olivia came running up, smiling. She stopped between them and looked up, puzzled at the grim faces. She turned her pretty auburn head from man to man, her face dropping. Oliver swept her possessively up in his arms and kissed her. She kissed him back and he was surprised when she addressed Clem.

'Have you brought Jessica to play, Clem?'

'No, not this time, Olivia,' Clem said, looking at Oliver, whom he was sure had not been told yet of the arrangement their wives had made about their children mixing and playing together.

'This time?' Oliver asked sharply.

'Aye,' Clem answered stoutly, 'there's been a lot of

changes since you took off. Since Kelynen's birth Kerensa and Alice have wanted your children and mine to grow up knowing each other. I don't like it but I agreed to it, eventually. They both went on at me about it, and they're anxious for it to continue.'

Oliver studied the handsome fair-haired young man and hated him three-fold for having so much to do with his family. He knew he could do nothing to alter the arrangement without causing a major upset and he was certain that Kerensa would not tolerate it if he tried. He was careful not to show his disapproval but he wanted to wipe the smugness off Clem's face.

Kissing Olivia again, he said, 'You must tell me all about it later, sweeting.'

'The boys fight,' Olivia said, hugging Oliver's neck and pulling at his hair.

Oliver began to walk back to the stable yard. He would tolerate Clem Trenchard's presence on his property no longer. Clem fell in step beside him.

'I can't imagine our sons getting along, Trenchard,' Oliver said dryly, over his shoulder.

'Kane's amiable enough, but the twins and Luke fight like he-goats.'

'So there's rivalry between the next generation, yours and mine, Trenchard.'

''Tis not unexpected. What could they possibly have in common?'

'Nothing I can think of, but I suppose only time will tell.'

Back in the stable yard Clem spotted Jack watching from his bedroom window and gave him a friendly wave. He wondered if Kerensa was behind one of the numerous windows, watching them too, anxious to know what was being said between the two men she professed to love.

He smiled gently at Olivia, whose face was so much like the one he loved, then looked at Oliver.

'I'm serious in the hope that the boy makes a full recovery,' he said briefly.

'At least I can thank you for that, Trenchard.'

Olivia asked to be put down and ran into the house. Oliver and Clem did not bid each other goodbye. They thought they knew the measure of each other and somehow both were content to leave it at that – for now.

As Clem returned to his family, Oliver went quickly to Luke's room. The sight of his own gathered there melted the uneasiness that Clem's visit had put round his heart. Kerensa looked up and smiled warmly as she sat cradling their baby beside Luke's bed. Luke was wide awake and quiet on his pillows. Kane and Olivia were sitting on the foot of the bed holding hands and wriggling their stockinged feet in the bedcovers. Oliver grinned as a mischievous glint came into Luke's dark eyes and he poked his tongue out at his brother and sister. Tomorrow he and Kerensa would ride to Marazion to tell another brood of brothers and sisters that they were part of the Pengarron family too.

Chapter 31

Jenifer Drannock looked proudly at all her children. At her request they had gathered round her bed after breakfast. They were all burning with curiosity, wanting to know why she had asked them to dress up and be on their best behaviour. Naomi and Hannah, her two eldest daughters, were secretly worried that Jenifer had felt her end had come and wanted one long last look at her children before she died. Charles and Jack, grumbling at having to wear neckcloths, wanted to get down on the floor and play, but warning looks from their big sisters kept them in line. Cordelia, the baby of the family, tiny and elfin-faced, looked like a sweetmeat wrapped in fancy paper in her frilled and flounced silk dress. Only Bartholomew looked the part, as a man of means, wearing his suit of tailored clothes with a natural, elegant flair.

'We must be expecting someone, Mother,' Hannah said, tidying things unnecessarily, 'or you wouldn't want us all up here like this else, would you?'

'You'll see, soon enough,' Jenifer said, her children becoming still so they could hear her faint voice.

'Are we having company, Mam?' Charles asked with an expression on his face that usually wound his mother round his little finger.

The others looked at Charles eagerly then quickly at

455

Jenifer. Charles had a knack of wheedling out secrets, but not this time. Jenifer just smiled mysteriously, then sighed. She was unsure how her children would take the news she and Sir Oliver Pengarron were soon to tell them. Bartholomew, of course, would not be surprised, and as an admirer of the baronet she was certain he would be delighted. Hannah and Naomi had always maintained that Bartholomew's suspicions that they, or he at least, might have Pengarron blood in their veins was nothing more than wishful thinking. The three little ones, Charles, Jack and Cordelia, were too young really to understand, but Jenifer thought they would be excited in varying degrees.

Jenifer knew that if the children allowed him, Oliver would take them fully under his wing and she had no qualms about this, especially since he had come back from his travels purged of his dangerous pride. And Kerensa would mother them, whatever their age; she had practically adopted the strapping eighteen-year-old Bartholomew, as well as the little ones, since she had become too ill to mother them herself. And the children would have cousins of position and influence. They would never have to feel they were inferior to her own family, the Milderns. Jenifer felt that no woman could die happier and have so few worries about the children she would leave behind.

Bartholomew was looking out of the window watching the fishing boats in the bay around Newlyn and Mousehole, picking out the luggers he recognised, hoping they had brought in a good catch, wishing them good luck for the morrow, glad that he wouldn't be going with them.

'I see Cap'n Solomon's ship is moored up at the Mount,' he said, then mischievously, 'Don't tell me 'tis he who's calling on us, Mother? You should have said, then I would have put my party suit on.'

'It is not Captain Solomon,' Jenifer replied.

'Then it is someone!' shouted Naomi, who was inclined to loud outbursts.

'Shush, child,' said her frail mother. 'Oh, very well, stop looking at me, all of you. Yes, we are expecting visitors, very important ones. I didn't tell you before because I didn't want you to get over-excited or anxious.'

Bartholomew looked at the flag fluttering in the wind on top of the castle on the Mount, across the causeway. 'Surely not the St Aubyns? They're in residence, but they have no business with us, have they?'

'Of course not,' Jenifer smiled.

'When are these visitors supposed to be coming?' Hannah asked, rather impatiently. 'Have I got time to see to my hair?'

Jenifer glanced at the carriage clock ticking gently on her bedside table. It was two minutes to ten o'clock.

'They'll be here any minute now, and your hair is fine, Hannah.'

'Oh, Mother, if you don't tell me I shall burst at the seams,' Naomi squealed; she was also inclined to be dramatic.

'No, let's wait and see, let it be a surprise. I love surprises,' said little Cordelia, and that decided the issue.

At a quarter past ten the younger children began to get restless and Bartholomew was pulling at the window sash when feet were heard coming up the stairs. Everyone held their breath at the tap on the door, and Mrs Parkin, the housekeeper, who looked quite overcome, announced the visitors and quickly departed.

'We do apologise for our late arrival,' Oliver said in a grim voice. 'Unfortunately we were delayed on the road on

457

the way here. The constable was there with some men, clearing away a body. I'm afraid that someone has been murdered.'

'Oh, not another one,' Bartholomew said, then remembering his manners he very humbly shook the hand Oliver was offering him.

Immediate concern fell upon Kerensa.

'What a dreadful shock for you, my dear,' Jenifer said weakly.

'Please, Lady Pengarron, do have this chair over here by Mother. Can I get you anything?' Hannah said, bobbing a curtsy.

'I'm quite all right,' Kerensa said, taking the seat and smiling lightly to reassure the company and to stop Bartholomew who was bent on pulling the bell rope for Mrs Parkin to fetch goodness knows what. 'I didn't see anything. I stayed on my pony and said a little prayer for the deceased.'

'Are you sure you are all right though, my dear?' Oliver was at her side.

Jenifer halted the rush of over-protectiveness. 'I think the experiences Lady Pengarron has undergone in recent times will have enabled her to cope quite ably with almost anything.'

'Jenifer is right. Shall we talk of something else?' Kerensa said firmly.

It was time for introductions and Oliver shook the hands of all the assembled company. Then Luke's condition was asked after and reported, and the Drannock children waited, respectfully agog, to discover the reason behind this visit from the Lord and Lady of the Manor.

But first Oliver took Bartholomew aside and asked, 'Did I hear you say "another one"? Have there been other murders of this kind?'

'Yes, I'm afraid there have,' Bartholomew answered. And the two men put their heads together so the women and children were spared the gory details.

'Dear God,' Oliver said. 'I saw something of the kind the day I sailed away. How many have there been since then?'

'This will make five, some men, some women. All low-life, drunkards, prostitutes and the like, so no one's been really that bothered about it. I must say I find it rather chilling.'

'And so do I. It was assumed the three rogues who attacked Her Ladyship and Jack were responsible, but they're tucked away in gaol so they had nothing to do with this one.'

'Well, I've a belief it could be a sailor coming in and out of port. There's a long interval between the murders, then usually more than one at a time. You see some rough types abroad in the town.'

'I think we should keep an eye on our families until the villains are apprehended, Bartholomew.'

The youth was pleased and honoured to be taken into the confidence of the baronet, to be spoken to man to man, as one head of a family to another, almost as a friend, or . . .

Bartholomew's eyes opened wide and he blurted out, 'I know why you've come here today.'

Jenifer let out a small gasp. 'Bartholomew! Where are your manners? That is no way to speak to Sir Oliver.'

But Oliver was amused by the youth's perceptiveness. 'Yes, I rather think you do.' He glanced at Kerensa and raised his brows lightheartedly then looked at his attentive nieces and nephews.

'Shall we all sit down and let your brothers and sisters in on our secret, Bartholomew?'

Jenifer had asked Mrs Parkin to put extra chairs in the

room and Oliver waited for the older girls to sit in a row next to Kerensa. Their eldest brother sat on the wide window ledge where he was joined by Charles, while Jack and Cordelia climbed up to nestle by their mother. He had a sea of faces all looking at him.

Jenifer's was ravaged by the malignancy that was sapping her life, but she looked strangely content. She cuddled her two youngest but held on to Kerensa's hand and he knew the revelations he was about to impart would have the same effect on Jenifer as if she was about to set out on an exciting journey. Hannah and Naomi, aged fifteen and sixteen, looked something of what Jenifer had as a girl, fair, medium build, good figures, and with their mother's influence they held themselves well. Charles was eleven years old now, he had Samuel's moody countenance but owned a good sense of humour. Jack and Cordelia were most like Bartholomew to look at, and thus most like their Pengarron relations.

'Well, shall I tell them or will you, Bartholomew?' Oliver asked his nephew.

Heads all turned to Bartholomew, but suddenly overcome with embarrassment he motioned the task back to Oliver.

'Your brother,' he spoke to the others, 'as you probably know, has for years, on the strength of his physical resemblance to me, wondered whether he might have Pengarron blood in him. I know that he has even made some inquiries into the possibility.'

Bartholomew coloured but gave his two grown-up sisters a superior look.

'The truth of the matter is that he has, and not only him, but all of you have. My father, Sir Daniel Pengarron, was in fact the father of your father, Samuel, not Caleb

460

Drannock. You are all Sir Daniel's grandchildren and my nieces and nephews.' Oliver looked from face to face. The younger ones just stared at him, not really taking it in. Naomi and Hannah were obviously stunned and Bartholomew beamed all round the room. Jenifer smiled confidently and Kerensa took Naomi and Hannah's hands.

'I hope you will welcome joining the family,' Kerensa said encouragingly.

'But it's incredible,' said Naomi, dramatically waving her other hand about. 'Us! Related to you, Your Lordship.'

'I'm rather hoping you will call me Uncle Oliver,' Oliver replied, coming across the room and standing in front of her and Hannah.

'But you don't have to acknowledge us, Sir Oliver,' Hannah said, meeting his eyes squarely. 'We know all about gentlemen having illegitimate children. We don't expect you to feel obligated. It's just one of those things, as folk do say.'

'But I want to acknowledge you, my dear,' Oliver returned, 'and not just privately. I want to announce you as my kin, and I'm hoping you will all agree to my doing so. I also want any of you, at any time you may desire it, to come and live at the manor house on equal standing with my own children. There are plenty of empty rooms, plenty of space to be yourselves if that is what you want.'

Cordelia tugged at Oliver's coat. 'Are you really my uncle, Mr Sir?'

Oliver laughed and lifted her up into his arms. She was as light as a feather and stared at him uncertainly from large dark eyes.

'Yes, young lady, I am your uncle. Ask your mother, she knows all about it.'

'All that Sir Oliver has told you is completely true, my

461

dears,' Jenifer said, and in a breathless voice she filled her children in on all the details.

'But Mother,' Charles spoke up, his face screwed up anxiously, 'if we're not really Drannocks then the money great-uncle Obadiah left doesn't actually belong to us. We're not entitled to it. The rightful heirs will have to be found and we'll have to give everything back!'

'No you won't. Have no fears about that, Charles,' Oliver said quickly. 'There is no such person as Obadiah Drannock. It was I who arranged to have that money sent to you. As I was away at the time I wanted to be certain you'd accept your "inheritance" so I invented a great-uncle for you.'

'You did that?' Bartholomew exclaimed and blew a short whistle. 'I never guessed it, it never crossed my mind.'

'Well then, you don't know everything,' Jack said cheek-ily.

'Are you my aunty then?' Cordelia chirruped, wriggling towards Kerensa and holding out her arms. Oliver passed her over, and Jack, who missed having his father about, plucked up his courage and shyly held up his arms to his uncle. Oliver cheerfully obliged.

'I hope all of you are happy with what I have told you,' Oliver said. 'Your Aunt Kerensa and I will be glad to have you over to the manor to spend the day as soon as your cousin Luke is well again.'

'I don't think any of us have any objections, but it takes some getting used to,' Hannah said, and tears were forming in her eyes.

Bartholomew looked out of the window and wondered how the good people of Mount's Bay would view him now. 'I always knew it,' he murmured.

'I would like you and Charles and Jack to receive a

proper education,' Oliver said, joining him and holding up Jack so he got an excellent view of the people milling about below. 'And I'll ensure Hannah and Naomi make good marriages.'

'Thank you . . . Uncle. After that I want to travel,' Bartholomew went on, his voice low, 'all round the world. But what about the time when Mother has gone, what about little Cordelia? Could she, and the boys, when they're not at school, come and live with you? I'd like to keep this house open as a base for us all to return to, somewhere to come back to and remember Mother.'

'It will all be done, Bartholomew,' Oliver answered, falling into Bartholomew's quiet, serious mood.

'But what will your children think about us?' Charles asked, adding himself to the male gathering and standing importantly with his hands clasped behind him. 'Will Masters Kane and Luke and Miss Olivia want to have anything to do with us? We might have come into money and live in a big house but most of the gentry folk still think we're beneath them and make no bones about it.'

'My children will accept you as their equals, have no worries on that score, Charles, and my servants will treat you as Pengarrons too,' or I shall have something to say about it! Oliver thought privately. 'As for the gentry, you will find some will always spurn you, but they are of no consequence. The others will fall over themselves to have society with you. I will make each of your brothers and sisters, and you, a person of position and high standing.'

'Sounds some exciting,' Charles said, puffing out his chest.

Bartholomew's was already well puffed out. 'You can say that again, brother.'

Kerensa sat and watched the roomful of happy, excited

463

faces. Oliver and his new male kin were conversing like equals already. Naomi and Hannah laughed and chattered about the new social life they were going to be able to take part in. Cordelia, too, had caught some of the new vitality pulsing in the room but she was content to sit on Kerensa's lap and receive a long cuddle.

'I was going to ask if all is well with you, my dear,' Jenifer said to her in her weak voice, smiling more than she had since Samuel had died, 'but I can see your contentment, it's clearly written all over your lovely face.'

'I don't care how silly or sentimental it sounds, Jenifer,' Kerensa smiled from deep within and gazed at the tall dark man talking to Jenifer's sons, 'but you could say my paradise has come home.'

Jenifer followed her gaze. 'And if I am any judge, he's here to stay for ever.'

Kerensa sat quietly. She was tired from her months of heartache, the events of those months, Kelynen's birth and Luke's accident. But Oliver was home and she would never have to bear anything alone again. Here he was, not only back from a long absence but from the hurts of the past, and with an enlargement of the family that meant so much to him.

Jenifer grew pleasantly sleepy. She let herself drift away, and soon she would not fight to come back. She could die content, knowing that she had taught her children their manners and the etiquette of society. They would have little trouble mixing in genteel company and while Samuel had rejected the idea that he belonged in it, his children would take their rightful places. And she was glad that they would have opportunities their father had refused.

'Bartholomew and the others took the news very well,'

Kerensa said, reaching over the bed and retrieving a pillow that had fallen on the floor.

'Mmm, they did,' Oliver agreed in a husky voice.

'Why are you smiling like that?' she asked pertly.

'Why do you think?'

She pretended modesty by covering herself with the sheet. 'Anything else?'

'I'm just very, very happy, my dear. Luke is much better, Kane and Olivia are happy to have me back home, my baby daughter is as beautiful as her mother and Bartholomew took the news just as I hoped he would.'

'I wasn't surprised,' Kerensa said, hammering the battered pillows into shape and lying back on them. 'I had a few words with him back along and he's grown up since and seen sense about a lot of things.'

Oliver chuckled, and catching her chin turned her head to look at him. 'My wife, the wise woman of West Cornwall. You spoke to Bartholomew while I was away, I presume.'

'No, actually it was a day or two before you left. I had reason to believe he was about to seduce Ameline. As she was under our care I decided something ought to be done about it. I was also concerned with the way he was neglecting Jenifer and the children.'

'You are a brave little thing.' He kissed the tip of her nose. 'Fancy a little bit of a thing like you taking on a strapping youth like Bartholomew.'

Kerensa kissed the tip of his nose and said teasingly in a superior voice, 'Perhaps you big brave men should stop looking on your women as "little bits of a thing" and realise just how tough and intelligent we are. And anyway, you're all little boys deep down when your thick skin is rubbed away.'

'Is that how you thought of me a few moments ago?'

The dangerous gleam was back in his dark eyes and she lowered her eyelashes provocatively. 'Not . . . exactly . . .'

'I still pride myself on some things even if I have changed a great deal,' he laughed at himself.

Kerensa moved to face him fully. It was time to be serious. 'A lot of things have changed here, Oliver. We have another child and we're going to have to help Luke grow up and cope with a possible disability. Ameline is contentedly married to James Mortreath. Rosie Trenchard is to marry Matthias Renfree very soon. But I want to know how you have changed. Can you tell me? Some of it? All of it? Or do you just want us to forget all the bad things that have happened and make a fresh start?'

Oliver let his hands fall away from Kerensa and clasped them on his firm stomach. 'We won't be able to have a completely fresh start if I don't tell you all about my months away and I want you to know everything, my love. My story is quite simple. I couldn't come to terms with myself or my reaction to learning about Samuel until I got away on my own. So I sailed with Hezekiah, leaving the *Free Spirit* at Roscoff. In France Hezekiah passes as a Frenchman, as you know. I had to be very careful, I didn't want to run the risk of being executed as a spy or putting Hezekiah into any danger. So from there, so as not to be conspicuous, I wore peasant clothes for the journey to— You're frowning, Kerensa. What's wrong?'

'Nothing is wrong, dearest, but it can't be easy to go unnoticed when you're six feet, five inches tall, broad-shouldered, dark-featured – and exceedingly handsome.'

'Well, yes, all right,' Oliver conceded lightheartedly. 'I don't know about the handsome bit but I did occasionally attract attention. I moved on, working for my food and passage until I arrived at Dettingen in the Low Countries.'

'The place where Arthur Beswetherick died in battle . . .' Kerensa said softly.

'I needed to lay Arthur's ghost. You were right about that. I stood on the very spot where nineteen years ago he was hit in the throat by a splinter of metal that had shirred off a wagon's wheel.'

'My dear Oliver, was it very awful?'

'Much less awful than what you were going through at the same time, but yes, it was painful to visit the place the field hospital had been. To go back over every minute as I watched his lifeblood ebb away while the Army surgeon was too drunk to be of any use at all.

'I camped out for days in the place where he was buried beside the river. There is no mass grave as is the custom when burying the military dead after battle. Ironically there was only one man killed in my regiment at the battle of Dettingen – my friend Arthur.'

Kerensa knelt up on the bed and hugged Oliver to her breast. 'It seems all the more terrible for that.'

'The King, the old King, had led us into battle. He was grieved when the news reached him. He sent his personal condolences to Martin and Lady Ameline, but it's hard to take the death of a youngest child . . . the death of your only close friend.'

Oliver pulled Kerensa down so he could hold her. 'I stayed there and mourned Arthur until I felt a sense of peace. Sometimes it was as if he was there with me, telling me to forget him, to go on with my life, and then . . . then I had to work out my feelings for you. It was the hardest thing I've ever had to do in my life. I wandered about the countryside like a lost soul, moving from village to village, from country to country, keeping away from people except to buy food and wine. I ended up in Brittany where there

467

was so much to remind me of my own beloved county. It was there, my precious love, that I began to get things straightened out in my mind.

'I had run out of money again but managed to get work on a farm for just my food and milk or water. The old couple who rented it were very poor and disapproved of alcohol. I suppose it helped to clear my head.' Laughing wryly, he swallowed from a glass of water at the bedside.

'Jules and Michelle – that's where I got our baby's other name from – were very old and practically infirm. They told me they had had four children, all of whom died in childhood. They'd had a tragic life, yet always they were content. They were so close to each other, their marriage was truly like the Biblical "one person".

'They knew I was no peasant, and a foreigner, yet even with my secrets they treated me as their own son. As time went on, although I didn't realise it, they broke down the barriers I'd put up. I asked them why they were always happy. They replied, just a simple trust in God, and love and trust in each other.

'Michelle knew her man well, and she soon began to know me. She didn't have to guess I was married, that it was an affair of the heart I was running away from. Eventually, she got the whole story out of me. She asked me if I loved you. I answered, of course I did. Then she asked if there was any reason on God's earth why I couldn't trust you. It only took a moment's thought to say there was not. Michelle made me see it wasn't you, my love, who was the problem, or the fact that you had kept a secret from me. It was my own petty pride. Stupid.

'I used to think I was strong, Kerensa, but all the time I had this terrible weakness in me. I couldn't bear to think I didn't have total control of my life, of those I loved and those around me. While I wanted so desperately to have had the opportunity to get to know Samuel and see if we could have got on as brothers, I hated him for having the same arrogant proud behaviour as I had myself, and it was that that made me treat you so badly.

'The truth stung me for days, but slowly I got used to it and one morning I woke longing to come home to you and the children. It was hard to say goodbye to Jules and Michelle, it was comforting and humbling to have had them as sort of foster parents for a few months. I took the first ship back, a French merchantman, working for my fare. The ship was a smuggler and when she met up with her English partner I transferred to her. The captains didn't care who I was, they gave me no trouble. One day, Kerensa, if it's possible I would like to go back and repay all the kindness Jules and Michelle showed me. I'd like you to come with me.'

Throughout his narration Kerensa had barely moved. Now she wound her arms round his neck and kissed him tenderly.

'I would love to go with you. One day it will happen,' she said, smiling into his soul. 'Perhaps we could take all the children with us, even Kelynen, whom they don't know about.'

He hugged her tightly with tears sprinkling his lower eyelashes. 'It's no wonder I love you so very much, Kerensa Pengarron.'

He banked down his fierce need to make love. Kerensa sensed he had more to say.

'What is it?' she whispered.

'When I spoke to Clem Trenchard last evening I realised it must have been him who suggested the baby's name to you. Does this mean you have a need for him, Kerensa? I'm sorry I have to ask this. I just want everything to be clear between us.'

'Clem and I have a special friendship, Oliver, nothing more, and certainly nothing that can hurt or come between us. The wonderful thing about me having Kelynen in Trecath-en is it made Clem realise he needs and loves Alice. We've both let go of the past, I went my different way years ago, and now so has Clem. There is nothing left of the boy and girl we once were. I didn't take the name Kelynen to hurt you, Oliver, it just seemed right at the time. But we don't have to call her that, if you would rather change it.'

'No, leave things as they are. I don't feel I have the right to come home and change things as if they had never happened. I'll live no more lies. I can't say that I trust Clem Trenchard, but I do trust you. Our baby has four names and each one tells a story. Kelynen says where she was born, Michelle where I was living when she was born, Jenifer tells of the aunt who was dying as she began her life, and Ann of brave, devoted Jack who lay beaten as she began her journey into the world. She's our special baby, to help us remember what we suffered and how we came out of it with our love all the stronger.'

They kissed and clung together, washed on a tide of passion. Of a sudden Oliver stopped.

'Did you say Rosie Trenchard is getting married?'

'Mmmm, yes, why?' Kerensa murmured.

'I'm glad.' Oliver leaned on his elbows and smiled. 'It's reminded me of something. Tomorrow, my precious love, I'm going to take you up to the oak plantation where I have a little hideout.'

'Why?' Kerensa's voice rippled through the night air on a note of interest.

'Because there should be some fox cubs I'd like you to see.'

'Really? Tell me more.'

'It can wait until tomorrow . . .'

More Compelling Fiction from Headline:

GWEN KIRKWOOD
FAIRLYDEN

A family saga of life on the land in 19th-century Scotland

Matthew Cameron's death ends the Camerons' three-life lease of the fertile farmstead of Nethertannoch. But Sandy Logan is determined to secure the tenancy in his name so that he can keep his promise to the dying Matthew - that he will love and protect his daughter, the beautiful and vulnerable Mattie, who has been deaf since childhood.

But the laird has other plans. Events explode into violence and Sandy is forced to flee with Mattie. They find refuge in the rundown farm of Fairlyden, which is owned by Daniel Munro. Daniel, crippled by rheumatism, does not welcome strangers, but something about the pair of fugitives touches his heart and he lets them stay.

Slowly they bring the farm to prosperity; Mattie with her hens and her sure touch with the cows, and Sandy with his strength and knowledge of horse breeding. But Daniel is the illegitimate son of the late Earl of Strathtod and Fairlyden belongs to him only for his lifetime; without heirs it will return to the estate of the present Earl, who has always hated Daniel. So Daniel comes up with a scheme to thwart his half-brother - a scheme that includes Mattie, and will have far-reaching consequences down the years.

FICTION/SAGA   0 7472 3692 5